The Makers of Modern Rome by Margaret Oliphant

In Four Books

Margaret Oliphant Wilson was born on April 4th, 1828 to Francis W. Wilson, a clerk, and Margaret Oliphant, at Wallyford, near Musselburgh, East Lothian.

Her youth was spent in establishing a writing style and by 1849 she had her first novel published: Passages in the Life of Mrs. Margaret Maitland.

Two years later, in 1851 Caleb Field was published and also an invitation gained to contribute to Blackwood's Magazine; the beginning of a lifelong business relationship.

In May 1852, Margaret married her cousin, Frank Wilson Oliphant. Their marriage produced six children but, tragically, three died in infancy. When her husband developed signs of the dreaded consumption (tuberculosis) they moved to Florence, and then to Rome where, sadly, he died.

Margaret was naturally devastated but was also now left without support and only her income from writing to support the family. She returned to England and took up the burden of supporting her three remaining children by her literary activity.

Her incredible and prolific work rate increased both her commercial reputation and the size of her reading audience. Tragedy struck again in January 1864 when her only remaining daughter, Maggie, died.

In 1866 she settled at Windsor to be closer to her sons, who were being educated at near-by Eton School.

For more than thirty years she pursued a varied literary career but family life continued to bring problems. Cyril Francis, her eldest son, died in 1890. The younger son, Francis, who she nicknamed 'Cecco', died in 1894.

With the last of her children now lost to her, she had little further interest in life. Her health steadily and inexorably declined.

Margaret Oliphant Wilson Oliphant died at the age of 69 in Wimbledon on 20th June 1897. She is buried in Eton beside her sons.

Index of Contents

LIST OF ILLUSTRATIONS

[THE COLOSSEUM]

PREFACE

Nobody will expect in this book, or from me, the results of original research, or a settlement—if any settlement is ever possible—of vexed questions which have occupied the gravest students. An individual glance at the aspect of these questions which most clearly presents itself to a mind a little exercised in the aspects of humanity, but not trained in the ways of learning, is all I attempt or desire. This humble endeavour has been conscientious at least. The work has been much interrupted by sorrow and suffering, on which account, for any slips of hers, the writer asks the indulgence of her unknown friends.

BOOK I

HONOURABLE WOMEN NOT A FEW

CHAPTER I

ROME IN THE FOURTH CENTURY

There is no place in the world of which it is less necessary to attempt description (or of which so many descriptions have been attempted) than the once capital of that world, the supreme and eternal city, the seat of empire, the home of the conqueror, the greatest human centre of power and influence which our race has ever known. Its history is unique and its position. Twice over in circumstances and by means as different as can be imagined it has conquered and held subject the world. All that was known to man in their age gave tribute and acknowledgment to the Cæsars; and an ever-widening circle, taking in countries and races unknown to the Cæsars, have looked to the spiritual sovereigns who succeeded them as to the first and highest of authorities on earth. The reader knows, or at least is assisted on all hands to have some idea and conception of the classical city—to be citizens of which was the aim of the whole world's ambition, and whose institutions and laws, and even its architecture and domestic customs, were the only rule of civilisation—with its noble and grandiose edifices, its splendid streets, the magnificence and largeness of its life; while on the other hand most people are able to form some idea of what was the Rome of the Popes, the superb yet squalid mediæval city with its great palaces and its dens of poverty, and that conjunction of exuberance and want which does not strike the eye while the bulk of a population remains in a state of slavery. But there is a period between, which has not attracted much attention from English writers, and which the reader passes by as a time in which there is little desirable to dwell upon, though it is in reality the moment of transition when the old is about to be replaced by the new, and when already the energy and enthusiasm of a new influence is making its appearance among the tragic dregs and abysses of the past. An ancient civilisation dying in the impotence of luxury and wealth from which all active power or influence over the world had departed, and a new and profound internal revolt, breaking up its false calm from within, before the raging forces of another rising power had yet begun to thunder at its gates without—form however a spectacle full of interest, especially when the scene of so many conflicts is traversed and lighted up by the most lifelike figures, and has left its record, both of good and evil, in authentic and detailed chronicles, full of individual character and life, in which the men and women of the age stand before us, occupied and surrounded by circumstances which are very different from our own, yet linked to us by that unfailing unity of human life and feeling which makes the farthest off foreigner a brother, and the most distant of our primeval predecessors like a neighbour of to-day.

The circumstances of Rome in the middle and end of the fourth century were singular in every point of view. With all its prestige and all its memories, it was a city from which power and the dominant forces of life had faded. The body was there, the great town with its high places made to give law and judgment to the world, even the officials and executors of the codes which had dispensed justice throughout the universe; but the spirit of dominion and empire had passed away. A great aristocracy, accustomed to the first place everywhere, full of wealth, full of leisure, remained; but with nothing to do to justify this greatness, nothing but luxury, the prize and accompaniment of it, now turned into its sole object and meaning. The patrician class had grown by use, by the high capability to fill every post and lead every expedition which they had constantly shown, which was their original cause and the reason of their existence, into a position of unusual superiority and splendour. But that reason had died away, the empire had departed from them, the world had a new centre: and the sons of the men who had conducted all the immense enterprises of Rome were left behind with the burden of their great names, and the weight of their great wealth, and nothing to do but to enjoy and amuse themselves: no vocations to fulfil, no important public functions to occupy their time and their powers. Such a position is perhaps the most dreadful that can come to any class in the history of a nation. Great and irresponsible wealth, the supremacy of high place, without those bonds of practical affairs which, in the case of all rulers—even of estates or of factories—preserve the equilibrium of humanity, are instruments of degradation rather than of elevation. To have something to do for it, something to do with it, is the condition which alone makes boundless wealth wholesome. And this had altogether failed in the imperial city. Pleasure and display had taken the place of work and duty. Rome had no longer any imperial affairs in hand. Her day was over: the absence of a court and all its intrigues might have been little loss to any community—but that those threads of universal dominion which had hitherto occupied them had been transferred to other hands, and that all the struggles, the great questions, the causes, the pleas, the ordinances of the world were now decided and given forth at Constantinople, was ruin to the once masters of the world. It was worse than destruction, a more dreadful overthrow than anything that the Goths and barbarians could bring—not death which brings a satisfaction of all necessities in making an end of them—but that death in life which fills men's blood with cold.

The pictures left us of this condition of affairs do indeed chill the blood. It is natural that there should be a certain amount of exaggeration in them. We read daily in our own contemporary annals, records of society of which we are perfectly competent to judge, that though true to fact in many points, they give a picture too dark in all its shadows, too garish in its lights, to afford a just view of the state of any existing condition of things. Contemporaries know how much to receive and how much to reject, and are apt to smile at the possibility of any permanent impression upon the face of history being made by lights and darks beyond the habit of nature. But yet when every allowance has been made, the contemporary pictures of Rome at this unhappy period leave an impression on the mind which is not contradicted but supported and enforced by the incidents of the time and the course of history. The populace, which had for ages been fed and nourished upon the bread of public doles and those entertainments of ferocious gaiety which deadened every higher sense, had sunk into complete debasement. Honest work and honest purpose, or any hope of improving their own position, elevating themselves or training their children, do not seem to have existed among them. A half-ludicrous detail, which reminds us that the true Roman had always a trifle of pedantry in his pride, is noted with disgust and disdain even by serious writers—which is that the common people bore no longer their proper names, but were known among each other by nicknames, such as those of Cabbage-eaters, Sausage-mongers, and other coarse familiar vulgarisms. This might be pardoned to the crowd which spent its idle days at the circus or spectacle, and its nights on the benches in the Colosseum or in the porch of a palace; but it is difficult to exaggerate the debasement of a populace which lived for amusement alone, picking up the miserable morsels which kept it alive from any chance or tainted source, without work to do or hope of amelioration. They formed the shouting, hoarse accompaniment of every pageant, they swarmed on the lower seats of every amphitheatre, howling much criticism as well as boisterous applause, and keeping in fear, and disgusted yet forced compliance with their coarse exactions, the players and showmen who supplied their lives with an object. According to all the representations that have reached us, nothing more degraded than this populace—encumbering every portico and marble stair, swarming over the benches of the Colosseum, basking in filth and idleness in the brilliant sun of Rome, or seeking, among the empty glories of a triumphal age gone by, a lazy shelter from it—has ever been known.

The higher classes suffered in their way as profoundly, and with a deeper consciousness, from the same debasing influences of stagnation. The descriptions of their useless life of luxury are almost too extravagant to quote. "A loose silken robe," says the critic and historian of the time, Ammianus Marcellinus, speaking of a Roman noble,—"for a toga of the lightest tissue would have been too heavy for him—linen so transparent that the air blew through it, fans and parasols to protect him from the light, a troop of eunuchs always round him." This was the appearance and costume of a son of the great and famous senators of Rome. "When he was not at the bath, or at the circus to maintain the cause of some charioteer, or to inspect some new horses, he lay half asleep upon a luxurious couch in great rooms paved with marble, panelled with mosaic." The luxurious heat implied, which makes the freshness of the marble, the thinness of the linen, so desirable, as in a picture of Mr. Alma Tadema's, bids us at the same time pause in receiving the whole of this description as unquestionable; for Rome has its seasons in which vast chambers paved with marble are no longer agreeable, though the manners and utterances of the race still tend to a complete ignoring of this other side of the picture: but yet no doubt its general features are true.

When this Sybarite went out it was upon a lofty chariot, where he reclined negligently, showing off himself, his curled and perfumed locks, his robes, with their wonderful embroideries and tissues of silk and gold, to the admiration of the world; his horses' harness were covered with ornaments of gold, his coachman armed with a golden wand instead of a whip, and the whole equipage followed by a procession of attendants, slaves, freedmen, eunuchs, down to the knaves of the kitchen, the hewers of wood and drawers of water, to give importance to the retinue, which pushed along through the streets with all the brutality which is the reverse side of senseless display, pushing citizens and passers-by out of the way. The dinner parties of the evening were equally childish in their extravagance: the tables covered with strange dishes, monsters of the sea and of the mountains, fishes and birds of unknown kinds and unequalled size. The latter seems to have been a special subject of pride, for we are told of the servants bringing scales to weigh them, and notaries crowding round with their tablets and styles to record the weight. After the feast came a "hydraulic organ," and other instruments of corresponding magnitude, to fill the great hall with resounding music, and pantomimical plays and dances to enliven the dulness of the luxurious spectators on their couches—"women with long hair, who might have married and given subjects to the state," were thus employed, to the indignation of the critic.

This chronicler of folly and bad manners would not be human if he omitted the noble woman of Rome from his picture. Her rooms full of obsequious attendants, slaves, and eunuchs, half of her time was occupied by the monstrous toilette which annulled all natural charms to give to the Society beauty a fictitious and artificial display of red and white, of painted eyelids, tortured hair, and extravagant dress. An authority still more trenchant than the heathen historian, Jerome, describes even one of the noble ladies who headed the Christian society of Rome as spending most of the day before the mirror. Like the ladies of Venice in a later age, these women, laden with ornaments, attired in cloth of gold, and with shoes that crackled under their feet with the stiffness of metallic decorations, were almost incapacitated from walking, even with the support of their attendants; and a life so accoutred was naturally spent in the display of the charms and wealth thus painfully set forth.

The fairer side of the picture, the revolt of the higher nature from such a life, brings us into the very heart of this society: and nothing can be more curious than the gradual penetration of a different and indeed sharply contrary sentiment, the impulse of asceticism and the rudest personal self-deprivation, amid a community spoilt by such a training, yet not incapable of disgust and impatience with the very luxury which had seemed essential to its being. The picturesqueness and attraction of the picture lies here, as in so many cases, chiefly on the women's side.

It is necessary to note, however, the curious mixture which existed in this Roman society, where Christianity as a system was already strong, and the high officials of the Church were beginning to take gradually and by slow degrees the places abandoned by the functionaries of the empire. Though the hierarchy was already established, and the Bishop of Rome had assumed a special importance in the Church, Paganism still held in the high places that sway of the old economy giving place to the new, which is at once so desperate and so nerveless—impotence and bitterness mingling with the false tolerance of cynicism. The worship of the gods had dropped into a survival of certain habits of mind and life, to which some clung with the angry revulsion of terror against a new revolutionary power at first despised: and some held with the loose grasp of an imaginative and poetical system, and some with a sense of the intellectual superiority of art and philosophy over the arguments and motives that moved the crowd. Life had ebbed away from these religions of the past. The fictitious attempt of Julian to re-establish the worship of the gods, and bring new blood into the exhausted veins of the mythological system, had in reality given the last proof of its extinction as a power in the world: but still it remained lingering out its last, holding a place, sometimes dignified by a gleam of noble manners and the graces of intellectual life—and often, it must be allowed, justified by the failure of the Church to embody that purity and elevation which its doctrines, but scarcely its morals or life, professed. Thus the faith in Christ, often real, but very faulty—and the faith in Apollo, almost always fictitious, but sometimes dignified and superior—existed side by side. The father might hold the latter with a superb indifference to its rites, and a contemptuous tolerance for its opponents, while the mother held the first with occasional hot impulses of devotion, and performances of penance for the pardon of those worldly amusements and dissipations to which she returned with all the more zest when her vigils and prayers were over.

This conjunction of two systems so opposite in every impulse, proceeding from foundations so absolutely contrary to each other, could not fail to have an extraordinary effect upon the minds of the generations moved by it, and affords, I think, an explanation of some events very difficult to explain on ordinary principles, and particularly the abandonment of what would appear the most unquestionable duties, by some of the personages, especially the women whose histories and manners fill this chapter of the great records of Rome. Some of them deserted their children to bury themselves in the deserts, to withdraw to the mountains, placing leagues of land and sea between themselves and their dearest duties—why? the reader asks. At the bidding of a priest, at the selfish impulse of that desire to save their own souls, which in our own day at least has come to mean a degrading motive—is the general answer. It would not be difficult, however, to paint on the other side a picture of the struggle with the authorities of her family for the training of a son, for the marriage of a daughter, from which a woman might shrink with a sense of impotence, knowing the prestige of the noble guardian against whom she would have to contend, and all the forces of family pride, of tradition and use and wont, that would be arrayed against her. Better perhaps, the mother might think, to abandon that warfare, to leave the conflict for which she was not strong enough, than to lose the love of her child as well, and become to him the emblem of an opposing faction attempting to turn him from those delights of youth which the hereditary authority of his house encouraged instead of opposing. It is difficult perhaps for the historians to take such motives into consideration, but I think the student of human nature may feel them to be worth a thought, and receive them as some justification, or at least apology, for the actions of some of the Roman women who fill the story of the time.

Unfortunately it is not possible to leave out the Church in Rome when we collect the details of depravity and folly in Society. One cannot but feel how robust is the faith which goes back to these ages for guidance and example when one sees the image in St. Jerome's pages of a period so early in the history of Christianity. "Could ye not watch with me one hour?" our Lord said to the chosen disciples, His nearest friends and followers, in the moment of His own exceeding anguish, with a reproach so sorrowful, yet so conscious of the weakness of humanity, that it silences every excuse. We may say, for a poor four hundred years could not the Church keep the impress of His teaching, the reality of the faith of those who had themselves fallen and fainted, yet found grace to live and die for their Master? But four centuries are a long time, and men are but men even with the inheritance of Christians. They belonged to their race, their age, and the manifold influences which modify in the crowd everything it believes or wishes. And they were exposed to many temptations which were doubly strong in that world to which by birth and training they belonged. How is an ordinary man to despise wealth in the midst of a society corrupted by it, and in which it is supreme? how learn to be indifferent to rank and prestige in a city where without these every other claim was trampled under foot? "The virtues of the primitive Church," says Villemain of a still later period, "had been under the guard of poverty and persecution: they were weak in success and triumph. Enthusiasm became less pure, the rules of life less severe. In the always increasing crowd of proselytes were many unworthy persons, who turned to Christianity for reasons of ambition and self-interest, to make way at Court, to appear faithful to the emperor. The Church, enriched at once by the spoil of the temples and the offerings of the Christian crowd, began to clothe itself in profane magnificence." Those who attained the higher clerical honours were sure, according to the evidence of Ammianus, "of being enriched by the offerings of the Roman ladies, and drove forth like noblemen in lofty chariots, clothed magnificently, and sat down at tables worthy of kings." The Church, endowed in an earlier period by converts, who offered sometimes all their living for the sustenance of the community which gave them home and refuge, had continued to receive the gifts of the pious after the rules of ordinary life regained their force; and now when she had yielded to a great extent to the prevailing temptations of the age, found a large means of endowment in the gifts of deathbed repentance and the weakness of dying penitents, of which she was reputed to take large advantage: wealth grew within her borders, and luxury with it, according to the example of surrounding society. It is Jerome himself who reports the saying of one of the highest of Roman officials to Bishop Damasus. "If you will undertake to make me Bishop of Rome, I will be a Christian to-morrow." Not even the highest place in the Government was so valuable and so great. It is Jerome also who traces for us— the fierce indignation of his natural temper, mingling with an involuntary perception of the ludicrous side of the picture—a popular young priest of his time, whose greatest solicitude was to have perfumed robes, a well fitting shoe, hair beautifully curled, and fingers glittering with jewels, and who walked on tip-toe lest he should soil his feet.

"What are these men? To those who see them pass they are more like bridegrooms than priests. Some among them devote their life and energies to the single object of knowing the names, the houses, the habits, the disposition of all the ladies in Rome. I will sketch for you, dear Eustochium, in a few lines, the day's work of one of them, great in the arts of which I speak, that by means of the master you may the more easily recognise his disciples.

"Our hero rises with the sun: he regulates the order of his visits, studies the shortest ways, and arrives before he is wanted, almost before his friends are awake. If he perceives anything that strikes his fancy, a pretty piece of furniture or an elegant marble, he gazes at it, praises it, turns it over in his hands, and grieves that he has not one like it—thus extorting rather than obtaining the object of his desires; for what woman would not hesitate to offend the universal gossip of the town? Temperance, modesty (castitas), and fasting are his sworn enemies. He smells out a feast and loves savoury meats.

"Wherever one goes one is sure to meet him; he is always there before you. He knows all the news, proclaims it in an authoritative tone, and is better informed than any one else can be. The horses which carry him to the four quarters of Rome in pursuit of this honest task are the finest you can see anywhere; you would say he was the brother of that King of Thrace known in story by the speed of his coursers.

"This man," adds the implacable satirist in another letter, "was born in the deepest poverty, brought up under the thatch of a peasant's cottage, with scarcely enough of black bread and millet to satisfy the cravings of his appetite; yet now he is fastidious and hard to please, disdaining honey and the finest flour. An expert in the science of the table, he knows every kind of fish by name, and whence come the best oysters, and what district produces the birds of finest savour. He cares only for what is rare and unwholesome. In another kind of vice he is not less remarkable; his mania is to lie in wait for old men and women without children. He besieges their beds when they are ill, serves them in the most disgusting offices, more humble and servile than any nurse. When the doctor enters he trembles, asking with a faltering voice how the patient is, if there is any hope of saving him. If there is any hope, if the disease is cured, the priest disappears with regrets for his loss of time, cursing the wretched old man who insists on living to be as old as Methusalem."

The last accusation, which has been the reproach of the Church in many different ages, had just been specially condemned by a law of the Emperor Valentinian I., declaring null and void all legacies made to priests, a law which called forth Jerome's furious denunciation, not of itself, but of the abuse which called it forth. This was a graver matter than the onslaught upon the curled darlings of the priesthood, more like bridegrooms than priests, who carried the news from boudoir to boudoir, and laid their entertainers under contribution for the bibelots and ancient bric-a-brac which their hearts desired. Thus wherever the eye turned there was nothing but luxury and the love of luxury, foolish display, extravagance and emulation in all the arts of prodigality, a life without gravity, without serious occupation, with nothing in it to justify the existence of those human creatures standing between earth and heaven, and capable of so many better things. The revulsion, a revulsion inspired by disgust and not without extravagance in its new way, was sure to come.

[THE PALATINE, FROM THE AVENTINE]

[THE RIPETTA]

CHAPTER II

THE PALACE ON THE AVENTINE

The strong recoil of human nature from those fatal elements which time after time have threatened the destruction of all society is one of the noblest things in history, as it is one of the most divine in life. There are evidences that it exists even in the most wicked individuals, and it very evidently comes uppermost in every commonwealth from century to century to save again and again from utter debasement a community or a nation. When depravity becomes the rule instead of the exception, and sober principle appears on the point of yielding altogether to the whirl of folly or the thirst of self-indulgence, then it may always be expected that some ember of divine indignation, some thrill of high disgust with the miserable satisfactions of the world will kindle in one quarter or another and set light to a thousand smouldering tires over all the face of the earth. It is one of the highest evidences of that charter of our being which is our most precious possession, the reflection of that image of God which amid all degradations still holds its place in human nature, and will not be destroyed. We may mourn indeed that so short a span of centuries had so effaced the recollection of the brightest light that ever shone among men, as to make the extravagance of a human revulsion and revolution necessary in order to preserve and restore the better life of Christendom. At the same time it is our salvation as a race that such revolutions, however imperfect they may be in themselves, are sure to come.

This revulsion from vice, degradation, and evil of every kind, public and personal, had already come with the utmost excess of self-punishment and austerity in the East, where already the deserts were mined with caverns and holes in the sand, to which hermits and coenobites, the one class scarcely less exalted in religious passion and suffering than the other, had escaped from the current of evil which they did not feel themselves capable of facing, and lived and starved and agonised for the salvation of their own souls and for a world lying in wickedness. The fame of the Thebaid and its saints and martyrs, slowly making itself known through the great distances and silences, had already breathed over the world, when Athanasius, driven by persecution from his see and his country, came to Rome, accompanied by two of the monks whose character was scarcely understood as yet in the West, and bringing with him his own book, the life of St. Antony of the desert, a work which had as great an effect in that time as the most popular of publications, spread over the world in thousands of copies, could have now. It puzzles the modern reader to think how a book should thus have moved the world and revolutionised hundreds of lives, while it existed only in manuscript and every example had to be carefully and tediously copied before it could touch even those who were wealthy enough to secure themselves such a luxury. What readings in common, what earnest circles of auditors, what rapt intense hanging upon the lips of the reader, there must have been before any work, even the most sacred, penetrated to the crowd!—but to us no doubt the process seems more slow and difficult than it really was when scribes were to be found everywhere, and manuscripts were treated with reverence and respect. When Athanasius found refuge in Rome, which was during the pontificate, or rather—for the full papal authority had as yet been claimed by no one—the primacy—of Liberius, and about the year 341, he was received by all that was best in Rome with great hospitality and sympathy. Rome so far as it was Christian was entirely orthodox, the Arian heresy having gained no part of the Christian society there—and a man of genius and imposing character, who brought into that stagnant atmosphere the breath of a larger world, who had shared the councils of the emperor and lived in the cells of Egypt—an orator, a traveller, an exile, with every kind of interest attaching to him, was such a visitor as seldom appeared in the city deserted by empire.

Something like the man who nine centuries later went about the Italian streets with the signs upon him of one who had been through heaven and hell, the Eastern bishop must have appeared to the languid citizens, with the brown of the desert still on his cheeks, yet something of the air of a courtly prelate, a friend of princes; while his attendants, one with all the wildness of a hermit from the desert in his eyes and aspect, in the unfamiliar robe and cowl—and the other mild and young like the ideal youth, shy and simple as a girl—were wonderful apparitions in the fatigued and blasé society, which longed above everything for something new, something real, among all the mocks and shows of their impotent life.

One of the houses in which Athanasius and his monks were most welcome was the palace of a noble widow, Albina, who lived the large and luxurious life of her class in the perfect freedom of a Roman matron, Christian, yet with no idea in her mind of retirement from the world, or renunciation of its pleasures. A woman of a more or less instructive mind and lively intelligence, she received with the greatest interest and pleasure these strangers who had so much to tell, the great bishop flying from his enemies, the monks from the desert. That she and her circle gathered round him with that rapt and flattering attention which not the most abstracted saint any more than the sternest general can resist, is evident from the story, and it throws a gleam of softer light upon the impassioned theologian who stood fast, "I, Athanasius, against the world" for that mysterious splendour of the Trinity, against which the heretical East had risen. In the Roman lady's withdrawingroom, in his dark and flowing Eastern robes, we find him amid the eager questionings of the women, describing to them the strange life of the desert which it was such a wonder to hear of—the evensong that rose as from every crevice of the earth, while the Egyptian after-glow burned in one great circle of colour round the vast globe of sky, diffusing an illumination weird and mystic over the fantastic rocks and dark openings where the singers lived unseen. What a picture to be set before that soft, eager circle, half rising from silken couches, clothed with tissues of gold, blazing with jewels, their delicate cheeks glowing in artificial red and white, their crisped and curled tresses surmounted by the fantastic towering headdress which weighed them down!

Among the ladies was the child of the house, the little girl who was her mother's excuse for retaining the freedom of her widowhood, Marcella: a thoughtful and pensive child, devouring all these wonderful tales, listening to everything and laying up a store of silent resolutions and fancies in her heart. Her elder sister Asella would seem to have already secluded herself in precocious devotion from the family, or at least is not referred to. The story which touched the general mind of the time with so strange and strong an enthusiasm, fell into the virgin soil of this young spirit like the seed of a new life. But the little Roman maiden was no ascetic. She had evidently no impulse, as some young devotees have had, to set out barefoot in search of suffering. When Athanasius left Rome, he left in the house which had received him so kindly his life of St. Antony, the first copy which had been seen in the Western world. This manuscript, written perhaps by the hand of one of those wonderful monks, the strangest figures in her luxurious world whom Marcella knew, became the treasure of her youth. Such a present, at such a time, was enough to occupy the visionary silence of a girl's life, often so full of dreams unknown and unsearchable even to her nearest surroundings. She went through however the usual routine of a young lady's life in Rome. Madame Albina the mother, though full of interest and curiosity in respect to all things intellectual and Christian, held still more dearly a mother's natural desire to see her only remaining child nobly married and established in the splendour and eminence to which she was born. We are told that Marcella grew up to be one of the beauties of Rome, but as this is an inalienable qualification of all these beautiful souls, it is not necessary to believe that the "insignem decorem corporis" meant any extraordinary distinction. She carried out at all events her natural fate and married a rich and noble husband, of whom however we know no details, except that he died some months after, leaving her without child or tie to the ordinary life of the world, in all the freedom of widowhood, at a very early age.

Thus placed in full command of her fate, she never seems to have hesitated as to what she should do with herself. She was, as a matter of course, assailed by many new suitors, among whom her historian, who is no other than St. Jerome himself, makes special mention of the exceptionally wealthy Cerealis ("whose name is great among the consuls"), and who was so splendid a suitor that the fact that he was old scarcely seems to have told against him. Marcella's refusal of this great match and of all the others offered to her, offended and alienated her friends and even her mother, and there followed a moment of pain and perplexity in her life. She is said to have made a sacrifice of a part of her possessions to relatives to whom, failing herself, it fell to keep up the continuance of the family name, hoping thus to secure their tolerance. And she acquired the reputation of an eccentric, and probably of a poseuse, so general in all times when a young woman forsakes the beaten way, as she had done by giving up the ridiculous fashions and toilettes of the time, putting aside the rouge and antimony, the disabling splendour of cloth of gold, and assuming a simple dress of a dark colour, a thing which shocked her generation profoundly. The gossip rose and flew from mouth to mouth among the marble salons where the Roman ladies languished for a new subject, or in the ante-rooms, where young priests and deacons awaited or forestalled the awakening of their patronesses. It might be the Hôtel Rambouillet of which we are reading, and a fine lady taking refuge at Port Royal who was being discussed and torn to pieces in those antique palaces. What was the meaning that lay beneath that brown gown? Was it some unavowed disappointment, or, more exciting still, some secret intrigue, some low-placed love which she dared not acknowledge? Withdrawn into a villa had she, into the solitude of a suburban garden, hid from every eye? and who then was the companion of Marcella's solitude? The ladies who discussed her had small faith in austerities, nor in the desire of a young and attractive woman to live altogether alone.

It is very likely that Marcella herself, as well as her critics, soon began to feel that the mock desert into which she had made the gardens of her villa was indeed a fictitious way of living the holy life, and the calumny was more ready and likely to take hold of this artificial retirement, than of a course of existence led within sight of the world. She finally took a wiser and more reasonable way. Her natural home was a palace upon the Aventine to which she returned, consecrating a portion of it to pious uses, a chapel for common worship and much accommodation for the friends of similar views and purposes who immediately began to gather about her. It is evident that there were already many of these women in the best society of Rome. A lively sentiment of feminine society, of the multiplied and endless talks, consultations, speculations, of a community of women, open to every pleasant curiosity and quick to every new interest, rises immediately before us in that first settlement of monasticism—or, as the ecclesiastical historians call it, the first convent of Rome, before our eyes. It was not a convent after all so much as a large and hospitable feminine house, possessing the great luxury of beautiful rooms and furniture, and the liberal ways of a large and wealthy family, with everything that was most elegant, most cultured, most elevated, as well as most devout and pious. The "Souls," to use our own jargon of the moment, would seem indeed to have been more truly represented there than the Sisters of our modern understanding, though we may acknowledge that there are few communities of Sisters in which this element does not more or less flourish. Christian ladies who were touched like herself with the desire of a truer and purer life, gathered about her, as did the French ladies about Port Royal, and women of the same class everywhere, wherever a woman of influential character leads the way.

The character and position of these ladies was not perhaps so much different as we might suppose from those of the court of Louis XIV. or any other historical period in which great luxuries and much dissipation had sickened the heart of all that was good and noble. Yet there were very special characteristics in their lot. Some of them were the wives of pagan officials of the empire, holding a sometimes devious and always agitated course through the troubles of a divided household: and there were many young widows perplexed with projects of remarriage, of whom some would be tempted by the prospects of a triumphant re-entry into the full enjoyments of life, although a larger number were probably resistant and alarmed, anxious to retain their freedom, or to devote themselves as Marcella had done to a higher life. Women of fashion not unwilling to add a devotion à la mode to their other distractions, women of intellectual aspirations, lovers of the higher education, seekers after a society altogether brilliant and new, without any special emotions of religious feeling, no doubt filled up the ranks. "A society," says Thierry, in his Life of Jerome, "of rich and influential women, belonging for the great part to patrician families, thus organised itself, and the oratory on the Aventine became a seat of lay influence and power which the clergy themselves were soon compelled to reckon with."

The heads of the community bore the noblest names in Rome, which however at that period of universal deterioration was not always a guarantee of noble birth, since the greatest names were sometimes assumed with the slenderest of claims to their honours. Marcella's sister, Asella, older than the rest, and a sort of mother among them, had for a long time before "lived the life" in obscurity and humbleness, and several others not remarkable in the record, were prominent associates. The actual members of the community, however, are not so much remarked or dwelt upon as the visitors who came and went, not all of them of consistent religious character, ladies of the great world. One of these, Fabiola, affords an amusing episode in the graver tale, the contrast of a butterfly of society, a grande dame of fascinating manners, airs, and graces, unfortunate in her husbands, of whom she had two, one of them divorced—and not quite unwilling to divorce the second and try her luck again. Another, one of the most important of all in family and pretensions, and by far the most important in history of these constant visitors, was Paula, a descendant (collateral, the link being of the lightest and easiest kind, as was characteristic of the time) of the great Æmilius Paulus, the daughter of a distinguished Greek who claimed to be descended from Agamemnon, and widow of another who claimed Æneas as his ancestor. These large claims apart, she was certainly a great lady in every sense of the word, delicate, luxurious, following all the fashions of the time. She too was a widow, with a family of young daughters, in that enviable state of freedom which the Roman ladies give every sign of having used and enjoyed to the utmost, the only condition in which they were quite at liberty to regulate their own fate. Paula is the most interesting of the community, as she is the one of whom we know the most. No fine lady more exquisite, more fastidious, more splendid than she. Not even her Christianity had beguiled her from the superlative finery of her Roman habits. She was one of the fine ladies who could not walk abroad without the support of her servants, nor scarcely cross the marble floor from one silken couch to another without tottering, as well she might, under the weight of the heavy tissues interwoven with gold, of which her robes were made. A widow at thirty-five, she was still in full possession of the charms of womanhood, and the sunshine of life (though we are told that her grief for her husband was profound and sincere)—with her young daughters growing up round her, more like her sisters than her children, and sharing every thought. Blæsilla, the eldest, a widow at twenty, was, like her mother, a Roman exquisite, loving everything that was beautiful and soft and luxurious. In the affectionate gibes of the family she is described as spending entire days before her mirror, giving herself up to all the extravagances of dress and personal decoration, the tower of curls upon her head, the touch of rouge on her cheeks. A second daughter, Paulina, was on the eve of marriage with a young patrician, as noble, as rich, and, as was afterwards proved, as devoutly Christian as the family into which he married. The third member of the family, Eustochium, a girl of sixteen, of a character contrasting strongly with those of her beautiful mother and sister, a saint from her birth, was the favourite, and almost the child, of Marcella, instructed by her from her earliest years, and had already fixed her choice upon a monastic life, and would seem to have been a resident in the Aventine palace to which the others were such frequent visitors. Of all this delightful and brilliant party she is the one born recluse, severe in youthful virtue, untouched by any of the fascinations of the world. The following very pretty and graphic story is told of her, in which we have a curious glimpse into the strangely mixed society of the time.

The family of Paula though Christian, and full of religious fervour, or at least imbued with the new spirit of revolt against the corruption of the time, was closely connected with the still existing pagan society of Rome. Her sister-in-law, sister of her husband and aunt of her children, was a certain lady named Prætextata, the wife of Hymettius, a high official under the Emperor Julian the Apostate, both of them belonging, with something of the fictitious enthusiasm of their master, to the faith of the old gods. No doubt one of the severest critics of that society on the Aventine, Prætextata saw with impatience and wrath, what no doubt she considered the artificial gravity, inspired by her surroundings, of the young niece who had already announced her intention never to marry, and to withdraw altogether from the world. Such resolutions on the part of girls who know nothing of the world they abandon have exasperated the most devout of parents, and it was not wonderful if this pagan lady thought it preposterous. The little plot which she formed against the serious girl was, however, of the most good-natured and innocent kind. Finding that words had no effect upon her, the elder lady invited Eustochium to her house on a visit. The young vestal came all unsuspicious in her little brown gown, the costume of humility, but had scarcely entered her aunt's house when she was seized by the caressing and flattering hands of the attendants, interested in the plot as the favourite maids of such an establishment would be, who unloosed her long hair and twisted it into curls and plaits, took away her humble dress, clothed her in silk and cloth of gold, covered her with ornaments and led her before the mirror which reflected all these charms, to dazzle her eyes with the apparition of herself, so different from the schoolroom figure with which she was acquainted. The little plot was clever as well as innocent, and might, no doubt, have made a heart of sixteen beat high. But Eustochium with her Greek name, and her virgin heart, was the grave girl we all know, the one here and there among the garden of girls, born to a natural seriousness which is beyond such temptations. She let them turn her round and round, received sweetly in her gentle calm the applauses of the collected household, looked at her image in the mirror as at a picture—and went home again in her little brown gown with her story to tell, which, no doubt, was an endless amusement and triumph to the ladies on the Aventine, repeated to every new-comer with many a laugh at the foolishness of the clever aunt who had hoped by such means to seduce Eustochium—Eustochium, the most serious of them all!

Such was the first religious community in Rome. It was the natural home of Marcella to which her friends gathered, without in most cases deserting their own palaces, or forsaking their own place in the world—a centre and home of the heart, where they met constantly, the residents ever ready to receive, not only their closer associates, but all the society of Roman ladies, who might be attracted by the higher aspirations of intellect and piety. Not a stone exists of that noble mansion now, but it is supposed to have stood close to the existing church of Sta. Sabina, an unrivalled mount of vision. From that mount now covered with so many ruins the ladies looked out upon the yet unbroken splendour of the city, Tiber far below sweeping round under the walls. Palatinus, with the "white roofs" of that home to which Horatius looked before he plunged into the yellow river, still stood intact at their right hand: and, older far, and longer surviving, the wealth of nature, the glory of the Roman sky and air, the white-blossomed daphne and the starry myrtle, and those roses which are as ancient inhabitants of the world as any we know flinging their glories about the marble balustrades and making the terraces sweet. There would they walk and talk, the recluses at ease and simple in their brown gowns, the great ladies uneasy under the weight of their toilettes, but all eager to hear, to tell, to read the last letter from the East, from the desert or the cloister, to exchange their experiences and plan their charities. There is nothing ascetic in the picture, which is a very different one from that of those austere solitudes of the desert, which had suggested and inspired it—the lady Paula tottering in, with a servant on either side to conduct her to the nearest couch, and young Blæsilla making a brilliant irruption in all her bravery, with her jewels sparkling and her transparent veil floating, and her golden heels tapping upon the marble floor. This is not how we understand the atmosphere of a convent; yet, if fact were taken into due consideration, the greatest convents have been very like it, in all ages—the finest ladies having always loved that intercourse and contrast, half envious of the peace of their cloistered sisters, half pleased to dazzle them with a splendour which never could be theirs.

"No fixed rule," says Thierry, in his Life of St. Jerome, "existed in this assembly, where there was so much individuality, and where monastic life was not even attempted. They read the Holy Scriptures together, sang psalms, organised good works, discussed the condition of the Church, the progress of spiritual life in Italy and in the provinces, and kept up a correspondence with the brothers and sisters outside of a more strictly monastic character. Those of the associates who carried on the ordinary life of the world came from time to time to refresh their spirits in these holy meetings, then returned to their families. Those who were free gave themselves up to devotional exercises, according to their taste and inclination, and Marcella retired into her desert. In a short time these exercises were varied by the pursuit of knowledge. All Roman ladies of rank knew a little Greek, if only to be able to say to their favourites, according to the mot of Juvenal, repeated by a father of the Church, [Greek: Zôê kai psuchê], my life and my soul: the Christian ladies studied it better and with a higher motive. Several later versions of the Old and New Testament were in general circulation in Italy, differing considerably from each other, and this very difference interested anxious minds in referring to the original Greek for the Gospels, and for the Hebrew books to the Greek of the Septuagint, the favourite guide of Western translators. The Christian ladies accordingly set themselves to perfect their knowledge of Greek, and many, among whom were Marcella and Paula, added the Hebrew language, in order that they might sing the psalms in the very words of the prophet-king. Marcella even became, by intelligent comparison of the texts, so strong in exegetical knowledge that she was often consulted by the priests themselves."

[ON THE PALATINE]

It was about the year 380 that this establishment was formed. "The desert of Marcella" above referred to was, as the reader will remember, a great garden in a suburb of Rome, which she had pleased herself by allowing to run wild, and where occasionally this great Roman lady played at a hermit's life in solitude and abstinence. Paula's desert, perhaps not so easy a one, was in her own house, where, besides the three daughters already mentioned, she had a younger girl Rufina, not yet of an age to show any marked tendencies, and a small boy Toxotius, her only son, who was jealously looked after by his pagan relatives, to keep him from being swept away by this tide of Christianity.

Such was the condition of the circle on the Aventine, when a great event happened in Rome. Following many struggles and disasters in the East, chiefly the continually recurring misfortune of a breach of unity, a diocese here and there exhibiting its freedom by choosing two bishops representing different parties at the same time, and thus calling for the exercise of some central authority—Pope Damasus had called a council in Rome. He was so well qualified to be a judge in such cases that he had himself won his see at the point of the sword, after a stoutly contested fight in which much blood was shed, and the church of S. Lorenzo, the scene of the struggle, was besieged and taken like a castle. If he had hoped by this means to establish the universal authority of his see, a pretension as yet undeveloped, it was immediately forestalled by the Bishop of Constantinople, who at once called together a rival council in that place. The Council of Rome, however, is of so much more importance to us that it called into full light in the Western world the great and remarkable figure of Jerome: and still more to our record of the Roman ladies of the Aventine, since it suddenly introduced to them the man whose name is for ever connected with theirs, who is supposed erroneously, as the reader will see, to have been the founder of their community, but who henceforward became its most trusted leader and guide in the spiritual life.

[THE WALLS BY ST. JOHN LATERAN]

CHAPTER III

It may be well, however, before continuing this narrative to tell the story of another Roman lady, not of their band, nor in any harmony with them, which had already echoed through the Christian world, a wild romance of enthusiasm and adventure in which the breach of all the decorums of life was no less remarkable than the abandonment of its duties. Some ten years before the formation of Marcella's religious household (the dates are of the last uncertainty) a young lady of Rome, of Spanish origin, rich and noble and of the highest existing rank, found herself suddenly left in the beginning of a splendid and happy life, in desolation and bereavement. Her husband, whose name is unrecorded, died early leaving her with three little children, and shortly after, while yet unrecovered from this crushing blow, another came upon her in the death of her two eldest children, one following the other. The young woman, only twenty-three, thus terribly stricken, seems to have been roused into a fever of excitement and passion by a series of disasters enough to crush any spirit. It is recorded of her that she neither wept nor tore her hair, but advancing towards the crucifix with her arms extended, her head high, her eyes tearless, and something like a smile upon her lips, thanked God who had now delivered her from all ties and left her free to serve Himself. Whether she had previously entertained this desire, or whether it was only the despair of the distracted mother which expressed itself in such words, we are not told. In the haste and restlessness of her anguish she arranged everything for a great funeral, and placing the three corpses on one bier followed them to Rome to the family mausoleum alone, holding her infant son, the only thing left to her, in her arms. The populace of Rome, eager for any public show, had crowded upon the course of many a triumph, and watched many a high-placed Cæsar return in victory to the applauding city, but never had seen such a triumphal procession as this, Death the Conqueror leading his captives. We are not told whether it was attended by the overflowing charities, extravagant doles and offerings to the poor with which other mourners attempted to assuage their grief, or whether Melania's splendour and solitude of mourning was unsoftened by any ministrations of charity; but the latter is more in accordance with the extraordinary fury and passion of grief, as of a woman injured and outraged by heaven to which she thus called the attention of the spheres.

The impression made by that funeral splendour and by the sight of the young woman following tearless and despairing with her one remaining infant in her arms, had not faded from the minds of the spectators when it was rumoured through Rome that Melania had abandoned her one remaining tie to life and gone forth into the outside world no one knew where, leaving her child so entirely without any arrangement for its welfare that the official charged with the care of orphans had to select a guardian for this son of senators and consuls as if he had been a nameless foundling. What bitterness of soul lay underneath such an incomprehensible desertion, who could say? It might be a sense of doom such as overwhelms some sensitive minds, as if everything belonging to them were fated and nothing left them but the tragic expedient of Hagar in the desert, "Let me not see the child die." Perhaps the courage of the heartbroken young woman sank before the struggle with pagan relations, who would leave no stone unturned to bring up this last scion of the family in the faith or no-faith of his ancestors; perhaps she was in reality devoid of those maternal instincts which make the child set upon the knee the best comforter of the woman to whom they have brought home her warrior dead. This was the explanation given by the world which tore the unhappy Melania to pieces and held her up to universal indignation. Not even the Christians already touched with the enthusiasm and passion of the pilgrim and ascetic could justify the sudden and mysterious disappearance of a woman who still had so strong a natural bond to keep her in her home. But whatever the character of Melania might be, whether destitute of tenderness, or only distracted by grief and bereavement, and hastening to take her fatal shadow away from the cradle of her child, she was at least invulnerable to any argument or persuasion. "God will take care of him better than I can," she said as she left the infant to his fate. It was probably a better one than had he been the charge of this apparently friendless young woman, with her pagan relations, her uncompromising enthusiasm and self-will, and with all the risks surrounding her feet which made the path of a young widow in Rome so full of danger; but it is fortunate for the world that few mothers are capable of counting those risks or of turning their backs upon a duty which is usually their best consolation.

There is, however, an interest in the character and proceedings of such an exceptional woman which has always excited the world, and which the thoughtful spectator will scarcely dismiss with the common imputation of simple heartlessness and want of feeling. Melania was a proud patrician notwithstanding that she flung from her every trace of earthly rank or wealth, and a high-spirited, high-tempered individual notwithstanding her subsequent plunge into the most self-abasing ministrations of charity. And these features of character were not altered by her sudden renunciation of all things. She went forth a masterful personage determined, though no doubt unconsciously, to sway all circumstances to her will, though in the utmost self-denial and with all the appearances and surroundings of humility. This is a paradox which meets us on every side, in the records of such world-abandonment as are familiar in every history of the beginnings of the monastic system, in which continually both men and women give up all things while giving up nothing, and carry their individual will and way through circumstances which seem to preclude the exercise of either.

The disappearance of Melania made a great sensation in Rome, and no doubt discouraged Christian zeal and woke doubts in many minds even while proving to others the height of sacrifice which could be made for the faith. On the other hand the adversary had boundless occasion to blaspheme and denounce the doctrines which, as he had some warrant for saying, thus struck at the very basis of society and weakened every bond of nature. What more dreadful influence could be than one which made a woman forsake her child, the infant whom she had carried in her arms to the great funeral, in the sight of all Rome, the son of her sorrow? Nobody except a hot-headed enthusiast could take her part even among her fellow-Christians, nor does it appear that she sought any support or made any apology for herself. Jerome, then a young student and scholar from the East, was in Rome, in obscurity, still a catechumen preparing for his baptism, at the time of Melania's flight; and though there is no proof that he was even known to her, and no probability that so unknown a person could have anything to do with her resolution, or could have influenced her mind, it was suggested in later times when he was well known, that probably he had much to do—who can tell if not the most powerful and guilty of motives?—in determining her flight. Such a vulgar explanation is always adapted to the humour of the crowd, and gives an easy solution of the problems which are otherwise so difficult to solve. As a matter of fact these two personages, not unlike each other in force and spirit, had much to do with each other, though mostly in a hostile sense, in the after part of their life.

We find Melania again in Egypt, to which presumably she at once directed her flight as the headquarters of austere devotion and self-sacrifice, on leaving Rome—alone so far as appears. This was in the year 372 (nothing can be more delightful than to encounter from time to time a date, like an angel, in the vague wilderness of letters and narratives), when Athanasius the great Bishop was near his end. The young fugitive, whose arrival in Alexandria would not be attended by such mystery as shrouded her departure from Rome, was received kindly by the dying saint, to whom she had probably been known in her better days, and who in his enthusiasm for the life of monastic privation and sacrifice probably considered her flight and her resolution alike inspired by heaven. He gave her, let us hope, his blessing, and much good counsel—in addition to the sacred sheepskin which had formed the sole garment of the holy Macarius in his cell in the desert, which she carried away with her as her most valued possession.

The great Roman lady then pursued her way into the wilderness, which was indeed a wilderness rather in name than in fact, being peopled on every side by communities both of men and women, while in every rocky fissure and cavern were hermits jealously shut each in his hole, the more inaccessible the better. Nothing can be more contradictory than the terms used. This desert of solitaries gave forth the evening hymn over all its extent as if the very sands and rocks sang, so many were the unseen worshippers. And the traveller went into the wilderness alone so to speak, in the utmost self-abnegation and humility, yet attended by an endless retinue of servants whose attendance was indispensable, if only to convey and protect the store of provisions and presents which she carried with her.

The conception of a lonely figure on the edge of a trackless sandy waste facing all perils, and encountering perhaps after toilsome days of solitude a still more lonely anchorite in his cell, to give her the hospitality of a handful of peas, and a shrine of prayer, which is the natural picture which rises before us—changes greatly when the details are examined. Melania evidently travelled with a great caravanserai, with camels laden with grain and every kind of provision that was necessary to sustain life in those regions. The times were more troublous even than usual. The death of Athanasius was the signal for one of those outbursts of persecution which rent the Christian world in its very earliest ages, and which alas! the Church herself has never been slow to learn the use of. The underground or overground population of the Egyptian desert was orthodox; the powers that were, were Arian; and hermits and coenobites alike were hunted out of their refuges and dragged before tribunals, where their case was decided before it was heard and every ferocity used against them. In a country so rent by the most violent of agitations Melania passed like an angel of charity. She became the providence of the hunted and suffering monks. She is said for a short period to have provided for five thousand in Nitria, which proves that however secret her disappearance from Rome had been, her address as we should say must have been well known to her bankers, or their equivalent. Thus it is evident that a robe of sackcloth need not necessarily imply poverty, much less humility, and that a woman may ride about on the most sorry horse (chosen it would seem because it was a more abject thing than the well-conditioned ass of the East) and yet demean herself like a princess.

There is one story told of this primitive Lady Bountiful by Palladius which if it did not recall the action of St. Paul in somewhat similar circumstances would be highly picturesque. The proconsul in Palestine, not at all aware who was the pestilent woman who persisted in supplying and defending the population of the religious which it was his mission to get rid of—even going so far as to visit and nourish them in his prisons—had her arrested to answer for her interference. There is nothing more likely than that Melania remembered the method adopted by St. Paul to bring his judges to his feet. She sent the consul a message in which a certain compassionate scorn mingles with pride. "You esteem me by my present dress," she said, "which it is quite in my power to change when I will. Take care lest you bring yourself into trouble by what you do in your ignorance." This incident happened at Cæsarea, the great city on the Mediterranean shore which Herod had built, and where the prodigious ruins still lie in sombre grandeur capable of restoration to the uses of life. The governor of the Syrian city trembled in his gilded chair. The names which Melania quoted were enough to unseat him half a dozen times over, though, truth to tell, they are not very clearly revealed to the distant student. He hastened to set free the sunburnt pilgrim in her brown gown, and leave her to her own devices. "One must answer a fool according to his folly," she said disdainfully, as she accepted her freedom. This lady's progress through the haunted deserts, her entrance into town after town, with the shield of rank ready for use in any emergency, attended by continual supplies from the stewards of her estates, and the power of shedding abundance round her wherever she went, could hardly be said to merit the rewards of privation and austerity even if her delicate feet were encased in rude sandals and the cloth of gold replaced by a tunic of rough wool.

[COLOSSEUM BY MOONLIGHT]

Melania had been, presumably for some time before this incident, accompanied by a priest named Rufinus, a fellow-countryman, schoolfellow and dear friend of Jerome, the future Father of the Church, at this period a young religious adventurer if we may use the word:—which indeed seems the only description applicable to the bands of young, devout enthusiasts, who roamed about the world, not bound to any special duties, supporting themselves one knows not how, aiming at one knows not what, except some devotion of mystical religious life, or indefinite Christian service to the world. The object of saving their souls was perhaps for most the prevailing object, and the greater part of them had at least passed a year or two in those Eastern deserts where renunciation of the world had been pushed to its furthest possibilities. But they were also hungry for learning, for knowledge, for disciples, and full of that activity of youth which is bound to go everywhere and see everything whether with possible means and motives or not. Whatever they were, they were not so far as can be made out missionaries in any sense of the word. They were received wherever they went, in devout households here and there, in any of the early essays at monasteries which existed by bounty and Christian charity, among the abounding dependents of great houses, or by the bishop or other ecclesiastical functionary. They were this man's secretary, that man's tutor—seldom so far as we can see were they employed as chaplains. Rufinus indeed was a priest, but few of the others were so, Jerome himself only having consented to be ordained from courtesy, and in no way fulfilling the duties of the priesthood. There were, however, many offices no doubt appropriate to them in the household of a bishop, who was often the distributor of great charities and the administrator of great possessions. But it is evident that there were always a number of these scholar-student monks available to join any travelling party, to serve their patron with their knowledge of the desert and their general experience of the ways of the world. "To lead about a sister":—St. Paul perhaps had already in his time some knowledge of the usefulness of such a functionary, and of the perfectly legitimate character of his office. Rufinus joined Melania in this way, to all appearance as the other head of the expedition, on perfectly equal terms, though it was her purse which supplied everything necessary. Jerome himself (with a train of brethren behind him) travelled in the same way with Paula—Oceanus with Fabiola. Nothing could be more completely in accordance with the fashion of the time. Perhaps the young men provided for their own expenses as we say, but the caravan was the lady's and all the immense and indiscriminate charity which flowed from it.

It is not necessary for us to follow the career of Rufinus any more than we intend to follow that of Jerome, into the violent controversy which is the chief link which connects their names, or indeed in any way except that of their association with the women of our tale. Rufinus was a Dalmatian from the shores of the Adriatic, learned enough according to the fashion of his time, though not such a scholar as Jerome, and apt to despise those elegances of literature which he was incapable of appreciating. He too, no doubt, like Jerome, had some following of other men like himself, ready for any adventure, and glad to make themselves the almoners of Melania and form a portion of her train. It is a strange conjunction according to our modern ideas, and no doubt there were vague and flying slanders, such as exist in all ages, accounting for anything that is unusual or mysterious by the worse reasons. But it must be remembered that such partnerships were habitual in those days, permitted by the usage of a time of which absolute purity was the craze and monomania, if we may so speak, as well as the ideal: and also that the solitude of those pilgrims was at all times that of a crowd—the supposed fugitive flying forth alone being in reality, as has been explained already, accompanied on every stage of the way by attendants enough to fill her ship and form her caravan wherever she went.

From Cæsarea, where Melania discomfited the government by her high rank and connections, it is but a little way to Jerusalem, where the steps of the party were directed after their prolonged journey through the desert. It had already become the end of many pilgrimages, the one place in the world which most attracted the hearts and imaginations of the devout throughout all the world; and we can well realise the sensation of the wanderers when they came in sight of that green hill, dominating the scene of so many tragedies, the still half-ruined but immortal city of which the very dust was dear to the primitive Christians. Who that has come suddenly upon that scene in quiet, without offensive guidance or ciceroneship, has not named to himself the Mount of Olives with such a thrill of identification as would move him in scarcely any other landscape in the world? It was still comparatively virgin soil in the end of the fourth century. The Empress Helena had been there, making, as we all feel now, but too easy and too exact discoveries: but the country was unexplored by any vain searchings of curiosity, and the calm of solitude, as perfect and far sweeter than amid the sands of the deserts, was still to be found there. The pilgrims went no further. They chose each their site upon the soft slope of that hill of divine memories. Rufinus took up his abode in a rocky cell, Melania probably in some house in the city, while their monasteries were being built. The great Roman lady with her faithful stewards, always sending those ever valuable supplies, no doubt provided for the expenses of both: and soon two communities arose near each other preserving the fellowship of their founders, where after some years of travel and movement Melania, with strength and courage restored, took up her permanent abode.

It is difficult to decide what is meant by sacrifice and self-abnegation in this world of human subterfuge and self-deception. It is very likely that Melania, like Paula after her, gave herself to the most humble menial offices, and did not scorn, great lady as she was, to bow the haughty head which had made the proconsul of Palestine tremble, to the modest necessities of primitive life. Perhaps she cooked the spare food, swept the bare cells with her own hands: undoubtedly she would superintend the flocks and herds and meagre fields which kept her community supplied. We know that she rode the sorriest horse, and wore the roughest gown. These things rank high in the catalogue of privations, as privations are calculated in the histories of the saints. And yet it is doubtful how far she is to be credited, if it were a merit, with any self-sacrifice. She had attained the full gratification of her own will and way, which is an advantage not easily or often computed. She had settled herself in the most interesting spot in the world, in the midst of a landscape which, notwithstanding all natural aridity and the depressing effects of ruin everywhere, is yet full of beauty as well as interest. Most of all perhaps she was in the way of the very best of company, receiving pilgrims of the highest eminence, bishops, scholars, princes, sometimes ladies of rank like herself, who were continually coming and going, bringing the great news of the world from every quarter to the recluses who thus commanded everything that wealth could supply. One may be sure that, as Jerome and Paula afterwards spent many a serene evening in Bethlehem under their trees, Melania and Rufinus would often sit under those hoary olives doubly grey with age, talking of all things in heaven and earth, looking across the little valley to the wall, all the more picturesque that it was broken, and lay here and there in heaps of ruin, of Jerusalem, and hearing, in the pauses of their conversation, the tinkling of that little brook which has seen so many sacred scenes and over which our Lord and His favourite disciples crossed to Gethsemane, on such a night as that on which His servants sat and talked of Him. It is true that the accursed Arians, and grave news of the fight going on between them and the Catholics, or perhaps the question of Origen's orthodoxy, or how the struggle was going between Paulinus and Meletius at Antioch, might occupy them more than those sacred memories. But it is much to be doubted whether any grandeur of Roman living would have been so much to Melania's mind as the convent on the Mount of Olives, the stream of distinguished pilgrims, and the society of her ever devoted companion and friend.

[THE TEMPLE OF VESTA]

[CHURCHES ON THE AVENTINE]

THE SOCIETY OF MARCELLA

The council which was held in Rome in 382 with the intention of deciding the cases of various contending bishops in distant sees, especially in Antioch where two had been elected for the same seat—a council scarcely acknowledged even by those on whose behalf it was held, and not at all by those opposed to them—was chiefly remarkable, as we have said, from the appearance for the first time, as a marked and notable personage, of one of the most important, picturesque, and influential figures of his time—Jerome: a scholar insatiable in intellectual zeal, who had sought everywhere the best schools of the time and was learned in all their science: and at the same time a monk and ascetic fresh from the austerities of the desert and one of those struggles with the flesh and the imagination which formed the epic of the solitary. It was not unnatural that the régime of extreme abstinence combined with utter want of occupation, and the concentration of all thought upon one's self and one's moods and conditions of mind, should have awakened all the subtleties of the imagination, and filled the brooding spirit with dreams of every wild and extravagant kind; but it would not occur to us now to represent the stormy passage into a life dedicated to religion as filled with dancing nymphs and visions of the grossest sensual enjoyment—above all in the case of such a man as Jerome, whose chief temptations one would have felt to be of quite another kind. This however was the fashion of the time, and belonged more or less to the monkish ideal, which exaggerated the force of all these lower fleshly impulses by way of enhancing the virtue of him who successfully overcame them. The early fathers all scourged themselves till they were in danger of their lives, rolled themselves in the snow, lay on the cold earth, and lived on a handful of dried grain, perhaps on the grass and wild herbs to be found in the crevices of the rocks, in order to get the body into subjection: which might have been more easily done, we should have supposed, by putting other more wholesome subjects in the place of these visionary temptations, or filling the vacancy of the hours with hard work. But the dulness of an English clown or athlete, in whom muscular exercise extinguishes all visions, would not have been at all to the mind of a monkish neophyte, to whom the sharpest stings of penitence and agonies of self-humiliation were necessary, whether he had done anything to call them forth or not.

Jerome had gone through all these necessary sufferings without sparing himself a pang. His face pale with fasting, and his body so worn with penance and privation that it was almost dead, he had yet felt the fire of earthly passions burning in his soul after the truest orthodox model. "The sack with which I was covered," he says, "deformed my members; my skin and flesh were like those of an Ethiop. But in that vast solitude, burnt up by the blazing sun, all the delights of Rome appeared before my eyes. Scorpions and wild beasts were my companions, yet I seemed to hear the choruses of dancing girls."

Finding no succour anywhere, I flung myself at the feet of Jesus, bathing them with tears, drying them with the hair of my head. I passed day and night beating my breast, I banished myself even from my cell, as if it were conscious of all my evil thoughts; and, rigid against myself, wandered further into the desert, seeking some deeper cave, some wilder mountain, some riven rock which I could make the prison of this miserable flesh, the place of my prayers.

Sometimes he endeavoured to find refuge in his books, the precious parchments which he carried with him even in those unlikely regions: but here another temptation came in. "Unhappy that I am," he cries, "I fasted yet read Cicero. After spending nights of wakefulness and tears I found Plautus in my hands."

To lay aside dramatist, orator, and poet, so well known and familiar, and plunge into the imperfectly known character of the Hebrew which he was learning, the uncomprehended mysteries and rude style of the prophets, was almost as terrible as to fling himself fasting on the cold earth and hear the bones rattle in the skin which barely held them together. Yet sometimes there were moments of deliverance: sometimes, when all the tears were shed, gazing up with dry exhausted eyes to the sky blazing with stars, "I felt myself transported to the midst of the angels, and full of confidence and joy, lifted up my voice and sang, 'Because of the savour of thy ointments we will run after thee.'" Thus both were reconciled, his imagination freed from temptation, and the poetry of the crabbed books, which were so different from Cicero, made suddenly clear to his troubled eyes.

This was however but a small part of the training of Jerome. From his desert, as his spirit calmed, he carried on a great correspondence, and many of his letters became at once a portion of the literature of his time. One in particular, an eloquent and oratorical appeal to one of his friends, the Epistle to Heliodorus, with its elaborate description of the evils of the world and impassioned call to the peace of the desert, went through the religious circles of the time with that wonderful speed and facility of circulation which it is so difficult to understand, and was read in Marcella's palace on the Aventine and learnt by heart by some fervent listeners, so precious were its elaborate sentences held to be. This letter boldly proclaimed as the highest principle of life the extraordinary step which Melania, as well as so many other self-devoted persons, had taken—and called every Christian to the desert, whatever duties or enjoyments might stand in the way. Perhaps such exhortations are less dangerous than they seem to be, for the noble ladies who read and admired and learned by heart these moving appeals do not seem to have been otherwise affected by them. Like the song of the Ancient Mariner, they have to be addressed to the predestined, who alone have ears to hear. Heliodorus, upon whom all that eloquence was poured at first hand, turned a deaf ear, and lived and died in peace among his own people, among the lagoons where Venice as yet was not, notwithstanding all his friend could say.

"What make you in your father's house, oh sluggish soldier?" cried that eager voice; "where are your ramparts and trenches, under what tent of skins have you passed the bitter winter? The trumpet of heaven sounds, and the great Leader comes upon the clouds to overcome the world. Let the little ones hang upon other necks; let your mother rend her hair and her garments; let your father stretch himself on the threshold to prevent you from passing: but arise, come thou! Are you not pledged to the sacrifice even of father and mother? If you believe in Christ, fight with me for His name and let the dead bury their dead." There were many who would dwell upon these entreaties as upon a noble song rousing the heart and charming the ear, but the balance of human nature is but rarely disturbed by any such appeal. Even in that early age we may in the greater number of cases permit it to move all hearers without any great fears for the issue.

Jerome, however, did not himself remain very long in his desert; he was invaded in his very cell by the echoes of polemical warfare drifting in from the world he had left: and was called upon to pronounce himself for one side or the other, while yet, according to his own account, unaware what it was all about. He left his retirement unwillingly after some three years, quoting Virgil as to the barbarity of the race which refused him the hospitality of a little sand, and plunged into the fight at Antioch between contending bishops and parties, the heresy of Apollinaris, and all the rage of religious polemics. It was probably his intimate acquaintance with all the questions so strongly contested in the East, and his power of giving information on points which the Western Council could only know at second hand, which led him to Rome on the eve of the Council already referred to, called by Pope Damasus, in 382. The primary object of this Council was to settle matters of ecclesiastical polity, and especially the actual question as to which of the competitors was lawful bishop of Antioch, besides other questions concerning other important sees. It was no small assumption on the part of the bishops of the West, an assumption supported in those days by no dogma as to the supremacy of the Bishop of Rome, to interfere in the affairs of the East to this extent. And it was at once crushed by the action of the Church in the East, which immediately held a council of its own at Constantinople, and authoritatively decided every practical question. Jerome was the friend of all those bishops whose causes would have been pleaded at Rome, had not their own section of the Church thus made short work with them: and this no doubt commended him to the special attention of Damasus, even after these practical questions were set aside, and the heresy of Apollinaris, which had been intended to be treated in the second place, was turned into the only subject before the house. Jerome was deeply learned on the subject of Apollinaris too. It was on account of this new heresy that his place in Egypt had become untenable. His knowledge could not but be of the utmost importance to the Western bishops, who were not as a rule scholars, nor given to the subtle reasoning of the East. He was very welcome therefore in Rome, especially after the illness of the great Ambrose had denuded that Council, shorn of so much of its prestige, of almost the only imposing name left to it. This was the opportunity of such a man as Jerome, in himself, as we have said, still not much different from the many young religious adventurers who scoured the world. He was already, however, a distinguished man of letters: he was known to Damasus, who had baptized him: he had learning enough to supplement the deficiencies of an entire Council, and for once these abilities were fully appreciated and found their right place. He had scarcely arrived in Rome when he was named Secretary of the Council—a temporary office which was afterwards prolonged and extended to that of Secretary to the Pope himself: thus the stranger became at once a functionary of the utmost importance in the proceedings of the See of Rome and in its development as a supreme power and authority in the Church.

There is something strangely familiar and quaint in the appearance, so perfectly known to ourselves, of the gathering of a religious congress, convocation, or general assembly, when every considerable house and hospitable family is moved to receive some distinguished clerical visitor—which thus took place in Rome in the end of the fourth century, while still all was classic in the aspect of the Eternal City, and the altars of the gods were still standing. The bishops and their trains arrived, making a little stir, sometimes even at the marble porticoes of great mansions where the master or mistress still professed a languid devotion to Jove or Mercury. Jerome, burnt brown by Egyptian suns, meagre and sinewy in his worn robe, with a humble brother or two in his train, accepted, after a little modest difficulty, the invitation or the allotment which led him to the Aventine, to the palace of Marcella, where he was already well known, and where, though his eyes were downcast with a becoming reserve at the sight of all the ladies, he yet felt it right to follow the example of the Apostle and industriously overcome his own bashfulness. It was not perhaps a quality very strong in his nature, and very soon his new and splendid habitation became to the ascetic a home more dear than any he had yet known.

It is curious to find how completely the principle of the association and friendship of a man and woman, failing closer ties, was adopted and recognised among these mystics and ascetics, without apparent fear of the comments of the world, or any of the self-consciousness which so often spoils such a relationship in ordinary society. Perhaps the gossips smiled even then upon the close alliance of Jerome with Paula, or Rufinus with Melania. There were calumnies abroad of the coarsest sort, as was inevitable; but neither monk nor lady seem to have been affected by them. It has constantly been so in the history of the Church, and it is interesting to collect such repeated testimony from the most unlikely quarter, to the advantage of this natural association. Women have had hard measure from Catholic doctors and saints. Their conventional position, so to speak, is that of the Seductress, always studying how to draw the thoughts of men away from higher things. The East and the West, though so much apart on other points, are at one in this. From the anguish of the fathers in the desert to the supposed difficulties of the humblest ordinary priest of modern times, the disturbing influence is always supposed to be that of the woman. Gruesome figure as he was for any such temptation, Antony of Egypt himself was driven to extremity by the mere thought of her: and it is she who figures as danger or as victim in every ultra-Protestant plaint over the condition of the priest (except in Ireland, wonderful island of contradictions! where priests and all men are more moved to fighting than to love). Yet notwithstanding there has been no founder of ecclesiastical institutions, no reformer, scarcely any saint, who has not been accompanied by the special friendship and affection of some woman. Jerome, who was so much the reverse, if we may venture to use these words, of a drawing-room hero, a man more used to vituperation than to gentleness of speech, often harsh as the desert from which he had come, was a notable example of this rule. From the time of his arrival on the Aventine to that of his death, his name was never dissociated from that of Paula, the pious lady par excellence of the group, the exquisite and delicate patrician who could scarcely plant her golden shoe firmly on the floor, but came tottering into Marcella's great house with a slave on either side to support her, in all the languid grace which was the highest fashion of the time. That such an example of conventional delicacy and luxury should have become the humble friend and secretary of Jerome, and that he, the pious solitary, acrid with opposition and controversy, should have found in this fine flower of society his life-long companion, both in labour and life, is more astonishing than words can say.

[THE STEPS OF THE CAPITOL]

His arrival in Marcella's hospitable house, with its crowds of feminine visitors, was in every way a great event. It brought the ladies into the midst of all the ecclesiastical questions of the time: and one can imagine how they crowded round him when he returned from the sittings of the Council—perhaps in the stillness of the evening after the dangerous hour of sunset, when all Rome comes forth to breathe again—assembling upon the marble terrace, from which that magical scene was visible at their feet: the long withdrawing distance beyond the river, out of which some gleam might be apparent of the great church which already covered the tombs of the Apostles, and the white crest of the Capitol close at hand, and the lights of the town scattered dimly like glowworms among the wide openings and level lines of classical building which made the Rome of the time. The subjects discussed were not precisely those which the lighter conventional fancy, Boccaccio or Watteau, has associated with such groups, any more than the dark monk resembled the troubadour. But they were subjects which up to the present day have never lost their interest. The debates of the Council were chiefly taken up with an extremely abstruse heresy, concerning the humanity of our Lord, how far the nature of man existed in him in connection with the nature of God, and whether the Redeemer of mankind had taken upon himself a mere ethereal appearance of flesh, or an actual human body, tempted as we are and subject to all the influences which affect man. It is a question which has arisen again and again at various periods and in various manners, and the subtleties of such a controversy have proved of the profoundest interest to many minds. Jerome was not alone to report to those eager listeners the course of the debates, and to demolish over again the intricate arguments by which that assembly of divines wrought itself to fever heat. The great Bishop Epiphanius, the great heresy-hunter of his day—who had fathomed all the fallacious reasonings of all the schismatics, and could detect a theological error at the distance of a continent, in whatever garb it might shield itself—was the guest of Paula, and no doubt, along with his hostess, would often join these gatherings. The two doctors thus brought together would vie with each other in making the course of the controversy clear to the women, who hung upon their lips with keen apprehension of every phrase and the enthusiastic partisanship which inspires debate. There could be no better audience for the fine-drawn arguments which such a controversy demands. How strange to think that these hot discussions were going on, and the flower of the artificial society of Rome keenly occupied by such a question, while still the shadow of Jove lingered on the Capitol, and the Rome of the heathen emperors, the Rome of the great Republic, stood white and splendid, a shadow, yet a mighty one, upon the seven hills!

Before his arrival in Rome, Jerome had been but little known to the general world. His name had been heard in connection with some eloquent letters which had flown about from hand to hand among the finest circles; but his true force and character were better known in the East than in the West, and it was in part this Council which gave him his due place in the ranks of the Church. He was no priest to be promoted to bishoprics or established in high places. He had indeed been consecrated against his will by an enthusiastic prelate, eager to secure his great services to the Church; but, monk and ascetic as he was, he had no inclination towards the sacerdotal character, and had said but one mass, immediately after his ordination, and no more. It was not therefore as spiritual director in the ordinary sense of the words that he found his place in Marcella's house, but at first at least as a visitor merely and probably for the time of the Council alone. But the man of the desert would seem to have been charmed out of himself by the unaccustomed sweetness of that gentle life. He would indeed have been hard to please if he had not felt the attraction of such a retreat, not out of, but on the edge of, the great world, with its excitements and warfare within reach, the distant murmur of the crowd, the prospect of the great city with its lights and rumours, yet sacred quiet and delightful sympathy within. The little community had given up the luxuries of the age, but they could not have given up the refinements of gentle breeding, the high-born manners and grace, the charm of educated voices and cultivated minds. And there was even more than these attractions to gratify the scholar. Not an allusion could be made to the studies of which he was most proud, the rugged Hebrew which he had painfully mastered, or ornate Greek, but some quick intelligence there would take it up; and the poets and sages of their native tongue, the Cicero and Virgil from whom he could not wean himself even in the desert, were their own literature, their valued inheritance. And not in the most devoted community of monks could the great orator have found such undivided attention and interest in his work as among the ladies of the Aventine, or secretaries so eager and ready to help, so proud to be associated with it. He was at the same time within reach of Bishop Damasus, a man of many experiences, who seems to have loved him as a son, and who not only made him his secretary, but his private counsellor in many difficulties and dangers: and Jerome soon became the centre also of a little band of chosen friends, distinguished personages in Roman society connected in faith and in blood with the sisterhood, whom he speaks of as Daniel, Ananias, Azarias, and Misael, some of whom were his own old companions and schoolfellows, all deeply attached to him and proud of his friendship. No more delightful position could have been imagined for the repose and strengthening of a man who had endured many hardships, and who had yet before him much more to bear.

Jerome remained nearly three years in this happy retreat, and it was here that he executed the first portion of his great work, that first authoritative translation of the entire Canon of Scripture which still retains its place in the Church of Rome—the Vulgate, so named when the Latin of Jerome, which is by no means that of Cicero, was the language of the crowd. In every generation what is called the higher education of women is treated as a new and surprising thing by the age, as if it were the greatest novelty; but we doubt whether Girton itself could produce graduates as capable as Paula and Marcella of helping in this work, discussing the turning of a phrase or the meaning of an abstruse Hebrew word, and often holding their own opinion against that of the learned writer whose scribes they were so willing to be. This undertaking gave a double charm to the life, which went on with much variety and animation, with news from all quarters, with the constant excitement of a new charity established, a new community founded: and never without amusement either, much knowledge of the sayings and doings of society outside, visits from the finest persons, and a daily entertainment in the flutterings of young Blæsilla between the world and the convent, and her pretty ways, so true a woman of the world, yet all the same a predestined saint: and the doings of Fabiola, one day wholly absorbed in the foundation of her great hospital, the first in Rome, the next not so sure in her mind that love, even by means of a second divorce, might not win the day over devotion. Even Paula in these days was but half decided, and came, a dazzling vision in her jewels and her crown, to visit her friends, in all the pomp of autumnal beauty, among her daughters, of whom that serious little maiden Eustochium was the only one quite detached from the world. For was there not also going on under their eyes the gentle wooing of Pammachius and Paulina to make it apparent to the world that the ladies on the Aventine did not wholly discredit the ordinary ties of life, although they considered with St. Paul that the other was the better way? The lovers were as devout and as much given up to good works as any of them, yet, as even Jerome might pardon once in a way, preferred to the cloister the common happiness of life. These good works were the most wonderful part of all, for every member of the community was rich. Their fortunes were like the widow's cruse. One hears of great foundations like that of Fabiola's hospital and Melania's provision for the monks in Africa, for which everything was sacrificed; yet, next day, next year, renewed beneficences were forthcoming, and always a faithful intendant, a good steward, to continue the bountiful supplies. So wonderful indeed are these liberalities, and so extraordinary the details, that it is surprising to find that no learned German, or other savant, has, as yet, attempted to prove that the fierce and vivid Jerome never existed, that his letters were the work of half a dozen hands, and the subjects of his brilliant narrative altogether fictitious—Melania and Paula being but mythical repetitions of the same incident, wrapt in the colours of fable. This hypothesis might be made to seem very possible if it were not, perhaps, a little too late in the centuries for the operations of that high-handed criticism, and Jerome himself a very hard fact to encounter.

But the great wealth of these ladies remains one of the most singular circumstances in the story. When they sell and sacrifice everything it is clear it must only be their floating possessions, leaving untouched the capital, as we should say, or the estates, perhaps, more justly, the wealthy source from which the continued stream flowed. This gave a splendour and a largeness of living to the home on the Aventine. There was no need to send any petitioner away empty, charity being the rule of life, and no thought having as yet entered the most elevated mind that to give to the poor was inexpedient for them, and apt to establish a pauper class, dependent and willing to be so. These ladies filled with an even and open hand every wallet and every mouth. They received orphans, they provided for widows, they filled the poor quarters below the hill—where all the working people about the Marmorata clustered near the river bank, in the garrets and courtyards of the old houses—with asylums and places of refuge. The miserable and idle populace of which the historian speaks so contemptuously, the fellows who hung about the circuses, and had no name but the nicknames of coarsest slang, the Cabbage-feeders, the Sausage-eaters, &c., the Porringers and Gluttons, were, no doubt, left all the more free to follow their own foul devices; but the poor women, who though perhaps far from blameless suffer most in the debasement of the population, and the unhappy little swarms of children, profited by this universal balm of charity, and let us hope grew up to something a little better than their sires. For however paganism might linger among the higher class, the multitudes were all nominally Christian. It was to the tombs of the Apostles that they made their pilgrimages, rather than to the four hundred temples of the gods. "For all its gilding the Capitol looks dingy," says Jerome himself in one of his letters; "every temple in Rome is covered with soot and cobwebs, and the people pour past those half-ruined shrines to visit the tombs of the apostles."

The house of Marcella was in the condition we have attempted to describe when Jerome became its guest. It was in no way more rigid in its laws than at the beginning. The little ecclesia domestica, as he happily called it, seems to have been entirely without rule or conventual order. They sang psalms together (sometimes we are led to believe, in the original Hebrew learned for the purpose—but it must have been few who attained to this height), they read together, they held their little conferences on points of doctrine, with much consultation of learned texts; but there is no mention even of any regular religious service, much less of matins, and vespers, and nones and compline, and the other ritualistic divisions of a monastic day; for indeed no rule had been as yet invented for any coenobites of the West. We do not hear even of a daily mass. Often there were desertions from the ranks, sometimes a young maiden withdrawing from the social enclosure, sometimes a young widow drawn back into the vortex of the fashionable world. But on the whole the record of the little domestic church, with its bodyguard of faithful friends and servitors outside, and Jerome, its pride and crown of glory, within, is one of serene and happy life, dignified by everything that was best in the antique world.

It was after the arrival of Jerome that the little tragedy of Blæsilla, the eldest daughter of Paula, occurred, rending their gentle hearts. "Our dear widow," as Jerome called her, had no idea of second marriage in her mind. The first, it would appear, had not been happy; and Blæsilla, fair and rich and young, had every mind to enjoy her freedom, her fine dresses, and all the pleasures of her youth. Safely lodged under her mother's wing, with those irreproachable friends 011 the Aventine about her, no gossip touched her gentle name. The community amused itself with her light-hearted ways. "Our widow loves to adorn herself. She is the whole day before her mirror," says Jerome, and there is no harsh tone in his voice. But in the midst of her gay and innocent life she fell ill of a fever, no unusual thing. It lingered, however, more than a month and took a dangerous form, so that the doctors began to despair.

When things were at this point Blæsilla had a dream or vision, in her fever, in which the Saviour appeared to her and bade her arise as He had done to Lazarus. It was the crisis of the disease, and she immediately began to recover, with the deepest faith that she had been cured by a miracle. The butterfly was touched beyond measure by this divine interposition, as she believed, in her favour, and as soon as she was well, made up her mind to devote herself to God. "An extraordinary thing has happened," cries Jerome. "Blæsilla has put on a brown gown! What a scandal is this!" He launches forth thereupon into a diatribe upon the fashionable ladies, with faces of gypsum like idols, who dare not shed a tear lest they should spoil their painted cheeks, and who are the true scandal to Christianity: then narrates with growing tenderness the change that has taken place in the habits of the young penitent. She, whose innocent head was tortured with curls and plaits and crowned with the fashionable mitella, now finds a veil enough for her. She lies on the ground who found the softest cushions hard, and is up the first in the morning to sing Alleluia in her silvery voice.

The conversion rang through Rome all the more that Blæsilla was known to have had no inclination toward austerity of life. Her relations, half pagan and altogether worldly, were hot against the fanatic monk, who according to the usual belief tyrannised over the whole house in which he had been so kindly received, and the weak-minded mother who had lent herself to his machinations. The question fired Rome, and became a matter of discussion under every portico and wherever men or women assembled. Was it lawful, had it any warrant in law or history, this new folly of opposing marriage and representing celibacy as a happier and holier state? It was against every tradition of the race; it tore families in pieces, abstracted from society its most brilliant members, alienated the patrimony of families, interfered with succession and every natural law. In the turmoil raised by this event, a noisy public controversy arose. Two assailants presented themselves, one a priest, who had been for a time a monk, and one a layman, to maintain the popular canon, the superiority of marriage and the natural life of the world. These arguments had a great effect upon the public mind, naturally prone to take fright at any interference with its natural laws. They had very serious results at a later period both in the life of Paula and that of Jerome, and they seem to have threatened for a time serious injury to the newly established convents which Marcella's community had planted everywhere, and from which half-hearted sisters took this opportunity of separating themselves. It is amusing to find that, by a curious and furious twist of the usual argument, Jerome in his indignant and not always temperate defence describes these deserters as old and ugly, and unable to find husbands notwithstanding the most desperate efforts. It has been very common to allege this as a reason for the self-dedication of nuns: and it is always a handy missile to throw.

Jerome was not the man to let any such fine opening for a controversy pass. He burst forth upon his opponents, thundering from the heights of the Aventine, reducing the feeble writers who opposed him to powder. Helvidius, the layman above mentioned, had taken up the question—a question always offensive and injurious to natural sentiment and prejudice, exclusive even of religious feeling, and which, whatever opinions may prevail, it must always be profane to touch—of the Virgin Mary herself, and the existence of persons called brothers and sisters of our Lord. To him Jerome replied by a flood of angry eloquence, as well as some cogent argument—though argument, however strong, is insupportable on such a subject. And he launched forth upon the other, Jovinian, the false monk, that famous letter on Virginity, nominally addressed to Eustochium, in which one of the most trenchant pictures ever made of society, both lay and clerical—the habits, the ideas, the follies of debased and fallen Rome—is of far more force and importance than the argument, and furnishes us with such a spectacle as very few writers at any time or in any place are capable of placing before the eyes of the world. I have already quoted from this wonderful composition the portrait of the popular priest.

The foolish virgin who puts on an appearance of indifference to worldly things, and "under the ensign of a holy profession draws towards her the regard of men," is treated with equal severity.

We cast out and banish from our sight those virgins who only wish to seem to be so. Their robes have but a narrow stripe of purple, they let their hair hang about their shoulders, their sleeves are short and narrow, and they have cheap shoes upon their feet. This is all their sanctity. They make by these pretences a higher price for their innocence. Avoid, dear Eustochium, the secret thought that having ceased to court attention in cloth of gold you may begin to do so in mean attire. When you come into an assembly of the brothers and sisters do not, like some, choose the lowest seat or plead that you are unworthy of a footstool. Do not speak with a faltering voice as if worn out with fasting, or lean upon the shoulders of your neighbours as if fainting. There are some who thus disfigure their faces that they may appear to men to fast. As soon as they are seen, they begin to groan, they look down, they cover their faces, all but one eye. Their dress is sombre, their girdles are of sackcloth. Others assume the mien of men, blushing that they have been born women, who cut their hair short, and walk abroad with effrontery, confronting the world with the impudent faces of eunuchs.... I have seen, but will not name, one among the noblest of Rome who in the very basilica of the blessed Peter gave alms with her own hands at the head of her retinue of servants, but struck in the face a poor woman who had twice held out her hand. Flee also the men who wear an iron chain, who have long hair like women against the rule of the Apostle, a miserable black robe, who go barefooted in the cold, and have in appearance at least an air of sadness and anxiety.

The following sketch of the married woman who thinks of the things of the world, how she may please her husband, while the unmarried are free to please God, has an interest long outliving the controversy, in the light it throws upon contemporary Roman life.

Do you think there is no difference between one who spends her time in fastings, and humbles herself night and day in prayer—and her who must prepare her face for the coming of her husband, ornament herself, and put on airs of fascination? The first veils her beauty and the graces which she despises; the other paints herself before a mirror, to make herself more fair than God has made her. Then come the children, crying, rioting, hanging about her neck, waiting for her kiss. Expenses follow without end, her time is spent in making up her accounts, her purse always open in her hand. Here there is a troop of cooks, their garments girded like soldiers for the battle, hashing and steaming. Then the women spinning and babbling. Anon comes the husband, followed by his friends. The wife flies about like a swallow from one end of the house to the other, to see that all is right, the beds made, the marble floors shining, flowers in the vases, the dinner prepared. Is there in all that, I ask, a thought of God? Are these happy homes? No, the fear of God is absent there, where the drum is sounded, the lyre struck, where the flute breathes out and the cymbals clash. Then the parasite abandons shame and glories in it, if he amuses the host who has invited him. The victims of debauch have their place at these feasts; they appear half naked in transparent garments which unclean eyes see through. What part is there for the wife in these orgies? She must learn to take pleasure in such scenes, or else to bring discord into her house.

He paints for us, in another letter, a companion picture of the widow remarried.

Your contract of marriage will scarcely be written when you will be compelled to make your will. Your new husband pretends to be very ill, and makes a will in your favour, desiring you to do the same. But he lives, and it is you who die. And if it happens that you have sons by your second marriage, war blazes forth in your house, a domestic contest without term or conclusion. Those who owe life to you, you are not permitted to love equally, fully. The second envies the caress which you give to the son of the first. If, on the contrary, it is he who has children by another wife, although you may be the most loving of mothers, you are condemned as a stepmother by all the rhetoric of the comedies, the pantomimes, and orators. If your stepson has a headache you have poisoned him. If he eats nothing you starve him, if you serve him his food it is worse still. What compensation is there in a second marriage to make up for so many woes?

This tremendous outburst and others of a similar kind raised up, as was natural, a strong feeling against Jerome. It was not likely that the originals of these trenchant sketches would forgive easily the man who put them up in effigy on the very walls of Rome. That the pictures were identified was clear from another letter, in which he asks whether he is never to speak of any vice or folly lest he should offend a certain Onasus, who took everything to himself. Little cared he whom he offended, or what galled jade might wince. But at last the remonstrances of his friends subdued his rage. "When you read this you will bend your brows and check my freedom, putting a finger on my mouth to stop me from speaking," he wrote to Marcella. It was full time that the prudent mistress of the house which contained such a champion should interfere.

While still the conflict raged which had been roused by the retirement of Blæsilla from the world, and which had thus widened into the general question, far more important than any individual case, between the reforming party in the Church, the Puritans of the time—then specially represented by the new development of monasticism—and the world which it called all elevated souls to abandon: incidents were happening which plunged the cheerful home on the Aventine into sorrow and made another noble house in Rome desolate. The young convert in the bloom of her youthful devotion, who had been raised up miraculously as they all thought from her sick bed in order that she might devote her life to Christ, was again struck down by sickness, and this time without any intervention of a miracle. Blæsilla died in the fulness of her youth, scarcely twenty-two, praying only that she might be forgiven for not having been able to do what she had wished to do in the service of her Lord. She was a great lady, though she had put her natural splendour away from her, and it was with all the pomp of a patrician funeral that she was carried to her rest. It is again Jerome who makes visible to us the sad scene of this funeral, and the feeling of the multitude towards the austere reformers who had by their cruel exactions cut off this flower of Roman society before her time. Paula, the bereaved mother, followed, as was the custom, the bier of her daughter through the crowded streets of Rome, scarcely able in the depths of her grief to support herself, and at last fell fainting into the arms of the attendants and had to be carried home insensible. At this sight, which might have touched their hearts, the multitude with one voice cried out against the distracted mother. "She weeps, the daughter whom she has killed with fastings," they cried. "Why are not these detestable monks driven from the city? why are they not stoned or thrown into the river? It is they who have seduced this miserable woman to be herself a monk against her will—this is why she weeps for her child as no woman has ever wept before." Paula, let us hope, did not hear these cries of popular rage. The streets rung with them, the populace always ready for tumult, and the disgusted and angry nobles encouraging every impulse towards revolt. No doubt many of the higher classes had looked on with anxiety and alarm at the new movement which dissipated among the poor so many fine inheritances and threatened to carry off out of the world, of which they had been the ornaments, so many of the most distinguished women. Any sudden rising which might kill or banish the pestilent monk or disperse the troublesome community would naturally find favour in their eyes.

[THE LATERAN FROM THE AVENTINE]

[PORTICO OF OCTAVIA]

CHAPTER V

PAULA

Paula was a woman of very different character from the passionate and austere Melania who preceded and resembled her in many details of her career. Full of tender and yet sprightly humour, of love and gentleness and human kindness, a true mother benign and gracious, yet with those individualities of lively intelligence, understanding, and sympathy which quicken that mild ideal and bring in all the elements of friendship and the social life—she was the most important of those visitors and associates who made the House on the Aventine the fashion, and filled it with all that was best in Rome. Though her pedigree seems a little delusive, her relationship to Æmilius Paulus resolving itself into a descent from his sister through her own mother, it is yet apparent that her claims of the highest birth and position were fully acknowledged, and that no Roman matron held a higher or more honourable place. She was rich as they all were, highly allied, the favourite of society, neglecting none of its laws, though always with a love of intellectual intercourse and a tendency to devotion. Which of these tendencies drew her first towards Marcella and her little society we cannot tell: but it is evident that both found satisfaction there, and were quickened by the strong impulse given by Jerome when he came out of the schools and out of the wilds, at once Scholar and Hermit, to this house of friendship, the Ecclesia Domestica of Rome. That all this rising tide of life, the books, the literary work, the ever-entertaining companionship, as well as the higher influence of a life of self-denial and renunciation, as understood in those days—should have at first added a charm even to that existence upon its border, the life in which every motive contradicted the new law, is very apparent. Many a great lady, deeply plunged in all the business of the world, has felt the same attraction, the intense pleasure of an escape from those gay commotions which in the light of the other life seem so insignificant and wearisome, the sensation of rest and tranquillity and something higher, purer, in the air—which yet perhaps at first gave a zest to the return into the world, in itself once more a relief from that higher tension and those deeper requirements. The process by which the attraction grew is very comprehensible also. Common pleasures and inane talk of society grow duller and duller in comparison with the conversation full of wonders and revelations which would keep every faculty in exercise, the mutual studies, the awe yet exhilaration of mutual prayers and psalms, the realisation of spiritual things. And no doubt the devout child's soul so early fixed, the little daughter who had thought of nothing from her cradle but the service of God, must have drawn the ever-tender, ever-sympathetic mother still nearer to the centre of all. The beautiful mother among her girls, one betrothed, one self-consecrated, one in all the gay emancipation of an early widowhood, affords the most charming picture among the graver women—women all so near to each other in nature,—mutually related, members of one community, linked by every bond of common association and tradition.

When Blæsilla on her recovery from her illness threw off her gaieties and finery, put on the brown gown, and adopted all the rules of the community, the life of Paula, trembling between two spheres, was shaken by a stronger impulse than ever before. But how difficult was any decision in her circumstances! She had her boy and girl at home as yet undeveloped—her only boy, dragged as much as might be to the other side, persuaded to think his mother a fanatic and his sisters fools. Paula did all she could to combine the two lives, indulging perhaps in an excess of austerities under the cloth of gold and jewels which, as symbols of her state and rank, she could not yet put off. The death of Blæsilla was the shock which shattered her life to pieces. Even the coarse reproaches of the streets show us with what anguish of mourning this first breach in her family overwhelmed her. "This is why she weeps for her child as no woman has ever wept before," the crowd cried, turning her sorrow into an accusation, as if she had thus acknowledged her own fault in leaving Blæsilla to privations she was not able to endure. Did the cruel censure perhaps awake an echo in her heart, ready as all hearts are in that moment of prostration to blame themselves for something neglected, something done amiss? At least it would remind Paula that she herself had never made completely this sacrifice which her child had made with such fatal effect. She was altogether overcome by her sorrow: her sobs and cries rent the hearts of her friends. She refused all food, and when exhausted by the paroxysms of violent grief fell into a lethargy of despair more alarming still. When every one else had tried their best to draw her from this excess of affliction, the ladies had recourse to Jerome in their extremity: for it was clear that Paula must be roused from this collapse of all courage and hope, or she must die.

Jerome did not refuse to answer the appeal: though helpless as even the most anxious affection is in face of this anguish of the mother which will not be comforted, he did what he could; he wrote to her from the house of their friends who shared yet could not still her sorrow, a letter full of grief and sympathy, in the forlorn hope of bringing her back to life. Such letters heaven knows are common enough. We have all written, and most of us have received them, and found in their tender arguments, in their assurances of final good and present fellow feeling, only fresh pangs and additional sickness of heart. Yet Jerome's letter was not of a common kind. No one could have touched the shrinking heart with a softer touch than this fierce controversialist, this fiery and remorseless champion: for he had yet a more effectual spell to move the mourner, in that he was himself a mourner, not much less deeply touched than she. "Who am I," he cries, "to forbid the tears of a mother who myself weep? This letter is written in tears. He is not the best consoler whom his own groans master, whose being is un-manned, whose broken words distil into tears. Yes, Paula, I call to witness Christ Jesus whom our Blæsilla now follows, and the angels who are now her companions, I, too, her father in the spirit, her foster-father in affection, could also say with you—Cursed be the day that I was born. Great waves of doubt surge over my soul as over yours. I, too, ask myself why so many old men live on, why the impious, the murderers, the sacrilegious, live and thrive before our eyes, while blooming youth and childhood without sin are cut off in their flower." It is not till after he has thus wept with her that he takes a severer tone. "You deny yourself food, not from desire of fasting, but of sorrow. If you believed your daughter to be alive, you would not thus mourn that she has migrated to a better world. Have you no fear lest the Saviour should say to you, 'Are you angry, Paula, that your daughter has become my daughter? Are you vexed at my decree, and do you with rebellious tears grudge me the possession of Blæsilla?' At the sound of your cries Jesus, all-clement, asks, 'Why do you weep? the damsel is not dead but sleepeth.' And when you stretch yourself despairing on the grave of your child, the angel who is there asks sternly, 'Why seek ye the living among the dead?'"

In conclusion Jerome adds a wonderful vow: "So long as breath animates my body, so long as I continue in life, I engage, declare and promise that Blæsilla's name shall be for ever on my tongue, that my labours shall be dedicated to her honour, and my talents devoted to her praise." It was the last word which the enthusiasm of tenderness could say: and no doubt the fervour and warmth of the promise, better kept than such promises usually are, gave a little comfort to the sorrowful soul.

When Paula came back to the charities and devotions of life after this terrible pause a bond of new friendship was formed between her and Jerome. They had wept together, they bore the reproach together, if perhaps their trembling hearts might feel there was any truth in it, of having possibly exposed the young creature they had lost to privations more than she could bear. But it is little likely that this modern refinement of feeling affected these devoted souls; for such privations were in their eyes the highest privileges of life, and in fasting man was promoted to eat the food of angels. At all events, the death of Blæsilla made a new bond between them, the bond of a mutual and most dear remembrance never to be forgotten.

This natural consequence of a common sorrow inflamed the popular rage against Jerome to the wildest fury. Paula's relations and connections, half of them, as in most cases in the higher ranks of society, still pagan—who now saw before them the almost certain alienation to charitable and religious purposes of Paula's wealth, pursued him with calumny and outrage, and did not hesitate to accuse the lady and the monk of a shameful relationship and every crime. To make things worse, Damasus, whose friend and secretary, almost his son, Jerome had been, died a few months after Blæsilla, depriving him at once of that high place to which the Pope's favour naturally elevated him. He complains of the difference which his close connection with Paula's family had made on the general opinion of him. "All, almost without exception, thought me worthy of the highest sacerdotal position; there was but one word for me in the world. By the mouth of the blessed Damasus it was I who spoke. Men called me holy, humble, eloquent." But all this had changed since the recent events in Paula's house. She on her side, wounded to the heart by the reproaches poured upon her, and the shameful slanders of which she was the object, and which had no doubt stung her into renewed life and energy, resolved upon a step stronger than that of joining the community, and announced her intention of leaving Rome, seeking a refuge in the holy city of Jerusalem, and shaking the dust of her native country, where she had been so vilified, from her feet. This resolution was put to Jerome's account as might have been expected, and when his patron's death left him without protection every enemy he had ever made, and no doubt they were many, was let loose. He whom courtiers had sought, whose hands had been kissed and his favour implored by all who sought anything from the Pope, was now greeted when he appeared in the streets by fierce cries of "Greek," "Impostor," "Monk," and his presence became a danger for the peaceful house in which he had found a refuge.

It is scarcely possible to be very sorry for Jerome. He had not minced his words; he had flung libels and satires about that must have stung and wounded many, and in such matters reprisals are inevitable. But Paula had done no harm. Even granting the case that Blæsilla's health had been ruined by fasting, the mother herself had gone through the same privations and exulted in them: and her only fault was to have followed and sympathised in, with enthusiasm, the new teaching and precepts of the divine life in the form which was most highly esteemed in her time. No cry from that silent woman comes into the old world, ringing with so many outcries, where the rude Roman crowd bellowed forth abuse, and the ladies on their silken couches whispered the scandal of Paula's liaison to each other, and the men scoffed and sneered over their banquets at the mere thought of such a friendship being innocent. Some one of their enemies ventured to speak or write publicly the vile accusation, and was instantly brought to book by Jerome, and publicly forswore the scandal he had spread. "But," as Jerome says, "a lie is hard to kill; the world loves to believe an evil story: it puts its faith in the lie, but not in the recantation." And the situation of affairs became such that he too saw no expedient possible but that of leaving Rome. He would seem to have been, or to have imagined himself, in danger of his life, and his presence was unquestionably a danger for his friends. A man of more patient temperament and quiet mind might have thought that Paula's resolution to go away was a reason for him to stay, and thus to bear the scandal and outrage alone, at least until she was safe out of its reach—giving no possible occasion for the adversary to blaspheme. But Jerome was evidently not disposed to any such self-abnegation, and indeed it is very likely that his position had become intolerable and that his only resource was departure. It was in the summer of 385, nearly three years after his arrival in Rome—in August, seven months after the death of Damasus, and not a year after that of Blæsilla, that he left "Babylon," as he called the tumultuous city, writing his farewell with tears of grief and wrath to the Lady Asella, now one of the eldest and most important members of the community, and thanking God that he was found worthy of the hatred of the world. We are apt to speak as if travelling were an invention of our time: but as a matter of fact facilities of travelling then existed little inferior to those we ourselves possessed thirty or forty years ago, and it was no strange or unusual journey from Ostia at the mouth of the Tiber, by the soft Mediterranean shores, past the vexed rocks of the Sirens in the blazing weather, to Cyprus that island of monasteries, and Antioch a vexed and heresy-tainted city yet full of friends and succour. Jerome had a cluster of faithful followers round him, and was escorted by a weeping crowd to the very point of his embarkation: but yet swept forth from Rome in a passion of indignation and distress.

[TEMPLE OF VENUS AND ROME FROM THE COLOSSEUM (1860)]

It was while waiting for the moment of departure in the ship that was to carry him far from his friends and the life he loved, that Jerome's letters to Asella were written. They were full of anger and sorrow, the utterance of a heart sore and wounded, of a man driven almost to despair. "I am said," he cries, "to be an infamous person, a deceiver full of guile, an impostor with all the arts of Satan at his fingers' ends.... These men have kissed my hands in public, and stung me in secret with a viper's tooth; they compassionate me with their lips and rejoice in their hearts. But the Lord saw them, and had them in derision, reserving them to appear with me, his unfortunate servant, at the last judgment. One of them ridicules my walk, and my laugh: another makes of my features a subject of accusation: to another the simplicity of my manners is the evil thing: and I have lived three years in the company of such men!" He continues his indignant self-defence as follows:

"I have lived surrounded by virgins, and to some of them I explained as best I could the divine books. With study came an increased knowledge of each other, and with that knowledge mutual confidence. Let them say if they have ever found anything in my conduct unbecoming a Christian. Have I not refused all presents, great or small? Gold has never sounded in my palm. Have they heard from my lips any doubtful word, or seen in my eyes a bold or hazardous look? Never, and no one dares say so. The only objection to me is that I am a man: and that objection only appeared when Paula announced her intention of going to Jerusalem. They believed my accuser when he lied: why do they not believe him when he retracts? He is the same man now as then. He imputed false crimes to me, now he declares me innocent. What a man confesses under torture is more likely to be true than that which he gives forth in a moment of gaiety: but people are more prone to believe such a lie than the truth.

"Of all the ladies in Rome Paula only, in her mourning and fasting, has touched my heart. Her songs were psalms, her conversations were of the Gospel, her delight was in purity, her life a long fast. But when I began to revere, respect, and venerate her, as her conspicuous virtue deserved, all my good qualities forsook me on the spot.

"Had Paula and Melania rushed to the baths, taken advantage of their wealth and position to join, perfumed and adorned, in one worship God and their wealth, their freedom and pleasure, they would have been known as great and saintly ladies; but now it is said they seek to be admired in sackcloth and ashes, and go down to hell laden with fasting and mortifications: as if they could not as well have been damned along with the rest, amid the applauses of the crowd. If it were Pagans and Jews who condemned them, they would have had the consolation of being hated by those who hated Christ, but these are Christians, or men known by that name.

"Lady Asella, I write these lines in haste, while the ship spreads its sails. I write them with sobs and tears, yet giving thanks to God to have been found worthy of the hatred of the world. Salute Paula and Eustochium, mine in Christ whether the world pleases or not, salute Albina your mother, Marcella your sister, Marcellina, Felicita: say to them that we shall meet again before the judgment seat of God, where the secrets of all hearts shall be revealed. Remember me, oh example of purity! and may thy prayers tranquillise before me the tumults of the sea!"

[TRINITA DE' MONTI]

The agitation with which the community of ladies must have received such a letter may easily be imagined. They were better able than any others to judge of the probity and honour of the writer who had lived among them so long: and no doubt all these storms raging about, the injurious and insulting imputations, all the evil tongues of Rome let loose upon the harmless house, their privacy invaded, their quiet disturbed, must, during the whole course of the deplorable incident, have been the cause of pain and trouble unspeakable to the gentle society on the Aventine. Marcella it is evident had done what she could to stop the mouth of Jerome when the trouble began; it is perhaps for this reason that the letter of farewell is addressed to the older Asella, perhaps a milder judge.

Paula's preparations had begun before Jerome had as yet thought of his more abrupt departure. They were not so easily made as those of a solitary already detached from the world. She had all her family affairs to regulate, and, what was harder still, her children to part with, the most difficult of all, and the special point in her conduct with which it is impossible for us to sympathise. But it must be remembered that Paula, a spotless matron, had been branded with the most shameful of slanders, that she had been shrieked at by the crowd as the slayer of her daughter, and accused by society of having dishonoured her name. She had been the subject of a case of libel, as we should say, before the public courts, and though the slanderer had confessed his falsehood (under the influence of torture it would seem, according to the words of Jerome), the imputation, as in most cases, remained. Outraged and wounded to the quick, it is very possible that she may have thought that it was well for her younger children that she should leave them, that they might not remain under the wing of a mother whose name had been bandied about in the mouths of men. Her daughter Paulina was by this time married to the good and faithful Pammachius, whose protection might be of greater advantage to the younger girl and boy than her own. And Paula had full knowledge of the tender mercies of her pagan relations, and of the influence they were likely to exercise against her, even in her own house. The staid young Eustochium, grave and calm, clung to her mother's side, her youthful head already covered by the veil of the dedicated virgin, a serene and unfaltering figure in the midst of all the agitations of the parting. All Rome poured forth to accompany them to the port, brothers and sisters with their wives and husbands, relations less near, a crowd of friends. All the way along the winding banks of the Tiber they plied Paula with entreaties and reproaches and tears. She made them no reply. She was at all times slow to speak, as the tender chronicle reports. "She raised her eyes to heaven, pious towards her children but more pious to God." She retained her self-command until the vessel began to move from the shore, where little Toxotius, the boy of ten years old, stood stretching out his hands to her in a last appeal, his sister Rufina silent, with wistful eyes, by his side. Paula's heart was like to burst. She turned her eyes away unable to bear that cruel sight, while Eustochium, firm and steadfast, supported her weaker mother in her arms.

Was it a cruel desertion, a heartless abandonment of duty? Who can tell? There are desertions, cruelties in this kind, which are the highest sacrifice, and sometimes the most bitter proof of self-devotion. Did Paula in her heart believe, most painful thought that can enter a mother's mind, that her boy would be better without her, brought up in peace among his uncles and guardians, who, had she been there, would have made his life a continual struggle between two sides? Was Rufina more likely to be happy in her gentle sister's charge, than with her mind disturbed, and perhaps her marriage spoiled, by her mother's religious vows, and all that was involved in them? She might be wrong in thinking so, as we are all wrong often in our best and most painfully pondered plans. But condemnation is very easy, and gives so little trouble—there is surely a word to be said on the other side of the question.

When these pilgrims leave Rome they cease to have any part in the story of the great city with which we have to do. Yet their after-fate may be stated in a few words. No need to follow the great lady in her journey over land and sea to the Holy Land with all its associations, where Jerusalem out of her ruins, decked with a new classic name, was already rising again into the knowledge and the veneration of the world. These were not the days of excursion trains and steamers, it is true; but the number of pilgrims ever coming and going to those more than classic shores, those holy places, animated with every higher hope, was perhaps greater in proportion to the smaller size and less population of the known world than are our many pilgrimages now, though this seems so strange a thing to say. But is there not a Murray, a Baedeker, of the fourth century, still existent, the Itinéraire de Bordeaux à Jerusalem, unquestioned and authentic, containing the most careful account of inns and places of refuge and modes of travel for the pilgrims? It is possible that the lady Paula may have had that ancient roll in her satchel, or slung about the shoulders of her attendant for constant reference. Her ship was occupied by her own party alone, and conveyed, no doubt, much baggage and many provisions as an emigration for life would naturally do; and it was hindered by no storms, as far as we hear, but only by a great calm which delayed the vessel much and made the voyage tedious, necessitating the use of the galley's oars, which very likely the ladies would like best, though it kept them so many more days upon the sea. They reached Cyprus at last, that holy island now covered with monasteries, where Epiphanius, once Paula's guest in Rome, awaited and received her with every honour, and where there were many visits to be paid to monks and nuns in their new establishments, the favourite dissipation of the cloister. The ladies afterwards continued their voyage to Antioch, where they met Jerome; and proceeded on their journey, having probably had enough of the sea, along the coast by Tyre and Sidon, by Herod's splendid city of Cæsarea, and Joppa with its memories of the Apostles—not without a thought of Andromeda and her monster as they looked over the dark and dangerous reefs which still scare the traveller: for they loved literature, notwithstanding their separation from the world. They formed by this time a great caravanserai, not unlike, to tell the truth, one of those parties which we are so apt to despise, under charge of guides and attendants who wear the livery of Cook. But such an expedition was far more dignified and important in those distant days. Jerome and his monks made but one family of sisters and brothers with the Roman ladies and their followers, who endured so bravely all the fatigues and dangers of the way. Paula the pilgrim was no longer a tottering fine lady, but the most animated and interested of travellers, with no mere mission of hermit-hunting like Melania, but the truest human enthusiasm for all the storied scenes through which she passed. When they reached Jerusalem she went in a rapture of tears and exaltation from one to another of the sacred sites, kissing the broken stone which was supposed to have been that which was rolled against the door of the Holy Sepulchre, and following with pious awe and joy the steps of Helena into the cave where the True Cross was found. The legend was still fresh in those days, and doubts there were none. The enthusiasm of Paula, the rapture and exaltation, which found vent in torrents of tears, in ecstasies of sacred emotion, joy and prayer, moved all the city, thronged with pilgrims, devout and otherwise, to whom the great Roman lady was a wonder: the crowd followed her about from point to point, marvelling at her devotion and the warmth of natural feeling which in all circumstances distinguished her. The reader cannot but follow still with admiring interest a figure so fresh, so unconventional, so profoundly touched by all those holy and sacred associations. Amid so many who are represented as almost more abstracted among spiritual thoughts than nature permits, her frank emotion and tender, natural enthusiasm are always a refreshment and a charm.

We come here upon a break in the hitherto redundant story. Melania and Rufinus were in possession of their convents, and fully established as residents on the Mount of Olives, when the other pilgrims arrived; and there can be but little doubt that every grace of hospitality was extended by the one Roman lady to the other, as well as by the old companions of Jerome to her friend. But in the course of the after-years these dear friends quarrelled bitterly, not on personal matters, so far as appears, but on points of doctrine, and fell into such prolonged warfare of angry and stinging words as hurt more than blows. By means of this very intimacy they knew everything that had ever been said or whispered of each other, and in the heat of conflict did not hesitate to use every old insinuation, every suggestion that could hurt or wound. The struggle ran so high that the after-peace of both parties was seriously affected by it; and one of its most significant results was that Jerome, a man great enough and little enough for anything, either in the way of spitefulness or magnanimity, cut off from his letters and annals all mention of this early period of peace, and all reference to Melania, whom he is supposed to have praised so highly in his first state of mind that it became impossible in his second to permit these expressions of amity to be connected with her name. This is a melancholy explanation of the silence which falls over the first period of Paula's residence in Palestine, but it is a very natural one: and both sides were equally guilty. The quarrel happened, however, years after the first visit, which we have every reason to believe was all friendliness and peace.

After this first pause at Jerusalem, the caravanserai got under way again and set out on a long journey through all the scenes of the Old Testament, the storied deserts and ruins of Syria, not much less ancient to the view and much less articulate than now. This was in the year 387, two years after their departure from Rome. Even now, with all our increased facilities for travel—neutralised as they are by the fact that these wild and desert lands will probably never be adapted to modern methods—the journey would be a very long and fatiguing business. Jerome and his party "went everywhere," as we should say; they were daunted by no difficulties. No modern lady in deer-stalker's costume could have shrunk less from any dangerous road than the once fastidious Paula. They stopped everywhere, receiving the ready hospitality of the convents in every awful pass of the rocks and stony waste where such homes of penance were planted. Those wildernesses of ruin, from which our own explorers have picked carefully out some tradition of Gilgal or of Ziklag, some Philistine stronghold or Jewish city of refuge—were surveyed by these adventurers fourteen hundred years ago, when perhaps there was greater freshness of tradition, but none of the aids of science to decipher what would seem even more hoary with age to them than it does to us. How trifling in our pretences at exploration do the luxurious parties of the nineteenth century seem, abstracted from common life for a few months at the most, and with all the resources of civilisation to fall back upon, in comparison with that of these patient wanderers, eating the Arab bread and clotted milk, and such fare as was to be got at, finding shelter among the dark-skinned ascetics of the desert communities, taking refuge in the cave which some saint but a day or two before had inhabited, wandering everywhere, over primeval ruin and recent shrine!

When they came back from these savage wildernesses to green Bethlehem standing up on its hillside over the pleasant fields, the calm and sweetness of the place went to their hearts. It was in this sacred spot that they decided to settle themselves, building their two convents, Jerome's upon the hill near the western gate, Paula's upon the smiling level below. He is said to have sold all that he had, some remains of personal property in Dalmatia belonging to himself and his brother, who was his faithful and constant companion, to provide for the expenses of the building, on his side; and no doubt the abundant wealth of Paula supplemented all that was wanting. Gradually a conventual settlement, such as was the ideal of the time, gathered in this spot. After her own convent was finished Paula built two others near it, which were soon filled with dedicated sisters. And she built a hospice for the reception of travellers, so that, as she said with tender smiles and tears, "If Joseph and Mary should return to Bethlehem, they might be sure of finding room for them in the inn." This soft speech shines like a gleam of tender light upon the little holy city with all its memories, showing us the great lady of old in her gracious kindness, full of noble natural kindness, and seeing in every poor pilgrim who passed that way some semblance of that simple pair, who carried the Light of the World to David's little town among the hills.

All these homes of piety and charity are swept away, and no tradition even of their site is left; but there is one storied chamber that remains full of the warmest interest of all. It is the rocky room, in one of the half caves, half excavations close to that of the Nativity, and communicating with it by rudely hewn stairs and passages, in which Jerome established himself while his convent was building, which he called his Paradise, and which is for ever associated with the great work completed there. All other traditions and memories grow dim in the presence of the great and sacred interest of the place. Yet it will be impossible even there for the spectator who knows their story to stand unmoved in the scene, practically unaltered since their day, where Jerome laboured at his great translation, and Paula and Eustochium copied, compared, and criticised his daily labours. A great part of the Vulgate had been completed in Rome, but since leaving that city Jerome had much increased his knowledge of Hebrew, losing no opportunity, during his travels, of studying the language with every learned Rabbi he encountered, and acquiring much information in respect to the views and readings of the doctors in the law. He took the opportunity of his retirement at Bethlehem to revise what was already done and to finish the work. His two friends had both learned Hebrew in a greater or less degree before leaving Rome. They had no doubt shared his studies on the way. They read with him daily a portion of the Scriptures in the original; and it was at their entreaty and with their help that he began the translation of the Psalms, so deeply appropriate to this scene, in which the voice of the shepherd of Bethlehem could almost be heard, singing as he led his flock about the little hills. I quote from M. Amédée Thierry a sympathetic description of the method of this work as it was carried out in the rocky chamber at Bethlehem, or in the convent close by.

His two friends charged themselves with the task of collecting all the materials, and this edition, prepared by their care, is that which remains in the Church under Jerome's name. We have his own instructions to them for this work, even to the lines traced for greater exactness, and the explanation of the signs which he had adopted in the collation of the different versions with his text, sometimes a line underscored, sometimes an obelisk or asterisk. A comma followed by two points indicated the cutting out of superfluous words coming from some paraphrase of the Septuagint; a star followed by two points showed, on the contrary, where passages had to be inserted from the Hebrew; another mark denoted passages borrowed from the translation of Theodosius, slightly different from the Septuagint as to the simplicity of the language. In reading these various symbols it is pleasant to think of the two noble Roman ladies seated before the vast desk upon which were spread the numerous manuscripts, Greek, Hebrew, and Latin—the Hebrew text of the Bible, the different editions of the Septuagint, the Hexapla of Origen, Theodosius, Symmachus, Aquila, and the Italian Vulgate—whilst they examined and compared, reducing to order under their hands, with piety and joy, that Psalter of St. Jerome which we still sing, at least the greater part of it, in the Latin Church at the present day.

It is indeed a touching association with that portion of Scripture which next to the Gospel is most dear to the devout, that the translation still in daily use throughout the churches of Continental Europe, the sonorous and noble words which amid all the babble of different tongues still form a large universal language, of which all have at least a conventional understanding—should have been thus transcribed and perfected for the use of the generations. Jerome is no gentle hero, and, truth to tell, has never been much loved in the Church which yet owes so much to him. Yet there is no other work of the kind which carries with it so many soft and tender associations. The cave at Bethlehem is as little adapted as a scene for that domestic combination as Jerome is naturally adapted to be its centre. And no doubt there are unkindly critics who will describe this austere yet beautiful interior as the workshop of two poor female slaves dragged after him by the tyranny of their grim taskmaster to do his work for him. No such idea is consistent with the record. The gentle Paula was a woman of high spirit as well as of much grace and courtesy, steadfastness and humour, the last the most unusual quality of all. The imaginative devotion which had induced her to learn Hebrew in order to sing the Psalmist's songs in the original, among the little band of Souls, under Marcella's gilded roof, had its natural evolution in the gentle pressure laid upon Jerome to make of them an authoritative translation: and where could so fit a place for this work have been found as in the delightful rest after their travels were over, in the very scene where these sacred songs were first begun? It would be almost as impertinent and foolish to suppose that any modern doubt of their authenticity existed in Paula's mind as to suggest that these were forced and dreary labours to which she was driven by a spiritual tyrant. To our mind this mutual labour and study adds the last charm to their companionship. The sprightly, gentle woman who shed so much light over that curious self-denying yet self-indulgent life, and the grave young daughter who never left her side, whose gentle shadow is one with her, so that while Paula lived we cannot distinguish them apart— must have found a quiet happiness above all they had calculated on in this delightful intercourse and work. Their minds and thoughts occupied by the charm of noble poetry, by the puzzle of words to be cleared and combined aright, and by constant employment in a matter which interested them so deeply, which is perhaps the best of all—must have drawn closer and ever closer, mother to child, and child to mother, as well as both to the friend and father whom they delighted to serve, and whose large intellect and knowledge kept theirs going in constant sympathy—not unmingled with now and then a little opposition, and the pleasant stir of independent opinion.

It is right to give Jerome himself, so fierce in quarrel and controversy, the advantage of this gentle lamp which burns for ever in his little Paradise. And can any one suppose that Paula, once so sensitive and exquisite, now strong and vigorous in the simplicity of that retirement, with her hands full and her mind, plenty to think of, plenty to do, had not her advantage also? The life would be ideal but for the thought that must have come over her by times, of the young ones left in Rome, and what was happening to them. She was indeed prostrated by grief again and again by the death of her daughters there, one after another, and mourned with a bitterness which makes us wonder whether that haunting doubt and self-censure, which perhaps gave an additional sting to her sorrow in the case of Blæsilla, may not have overwhelmed her heart again though on a contrary ground—the doubt whether perhaps the austerities she enjoined and shared had been fatal to one, the contradictory doubt whether to leave them to the usual course of life might not have been fatal to the others. Such a woman has none of the self-confidence which steels so many against fate—and, finding nothing effectual for the safety of those she loved, neither a sacred dedication nor that consent to commonplace happiness which is the ordinary ideal of a mother's duty, might well sometimes fall into despair—a despair silently shared by many a trembling heart in all ages, which finds its best-laid plans, though opposite to each other, fall equally into downfall and dismay.

[FROM THE AVENTINE]

But she had her compensations. She had her little glory, too, in the books which went forth from that seclusion in Bethlehem, bearing her name, inscribed to her and her child by the greatest writer of the time. "You, Paula and Eustochium, who have studied so deeply the books of the Hebrews, take it, this book of Esther, and test it word by word; you can tell whether anything is added, anything withdrawn: and can bear faithful witness whether I have rendered aright in Latin this Hebrew history." Few women would despise such a tribute, and fewer still the place of these two women in the Paradise of that laborious study, and at the doors of that beautiful Hospice on the Jerusalem road, where Joseph and Mary had they but come again would have run no risk of finding room!

They died all three, one after another, and were laid to rest in the pure and wholesome rock near the sacred spot of the Nativity. There is a touching story told of how Eustochium, after her mother's death, when Jerome was overwhelmed with grief and unable to return to any of his former occupations, came to him with the book of Ruth still untranslated in her hand, at once a promise and an entreaty. "Where thou goest I will go. Where thou dwellest I will dwell"—and a continuation at the same time of the blessed work which kept their souls alive.

[THE CAPITOL FROM THE PALATINE]

CHAPTER VI

THE MOTHER HOUSE

Amid all these changes the house on the Aventine—the mother house as it would be called in modern parlance—went on in busy quiet, no longer visible in that fierce light which beats upon the path of such a man as Jerome, doing its quiet work steadily, having a hand in many things, most of them beneficent, which went on in Rome. Albina the mother of Marcella, and Asella her elder sister, died in peace: and younger souls, with more stirring episodes of life, disturbed and enlivened the peace of the cloister, which yet was no cloister but open to all the influences of life, maintaining a large correspondence and much and varied intercourse with the society of the times. In the first fervour of the settlement in Bethlehem both Paula and Jerome (she by his hand) wrote to Marcella urging her to join them, to forsake the world in a manner more complete than she had yet done. "... You were the first to kindle the fire in us" (the letter is nominally from Paula and Eustochium): "the first by precept and example to urge us to adopt our present life. As a hen gathers her chickens, who fear the hawk and tremble at every shadow of a bird, so did you take us under your wing. And will you now let us fly about at random with no mother near us?"

This letter is full not only of affectionate entreaties but of delightful pictures of their own retired and peaceful life. "How shall I describe to you," the writer says, "the little cave of Christ, the hostel of Mary? Silence is more respectful than words, which are inadequate to speak its praise. There are no lines of noble colonnades, no walls decorated by the sweat of the poor and the labour of convicts, no gilded roofs to intercept the sky. Behold in this poor crevice of the earth, in a fissure of the rock, the builder of the firmament was born." She goes on with touching eloquence to put forth every argument to move her friend.

Read the Apocalypse of St. John and see there what he says of the woman clothed in scarlet, on whose forehead is written blasphemy, and of her seven hills, and many waters, and the end of Babylon. "Come out of her, my people," the Lord says, "that ye be not partakers of her sins." There is indeed there a holy Church; there are the trophies of apostles and martyrs, the true confession of Christ, the faith preached by the apostles, and heathendom trampled under foot, and the name of Christian every day raising itself on high. But its ambition, its power, the greatness of the city, the need of seeing and being seen, of greeting and being greeted, of praising and detracting, hearing or talking, of seeing, even against one's will, all the crowds of the world—these things are alien to the monastic profession and they have spoiled Rome, they all oppose an insurmountable obstacle to the quiet of the true monk. People visit you: if you open your doors, farewell to silence: if you close them, you are proud and unfriendly. If you return their politeness, it is through proud portals, through a host of grumbling insolent lackeys. But in the cottage of Christ all is simple, all is rustic: except the Psalms, all is silence: no frivolous talk disturbs you, the ploughman sings Allelujah as he follows his plough, the reaper covered with sweat refreshes himself with chanting a psalm, and it is David who supplies with a song the vine dresser among his vineyards. These are the songs of the country, its ditties of love, played upon the shepherd's flute. Will the time never come when a breathless courier will bring us the good news, your Marcella has landed in Palestine? What a cry of joy among the choirs of the monks, among all the bands of the virgins! In our excitement we wait for no carriage but go on foot to meet you, to clasp your hand, to look upon your face. When will the day come when we shall enter together the birthplace of Christ: when, leaning over the divine sepulchre, we weep with a sister, a mother, when our lips touch together the sacred wood of the Cross: when on the Mount of Olives our hearts and souls rise together in the rising of our Lord? Would not you see Lazarus coming out of his tomb, bound in his shroud? and the waters of Jordan purified for the washing of the Lord? Then we shall hasten to the shepherds' folds, and pray at the tomb of David. Listen, it is the prophet Amos blowing his shepherd's horn from the height of his rock; we shall see the monuments of Abraham, Isaac and Jacob, and the three famous women, and Samaria and Nazareth, the flower of Galilee, and Shiloh and Bethel and other holy places, accompanied by Christ, where churches rise everywhere like standards of the victories of Christ. And when we return to our cavern we will sing together always, and sometimes we shall weep; our hearts wounded with the arrow of the Lord, we will say one to another, "I have found Him whom my soul loveth; I will hold Him, and will not let Him go!"

Similar words upon the happiness of rural life and retirement Jerome had addressed to Marcella before. He had warned her of the danger of the tumultuous sea of life, and how the frail bark, beaten by the waves, ought to seek the shelter of the port before the last hurricane breaks. The image was even more true than he imagined; but it was not of the perils of Rome in the dreadful time of war and siege which was approaching that he spoke, but of the usual dangers of common life to the piety of the recluse. "The port which we offer you, it is the solitude of the fields," he says:

Brown bread, herbs watered by our own hands, and milk, the daintiest of the country, supply our rustic feasts. We have no fear of drowsiness in prayer or heaviness in our readings, on such fare. In summer we seek the shade of our trees; in autumn the mild weather and pure air invite us to rest on a bed of fallen leaves; in spring, when the fields are painted with flowers, we sing our psalms among the birds. When winter comes, with its chills and snows, the wood of the nearest forest supplies our fire. Let Rome keep her tumults, her cruel arena, her mad circus, her luxurious theatres; let the senate of matrons pay its daily visits. It is good for us to cleave to the Lord and to put all our hope in Him.

But Marcella turned a deaf ear to these entreaties. Perhaps she still loved the senate of matrons, the meetings of the Souls, the irruption of gentle visitors, the murmur of all the stories of Rome, and the delicate difficulties of marriage and re-marriage brought to her for advice and guidance. The allusions in both these letters point to such a conclusion, and there is no reason why it should not have been so. The Superior of a convent has in this fashion in much later days fulfilled more important uses than the gentle nun of the fields. At all events this lady remained in her home, her natural place, and continued to pour forth her bounty upon the poor of her native city: which many would agree was perhaps the better, though it certainly was not the safer, way. The death of her mother, which made a change in her life, and might have justified a still greater breaking up of all old customs and ties, was perhaps the occasion of these affectionate arguments; but Marcella would herself be no longer young and in a position much resembling that of a mother in her own person, the trusted friend of many in Rome, and their closest tie to a more spiritual and better life. The light of such a guest as Jerome, attracting all eyes to the house and bringing it within the records of literary history, that sole mode of saving the daily life of a household from oblivion—had indeed died away, leaving life perhaps a little flat and blank, certainly much less agitated and visible to the outer world than when he was pouring forth fire and flame upon every adversary from within the shelter of its peaceful walls. But no other change had happened in the circumstances under which Marcella opened her palace to a few consecrated sisters, and made it a general oratory and place of pious counsel and retreat for the ladies of Rome. The same devout readings, the same singing of psalms (sometimes in the original), the same life of mingled piety and intellectualism must have gone on as before: and other fine ladies perhaps not less interesting than Paula must have sought with their confessions and confidences the ear of the experienced woman, who as Paula says in respect to herself and her daughters, "first carried the sparkle of light to our hearts, and collected us like chickens under your wing." She was the same, "our gentle, our sweet Marcella, sweeter than honey," open to every charity and kindness: not refusing, it would seem, to visit as well as to be visited, and willing to "live the life" without forsaking any ordinary bonds or traditions of existence. There is less to tell of her for this reason, but not perhaps less to praise.

Marcella had her share no doubt in forming the minds of the two younger spirits, vowed from their cradle to the perfect life of virginhood, the second Paula, daughter of Toxotius and his Christian wife; and the younger Melania, daughter also of the son whom his mother had abandoned as an infant. It is a curious answer to the stern virtue which reproaches these two Roman ladies with the cruel desertion of their children, to find that both those children, grown men, permitted or encouraged the vocation of their daughters, and were proud of the saintly renown of the mothers who had left them to their fate. The consecrated daughters however leave only a faint trace as of two spotless catechumens in the story. Incidents of a more exciting character broke now and then the calm of life in the palace on the Aventine. M. Thierry in his life of Jerome gives us perhaps a sketch too entertaining of Fabiola, one of the ladies more or less associated with the house of Marcella, a constant visitor, a penitent by times, an enthusiast in charity, a woman bent on making, or so it seemed, the best of both worlds. She had made early what for want of a better expression we may call a love match, in which she had been bitterly disappointed. That a divorce should follow was both natural and lawful in the opinion of the time, and Fabiola had already formed a new attachment and made haste to marry again. But the second marriage was a disappointment even greater than the first, and this repeated failure seems to have confused and excited her mind to issues by no means clear at first, probably even to herself. She made in the distraction of her life a sudden and unannounced visit to Paula's convent at Bethlehem, where she was a welcome and delightful visitor, carrying with her all the personal news that cannot be put into writing, and the gracious ways of an accomplished woman of the world. She is supposed to have had a private object of her own under this visit of friendship, but the atmosphere and occupations of the place must have overawed Fabiola, and though her object was hidden in an artful web of fiction she was not bold enough to reveal it, either to the stern Jerome or the mild Paula. What she did was to make herself delightful to both in the little society upon which we have so many side-lights, and which doubtless, though so laborious and full of privations, was a very delightful society, none better, with such a man as Jerome, full of intellectual power, and human experience, at its head, and ladies of the highest breeding like Paula and her daughter to regulate its simple habits. We are told of one pretty scene where—amid the talk which no doubt ran upon the happiness of that peaceful life amid the pleasant fields where the favoured shepherds heard the angels' song—there suddenly rose the voice of the new-comer reciting with the most enchanting flattery a certain famous letter which Jerome long before had written to his friend Heliodorus and which had been read in all the convents and passed from hand to hand as a chef d'oeuvre of literary beauty and sacred enthusiasm. Fabiola, quick and adroit and emotional, had learned it by heart, and Jerome would have been more than man had he not felt the charm of such flattery.

For a moment the susceptible Roman seems to have felt that she had attained the haven of peace after her disturbed and agitated life. Her hand was full and her heart generous: she spread her charities far and wide among poor pilgrims and poor residents with that undoubting liberality which considered almsgiving as one of the first of Christian duties. But whether the little busy society palled after a time, or whether it was the great scare of the rumour that the Huns were coming that frightened Fabiola, we cannot tell, nor precisely how long her stay was. Her coming and going were at least within the space of two years. She was not made to settle down to the revision of manuscripts like her friends, though she had dipped like them into Hebrew and had a pretty show of knowledge. She would seem to have evidenced this however more by curious and somewhat frivolous questions than by any assistance given in the work which was going on. Nothing could be more kind, more paternal, than Jerome to the little band of women round him. He complains, it is true, that Fabiola sometimes propounded problems and did not wait for an answer, and that occasionally he had to reply that he did not know, when she puzzled him with this rapid stream of inquiry. But it is evident also that he did his best sincerely to satisfy her curiosity as if it had been the sincerest thing in the world. For instance, she was seized with a desire to know the symbolical meaning of the costume of the high priest among the Jews: and to gratify this desire Jerome occupied a whole night in dictating to one of his scribes a little treatise on the subject, which probably the fine lady scarcely took time to read. Nothing can be more characteristic than the indications of this bright and charming visitor, throwing out reflections of all that was going on round her, so brilliant that they seemed better than the reality, fluttering upon the surface of their lives, bringing all under her spell.

There seems but little ground however for the supposition of M. Thierry that it was in the interest of Fabiola that Amandus, a priest in Rome, wrote a letter laying before Jerome a case of conscience, that of a woman who had divorced her husband and married again, and who now was troubled in her mind as to her duty; whether the second husband was wholly unlawful, and whether she could remain in full communion with the Church, having made this marriage? If she was the person referred to no one has been able to divulge what the question meant—whether she had a third marriage in her mind, or if a wholly unnecessary fit of compunction had seized her; for as a matter of fact she had never been subjected by the Church to any pains or penalties in consequence of her second marriage. Jerome however, as might have been expected of him, gave forth no uncertain sound in his reply. According to the Church, he said, there could be but one husband, the first. Whatever had been his unworthiness, to replace him by another was to live in sin. Whether it was this answer which decided her action, or whether she had been moved by the powerful fellowship of Bethlehem to renounce the more agitating course of worldly life, at least it is certain that Fabiola's career was changed from this time. Perhaps it was her desire to shake off the second husband which moved her. At all events on her return to Rome she announced to the bishop that she felt herself guilty of a great sin, and that she desired to make public penance for the same.

[SAN BARTOLOMMEO]

Accordingly on the eve of Easter, when the penitents assembled under the porch of the great Church of St. John Lateran, amid all the wild and haggard figures appearing there, murderers and criminals of all kinds, the delicate Fabiola, with her hair hanging about her shoulders, ashes on her head and on the dark robe that covered her, her face pale with fasting and tears, stood among them, a sight for the world. Under many aspects had all Rome seen this daughter of the great Fabian race, in the splendour of her worldly espousals, and at all the great spectacles and entertainments of a city given up to display and amusement. Her jewels, her splendid dresses, her fine equipages, were well known. With what curiosity would all her old admirers, her rivals in splendour, those who had envied her luxury and high place, gather to see her now in her voluntary humiliation, descending to the level of the very lowest as she had hitherto been on the very highest apex of society! All Rome we are told was there, gazing, wondering, tracing her movements under the portico, among these unaccustomed companions. Perhaps there might be a supreme fantastic satisfaction to the penitent—with that craving for sensation which the exhaustion of all kinds of triumphs and pleasures brings—in thus stepping from one extreme to the other, a gratification in the thought that Rome which had worshipped her beauty and splendour was now gazing aghast at her bare feet and dishevelled hair. One can have no doubt of the sensation experienced by the Tota urbe spectante Romana. It was worth while frequenting religious ceremonies when such a sight was possible! Fabiola,—once with mincing steps, and gorgeous liveried servants on either hand, descending languidly the great marble steps from her palace to the gilded carriage in which she sank fatigued when that brief course was over, the mitella blazing with gold upon her head, her robe woven with all the tints of the rainbow into metallic splendour of gold and silver threads. And now to see her amid that crowd of ruffians from the Campagna, and unhappy women from the purlieus of the city, her splendid head uncovered, her thin hands crossed in the rough sleeves of the penitent's gown! It might be to some perhaps a salutary sight—moving other great ladies with heavier sins on their heads than Fabiola's to feel the prickings of remorse; though no doubt it is equally possible that they might think they saw through her, and the new form of self-exhibition which attracted all the world to gaze. We are not told whether Fabiola found refuge in the house on the Aventine with Marcella, who had lit the fire of Christian faith in her heart as well as in that of Paula: or whether she remained, like Marcella, in her own house, making it another centre of good works. But at all events her life from this moment was entirely given up to charity and spiritual things. Her kinsfolk and noble neighbours still more or less Pagan, were filled with fury and indignation and that sharp disgust at the loss of so much good money to the world, which had so much to do in embittering opposition: but the Christians were deeply impressed, the homage of such a great lady to the faith, and her recantation of her errors affecting many as a true martyrdom.

If it was really compunction for the sin of the second marriage which so moved her, her position would much resemble that of the fine fleur of French society as at present constituted, in its tremendous opposition to the law of divorce, now lawful in France of the nineteenth century as it was in Rome of the fourth—but resisted with a splendid bigotry of feeling, altogether independent of morality or even of reason, by all that is noblest in the country. Fabiola's divorce had been perfectly lawful and according to all the teaching and traditions of her time. The Church had as yet uplifted no voice against it. She had not been shut out from the society even of the most pious, or condemned to any penance or deprivation. Not even Jerome (till forced to give a categorical answer), nor that purest circle of devout women at Bethlehem, had refused her any privilege. Her action was unique and unprecedented as a protest against the existing law of the land, as well as universal custom and tradition. We are not informed whether it had any lasting effect, or formed a precedent for other women. No doubt it encouraged the formation of the laws against divorce which originated in the Church itself but have held through the intervening ages a doubtful sway, broken on every side by Papal dispensations, until now that they have settled down into a bond of iron on the consciences of the devout—chiefly the women, more specially still the gentlewomen—of Catholic Europe, where as in Fabiola's time they are once more against the law of the land.

The unworthy second husband we are informed had died even before Fabiola's public act of penitence; but no further movements towards the world, or the commoner ways of life reveal themselves in her future career. If she returned to life with the veiled head and bare feet of her penitence, or if she resumed, like Marcella, much of the ordinary traffic of society, we have no information. But she was the founder of the first public hospital in Rome, besides the usual monasteries, and built in concert with Pammachius a hospice at Ostia at the mouth of the Tiber, where strangers and travellers from all parts of the world were received, probably on the model of that hospice for pilgrims which Paula had established. And she was herself the foremost nurse in her own hospital, shrinking from no office of charity. The Church has always and in all circumstances encouraged such practical acts of self-devotion.

The ladies of the Aventine and all the friends of Jerome had been disturbed a little before by the arrival of a stranger in Rome, also a pretended friend of Jerome, and at first very willing to shelter himself under that title, Rufinus, who brought with him—after a moment of delusive amiability during which he had almost deceived the very elect themselves—a blast of those wild gales of polemical warfare which had been echoing for some time with sacrilegious force and inappropriateness from the Mount of Olives itself. The excitement which he raised in Rome in respect to the doctrines of Origen caused much commotion in the community, which lived as much by news of the Church and reports of all that was going on in theology as by the daily bread of their charities and kindness. It was to Marcella that Jerome wrote, when, reports having been made to him of all that had happened, he exploded, with the flaming bomb of his furious rhetoric, the fictitious statements of Rufinus, by which he was made to appear a supporter of Origen. Into that hot and fierce controversy we have no need to enter. No one can study the life of Jerome without becoming acquainted with this episode and finding out how much the wrath of a Father of the Church is like the rage of other men, if not more violent; but happily as Rome was not the birthplace of this fierce quarrel it is quite immaterial to our subject or story. It filled the house of Marcella with trouble and doubt for a time, with indignation afterwards when the facts of the controversy were better known; but interesting as it must have been to the eager theologians there, filling their halls with endless discussions and alarms, lest this new agitation should interfere with the repose of their friend, it is no longer interesting except to the student now. Rufinus was finally unmasked, and condemned by the Bishop of Rome, chiefly by the exertions of Marcella, whom Oceanus, coming hot from the scene of the controversy, and Paulinian the brother of Jerome, had instructed in his true character. Events were many at this moment in that little Christian society. The tumult of controversy thus excited and all the heat and passion it brought with it had scarcely blown aside, when the ears of the Roman world were made to tingle with the wonderful story of Fabiola, and the crowd flew to behold in the portico of the Lateran her strange appearance as a penitent; and the commotion of that event had scarcely subsided when another wonderful incident appears in the contemporary history filling the house with lamentation and woe.

The young Paulina, dear on all accounts to the ladies of the Aventine as her mother's daughter, and as her husband's wife (for Pammachius, the friend and schoolfellow of Jerome, was one of the fast friends and counsellors of the community), as well as for her own virtues, died in the flower of life and happiness, a rich and noble young matron exhibiting in her own home and amid the common duties of existence, all the noblest principles of the Christian faith. She had not chosen what these consecrated women considered as the better way: but in her own method, and amid a world lying in wickedness, had unfolded that white flower of a blameless life which even monks and nuns were thankful to acknowledge as capable of existing here and there in the midst of worldly splendours and occupations. She left no children behind her, so that her husband Pammachius was free of the anxieties and troubles, as well as of the joy and pride, of a family to regulate and provide for. His young wife left to him all her property on condition that it should be distributed among the poor, and when he had fulfilled this bequest the sorrowful husband himself retired from life, and entered a convent, in obedience to the strong impulse which swayed so many. Before this occurred however "all Rome" was roused by another great spectacle. The entire city was invited to the funeral of Paulina as if it had been to her marriage, though those who came were not the same wondering circles who crowded round the Lateran gate to see Fabiola in her humiliation. It was the poor of Rome who were called by sound of trumpet in every street, to assemble around the great Church of St. Peter, where were those tombs of the Apostles which every Christian visited as the most sacred of shrines, and where Paulina was laid forth upon her bier, the mistress of the feast. The custom was an old one, and chambers for these funeral repasts were attached to the great catacombs and all places of burial. The funeral feast of Paulina however meant more than ordinary celebrations of the kind, as the place in which it was held was more impressive and imposing than an ordinary sepulchre however splendid. She must have been carried through the streets in solemn procession, from the heights on which stood the palaces of her ancient race, across the bridge, and by the tomb of Hadrian to that great basilica where the Apostles lay, her husband and his friends following the bier: and in all likelihood Marcella and her train were also there, replacing the distant mother. St. Peter's it is unnecessary to say was not the St. Peter's we know; but it was even then a great basilica, with wide extending porticoes and squares, and lofty roof, though the building was scarcely quite detached from the rock out of which the back part of the cathedral had been hewn.

[ST. PETER'S, FROM THE JANICULUM]

Many strange sights have been seen in that spot which once was the centre of the civilised world, and this which seems to us one of the strangest was in no way unusual or against the traditions of the age in which it occurred. The church itself, and all its surroundings, nave and aisles and porticoes, and the square beyond, were filled with tables, and to these from all the four quarters of Rome, from the circus and the benches of the Colosseum, where the wretched slept and lurked, from the sunny pavements, and all the dens and haunts of the poor by the side of the Tiber, the crowds poured, in those unconceivable yet picturesque rags which clothe the wretchedness of the South. They were ushered solemnly to their seats, the awe of the place, let us hope, quieting the voices of a profane and degraded populace, and overpowering the whispering, rustling, many-coloured multitude. Outside the later comers would be more unrestrained, and the roar, even though subdued, of thronging humanity must have come in strangely to the silence of the great church, and of the mourners, bent upon doing Paulina honour in this curious way. Did she lie there uplifted on her high bier to receive her guests? Or was the heart-broken Pammachius the host, standing pale upon the steps, over the grave of the Apostles? When they were "saturated" with food and wine, the first assembly left their places and were succeeded by another, each as he went away receiving from the hands of Pammachius himself a sum of money and a new garment. "Happy giver, unwearied distributor!" says the record. The livelong day this process went on; a winter day in Rome, not always warm, not always genial, very cold outside in the square under the evening breeze, and no doubt growing more and more noisy as one band continued to succeed another, and the first fed lingered about comparing their gifts, and hoping perhaps for some remnants to be collected at the end from the abundant and oft-renewed meal. There were no doubts in anybody's mind, as we have said, about encouraging pauperism or demoralising the recipients of these gifts; perhaps it would have been difficult to demoralise further that mendicant crowd. But one cannot help wondering how the peace was kept, whether there were soldiers or some manner of classical police about to keep order, or if the disgusted Senators would have to bestir themselves to prevent this wild Christian carnival of sorrow and charity from becoming a danger to the public peace.

We are told that it was the sale of Paulina's jewels, and her splendid toilettes which provided the cost of this extraordinary funeral feast. "The beautiful dresses woven with threads of gold were turned into warm robes of wool to cover the naked; the gems that adorned her neck and her hair filled the hungry with good things." Poor Paulina! She had worn her finery very modestly according to all reports; it had served no purposes of coquetry. The reader feels that something more congenial than that coarse and noisy crowd filling the church with its deformities and loathsomeness might have celebrated her burial. But not so was the feeling of the time; that they were more miserable than words could say, vile, noisome, and unclean, formed their claim of right to all these gifts—a claim from which their noisy and rude profanity, their hoarse blasphemy and ingratitude took nothing away. Charity was more robust in the early centuries than in our fastidious days. "If such had been all the feasts spread for thee by thy Senators," cried Bishop Paulinus, the historian of this episode, "oh Rome thou might'st have escaped the evils denounced against thee in the Apocalypse." We must remember that whatever might have been the opinion later, there was no doubt in any Christian mind in the fourth century that Rome was the Scarlet Woman of the Revelation of St. John, and that a dreadful fate was to overwhelm her luxury and pride.

Pammachius, when he had fulfilled the wishes of his wife in this way, thrilling the hearts of the mourning mother and sister in Bethlehem with sad gratification, and edifying the anxious spectators on the Aventine, carried out her will to its final end by becoming a monk, but with the curious mixture of devotion and independence common at the time, retired to no cloister, but lived in his own house, fulfilling his duties, and appearing even in the Senate in the gown and cowl so unlike the splendid garb of the day. He was no doubt one of the members for the poor in that august but scarcely active assembly, and occupied henceforward all his leisure in works of charity and religious organisations, in building religious houses, and protecting Christians in every necessity of life.

We have said that Rome in these days was as freely identified with the Scarlet Woman of the Apocalypse as ever was done by any Reformer or Puritan in later times. To Jerome she was as much Babylon, and as damnable and guilty in every way as if he had been an Orangeman or Covenanter. Mildness was not general either in speech or thought: it has seldom been so perhaps in religious controversy. It is curious indeed to mark how, so near the fount of Christianity, the Church had already come to rend itself with questions of doctrine, and expend on discussions of philosophical subtlety the force that was wanted for the moral advantage of the world. But that no doubt was one of the defects of the great principle of self-devotion which aimed at emptying the mind of everything worldly and practical, and fixing it entirely upon spiritual subjects, thus substituting them for the ruder obstacles which occupied in common life the ruder forces of nature.

All things however were now moving swiftly towards one of the great catastrophes of the ages. Though Christianity was young, the entire system of the world's government was old and drawing towards its fall. Rome was dead, or virtually so, and all the old prestige, the old pride and pretension of her race, were perishing miserably in those last vulgarities of luxury and display which were all that was left to her. It is no doubt true that the crumbling of all common ties which took place within her bosom, under the invasion of the monkish missionaries from the East, and the influence of Athanasius, Jerome, and others—had been for some time undermining her unity, and that the rent between that portion of the aristocracy of Rome which still held by the crumbling system of Paganism, and those who had adopted the new faith, was now complete. Rome which had been the seat of empire, the centre from which law and power had gone out over all the earth, the very impersonation of the highest forces of humanity, the pride of life, the eminence of family and blood—now saw her highest names subjected voluntarily to strange new laws of humiliation, whole households trooping silently away in the garb of servants to the desert somewhere, to the Holy Land on pilgrimages, or living a life of hardship and privation and detachment from all public interests, in the very palaces which had once been the seats of authority.

[ST. PETER'S, FROM THE PINCIO]

All things however were now moving swiftly towards one of the great catastrophes of the ages. Though Christianity was young, the entire system of the world's government was old and drawing towards its fall. Rome was dead, or virtually so, and all the old prestige, the old pride and pretension of her race, were perishing miserably in those last vulgarities of luxury and display which were all that was left to her. It is no doubt true that the crumbling of all common ties which took place within her bosom, under the invasion of the monkish missionaries from the East, and the influence of Athanasius, Jerome, and others—had been for some time undermining her unity, and that the rent between that portion of the aristocracy of Rome which still held by the crumbling system of Paganism, and those who had adopted the new faith, was now complete. Rome which had been the seat of empire, the centre from which law and power had gone out over all the earth, the very impersonation of the highest forces of humanity, the pride of life, the eminence of family and blood—now saw her highest names subjected voluntarily to strange new laws of humiliation, whole households trooping silently away in the garb of servants to the desert somewhere, to the Holy Land on pilgrimages, or living a life of hardship and privation and detachment from all public interests, in the very palaces which had once been the seats of authority. Her patricians moved silent about the streets in the rude sandals and mean robes of the monk: her great ladies drove forth no longer resplendent as Venus on her car, but stood like penitent Magdalenes upon the steps of a church; and bridegroom and bride no longer linked with flowery garlands, but with the knotted cord of monastic rule, lived like vestals side by side. What was to come to a society so broken up and undermined, knowing no salvation save in its own complete undoing, preparing unconsciously for some convulsion at hand? The interpreter of the dark sayings of prophecy goes on through one lingering age after another, holding the threats of divine justice as still and always unfulfilled, and will never be content that it is any other than the present economy which is marked with the curse and threatened with the ruin of Apocalyptic denunciations. But no one could doubt that the wine was red in that cup of the wrath of God which the city of so many sins held in her hand. The voice that called "Come out of her, my people," had rung aloud in tones unmistakable, calling the best of her sons and daughters from her side; her natural weapons had fallen from her nerveless hands; she had no longer any heart even to defend herself, she who had once but to lift her hand and the air had tingled to the very boundaries of the known world as if a blazing sword had been drawn. It requires but little imagination to appropriate to the condition of Rome on the eve of the invasion of Alaric every strophe of the magnificent ode in the eighteenth chapter of Revelation. There are reminiscences in that great poem of another, of the rousing of Hell to meet the king of the former Babylon echoing out of the mists of antiquity from the lips of the Hebrew prophet. Once more that cry was in the air—once more the thrill of approaching destruction was like the quiver of heat in the great atmosphere of celestial blue which encircled the white roofs, the shining temples, the old forums as yet untouched, and the new basilicas as yet scarce completed, of Rome. The old order was about to change finally, giving place to the new.

All becomes confused in the velocity and precipitation of descending ruin. We can trace the last hours of Paula dying safe and quiet in her retreat at Bethlehem, and even of the less gentle Melania; but when we attempt to follow the course of the events which overwhelmed the home of early faith on the Aventine, the confusion of storm and sack and horrible sufferings and terror fills the air with blackness. For years there had existed a constant succession of danger and reprieve, of threatening hosts (the so-called friends not much better than the enemies) around the walls of the doomed city, great figures of conquerors with their armies coming and going, now the barbarian, now the Roman general upon the height of the wave of battle, the city escaping by a hair's breadth, then plunged into terror again. And Marcella's house had suffered with the rest. No doubt much of the gaiety, the delightful intellectualism of that pleasant refuge, had departed with the altering time. Age had subdued the liveliness and brightness of a community still full of the correspondences, the much letter-writing which women love. Marcella's companions had died away from her side; life was more quickly exhausted in these days of agitation, and she herself, the young and brilliant founder of that community of Souls, must have been sixty or more when the terrible Alaric, a scourge of God like his predecessor Attila, approached Rome. What had become of the rest we are not told, or if the relics of the community, nameless in their age and lessened importance, were still there: the only one that is mentioned is a young sister called Principia, her adopted child and attendant. Nothing can be more likely than that the remainder of the community had fled, seeking safety, or more likely an unknown death, in less conspicuous quarters of the city than the great palace of the Aventine with its patrician air of wealth and possible treasure. In that great house, so far as appears, remained only its mistress, her soul wound up for any martyrdom, and the girl who clung to her. If they dared to look forth at all from the marble terrace where so often they must have gazed over Rome shining white in the sunshine in all her measured lines and great proportions, her columns and her domes, what a dread scene must have met their eyes, clouds of smoke and wild gleams of flame, and the roar of outcry and slaughter mounting up into the air, soiling the very sky. There the greatest ladies of Rome had come in their grandeur to enjoy the piquant contrast and the still more piquant talk, the philosophies which they loved to penetrate and understand, the learning which went over their heads. There Jerome, surrounded with soft flatteries and provocations, had talked his best, giving forth out of his stores the tales of wonder he had brought from Eastern cells and caves and all the knowledge of the schools, to dazzle the amateurs of the Roman gynæceum. What gay, what thrilling, what happy memories!—mingled with the sweetness of remembrance of gentle Paula who was dead, of Asella dead, of Fabiola in all her fascinations and caprices, dead too so far as appears—and no doubt in those thirty years since first Marcella opened her house to the special service of God, many more; till now that she was left alone, grey-headed, on that height whither the fierce Goths were coming, raging, flashing round them fire and flame, with the girl who would not leave her, the young maiden in her voiceless meekness whom we see only at this awful moment, she who might have a sharper agony than death before her, the most appalling of martyrdoms.

One final triumph however remained for Marcella. By what wonderful means we know not, by her prayers and tears, by supplication on her knees, to the rude Goths who after their sort were Christians, and sometimes spared the helpless victims and sometimes listened to a woman's prayer, she succeeded in saving her young companion from outrage, and in dragging her somehow to the shelter of the nearest church, where they were safe. But she was herself in her age and weakness, tortured, flogged, and treated with the utmost cruelty, that she might disclose the hiding-place in which she had put her treasure. The treasure of the house of the Aventine was not there: it had fed the poor, and supplied the wants of the sick in all the most miserable corners of Rome. The kicks and blows of the baffled plunderers could not bring that long-expended gold and silver together again. But these sufferings were as nothing in comparison to the holy triumph of saving young Principia, which was the last and not the least wonderful work of her life. The very soldiers who had struck and beaten the mistress of the desolate house were overcome by her patience and valour, "Christ softened their hard hearts," says Jerome. "The barbarians conveyed both you and her to the basilica that you might find a place of safety or at least a tomb." Nothing can be more extraordinary in the midst of this awful scene of carnage and rapine than to know that the churches were sanctuaries upon which the rudest assailants dared not to lift a hand, and that the helpless women, half dead of fright and one of them bleeding and wounded with the cruel treatment she had received, were safe as soon as they had been dragged over the sacred threshold.

[TEMPLE OF VESTA]

The church in which Marcella and her young companion found shelter was the great basilica of St. Paul fuori le mura, beyond the Ostian gate. They were conducted there by their captors themselves, some compassionate Gaul or Frank, whose rude chivalry of soul had been touched by the spectacle of the aged lady's struggle for her child. What a terrible flight through the darkness must that have been "in the lost battle borne down by the flying" amid the trains of trembling fugitives all bent on that one spot of safety, the gloom lighted up by the gleams of the burning city behind, the air full of shrieks and cries of the helpless, the Tiber rushing swift and strong by the path to swallow any helpless wayfarer pushed aside by stronger fugitives. The two ladies reached half-dead the great church on the edge of the Campagna, the last refuge of the miserable, into which were crowded the wrecks of Roman society, both Pagan and Christian, patrician and slave, hustled together in the equality of doom. A few days after, in the church itself, or some of its dependencies, Marcella died. Her palace in ruins, her companions dead or fled, she perished along with the old Rome against whose vices she had protested, but which she had loved and would not abandon: whose poor she had fed with her substance, whose society she had attempted to purify, and in which she had led so honourable and noble—may we not also believe amid all her austerities, in the brown gown which was almost a scandal, and the meagre meals that scarcely kept body and soul together?—so happy a life. There is no trace now of the noble mansion which she devoted to so high a purpose, and few of the many pilgrims who love to discover all that is interesting in the relics of Rome, have even heard the name of Marcella—"Illam mitem, illam suavem, illam omni melle et dulcedine dulciorem"—whose example "lured to higher worlds and led the way." But her pleasant memory lingers on the leafy crest of the Aventine where she lived, and where the church of Sta. Sabina now stands: and her mild shadow lies on that great church outside the gates, often destroyed, often restored, the shrine of Paul the Apostle, where, wounded and broken, but always faithful to her trust, she died. The history of the first dedicated household, the first convent, the ecclesia domestica, which was so bright a centre of life in the old Rome, not yet entirely Christian, is thus rounded into a perfect record. It began in 380 or thereabouts, it ended in 410. Its story is but an obscure chapter in the troubled chronicles of the time; but there is none more spotless, and scarcely any so serenely radiant and bright.

[PORTA SAN PAOLO]

Pammachius also died in the siege, whether among the defenders of the city or in the general carnage is not known, "with many other brothers and sisters whose death is announced to us" Jerome says, whom that dreadful news threw into a stupor of horror and misery, so that it was some time before he could understand the details or discover who was saved and who lost. The saved indeed were very few, and the losses many. Young Paula, the granddaughter of the first, the child of Toxotius, who also was happily dead before these horrors, had been for some years in Bethlehem peacefully learning how to take the elder Paula's place, and shedding sweetness into the life of the old prophet in his rocky chamber at Bethlehem, and of the grave Eustochium in her convent. Young Melania, standing in the same relationship to the heroine of that name, whose fame is less sweet, was out of harm's way too. They and many humbler members of the community had escaped by flight, among the agitated crowds which had long been pouring out of Italy towards the East, some from mere panic, some by the vows of self-dedication and retirement from the world. Many more as has been seen escaped in Rome itself, before its agony began, by the still more effectual way of death. Only Marcella, the first of all, the pupil of Athanasius, the mother and mistress of so many consecrated souls, fell on the outraged threshold of her own house, over which she had come and gone for thirty years, with those feet that are beautiful on the mountains, the feet of those who bring good tidings, and carry charity and loving kindness to every door.

[THE STEPS OF SAN GREGORIO]

BOOK II

THE POPES WHO MADE THE PAPACY

CHAPTER I

GREGORY THE GREAT

When Rome had fallen into the last depths of decadence, luxury, weakness, and vice, the time of fierce and fiery trial came. The great city lay like a helpless woman at the mercy of her foes—or rather at the mercy of every new invader who chose to sack her palaces and throw down her walls, without even the pretext of any quarrel against the too wealthy and luxurious city, which had been for her last period at least nobody's enemy but her own. Alaric, who, not content with the heaviest ransom, returned to rage through her streets with all those horrors and cruelties which no advance in civilisation has ever yet entirely dissociated from the terrible name of siege: Attila, whose fear of his predecessor's fate and the common report of murders and portents, St. Peter with a sword of flame guarding his city, and other signs calculated to melt the hearts of the very Huns in their bosoms, kept at a distance: passed by without harming the prostrate city. But Genseric and his Vandals were kept back by no such terrors. The ancient Rome, with all her magnificent relics of the imperial age, fell into ruin and was trampled under foot by victor after victor in the fierce license of barbarous triumph. Her secret stores of treasure, her gold and silver, her magnificent robes, her treasures of art fell, like her beautiful buildings, into the rude hands which respected nothing, neither beauty nor the traditions of a glorious past. How doth the city sit solitary that was full of people! All the pathetic and wonderful plaints of the Hebrew prophet over a still holier and more ancient place, trodden under foot and turned into a desert, rise to the mind during this passion and agony of imperial Rome. But the mistress of the world had no such fierce band of patriots to fight inch by inch for her holy places as had the old Jerusalem. There were few to shed their blood for her in the way of defence. The blood that flowed was that of murdered weakness, not that freely shed of valiant men.

During this terrible period of blood and outrage and passion and suffering, one institution alone stood firm amid the ruins, wringing even from the fiercest of the barbarians a certain homage, and establishing a sanctuary in the midst of sack and siege in which the miserable could find shelter. As every other public office and potency fell, the Church raised an undaunted front, and took the place at once of authority and of succour among the crushed and downtrodden people. It is common to speak of this as the beginning of that astute and politic wisdom of Rome which made the city in the middle ages almost a greater power than in her imperial days, and equally mistress of the world. But there is very little evidence that any great plan for the aggrandisement of the Church, or the establishment of her supremacy, had yet been formed, or that the early Popes had any larger purpose in their minds than to do their best in the position in which they stood, to avert disaster, to spread Christianity, and to shield as far as was possible the people committed to their care. No formal claim of supremacy over the rest of the Church had been as yet made: it was indeed formally repudiated by the great Gregory in the end of the sixth century as an unauthorised claim, attributed to the bishops of Rome only by their enemies, though still more indignantly to be denounced when put forth by any other ecclesiastical authority such as the patriarch of Constantinople. To Peter, he says in one of his epistles, was committed the charge of the whole Church, but his successors did not on that account call themselves rulers of the Church universal—how much less a bishropic of the East who had no such glorious antecedents!

But if pretension to the primacy had not yet been put forth, there had arisen the practical situation, which called the bishops of Rome to a kind of sovereignty of the city. The officials of the empire, a distant exarch at Ravenna, a feeble prætor at Rome, had no power either to protect or to rescue. The bishop instinctively, almost involuntarily, whenever he was a man of strength or note, was put into the breach. Whatever could be done by negotiation, he, a man of peace, was naturally called to do. Innocent procured from Alaric the exemption of the churches from attack even in the first and most terrible siege; there wounded men and flying women found refuge in the hottest of the pillage, and Marcella struggling, praying for the deliverance of her young nun, through the brutal crowd which had invaded her house, was in safety with her charge, as we have seen, as soon as they could drag themselves within the sanctuary. This was already a great thing in that dread conflict of force with weakness—and it continued to be the case more or less in all the successive waves of fire and flame which passed over Rome. And when the terrible tide of devastation was over, one patriot Pope at least took the sacred vessels of gold and silver, which had been saved along with the people in their sanctuaries, and melted them down to procure bread for the remnant, thus doubly delivering the flock committed to his care. These facts worked silently, and there seems no reason to believe other than unconsciously at first, towards the formation of the great power which was once more to make Rome a centre of empire. The historian is too apt to perceive in every action an early-formed and long-concealed project tending towards one great end; and it is common to recognise, even in the missionary expeditions of the Church, as well as in the immediate protection exercised around her seat, this astute policy and ever-maturing, ever-growing scheme. But neither Leo nor Gregory require any such explanation of their motives; their duty was to protect, to deliver, to work day and night for the welfare of the people who had no other protectors: as it was their first duty to spread the Gospel, to teach all nations according to their Master's commission. It is hard to take from them the credit of those measures which were at once their natural duty and their delight, in order to make all their offices of mercy subservient to the establishment of a universal authority to which neither of them laid any claim.

While Rome still lay helpless in the midst of successive invasions, now in one conqueror's hands, now in another, towards the middle of the sixth century a young man of noble race—whose father and mother were both Christians, the former occupying a high official position, as was also the case with the son, in his earlier years—became remarkable among his peers according to the only fashion which a high purpose and noble meaning seems to have been able to take at that period. Perhaps such a spirit as that of Gregory could never have been belligerent; yet it is curious to note that no patriotic saviour of his country, no defender of Rome, who might have called forth a spirit in the gilded youth, and raised up the ancient Roman strength for the deliverance of the city, seems to have been possible in that age of degeneration. No Maccabæus was to be found among the ashes of the race which once had ruled the world. Whatever excellence remained in it was given to the new passion of the cloister, the instinct of sacrifice and renunciation instead of resistance and defence. It may be said that the one way led equally with the other to that power which is always dear to the heart of man: yet it is extraordinary that amid all the glorious traditions of Rome,—notwithstanding the fame of great ancestors still hanging about every noble house, and the devotion which the city itself, then as now, excited among its children, a sentiment which has made many lesser places invulnerable, so long as there was a native arm to strike a blow for them, no single bold attempt was ever made, no individual stand, no popular frenzy of patriotism ever excited in defence of the old empress of the world. The populace perhaps was too completely degraded to make any such attempt possible, but the true hero when he appears does not calculate, and is able to carry out his glorious effort with sometimes the worst materials. However, it is needless to attempt to account for such an extraordinary failure in the very qualities which had made the Roman name illustrious. Despair must have seized upon the very heart of the race. That race itself had been vitiated and mingled with baser elements by ages of conquest, repeated captivities, and overthrows, and all the dreadful yet monotonous vicissitudes of disaster, one outrage following another, and the dreadful sense of impotence, which crushes the very being, growing with each new catastrophe. It must have appeared to the children of the ancient conquerors that there was no refuge or hope for them, save in that kingdom not of this world, which had risen while everything else crumbled under their feet, which had been growing in silence while the old economy fell into ashes, and which alone promised a resurrection and renewal worthy of the highest hopes.

This ideal had been growing throughout the world, and had penetrated into almost every region of Christendom before the period of Gregory's birth. Nearly a hundred and fifty unhappy years had passed since Marcella ended her devout life amid the fire and flame of the first siege; but the times had so little changed that it was at first under the same aspect which attracted that Roman lady and so many of her contemporaries, that the monastic life recommended itself to the young patrician Gregorius, in the home of his parents, the Roman villa on the edge of that picturesque and splendid wood of great oak-trees which gave to the Coelian Hill its first title of Mons Querquetulanus. It had been from the beginning of his life a devout house, full of the presence and influence of three saintly women, all afterwards canonised, his mother Silvia and his father's sisters. That father himself was at least not uncongenial to his surroundings, though living the usual life, full of magnificence and display, of the noble Roman, filling in his turn great offices in the state, or at least the name and outward pomp of offices which had once been great. Some relics of ancient temples gleaming through the trees beyond the gardens of the villa must still have existed among the once sacred groves; and the vast buildings of the old economy, the Colosseum behind, the ruined and roofless palaces of the Palatine, would be visible from the terrace on which the meditative youth wandered, pondering over Rome at his feet and the great world lying beyond, in which there were endless marchings and countermarchings of barbarous armies, one called in to resist the other, Huns and Vandals from one quarter, irresistible Franks, alien races all given to war, while the secret and soul of peace lay in that troubled and isolated stronghold of Him whose kingdom was not of this world. Gregory musing can have had no thought, such as we should put instinctively into the mind of a noble young man in such circumstances, of dying upon the breached and crumbling walls for his country, or leading any forlorn hope; and if his fancy strayed instead far from those scenes of battle and trouble to the convent cells and silent brotherhoods, where men disgusted and sick of heart could enter and pray, it was as yet with no thought or intention of following their example. He tells us himself that he resisted as long as he could "the grace of conversion," and as a matter of fact entered into the public life such as it was, of the period, following in his father's footsteps, and was himself, like Gordianus, prætor urbis in his day, when he had attained the early prime of manhood. The dates of his life are dubious until we come to his later years, but it is supposed that he was born about 540; and he was recommended for the Prætorship by the Emperor Julius, which must have been before 573, at which date he would have attained the age of thirty-three, that period so significant in the life of man, the limit, as is believed, of our Lord's existence on earth, and close to that mezzo del cammin which the poet has celebrated as the turning-point of life. In his splendid robes, attended by his throng of servants, he must no doubt have ruffled it with the best among the officials of a state which had scarcely anything but lavish display and splendour to justify its pretence of government; but we hear nothing either of the early piety or early profanity which generally distinguish, one or the other, the beginning of a predestined saint. Neither prodigal nor devotee, the son of Gordianus and Silvia did credit to his upbringing, even if he did not adopt its austerer habits. But when his father died, the attraction which drew so many towards the cloister must have begun to operate upon Gregory. When all the wealth came into his hands, when his devout mother retired to her nun's cell on the Aventine, close to the old basilica of S. Sabba, giving up the world, and the young man was left in full possession of his inheritance and the dwelling of his fathers, he would seem to have come to a serious pause in his life. Did he give a large slice of his fortune to endow monasteries in distant Sicily, as far out of the way, one might say, as possible, by way of compromising with his conscience, and saving himself from the sweep of the current which had begun to catch his feet? Perhaps it was some family connection with Sicily—estates, situated there as some think, which prompted the appropriation of his gifts to that distant island; but this is mere speculation, and all that the authorities tell us is that he did establish and endow six monasteries in Sicily, without giving any reason for it. This was his first step towards the life to which later all his wishes and interests were devoted.

It would seem, however, if there is any possible truth in the idea, that the Sicilian endowments were a sort of ransom for himself and the personal sacrifice of the world which his growing fervour demanded of him, that the expedient was not a successful one. He did not resist the grace of conversion very long; but it is curious to find him, so long after, adopting the same expedient as that which had formed a middle ground for his predecessors in an earlier age, by converting his father's house into a convent. St. Benedict, the first of monastic founders in Europe, was scarcely born when Marcella first called about her the few pious maidens and widows who formed her permanent household in Rome; but by the time of Gregory, the order of Benedict had become one of the great facts and institutions of the time—and his villa was soon filled with a regular community of black-robed monks with their abbot and other leaders. Remaining in the beloved shelter of his natural home, he became a member of this community. He did not even retain, as Marcella did, the government of the new establishment in his own hand, but served humbly, holding no office, as an undistinguished brother. It was not without difficulty that he made up his mind to this step. In the letter to Leander which forms the dedication of his commentary on Job, he gives a brief and vague account of his own hesitations and doubts. The love of things eternal, he says, had taken hold upon his mind while yet custom had so wound its chains round him that he could not make up his mind to change his outward garb. But the new influence was so strong that he engaged in the service of the world as it were in semblance only, his purpose and inclination turning more and more towards the cloister. When the current of feeling and spiritual excitement carried him beyond all these reluctances and hesitations, and he at last "sought the haven of the monastery," having, as he says, "left all that is of the world as at that time I vainly believed, I came out naked from the shipwreck of human life." His intention at this crisis was evidently not that of fitting himself for the great offices of the Church or entering what was indeed one of the greatest professions of the time, the priesthood, the one which, next to that of the soldier, was most apt for advancement. Like Jerome, Gregory's inclination was to be a monk and not a priest, and he expressly tells us that "the virtue of obedience was set against my own inclination to make me take the charge of ministering at the holy altar," which he was obliged to accept upon the ground that the Church had need of him. This disinclination to enter the priesthood is all the more remarkable that Gregory was evidently a preacher born, and seems early in his monastic life to have developed this gift. The elucidation of so difficult and mysterious a book as that of Job was asked of him by his brethren at an early period of his career.

We have no guidance of dates to enable us to know how long a time he passed in the monastery, which was dedicated to St. Andrew, after he turned it from a palace-villa into monastic cells and cloisters; but the legend which comes in more or less to every saintly life here affords us one or two delightful vignettes to illustrate the history. His mother Silvia in her nun's cell, surrounded by its little garden, at S. Sabba, sent daily, the story goes—and there is no reason to doubt its truth—a mess of vegetables to her son upon the Coelian, prepared by her own tender hands. One can imagine some shockheaded Roman of a lay brother, old servant or retainer, tramping alone, day by day, over the stony ways, across the deep valley between the two hills, with the simple dish tied in its napkin, which perhaps had some savour of home and childhood, the mother's provision for her boy.

Another story, less original, relates how having sold everything and given all his money to the poor, Gregory was beset by a shipwrecked sailor who came to him again and again in the cell where he sat writing, and to whom at last, having no money, he gave the only thing of value he had left, a silver dish given him by his mother—perhaps the very bowl in which day by day his dinner of herbs was sent to him. Needless to say that the mysterious sailor assumed afterwards a more glorious form, and Gregory found that he had given alms, if not as in most such cases to his Master, at least to a ministering angel. Then, too, in those quiet years arose other visionary legends, that of the dove who sat on his shoulder and breathed inspiration into his ear, and the Madonna who spoke to him as he sat musing—a Madonna painted by no mortal hands, but coming into being on the wall—a sweet and consoling vision in the light that never was by sea or shore. These are the necessary adjuncts of every saintly legend. It is not needful that we should insist upon them; but they help us to realise the aspect of the young Roman who had, at last, after some struggles attained that "grace of conversion" which makes the renunciation of every worldly advantage possible, but who still dwelt peacefully in his own house, and occupied the cell he had chosen for himself with something of the consciousness of the master of the house, although no superiority of rank among his brethren, finding no doubt a delightful new spring of life in the composition of his homilies, and the sense that a higher sphere of work and activity was thus opening before his feet.

The cell of St. Gregory and his marble chair in which he worked and rested, are still shown for the admiration of the faithful on the right side of the church which bears his name: but neither church nor convent are of his building, though they occupy the sites consecrated by him to the service of God. "Here was the house of Gregory, converted by him into a monastery," says the inscription on the portico. And in one spot at least the steps of the Roman gentleman turned monk, may still be traced in the evening freshness and among the morning dews—in the garden, from which the neighbouring summits of the sun-crowned city still rise before the rapt spectator with all their memories and their ruins. There were greater ruins in Gregory's day, ruins still smoking from siege and fire, roofless palaces telling their stern lesson of the end of one great period of empire, of a mighty power overthrown, and new rude overwhelming forces, upon which no man could calculate, come in, in anarchy and bloodshed, to turn the world upside down. We all make our own somewhat conventional comparisons and reflections upon that striking scene, and moralise at our leisure over the Pagan and the Christian, and all that has been signified to the world in such an overthrow and transformation. But Gregory's thoughts as he paced his garden terrace must have been very different from ours. He no doubt felt a thrill of pleasure as he looked at the desecrated places over which Goth and Vandal had raged, in the thought that the peaceful roof of his father's house was safe, a refuge for the chosen souls who had abjured the world; and self-withdrawn from all those conflicts and miseries, mused in his heart over the new world which was dawning, under the tender care of the Church and the ministration of those monks denuded of all things, whose sole inspiration was to be the love of God and the succour of the human race. The world could not go on did not every new economy form to itself some such glorious dream of the final triumph of the good, the noble, and the true. Great Rome lay wrecked and ended in the sight of the patrician monk who had schooled himself out of all the bitterness of the vanquished in that new hope and new life of the cloister. Did he already see his brethren, the messengers of the faith, going forth to all the darkest corners of the unknown world with their gospel, and new skies and new lands turning to meet the shining of the new day?—or with thoughts more profound in awe, more sacred in mysterious joy, did he hold his breath to think what all these ragings of nations and overturning of powers might portend, the glorious era when all misery should be ended, and the Lord come in the clouds to judge the earth and vindicate His people? The monks have failed like the emperors since Gregory's day—the Popes have found no more certain solution for the problems of earth than did the philosophers. But it is perhaps more natural on one of those seven hills of Rome, to think of that last great event which shall fulfil all things, and finally unravel this mortal coil of human affairs, than it is on any other spot of earth except the mystic Mount of the Olives, from which rose the last visible steps of the Son of Man.

We have no knowledge how long this quiet life lasted, or if he was long left to write his sermons in his cell, and muse in his garden, and receive his spare meal from his mother's hands, the mess of lentils, or beans, or artichokes, which would form his only fare; but it is evident that even in this seclusion he had given assurance of a man to the authorities of the Church and was looked upon as one of its hopes. He had no desire, as has been said, to become a priest, but rather felt an almost superstitious fear of being called upon to minister at the holy altar, a sentiment very usual in those days among men of the world converted to a love of the life of prayer and penitence, but not of the sacerdotal charge or profession. It is curious indeed how little the sacramental idea had then developed in the minds of the most pious. The rule of Benedict required the performance of the mass only on Sundays and festivals, and there is scarcely any mention of the more solemn offices of worship in the age of Jerome, who was a priest in spite of himself, and never said but one mass in his life. It was to "live the life," as in the case of a recent remarkable convert from earthly occupations to mystical religionism, that the late prætor, sick of worldly things, devoted himself: and not to enter into a new caste, against which the tradition that discredits all priesthoods and the unelevated character of many of its members, has always kept up a prejudice, which exists now as it existed then.

But Gregory could not struggle against the fiat of his ecclesiastical superiors, and was almost compelled to receive the first orders. After much toiling and sifting of evidence the ever careful Bollandists have concluded that this event happened in 578 or 579—while Baronius, perhaps less bigoted in his accuracy, fixes it in 583. Nor was it without a distinct purpose that this step was taken; there was more to do in the world for this man than to preach homilies and expound Scripture in the little Roman churches. Some one was wanted to represent Pope Benedict the First in Constantinople, some one who knew the world and would not fear the face of any emperor; and it was evidently to enable him to hold the post of Apocrisarius or Nuncio, that Gregory was hastily invested with deacon's orders, and received the position later known as that of a Cardinal deacon. It is a little premature, and harmonises ill with the other features of the man, to describe him as a true mediæval Nuncio, with all the subtle powers and arrogant assumptions of the Rome of the middle ages. This however is Gibbon's description of him, a bold anachronism, antedating by several ages the pretensions which had by no means come to any such development in the sixth century. He describes the Apocrisarius of Pope Benedict as one "who boldly assumed in the name of St. Peter a tone of independent dignity which would have been criminal and dangerous in the most illustrious layman of the empire."

There is little doubt that Gregory would be an original and remarkable figure among the sycophants of the imperial court, where the vices of the East mingled with those of the West, and everything was venal, corrupt, and debased. Gregory was the representative of a growing power, full of life and the prospects of a boundless future. There was neither popedom nor theories of universal primacy as yet, and he was confronted at Constantinople by ecclesiastical functionaries of as high pretensions as any he could put forth; but yet the Bishop of Rome had a unique position, and the care of the interests of the entire Western Church was not to be held otherwise than with dignity and a bold front whoever should oppose.

[VILLA DE' MEDICI]

There was however another side to the life of the Nuncio which is worthy of note and very characteristic of the man. He had been accompanied on his mission by a little train of monks; for these coenobites were nothing if not social, and their solitude was always tempered by the proverbial companion to whom they could say how delightful it was to be alone. This little private circle formed a home for the representative of St. Peter, to which he retired with delight from the wearisome audiences, intrigues, and ceremonies of the imperial court. Another envoy, Leander, a noble Spaniard, afterwards Bishop of Seville, and one of the favourite saints of Spain, was in Constantinople at the same time, charged with some high mission from Rome "touching the faith of the Visigoths," whose conversion from Arianism was chiefly the work of this apostolic labourer. And he too found refuge in the home of Gregory among the friends there gathered together, probably bringing with him his own little retinue in the same Benedictine habit. "To their society I fled," says Gregory, "as to the bosom of the nearest port from the rolling swell and waves of earthly occupation; and though that office which withdrew me from the monastery had with the point of its employments stabbed to death my former tranquillity of life, yet in their society I was reanimated." They read and prayed together, keeping up the beloved punctilios of the monastic rule, the brethren with uninterrupted attention, the Nuncio and the Bishop as much as was possible to them in the intervals of their public work. And in the cool atrio of some Eastern palace, with the tinkling fountain in the midst and the marble benches round, the little company with one breath besought their superior to exercise for them those gifts of exposition and elucidation of which he had already proved himself a master. "It was then that it seemed good to those brethren, you too adding your influence as you will remember, to oblige me by the importunity of their requests to set forth the book of the blessed Job—and so far as the Truth should inspire me, to lay open to them these mysteries." We cannot but think it was a curious choice for the brethren to make in the midst of that strange glittering world of Constantinople, where the ecclesiastical news would all be of persecuting Arians and perverse Eastern bishops, and where all kinds of subtle heresies, both doctrinal and personal, were in the air, fine hair-splitting arguments as to how much or how little of common humanity was in the sacred person of our Lord, as well as questions as to the precise day on which to keep Easter and other regulations of equal importance. But to none of these matters did the monks in exile turn their minds. "They made this too an additional burden which their petition laid upon me, that I would not only unravel the words of the history in allegorical senses, but that I would go on to give to the allegorical sense the turn of a moral exercise: with the addition of something yet harder, that I would fortify the different meanings with analogous passages, and that these, should they chance to be involved, should be disentangled by the aid of additional explanation."

This abstruse piece of work was the recreation with which his brethren supplied the active mind of Gregory in the midst of his public employments and all the distractions of the imperial court. It need not be said that he did not approach the subject critically or with any of the lights of that late learning which has so much increased the difficulty of approaching any subject with simplicity. It is not supposed even that he had any knowledge of the original, or indeed any learning at all. The Nuncio and his monks were not disturbed by questions about that wonderful scene in which Satan stands before God. They accepted it with a calm which is as little concerned by its poetic grandeur as troubled by its strange suggestions. That extraordinary revelation of an antique world, so wonderfully removed from us, beyond all reach of history, was to them the simplest preface to a record of spiritual experience, full of instruction to themselves, lessons of patience and faith, and all the consolations of God. Nothing is more likely than that there were among the men who clustered about Gregory in his Eastern palace, some who like Job had seen everything that was dear to them perish, and had buried health and wealth and home and children under the ashes of sacked and burning Rome. We might imagine even that this was the reason why that mysterious poem with all its wonderful discoursings was chosen as the subject to be treated in so select an assembly. Few of these men if any would be peaceful sons of the cloister, bred up in the stillness of conventual life; neither is it likely that they would be scholars or divines. They were men rescued from a world more than usually terrible and destructive of individual happiness, saddened by loss, humiliated in every sensation either of family or national pride, the fallen sons of a great race, trying above all things to console themselves for the destruction of every human hope. And the exposition of Job is written with this end, with strange new glosses and interpretations from that New Testament which was not yet six hundred years old, and little account of any difference between: for were not both Holy Scripture intended for the consolation and instruction of mankind? and was not this the supreme object of all—not to raise antiquarian questions or exercise the mind on metaphysical arguments, but to gather a little balsam for the wounds, and form a little prop for the weakness of labouring and heavily laden men? Moralia: "The Book of the Morals of St. Gregory the Pope" is the title of the book—a collection of lessons how to endure and suffer, how to hope and believe, how to stand fast—in the certainty of a faith that overcomes all things, in the very face of fate.

"Whosoever is speaking concerning God," says Gregory, "must be careful to search out thoroughly whatsoever furnishes moral instruction to his hearers; and should account that to be the right method of ordering his discourse which permits him when opportunity for edification requires it, to turn aside for a useful purpose from that which he had begun to speak of. He that treats of sacred writ should follow the way of a river: for if a river as it flows along its channel meets with open valleys on its side, into these it immediately turns the course of its current, and when they are copiously supplied presently it pours itself back into its bed. Thus unquestionably should it be with every one that treats the Divine word, so that if discussing any subject he chances to find at hand any occasion of seasonable edification he should as it were force the streams of discourse towards the adjacent valley, and when he has poured forth enough upon its level of instruction fall back into the channel of discourse which he had proposed to himself."

We do not know what the reader may think of Gregory's geography; but certainly he carries out his discursive views to the full, and fills every valley he may chance to come to in his flowing, with pools and streams—no doubt waters of refreshing to the souls that surrounded him, ever eager to press him on. A commentary thus called forth by the necessities of the moment, spoken in the first place to anxious listeners who had with much pressure demanded it, and who nodded their heads over it with mingled approbation and criticism as half their own, has a distinctive character peculiar to itself, and requires little aid from science or learning. A large portion of it was written as it fell from his lips, without revision Gregory informs us, "because the brethren drawing me away to other things, would not leave time to correct this with any great degree of exactness."

A gleam of humour comes across the picture as he describes his position among this band of dependent and applauding followers, who yet were more or less the masters of his leisure and private life. "Pursuing my object of obeying their instructions, which I must confess were sufficiently numerous, I have completed this work," he says. The humour is a little rueful, the situation full of force and nature. The little group of lesser men would no doubt have fully acknowledged themselves inferior to the eloquent brother, their founder, their instructor, so much greater a man in every way than themselves: but yet not able to get on without the hints of Brother John or Brother Paul, helped so much by that fine suggestion of the Cellarius, and the questions and sagacious remarks of the others. The instructions of the brethren! who does not recognise the scene, the nods aside, the objections, the volunteered information and directions how to say this or that, which he knew so much better how to say than any of them! while he sat listening all the time, attending to every criticism, taking up a hint here and there, with that curious alchemy of good humour and genius, turning the dull remarks to profit, yet always with a twinkle in his eye at those advices "sufficiently numerous" which aimed at teaching him how to teach them, a position which many an ecclesiastic and many an orator must have realised since then. Gregory reveals his consciousness of the state of affairs quite involuntarily, nothing being further from his mind than to betray to his reverend and saintly brother anything so human and faulty as a smile; and it is clear that he took the animadversions in good part with as much good nature as humour. To make out the features of the same man in Gibbon's picture of an arrogant priest assuming more than any layman durst assume, is very difficult. The historian evidently made his study from models a few hundred years further down in the record.

Gregory seems to have held the place of Apocrisarius twice under two different Popes—Benedict I. and Pelagius II.; but whether he returned to Rome between the two is not clear. One part of his commission from Pelagius was to secure help from the Emperor against the Lombards who were threatening Rome. The Pope's letter with its lamentable account of the undefended and helpless condition of the city, and the urgency with which he entreats his representative to support the pleading of a special envoy sent for that purpose, is interesting. It is sent to Gregory by the hands of a certain Sebastian, "our brother and coadjutor," who has been in Ravenna with the general Decius, and therefore is able to describe at first hand the terrible state of affairs to the Emperor. "Such misfortunes and tribulations," says the Pope, "have been inflicted upon us by the perfidy of the Lombards contrary to their own oath as no one could describe. Therefore speak and act so as to relieve us speedily in our danger. For the state is so hemmed in, that unless God put it into the heart of our most pious prince to show pity to his servants, and to vouchsafe us a grant of money, and a commander and leader, we are left in the last extremity, all the districts round Rome being defenceless, and the Exarch unable to do anything to help us. Therefore may God persuade the Emperor to come quickly to our aid before the armies of that most accursed race have overrun our lands."

What a strange overturn of all things is apparent when such a piteous appeal is conveyed to the Eastern empire already beginning to totter, from what was once imperial and triumphant Rome!

It was in 586, four years before the end of the life of Pelagius, that Gregory returned home. The abbot of his convent, Maximianus, had been promoted to the see of Syracuse, though whether for independent reasons or to make room for Gregory in that congenial position we are not informed; and the Nuncio on his return succeeded naturally to the vacant place. If it was now or at an earlier period that he bestowed all his robes, jewels, etc., on the convent it is difficult to decide, for there seems always to have been some reserve of gifts to come out on a later occasion, after we have heard of an apparent sacrifice of all things for the endowment of one charity or another. At all events Gregory's charities were endless and continued as long as he lived.

No retirement within the shadow of the convent was however possible now for the man who had taken so conspicuous a position in public life. He was appointed secretary to the Pope, combining that office with the duties of head of his convent, and would appear besides to have been the most popular preacher in Rome, followed from one church to another by admiring crowds, and moving the people with all the force of that religious oratory which is more powerful than any other description of eloquence: though to tell the truth we find but little trace of this irresistible force in his discourses as they have come down to us. Popular as he was he does not seem to have had any special reputation either for learning or for literary style.

One of the best known of historical anecdotes is the story of Gregory's encounter with the group of English children brought to Rome as slaves, whom he saw accidentally, as we say, in one of his walks. It belongs in all probability to this period of his life, and no doubt formed an episode in his daily progress from St. Andrew's on its hill to the palace of the Bishop of Rome which was then attached to the great church of the Lateran gate. In this early home of the head of the Roman hierarchy there would no doubt be accommodation for pilgrims and strangers, in addition to the spare court of the primitive Pope, but probably little anticipation of the splendours of the Vatican, not yet dreamed of. Gregory was pursuing his musing way, a genial figure full of cheerful observation and interest in all around him, when he was suddenly attracted as he crossed some street or square, amid the crowd of dark heads and swarthy faces by a group, unlike the rest, of fair Saxon boys, long-limbed and slender, with their rose tints and golden locks. The great ecclesiastic appears to us here all at once in a new light, after all we have known of him among his monastic brethren. He would seem to have been one of those inveterate punsters who abound among ecclesiastics, as well as a tender-hearted man full of fatherly instincts. He stopped to look at the poor children so unlike anything he knew. Who were they? Angles. Nay, more like angels, he said in his kind tones, with no doubt a smile in return for the wondering looks suddenly raised upon him. And their country? Deiri. Ah, a happy sign! de ira eruti, destined to rise out of wrath into blessedness. And their king? the boys themselves might by this time be moved to answer the kind monk, who looked at them so tenderly. Ella—Alle, as it is reported in the Latin, softening the narrower vowel. And was it still all heathen that distant land, and unknown rude monarch, and the parents of these angelic children? Then might it soon be, good Lord, that Allelujah should sound wherever the barbarous Alle reigned! Perhaps he smiled at his own play upon words, as punsters are apt to do, as he strolled away, not we may be sure without a touch of benediction upon the shining tawny heads of the little Saxon lions. But smiling was not all it came to. The thought dwelt with him as he pursued his way, by the great round of the half-ruined Colosseum, more ruinous probably then than now, and down the long street to the Latin gate, where Pelagius and all the work of his secretaryship awaited him. The Pope was old and wanted cheering, especially in those dark days when the invader so often raged without, and Tiber was slowly swelling within, muttering wrath and disaster; while no force existed, to be brought against one enemy or another but the prayers of a few old men. Gregory told the story of his encounter, perhaps making the old Pope laugh at the wit so tempered with devotion, before he put forth his plea for a band of missionaries to be sent to those unknown regions to convert that beautiful and wonderful fair-haired race. Pelagius was very willing to give his consent; but where were men to be found to risk themselves and their lives on such a distant expedition among the savages of that unknown island? When it was found that nobody would undertake such a perilous mission, Gregory, who would naturally have become more determined in respect to it after every repulse, offered himself; and somehow managed to extort a consent from the Pope, of which he instantly took advantage, setting out at once with a band of faithful brethren, among whom no doubt must have been some of those who had accompanied him when he was Nuncio into scenes so different, and pressed him on with their advice and criticism while he opened to them the mysteries of Scripture. They might be tyrannical in their suggestions, but no doubt the impulse of the apostles—"let us die with him"—was strong in their hearts.

No sooner was it known, however, in Rome that Gregory had left the city on so distant and perilous a mission than the people rose in a sudden tumult. They rushed together from all the quarters of the city in excited bands towards the Lateran, surrounding the Pope with angry cries and protests, demanding the recall of the preacher, whose eloquence as well as his great benefactions to the poor had made him to the masses the foremost figure in the Church. The Pope, frightened by this tumult, yielded to the demand, and sent off messengers in hot haste to bring the would-be missionary back. The picture which his biographers afford us is less known than the previous incidents, yet full of character and picturesque detail. The little band had got three days on in their journey—one wonders from what port they meant to embark, for Ostia, the natural way, was but a few hours from Rome—when they made their usual halt at noon for refreshment and rest "in the fields." Gregory had seated himself under the shade of a tree with a book to beguile the warm and lingering hours. And as he sat thus reading with all the bustle of the little encampment round him, men and horses in the outdoor freedom enjoying the pause, the shade, and needful food—a locust suddenly alighted upon his page, on the roll of parchment which was then the form of the latest editions. Such a visitor usually alights for a moment and no more; but

Gregory was too gentle a spectator of all life to dash the insect off, and it remained there with a steadiness and "mansuetude" unlike the habits of the creature. The good monk began to be interested, to muse and pun, and finally to wonder. "Locusta," he said to himself, groping for a meaning, "loca sta." What could it signify but that in this place he would be made to stay? He called to his attendants to make ready with all speed and push on, eager to get beyond the reach of pursuit; but before the cumbrous train could be got under way again, the Pope's messengers arrived "bloody with spurring, fiery red with haste," and the missionaries were compelled to return to Rome. Thus his first attempt for the conversion of England was to have been made, could he have carried out his purpose, by himself.

There is a curious story also related of Gregory in his walks through Rome, the issue of which, could an unbelieving age put faith in it, would be even more remarkable. One day as he passed by the Forum of Trajan—then no doubt a spot more wildly ruinous than now, though still with some of its great galleries and buildings standing among overthrown monuments and broken pillars—some one told him the story of Trajan and the widow, which must have greatly affected the mediæval imagination since Dante has introduced it in his great poem. The prayer addressed to the Emperor on his way to the wars was the same as that of the widow in the parable, "Avenge me of mine adversary." "I will do so when I return," the Emperor replied. "But who will assure me that you will ever return?" said the importunate widow; upon which the Emperor, recognising the justice of the objection, stopped his warlike progress until he had executed the vengeance required, upon one of his own officials (is it not said by one authority his own son?) who had wronged her. Gregory was as much impressed by this tale as Dante. He went on lamenting that such a man, so just, so tolerant of interruption, so ready to do what was right, should be cut off from the Divine mercy. He carried this regret with him all the way to the tomb of the apostles, where he threw himself on his knees and prayed with all his heart that the good Trajan, the man who did right according to the light that was in him, at all costs, should be saved. Some versions of the story add that he offered to bear any penance that might be put upon him for his presumption, and was ready to incur any penalty to secure this great boon. It can never be put to proof in this world whether Gregory's petition was heard or not, but his monks and biographers were sure of it, and some of them allege that his own bodily sufferings and weakness were the penalty which he accepted gladly for the salvation of that great soul. The story proves at least the intense humanity and yearning over the unhappy, which was in his heart. Whether he played and punned in tender humour with the objects of his sympathy, or so flung himself in profoundest compassion into the abyss of hopelessness with them, that he could wish himself like Paul accursed for his brethren's sake—Gregory's being was full of brotherly love and fervent feeling, a love which penetrated even beyond the limits of visible life.

The four years that elapsed between his return to his convent and his election to the Popedom (or to speak more justly the bishopric of Rome) were years of trouble. In addition to the constant danger of invasion, the misery, even when that was escaped, of the tales brought to Rome by the fugitives who took refuge there from all the surrounding country, in every aggravation of poverty and wretchedness, and the efforts that had to be made for their succour—a great inundation of the Tiber, familiar yet terrible disaster from which Rome has not even now been able to secure herself, took place towards the end of the period, followed by a terrible pestilence, its natural result. Gregory was expounding the prophet Ezekiel in one of the Roman churches at the time of this visitation: but as the plague increased his sorrowful soul could not bear any bondage of words or thoughts apart from the awful needs of the moment, and closing the book, he poured forth his heart to the awed and trembling people, exhorting all to repent, and to fling themselves upon God's mercy that the pestilence might be stayed. In all such terrible emergencies it is the impulse of human nature to take refuge in something that can be done, and the impulse is no doubt itself of use to relieve the crushing weight of despair, whatever may be the form it takes.

[SAN GREGORIO MAGNO, AND ST. JOHN AND ST. PAUL]

We clean and scrub and whitewash in our day, and believe in these ways of arresting the demons; but in old Rome the call for help was more impressive at least, and probably braced the souls of the sufferers as even whitewash could not do. The manner in which Gregory essayed to turn the terrible tide was by a direct appeal to Heaven. He organised a great simultaneous procession from all the quarters of Rome to meet at "the Church of the Virgin"—we are not informed which—in one great united outcry to God for mercy. The septiform litany, as it was called, was chanted through the desolate streets by gradually approaching lines, the men married and unmarried, the priests and monks each approaching in a separate band; while proceeding from other churches came the women in all their subdivisions, the wives, the widows, the maidens, the dedicated virgins, Ancillæ Dei, each line converging towards the centre, each followed no doubt from windows within which the dying lay with tears and echoes of prayers. Many great sights there have been in old Rome, but few could have been more melancholy or impressive than this. We hear of no miraculous picture, no saintly idol as in later ceremonials, but only the seven processions with their long-drawn monotones of penitence, the men by themselves, the women by themselves, the widows in their mourning, the veiled nuns, the younger generation, boys and girls, most precious of all. That Gregory should have had the gift to see, or believe that he saw, a shining angel upon Hadrian's tomb, pausing and sheathing his sword as the long line of suppliants drew near, is very soothing and human to think of. Fresh from his studies of Ezekiel or Job, though too sick at heart with present trouble to continue them, why should he have doubted that the Hearer of Prayer might thus grant a visible sign of the acceptance which He had promised? We do not expect such visions nowadays, nor do we with such intense and united purpose seek them; but the same legend connects itself with many such periods of national extremity. So late as the Great Plague of London a similar great figure, radiant in celestial whiteness, was also reported to be seen as the pestilence abated, sheathing, in the same imagery, a blazing sword.

The story of the septiform litany relates how here and there in the streets as they marched the dead and dying fell out of the very ranks of the suppliants. But yet the angel sheathed his sword. It is hard to recall the splendid monument of Hadrian with its gleaming marbles and statues as the pilgrim of to-day approaches the vast but truncated and heavy round of the Castle of St. Angelo; but it does not require so great an effort of the mind to recall that scene, when the great angel standing out against the sky existed but in Gregory's anxious eyes, and was reflected through the tears of thousands of despairing spectators, who stood trembling between the Omnipotence which could save in a moment and the terrible Death which seized and slew while they were looking on. No human heart can refuse to beat quicker at such a spectacle—the good man in his rapture of love and earnestness with his face turned to that radiant Roman sky, and all the dark lines of people arrested in their march gazing too, the chant dying from their lips, while the white angel paused for a moment and sheathed the sword of judgment over their heads.

It was not till many centuries later, when every relic of the glories of the great Emperor's tomb had been torn from its walls, that the angel in marble, afterwards succeeded by the present angel in bronze, was erected on the summit of the Castle of St. Angelo, which derives from this incident its name—a name now laden with many other associations and familiar to us all.

Pope Pelagius was one of the victims of this great plague; and it is evident from all the circumstances recorded that Gregory was already the most prominent figure in Rome, taking the chief place, not only in such matters as the public penitence, but in all the steps necessary to meet so great a calamity. Not only were his powers as an administrator very great, but he had the faculty of getting at those sacred hordes of ecclesiastical wealth, the Church's treasures of gold and silver plate, which a secular ruler could not have touched. Gregory's own liberality was the best of lessons, and though he had already sacrificed so much he had yet, it would appear, something of his own still to dispose of, as we have already found to be the case in so many instances, no doubt rents or produce of estates which could not be alienated, though everything they produced was freely given up. Already the wealth of the Church had been called into requisition to provide for the fugitives who had taken refuge from the Lombards in Rome. These riches, however, were now almost exhausted by the wants of the disorganised commonwealth, where every industry and occupation had been put out of gear, and nothing but want and misery, enfeebled bodies, and discouraged hearts remained. It was inevitable that at such a time Gregory should be the one man to whom every eye turned as the successor of Pelagius. The clergy, the nobles, and the populace, all accustomed to take a part in the choice of the bishop, pronounced for him with one voice. It is a kind of fashion among the saints that each one in his turn should resist and refuse the honours which it is wished to thrust upon him; but there was at least sufficient reason in Gregory's case for resistance. For the apostolical see, which was far from being a bed of roses at any time, was at that period of distress and danger one of the most onerous posts in the world.

Pelagius died in January 590, but it was late in that year before his successor was forced into the vacant place. In the meantime Gregory had appealed to the Emperor, begging that he would oppose the election and support him in his resistance. This letter fell into the hands of the Præfect of Rome, who intercepted it, and wrote in his own name and that of the people a contrary prayer, begging the Emperor Maurice to sanction and give authority to their choice. It was only when the answer was received confirming the election, that Gregory became aware of the trick played upon him; and all his natural aversion strengthened by this deceitful proceeding, he withdrew secretly from the city, hiding himself, it is said, in a cave among the woods. Whether this means that he had made his way to the hills, and found this refuge among the ruins of Tusculum, or in some woodland grotto about Albano, or that some of the herdsmen's huts upon the Campagna amid the broken arches of the aqueducts received and concealed him, it is impossible to tell. It is said that the place of his retreat was made known by a light from heaven which made an illumination about him in his stony refuge, for the legend is unsparing in the breadth of its effects and easily appropriates the large miracle which in the Old Testament attends the passage of a whole nation to the service of an individual, without any of that sense of proportion which is to be found in older records. This light suggests somehow the wide breadth of the Campagna where its distant glow could be seen from afar, from the battlements of Rome herself, rather than the more distant hills. And we must hope that this direct betrayal by Heaven of his hiding-place showed Gregory that the appointment against which he struggled had in fact the sanction of the higher powers.

He speaks, however, in many of his works of the great repugnance he felt to take the cares of such an office upon him. He had allowed himself to be ordained a deacon with reluctance, and only apparently on an understanding that when the emergency which called for his services was over he might be permitted to retire again to his cloister. His letter to Leander already referred to is full of the complaint that "when the ministry of the altar was so heavy a weight, the further burden of the pastoral charge was fastened on me, which I now find so much the more difficulty in bearing as I feel myself unequal to it, and cannot find consolation in any comfortable confidence in myself." To another correspondent he remonstrates against the censure he met with for having endeavoured to escape from so heavy a charge. These hesitations are not like those with which it is usual to find the great men of the Church refusing honours, since it is no profession of humility which moves Gregory, but his overwhelming sense of the difficulties and danger to which the chief pastor of the Church would necessarily be exposed. His idea of his position is indeed very different from that of those who consider him as one of the first to conceive the great plan of the papacy, and as working sedulously and with intention at the foundations of an institution which he expected to last for hundreds of years and to sway the fortunes of the world. He was on the contrary fully persuaded that all the signs of the times foretold instead, the end of the world and final winding up of human history. The apostles had believed so before him, and every succeeding age had felt the catastrophe to be only for a little while delayed. Nation was rising against nation under his very eyes, earthquakes destroying the cities of the earth, and pestilence their populations. There had been signs in heaven generally reported and believed, fiery ranks of combatants meeting in conflict in the very skies, and every token of judgment about to fall. Little thought was there in his mind of a triumphant and potent ecclesiastical economy which should dominate all things. "I being unworthy and weak have taken upon me the care of the old and battered vessel," he says in one of his epistles written soon after his election; "the waves make their way in on all sides, and the rotten planks, shattered by daily and violent storms, threaten imminent shipwreck." An old and battered vessel, it had borne the strain of six centuries—a long time to those who knew nothing of the ages to come: and now struggled on its way beaten by winds and waves, not knowing when the dreadful moment expected by so many generations might come, when the sun should be turned into darkness and the moon into blood—the only signs that were yet wanting of the approach of that great and terrible day. How different were these anticipations from any conscious plan of conquest or spiritual empire; and how much more fully justified by all that was happening around that broken, suffering, poor, breathless and hopeless capital of the world!

Yet it is evident enough that this one resolute man, toiling in every possible way for the protection of the people round him, did put a certain heart in the city which had come through so many convulsions. Crowded with fugitives, decimated with pestilence, left for many months without any more able head than the half-hearted prætors and officials of the state and the distant exarch at Ravenna, with all of whom, according to Gregory's own witness, the exaction of taxes was the chief object—a strong and steadfast ruler in the midst of this distracted people changed in every way the disposition of affairs. For one thing he seems to have taken upon him from the beginning the care and nourishment of the poor. It had been the principle of the Church from her earliest days that almsgiving was one of the first of duties, and the care of the poor her inalienable right; but such a time of disaster made something more heroic needful than the usual doles and charities. A large proportion of the population of Rome came upon Gregory's hands to be fed and provided for. Lists of the destitute poor, of their houses and circumstances, were kept with the greatest care; and we are told that before the Pope sat down to any meal the tables for the poor outside were first supplied. How dreadful to any philanthropist now this straightforward and matter-of-fact feeding of the hungry! but it was the manner of Christianity, most understood and approved in the early ages, the one with which even the most enlightened of politicians had no fault to find. This was the first idea in every evangelical soul, but it was by no means the limit of Gregory's exertions. He had learned diplomacy as well as charity in the experiences of his past life, and every resource of his skill and knowledge were needed for the salvation of the otherwise hopeless city. In all the dignity of his spiritual office, yet with all the arts of a statesman, we can see him standing as it were before the gates of Rome, as Horatius stood on the banks of the Tiber. It is sometimes to Constantinople, sometimes to the host of the invaders, that he turns explaining, arguing, pleading on one side and another for the safety of his city and people. His letters to the Emperor and to the Empress on one hand, and those to Queen Theodolinda on the other hand, the wife of the invader—show with what persistency and earnestness he defended Rome and its people who were his special charge and flock, and who had neither ruler nor defender save himself. This was one of his ways of establishing the sway of the papacy, it is said; it was at the same time, and primarily, the stepping forth of the only man who could or would put himself at the head of a disorganised and trembling host without leader or defender. He, only he, stood fast to strike for them, to intercept destruction hanging over their heads, and it, would be a curious fact indeed in human nature if such a man performed his first duty for the sake of an unformed empire to come after hundreds of years had passed. He succeeded with the barbarians, preserving Rome from the attacks which were often threatened but never carried out; but he did little good with Maurice, who on his side had few troops to send and no general able to make a successful campaign against the Lombards. The officers and the armies of the empire were of use in exacting taxes for the imperial treasury, but not for opposing a vigorous invader or rescuing a defenceless people.

It is never pretended by any of his biographers or admirers that Gregory was a man of learning, or even interested very much in the preservation of letters, or the progress of intellectual life. Learning and philosophy were the inheritance of the Greek Church, which was the very presumptuous and arrogant rival of Rome, and the cradle of most of the heresies and all the difficult and delicate questions which had troubled the peace of the Church. He is accused, though without sufficient evidence, of burning a library of Latin poets, a thing which he might well have done, according to his ideas, without much sense of guilt. There has never been an age in which certain books have not been liable to that reformation by fire, and the principle is quite as strong now as in the sixth century, so we need not take pains to exonerate Gregory from such an imputation. He did not, like Jerome, love the literature which was full of classical images and allusions. Neither Cicero nor Plato would have tempted him to occupy himself with vain studies. "The same mouth," he says, "should not pronounce the name of Jupiter and that of Christ;" yet at the same time he expresses strong regret that letters had died out of Rome, amid all the tumults through which she had passed. Amid the jargon of barbarians heard on every side, Greek, he complains, had fallen almost out of knowledge. There were few men learned enough to settle a question of doctrine by reference to the original text of Scripture. "Those we have are good for little but to translate word by word; they are unable to grasp the sense, and it is with difficulty that we understand their translations." He does not take any credit for his own style, which indeed is anything but Ciceronian. He complains with great simplicity, at the end of his dedication to Leander of his Moralia, of the "collisions of metacism," a difficulty about the letter m which would seem to have been as troublesome as the letter h in our own day; and anticipates criticism by confessing that he has neglected the "cases of prepositions." "For I account it far from meet," he says, taking as we should say in Scotland, "the first word of flyting," and with a high hand, "to submit the words of the Divine Oracle to the rules of (the grammarian) Donatus." As who should say Lindley Murray has nothing to do with the language of a sermon. This was a great deal for a man to say, one of whose early feats in life had been the conviction and conversion by argument of Eutychius, whose heresy in respect to the body of the resurrection (a sufficiently distant and far-off subject to disturb the Church about—but such twists of impossible doctrine have always affected some minds) survived himself—but who acknowledged with his dying breath that he was wrong and Gregory right.

[ARCH OF CONSTANTINE]

Doctrine, however, was not the point on which Gregory was most strong—his Dialogues, written it is said for the edification and strengthening in the faith of the Empress Theodolinda, are nothing more than pious discussions and sanctions of the miracles performed by the saints, which we fear would have a very contrary effect if published in our day. His works upon the pastoral law and the discipline of the Church are the most valuable and important of his productions; though in these also his point of view is extraordinarily different from ours, and he advises a kind and degree of toleration which is somewhat appalling to hear of. For instance, in his instructions to Augustine and his band of missionaries Gregory instructs them to interfere as little as possible with the customs, especially in the matter of religious observances, of the people among whom they were sent. They were not to put down the familiar accompaniments of their converts' native rites and ceremonies. The old temples of Woden and Thor were not to be abandoned but turned to a new and better use; even the system of sacrifice to these gods was not to be altogether set aside. "Let there be no more victims to demons," he says with curious casuistry, "but let them kill and eat giving thanks to God; for you must leave them some material enjoyments that they may so much more easily enter into the delights of the soul." On the other hand, his instructions to a bishop of Sardinia bear a curiously different character. He recommended this prelate to put a pressure more or less gentle upon the peasants there who still remained pagan, in the form of an increased rent and taxes until such time as they should become Christian. "Though, conversion does not come by force," he says with sagacious cynicism, "yet the children of these mercenary converts will receive baptism in their innocence and will be better Christians than their fathers;" an argument which certainly embodies much economic truth if not exactly the spirit of the Gospel.

[THE PIAZZA DEL POPOLO]

Strangely different from these worldly-wise suggestions, however, are the detailed instructions for pastoral work, quoted by Bede, in Gregory's answer to the questions of Augustine, in which the artificial conscience of the confessional suddenly appears in full development, by the side of those strange counsels of a still semi-pagan age. Nothing can be more remarkable than this contrast, which exacts a more than Levitical punctilio of observance from the devout, while leaving open every door for the entrance of the profane. Though he entered with so much reluctance upon the pastoral care of the Church, no one has laid down more detailed directions for the cure of souls. It would seem to have been in reality one of the things which interested him most. His mind was in some respects that of a statesman full of the broadest sense of expediency and of the practicable, and of toleration and compromise carried to a length which fills us with dismay; while on the other it was that of a parish legislator, an investigator of personal details, to whom no trifle was unimportant, and the most fantastic stipulations of ritualistic purification of as great moment as morality itself.

In contrast however with those letters which recommended what was little more than a forced conversion, and which have been frequently cited as examples of the unscrupulousness of the early missionaries, we must here quote some of Gregory's pastoral instructions in which the true spirit of a pastor shines forth. "Nothing," he says in one of his epistles to the bishops with whom he kept up constant communications, "is so heavy a burden upon a priest as so to bend the force of his own mind in sympathy, as to change souls (cum personis supervenientibus animam mutare) with each new person who approaches him; yet this is very necessary." Nothing could be more happy in expression or fine in sentiment, and it shows how completely the monk-Pope, in cloister and on throne, understood the essential character of his great profession. Still more remarkable, as more involved in personal matters, is his advice to Augustine, who had consulted him as to the differences in worship between the Gallican churches and those of Rome.

"You know, my brother, the custom of the Roman Church in which you were bred up. But it will please me if when you have found anything, either in the Roman or Gallican or any other Church, which may be more acceptable to Almighty God, you will carefully make choice of the same, and sedulously teach the

Church of the English, which as yet is new in the faith, whatsoever good thing you can gather from the several Churches. For things are not to be loved for the sake of places, but places for the sake of good things. Choose therefore from every Church those things that are pious, religious and upright, and when you have as it were made them into one system, let the minds of the English be accustomed thereto."

This is surely the truest and highest toleration.

The Papacy of Gregory began in trouble and distress; Rome was more disorganised, more miserable, more confused and helpless than almost ever before, although she had already passed through many a terrible crisis; and he had shrunk from the terrible task of setting her right. But when he had once undertaken that task there was neither weakness nor hesitation in the manner with which he carried it out. The public penance and humiliation to which he moved the people, the septiform litany with its chanting and weeping crowds, the ceaseless prayers and intercessions in the Church were not all, though no doubt the chief part to Gregory, of those methods by which he sustained the courage, or rather put a heart into, the broken-down population, so that for once a show of resistance was made when the Lombards threatened the city. And his anxious negotiations never ceased. The Emperor, far off and indifferent, not to say helpless, in Constantinople, had no rest from the constant remonstrances and appeals of the ever-watchful Bishop. Gregory complained and with reason that no efforts, or at least but fictitious ones, were made for the help of Rome, and that the indifference or hostility of the Emperor was more dangerous to her than the arms of the Lombards. On the other hand he addressed himself to the headquarters of the invaders, taking as his champion—as was his custom, as it has always been the custom of the Churchman—the Queen Theodolinda, who had become a Catholic and baptized her son in that faith, notwithstanding the opposition of her Arian husband, and was therefore a very fitting and natural intercessor. "What an overwhelming charge it is!" he cries to one of his correspondents, "to be at once weighted with the supervision of the bishops and clergy, of the monasteries and the entire people, and to remain all the time watchful to every undertaking of the enemy and on my guard against the robbery and injustice of our rulers." It was indeed a burden under which few men could have stood.

Gregory appears to have neglected no movement of the foe, to have noted every exaction and treachery from Constantinople, to have remembered every bishop in the furthest-off regions, and to have directed to each in turn his expostulations, his entreaties, his reproofs. We have been told in our own day of the overwhelming weight of business (attributed to facilities of post and daily communications) which almost crushes an English archbishop, although that dignitary besides the care of the Church has but such an amount of concern in public matters as a conscientious adviser must have. But Gregory was responsible for everything, the lives and so far as was possible the liberties of his city and people, their daily bread, their safety, their very existence, besides that cure of souls which was his special occupation. The mass of correspondence, which beside all his other work he managed to get through, forgetting nothing, is enough to put any modern writer of hasty notes and curt business letters to shame. On this point there may be said a word of apology for the much-harassed Pope in respect to that one moment in his history, in which his conduct cannot be defended by his warmest admirer. His prayers and appeals were treated with contempt at Constantinople, a contempt involving not his own person alone, but Rome and the Church, for which the Emperor Maurice did not even pretend to care. And when that Emperor was suddenly swept away, it is natural enough that a sensation of relief, a touch of hope in the new man who, notwithstanding the treachery and cruelty of the first step in his career, might turn out better than his predecessor, should have gleamed across the mind of a distant, and perhaps at first imperfectly informed spectator, whose interests were so closely concerned. The complacency with which Gregory wrote to Phocas, the amazing terms he used to that murderer and tyrant, will always be the darkest stain on his reputation. Under Maurice the ministers of the empire had been more oppressive than the invaders. Perhaps under Phocas better things might be hoped for. It is all that can be said for this unfortunate moment of his career; but it is something nevertheless.

It was not till 597, when he had occupied his bishopric for seven years, that Gregory succeeded in carrying out the long-cherished scheme of the mission to England, which had been for many years so near his heart. It is said that he himself had purchased some of the captive boys who caught his eye in the streets, and trained them in the Christian doctrine and faith, in order that they might act as interpreters and commend the missionaries to their people, an expedient which has been so largely followed (and of course boasted of as an original thought) in recent missions. These boys would by this time have attained the age of manhood, and perhaps this determined the moment at which Augustine and his companions were sent forth. They were solemnly consecrated in the chapel of the convent on the Coelian hill, Gregory's beloved home, to which he always returned with so much affection, and to which they also belonged, monks of the same house. Their names are inscribed in the porch of the present church after that of their master, with designations strangely familiar to our British ears—S. Augustine, Apostle of England; S. Lawrence, Archbishop of Canterbury; S. Mellitus, of London and Canterbury; S. Justus, of Rochester; S. Paulinus, of York, appear in the record, the first teachers and ecclesiastical dignitaries of Saxon England. The church in which this consecration took place exists no longer; the present building, its third or fourth successor, dates only from the eighteenth century, and is dedicated to S. Gregory himself; but the little piazza now visited by so many pilgrims is unchanged, and it was from this small square, so minute a point amid the historic places of Rome, that the missionary party set forth, Augustine and his brethren kneeling below, while the Pope, standing at the head of the steps, gave them his parting blessing. No doubt the young Angles, with their golden locks of childhood matured into russet tones, who had filled Gregory's mind with so many thoughts, were in the group, behind the black-robed Benedictine brothers whose guides and interpreters they were to be.

This is an association full of interest for every Englishman, and has attracted many pilgrims from the nation whose faith has undergone so many vicissitudes, and in which the Pope's authority has been as vehemently decried in one age as strongly upheld in another; but whatever our opinions on that point may be, there can be nothing here but affectionate and grateful remembrance of the man of God who had so long cherished the scheme, which thus at length with fatherly benedictions and joy at heart, he was able to carry out. He himself would fain have gone on this mission many years before; but the care of all the Churches, and the tribulations of a distracted world, had made that for ever impossible, and he was now growing old, in feeble health, and with but a few years of work before him. The hearts of the missionaries were not so strong as that of this great Servant of the servants of God who sent them away with his blessing. Terrors of the sea and terrors of the wilds, the long journey and the savage tribes at the end of it, were in their hearts. When they had got nearly over their journey and were resting a little to recover their health among the Gauls,—fierce enough indeed, but still with sanctuaries of peace and holy brethren among them—before crossing the terrible channel, Augustine wrote beseeching letters, begging to be recalled. But let us hope that at the moment of dedication these terrors had scarcely yet got hold upon them. And to Gregory the occasion was one of unmingled satisfaction and joy. The Pope did not in those days wear the white robes which distinguish his dignity now. Gregory was presumably indifferent to such signs and tokens; for in the portrait of him which still exists in the description given of it by John the Deacon, he wears a dress scarcely distinguishable from the ordinary dress of a layman. But as he stood upon the steps in front of the church, separated from all the attendants, and raised his hands in blessing, the scene is one that any painter might covet, and which to many a visitor from these distant islands of the seas will make the little Piazza di San Gregorio more interesting in its simplicity than any other spot in storied Rome.

It would occupy too much time to quote here his long and careful letters to the bishops of the West generally—from Sicily which always seems to have been the object of his special care, to those in Gaul and his missionaries in England. That he assumed an unquestioned authority over them is clear, an authority which had more or less been exercised by the Bishop of Rome for many generations before him: and that he was unfeignedly indignant at the pretensions of John of Constantinople to be called Universal Bishop is also certain. These facts however by no means prove that a great scheme of papal authority was the chief thing in his mind, underlying all his undertakings. When the historians speak of Gregory as spreading the supremacy of the Church of Rome by his missions, notably by that mission to England of which I have just spoken, they forget that the salvation of the souls lying in darkness is a motive which has moved men in every age to the greatest sacrifices, and that we have no reason in the world to believe that it was not the faith of Christ rather than the supremacy of Rome which was Gregory's object. The Apostles themselves might be said in the same way to have been spreading their own supremacy when they obeyed the injunction of their Master to go over the whole world and preach the Gospel to every creature. The one sovereignty was actually implied in the other—but it requires a very robust faith in a preconceived dogma, and a very small understanding of human nature, to be able to believe that when the meditative monk paused in his walk, with compassion and interest, to look at the angelic boys, and punned tenderly with tears in his eyes over their names and nation and king, the idea immediately sprang up in his mind not that Allelujah should be sung in the dominions of King Alle, but that this wild country lost in the midst of the seas should be brought under a spiritual sceptre not yet designed.

Gregory thought as the Apostles thought, that the days of the world were numbered, and that his own generation might see its records closed. That is an idea which never has stopped any worthy man in undertakings for the good of the world—but it was a belief better established, and much more according to all the theories and dogmas of the age, than a plan of universal dominion for the Church such as is attributed to him. He did his duty most energetically and strenuously in every direction—never afraid of being supposed to interfere, using the prestige of the Apostolical See freely for every ecclesiastical purpose. And he became prince in Rome, an absolute sovereign by stress of circumstance and because every other rule and authority had failed. Whether these practical necessities vaguely formed themselves into visions of spiritual empire before the end of his life it is impossible to tell: as it is equally impossible to tell what dreams of happiness or grandeur may enter into any poor man's brain. But so large and world-embracing a plan seldom springs fully formed into any mind, and in his words he never claimed, nay, vehemently denied and repudiated, any pretension of the kind. It is curious how difficult it is to get the world to believe that a man placed in a position of great responsibility, at the head of any institution, is first of all actuated by the desire of doing his work, whatever the ulterior results may be.

Gregory's activity was boundless, though his health was weak, and his sufferings many. Fastings in his youth and neglect at all times told early upon his constitution. The dinner of herbs which his mother sent him daily, and which is sometimes described as uncooked—salad to wit, which enters so largely into the sustenance of the Italian poor—is a kind of fare which does not suit a delicate digestion; but he spared himself nothing on this account, though he had reached such a pitch of weakness that he was at last, as he bitterly laments, unable to fast at all, even on Easter Eve, when even little children abstain from food. Beside all the labours which I have already noted, there remains one detail which has done perhaps more to make the common world familiar with his name than all the rest; and that is the reformation in music which he accomplished among all his other labours. Church music is the only branch of the art of which we have any authentic record which dates so far back, and the Gregorian chant still exists among us, with that special tone of wailing mingled with its solemn measures which is characteristic of all primitive music.

"Four scales," says Mr. Helmore in The Dictionary of Music, "traditionally ascribed to St. Ambrose, existed before the time of St. Gregory. These, known as the Authentic Modes, and since the thirteenth century named after the ancient Greek scales from which they were supposed to be derived, are as follows: 1, Dorian; 2, Phrygian; 3, Lydian; 4, Mixo-Lydian. To the four Authentic St. Gregory added four Plagal, i.e. collateral or relative Modes. Each is a fourth below its corresponding original, and is called by the same name with the prefix hypo ([Greek: hypo], below), as follows: 5, Hypo-Dorium; 6, Hypo-Phrygian; 7, Hypo-Lydian; 8, Hypo-Mixo-Lydian.... Handel's 'Hanover' among modern tunes, which ranges from F to F has its finale on B flat. 'Should auld acquaintance be forgot' is also a specimen of a tune in a Plagal Mode descending about a fourth below its final, and rising above it only six notes, closing upon the final of its tone."

This may be a little too learned for the ordinary reader, but it is interesting to find how far the influence of the busy old Pope, who had a finger in every pie, could go. There is a very curious commentary by John the Deacon, Gregory's later biographer, upon this new musical system and its adoption throughout Europe, which makes a good pendant to the scientific description. The Italians seem then as now to have had a poor opinion of German modes of singing.

"This music was learned easily by the Germans and Gauls, but they could not retain it because of making additions of their own, and also because of their barbarous nature. Their Alpine bodies resounding to their depths with the thunders of their voices, do not properly give forth the sweetness of the modulation, the savage roughness of their bibulous throat when it attempts to give forth a delicate strain, producing rather harsh sounds with a natural crash, as of waggons sounding confusedly over the scales."

This is not flattering; but one can imagine something very like it coming from the lips of an Italian Maestro in our own day. The tradition goes that Gregory himself instructed the choristers, for whom he had established schools endowed each with its little property, one in the precincts of St. Peter's, the other in those of St. John Lateran, where his own residence was. And a couch is still shown on which he lay while giving or superintending their lessons, and even the whip with which he is said to have threatened the singers when they made false notes. The last is little in accord with the Pope's character, and we can scarcely imagine the twang through the air of any whip in Gregory's hand: but it is probably as true as other more agreeable circumstances of the legend. One can scarcely believe however that amid his multitudinous occupations he could have had time for more than a flying visit to the schools, however they might interest him.

Nor did he limit his exertions on behalf of ritual to the arrangement of the music. We are told that the Missal of Pope Gelasius then used in the Church was revised by him, and that he took away much, altered some things and added a little, among other things a confession of faith or Credo of his own writing, which is something between the Athanasian and Nicene Creeds. The Ordinary of the Mass remains now, another authority tells us, very much as it came from his hands. Thus his immediate authority and the impress of his mind remain on things which are still in daily use.

[MONTE PINCIO, FROM THE PIAZZA DEL POPOLO]

And there could be no more familiar or characteristic figure in Rome than that of this monk-Pope threading everywhere those familiar streets, in which there were more ruins, and those all fresh and terrible in their suggestions of life destroyed—than now: the gentle spectator full of meditation, who lingered among the group of slaves, and saw and loved and smiled at the Saxon boys: who passed by Trajan's Forum which we all know so well, that field of broken pillars, not then railed off and trim in all the orderliness of an outdoor museum, but wild in the neglect of nature: and heard the story of the Emperor, and loved him too, and poured out his soul to God for the great heathen, so that the gates of Hades were rolled back and the soul set free—strange parable of brotherly kindness as the dominant principle of heart and life. We can follow him through all the lists of the poor laid up in his Scrivii, like the catalogues of books enclosed in caskets, in an old-fashioned library—with careful enumeration of every half-ruined tenement and degraded palace where the miserable had found shelter: or passing among the crowds who received their portions before, not after, the Pope in the precincts of the great basilica; or "modulating," with a voice broken by age and weakness, the new tones of his music which the "bibulous throats" of the barbarian converts turned into thunder, and of which even his own choristers, careless as is their use, would make discords, till the whip of the Master trembled in the air, adding the sting of a sharper sound to the long-drawn notes of the monotone, and compelling every heedless tenor and frivolous soprano to attention. These are his simpler aspects, the lower life of the great Benedictine, the picture of the Pope as he endeared himself to the popular imagination, round which all manner of tender legends grew. His aspect is less familiar yet not less true as he sits at the head of affairs, dictating or writing with his own hand those innumerable letters which treat of every subject under heaven, from the safety of Rome to the cross which is to be hung round a royal infant's neck, or the amethyst ring for the finger of a little princess; from the pretensions of John of Constantinople, that would-be head of the Church, down to the ass sent by the blundering intendant from Sicily. Nothing was too great, nothing too little for his care. He had to manage the mint and cummin without leaving graver matters undone.

And the reader who has leisure may follow him into the maze of those Dialogues in which Peter the Deacon serves as questioner, and the Pope discourses gently, to improve his ignorance, of all the wonderful things which the saints have done, chiefly in Italy, turning every law of nature upside down: or follow him through the minute and endless rules of his book of discipline, and note the fine-drawn scruples with which he has to deal, the strange cases of conscience for which he provides, the punctilio of extravagant penitence, so strangely contrasted with the other rough and ready modes of dealing with the unconverted, to which he gives the sanction of his recommendation. He was a man of his time, not of ours: he flattered Phocas while his hands were still wet with his predecessor's blood—though we may still hope that at such a distance Gregory did not know all that had happened or what a ruffian it was whom he thus addressed. He wrote affectionately and with devotion to Queen Brunhild without inquiring into that lady's character, which no doubt he knew perfectly. Where the good of Rome, either the city or the Church, was concerned, he stopped at nothing. I have no desire to represent him as faultless. But the men who are faultless, if any are to be found, leave but a limited record, and there is little more to say of perfection than that it is perfect. Gregory was not so. He got very angry sometimes, with bishops in Sicily, with stupid intendants, above all with that Eastern John—and sometimes, which is worse, he was submissive and compliant when he ought to have been angry and denounced a criminal. But on the other hand he was the first of the great ecclesiastical princes who have made Modern Rome illustrious—he was able, greatest of miracles, to put a heart into the miserable city which had allowed herself to be overrun by every savage: and stood between her and all creation, giving the whole world assurance of a man, and fighting for her with every weapon that came to his hand. Doing whatsoever he found to do thoroughly well, he laid the foundations of that great power which still extends over the whole world. I do not believe that he acted on any plan or had the supremacy of the Pontificate in his mind, or had conceived any idea of an ecclesiastical empire which should grasp the universe. To say, for instance, that the mission to England which he had cherished so long was undertaken with the idea of extending the sway of the Papacy seems one of those follies of the theorist which requires no answer. St. Paul might as well be accused of intending to spread a spiritual empire when he saw in his dream that man of Macedonia, and immediately directed his steps thither, obeying the vision. What Gregory hoped and prayed for was to bring in a new nation, as he judged a noble and vigorous race, to Christianity. And he succeeded in doing so: with such secondary consequences as the developments of time, and the laws of progress, and the course of Providence brought about.

There is a certain humour in the indignation, which has been several times referred to, with which he turned against the Patriarch of Constantinople and his pretensions to a supremacy which naturally was in the last degree obnoxious to the Bishop of Rome. The Eastern and Western Churches had already diverged widely from each other, the one nourished and subdued under the shadow of a Court, in a leisure which left it open to every refinement and every temptation, whether of asceticism or heresy— both of which abounded: the other fighting hard for life amid the rudest and most practical dangers, obliged to work and fight like Nehemiah on the walls of Jerusalem with the tool in one hand and the sword in the other. John the Faster, so distinguished because of the voluntary privations which he imposed upon himself, forms one of the most startling contrasts of this age with Gregory, worn by work and warfare, whose spare and simple meal could not be omitted even on the eve of Easter. That he who, sitting in St. Peter's seat, with all the care of Church and country upon his shoulders, obeyed by half the world, yet putting forth in words no such pretension—should be aggrieved almost beyond endurance by the dignity conferred on, or assumed by, the other bishop, whose see was not apostolical but the mere creation of an emperor, and the claim put forth by him and the Council called by him for universal obedience, is very natural; yet Gregory's wrath has a fiercely human sense of injury in it, an aggrieved individuality to which we cannot deny our sympathy. "There is no doubt," he says with dignity, writing to the Emperor on the subject, "that the keys of heaven were given to Peter, the power of binding and loosing, and the care of the whole Church; and yet he is not called Universal Apostle. Nor does it detract from the honour of the See that the sins of Gregory are so great that he ought to suffer; for there are no sins of Peter that he should be treated thus. The honour of Peter is not to be brought low because of us who serve him unworthily." "Oh tempora, oh mores!" he exclaims; "Europe lies prostrate under the power of the barbarians. Its towns are destroyed, its fortresses thrown down, its provinces depopulated, the soil has no longer labourers to till it; and yet priests who ought to humble themselves with tears in the dust strive after vain honours and glorify themselves with titles new and profane!" To John himself he writes with more severity, reminding him of the vaunt of Lucifer in Isaiah, "I will exalt my throne above the stars of heaven." Now bishops, he says, are the stars of heaven, they shine over men; they are clouds (the metaphors are mixed) that rain words and are lighted up by the rays of good works. "What, then," he asks, "is the act of your paternity, in looking down upon them and pressing them into subjection, but following the example of the ancient enemy? When I see this I weep that the holy man, the Lord John, a man so renowned for self-sacrifice, should so act. Certainly Peter was first in the whole Church. Andrew, James, and the others were but heads of the people; yet all made up one body, and none were called Universal."

[THE FORUM]

The argument with which Gregory replies to a letter from Eulogius, Bishop of Alexandria, who had wished him to assume himself a similar title, is curious. The Apostolical See, he says, consists of three bishoprics, all held by St. Peter, that of Antioch, that of Alexandria, and that of Rome, and the honour of the title is shared between them. "If you give me more than my due," he adds, "you rob yourself. If I am named Pope, you own yourself to be no pope. Let no such thing be named between us. My honour is the honour of the Universal Church. I am honoured in the honour paid to my brethren." Nothing could be more determined than this oft-repeated refusal. Yet he never fails to add that it was Peter's right. The Council of Chalcedon, he says, offered that supreme title to the Church of Rome, which refused it. How much greater then, was the guilt of John, to whom it was never offered, but who assumed it, injuring all priests by setting himself above them, and the Empire itself by a position superior to it? Such were the sentiments of Gregory, in which the wrath of a natural heir, thus supplanted by a usurper, gives fervour to every denunciation. The French historian Villemain points out, what will naturally occur to the reader, that many of these arguments were afterwards used with effect by Luther and his followers against the assumptions of the Church of Rome. It will also be remembered that Jerome put the case more strongly still, denouncing the Scarlet Woman with as much fervour as any No-Popery orator.

But while he rejected all such titles and assumed for himself only that, conceived no doubt in all humility and sincere meaning, but afterwards worn with pride surpassing that of any earthly monarch, of Servus Servorum Dei, the servant of the servants of God, Gregory occupied himself, as has been said, with the care of all the churches in full exercise of the authority and jurisdiction of an overseer, at least over the western half of Christendom. Vain titles he would have none, and we cannot doubt his sincerity in rejecting them; but the reality of the pastoral supervision, never despotic, but continual, was clearly his idea of his own rights and duties. It has been seen what license he left to Augustine in the regulation of the new English Church. He acted with an equally judicious liberality in respect to the rich and vigorous Gallican bishops, never demanding too servile an obedience, but never intermitting his superintendence of all. But he does not seem to have put forth the smallest pretension to political independence, even when that was forced upon him by his isolated and independent position, and he found himself compelled to make his own terms with the Lombard invaders. At the moment of his election as Bishop of Rome, he appealed to the Emperor against the popular appointment, and only when the imperial decision was given against him allowed himself to be dragged from his solitude. And one of his accusations against John of Constantinople was that his assumption injured the very Empire itself in its supreme authority. Thus we may, and indeed I think must, conclude that Gregory's supposed theory of the universal papal power was as little real as are most such elaborate imputations of purpose conceived long before the event. He had no intention, so far as the evidence goes, of making himself an arbitrator between kings, and a judge of the world's actions and movements. He had enough and too much work of his own which it was his determination to do, as vigorously and with as much effect as possible—in the doing of which work it was necessary to influence, to conciliate, to appeal, as well as to command and persuade: to make terms with barbarians, to remonstrate with emperors, as well as to answer the most minute questions of the bishops, and lay out before them the proper course they were to pursue. There is nothing so easy as to attribute deep-laid plans to the great spirits among men. I do not think that Gregory had time for any such ambitious projects. He had to live for the people dependent upon him, who were a multitude, to defend, feed, guide and teach them. He had never an unoccupied moment, and he did in each moment work enough for half a dozen men. That it was his duty to superintend and guide everything that went on, so far as was wise or practicable, in the Church as well as in his immediate diocese, was clearly his conviction, and the reader may find it a little difficult to see why he should have guarded that power so jealously, yet rejected the name of it: but that is as far as any reasonable criticism can go.

What would seem an ancient complaint against Gregory appears in the sketch of his life given by Platina, in his Lives of the Popes—who describes him as having been "censured by a few ignorant men as if the ancient stately buildings were demolished by his order, lest strangers coming out of devotion to Rome should less regard the consecrated places, and spend all their gaze upon triumphal arches and monuments of antiquity." This curious accusation is answered by the author in words which I quote from an almost contemporary translation very striking in its forcible English. "No such reproach," says Platina in the vigorous version of Sir Paul Rycant, Knight, "can justly be fastened on this great Bishop, especially considering that he was a native of the city, and one to whom, next after God, his country was most dear, even above his life. 'Tis certain that many of those ruined structures were devoured by time, and many might, as we daily see, be pulled down to build new houses; and for the rest 'tis probable that, for the sake of the brass used in the concavity of the arches and the conjunctures 'of the marble or other square stones, they might be battered or defaced not only by the barbarous nations but by the Romans too, if Epirotes, Dalmatians, Pannonians, and other sorry people who from all parts of the world resorted hither, may be called Romans."

This is a specious argument which would not go far toward establishing Gregory's innocence were he seriously accused: but the accusation, like that of burning classical manuscripts, has no proof. Little explanation, however, is necessary to account for the ruins of a city which has undergone several sieges. That Gregory would have helped himself freely as everybody did, and has done in all ages, to the materials lying so conveniently at hand in the ruined palaces which nobody had any mission to restore, may be believed without doubt; for he was a man far too busy and preoccupied to concern himself with questions of Art, or set any great price upon the marble halls of patrician houses, however interesting might be their associations or beautiful their structure. But he built few new churches, we are expressly told, though he was careful every year to look into the condition of all existing ecclesiastical buildings and have them repaired. It seems probable that it might be a later Gregory however against whom this charge was made. In the time of Gregory the First these ruins were recent, and it was but too likely that at any moment a new horde of unscrupulous iconoclasts might sweep over them again.

There came however a time when the Pope's suffering and emaciated body could bear no longer that charge which was so burdensome. He had been ill for many years, suffering from various ailments and especially from weakness of digestion, and he seems to have broken down altogether towards the year 601. Agelulphus thundering at his gates had completed what early fastings and the constant work of a laborious life had begun, and at sixty Gregory took to his bed, from which, as he complains in one of his letters, he was scarcely able to rise for three hours on the great festivals of the Church in order to celebrate Mass. He was obliged also to conclude abruptly that commentary on Ezekiel which had been so often interrupted, leaving the last vision of the prophet unexpounded, which he regretted the more that it was one of the most dark and difficult, and stood in great need of exposition. "But how," he says, "can a mind full of trouble clear up such dark meanings? The more the mind is engaged with worldly things the less is it qualified to expound the heavenly." It was from Ezekiel that Gregory was preaching when the pestilence which swept away his predecessor Pelagius was raging in Rome, and when, shutting the book which was no longer enough with its dark sayings to calm the troubles of the time, he had called out to the people, with a voice which was as that of their own hearts, to repent. All his life as Pope had been threaded through with the study of this prophet. He closed the book again and finally when all Rome believed that another invasion was imminent, and his courage failed in this last emergency. It is curious to associate the name of such a man, so full of natural life and affection, so humorous, so genial, so ready to take interest in everything that met his eyes, with these two saddest figures in all the round of sacred history, the tragic patriarch Job, and the exiled prophet, who was called upon to suffer every sorrow in order to be a sign to his people and generation. Was it that the very overflowing of life and sympathy in him made Gregory seek a balance to his own buoyant spirit in the plaints of those two melancholy voices? or was it the misfortunes of his time, so distracted and full of miserable agitation, which directed him at least to the latter, the prophet of a fallen nation, of disaster and exile and penitence?

Thus he lay after his long activities, suffering sorely, and longing for the deliverance of death, though he was not more, it is supposed, than sixty-two when the end came. From his sick bed he wrote to many of his friends entreating that they would pray for him that his sufferings might be shortened and his sins forgiven. He died finally on the 12th of March, ever afterwards consecrated to his name, in the year 603. This event must have taken place in the palace at the Lateran, which was then the usual dwelling of the Popes. Here the sick and dying man could look out upon one of the finest scenes on earth, the noble line of the Alban Hills rising over the great plains of the Campagna, with all its broken lines of aqueduct and masses of ruin. The features of the landscape are the same, though every accessory is changed, and palace and basilica have both crumbled into the dust of ages, to be replaced by other and again other buildings, handing down the thread of historic continuity through all the generations. There are scarcely any remains of the palace of the Popes itself, save one famous mosaic, copied from a still earlier one, in which a recent learned critic sees the conquest of the world by papal Rome already clearly set forth. But we can scarcely hope that any thought of the first Gregory will follow the mind of the reader into the precincts of St. John of the Lateran Gate. His memory abides in another place, in the spot where stood his father's house, where he changed the lofty chambers of the Roman noble into Benedictine cells, and lived and wrote and mused in the humility of an obedient brother. But still more does it dwell in the little three-cornered piazza before the Church of St. Gregorio, from whence he sent forth the mission to England with issues which he could never have divined—for who could have told in those days that the savage Angles would have overrun the world further than ever Roman standard was carried? The shadow of the great Pope is upon those time-worn steps where he stood and blessed his brethren, with moisture in his eyes and joy in his heart, sending them forth upon the difficult and dangerous way which he had himself desired to tread, but from which their spirits shrank. We have all a sacred right to come back here, to share the blessing of the saint, to remember the constant affection he bore us, his dedication of himself had it been permitted, his never-ending thought of his angel boys which has come to such wonderful issues. He would have been a more attractive apostle than Augustine had he carried out his first intention; but still we find his image here, fatherly, full of natural tenderness, interest and sympathy, smiling back upon us over a dozen centuries which have changed everything—except the historical record of Pope Gregory's blessing and his strong desire and hope.

[PONTE MOLLE]

[THE PALATINE]

He was buried in St. Peter's with his predecessors, but his tomb, like so many others, was destroyed at the rebuilding of the great church, and no memorial remains.

CHAPTER II

THE MONK HILDEBRAND

It is a melancholy thing looking back through the long depths of history to find how slow the progress is, even if it can be traced at all, from one age to another, and how, though the dangers and the evils to which they are liable change in their character from time to time, their gravity, their hurtfulness, and their rebellion against all that is best in morals, and most advantageous to humanity, scarcely diminish, however completely altered the conditions may be. We might almost doubt whether the vast and as yet undetermined possibilities of the struggle which has begun in our days between what is called Capital and Labour, the theories held against all experience and reason of a rising Socialism, and the mad folly of Anarchism, which is their immediate climax—are not quite as dangerous to the peace of nations as were the tumults of an age when every man acted by the infallible rule that

He should take who had the power
And he should keep who can—

the principle being entirely the same, though the methods may be different. This strange duration of trouble, equal in intensity though different in form, is specially manifest in a history such as that which we take up from one age to another in so remarkable a development of life and government as Mediæval Rome. We leave the city relieved of some woes, soothed from some troubles, fed by much charity, and weeping apparently honest tears over Gregory the first of the name—although that great man was scarcely dead before the crowd was taught to believe that he had impoverished the city by feeding them, and were scarcely prevented from burning his library as a wise and fit revenge. Still it might have been expected that Rome and her people would have advanced a step upon the pedestal of such a life as that of Gregory: and in fact he left many evils redressed, the commonwealth safer, and the Church more pure.

But when we turn the page and come, four hundred years later, to the life of another Gregory, upon what a tumultuous world do we open our eyes: what blood, what fire, what shouts and shrieks of conflict: what cruelty and shame have reigned between, and still remained, ever stronger than any influence of good men, or amelioration of knowledge! Heathenism, save that which is engrained in the heart of man, had passed away. There were no more struggles with the relics of the classical past: the barbarians who came down in their hordes to overturn civilisation had changed into settled nations, with all the paraphernalia of state and great imperial authority—shifting indeed from one race to another, but always upholding a central standard. All the known world was nominally Christian. It was full of monks dedicated to the service of God, of priests, the administrants of the sacraments, and of bishops as important as any secular nobles—yet what a scene is that upon which we look out through endless smoke of battle and clashing of swords! Rome, at whose gates Alaric and Attila once thundered, was almost less secure now, and less easily visited than when Huns and Goths overran the surrounding country. It was encircled by castles of robber nobles, who infested every road, sometimes seizing the pilgrims bound for Rome, with their offerings great and small, sometimes getting possession of these offerings in a more thorough way by the election of a subject Pope taken from one of their families, and always ready on every occasion to thrust their swords into the balance and crush everything like freedom or purity either in the Church or in the city. In the early part of the eleventh century there were two if not three Popes in Rome. "Benedict IX. officiated in the church of St. John Lateran, Sylvester III. in St. Peter's, and John XX. in the church of St. Mary," says Villemain in his life of Hildebrand: the name of the last does not appear in the lists of Platina, but the fact of this profane rivalry is beyond doubt.

The conflict was brought to an end for the moment by a very curious transaction. A certain dignified ecclesiastic, Gratiano by name, the Cardinal-archdeacon of St. John Lateran, who happened to be rich, horrified by this struggle, and not sufficiently enlightened as to the folly and sin of doing evil that good might come—always, as all the chronicles seem to allow, with the best motives—bought out the two competitors, and procured his own election under the title of Gregory VI. But this mistaken though well-meant act had but brief success. For, on the arrival in 1046 of the Emperor Henry III. in Italy, at a council called together by his desire, Gregory was convicted of the strange bargain he had made, or according to Baronius of the violent means taken to enforce it, and was deposed accordingly, along with his two predecessors. It was this Pope, in his exile and deprivation, who first brought in sight of a universe which he was born to rule, a young monk of Cluny, Hildebrand—German by name, but Italian in heart and race—who had already moved much about the world with the extraordinary freedom and general access everywhere which we find common to monks however humble their origin. From his monastic home in Rome he had crossed the Alps more than once; he had been received and made himself known at the imperial court, and was on terms of kindness with many great personages, though himself but a humble brother of his convent. No youthful cleric in our modern world nowadays would find such access everywhere, though it is still possible that a young Jesuit for instance, noted by his superiors for ability or genius, might be handed on from one authority to another till he reached the highest circle. But it is surprising to see how free in their movements, how adventurous in their lives, the young members of a brotherhood bound under the most austere rule then found it possible to be.

Hildebrand was, like so many other great Churchmen, a child of the people. He was the son of a carpenter in a Tuscan village, who, however, possessed one of those ties with the greater world which a clergy drawn from the people affords to the humblest, a brother or other near relation who was the superior of a monastery in Rome. There the little Tuscan peasant took his way in very early years to study letters, having already given proof of great intelligence such as impressed the village and called forth prophecies of the highest advancement to come. His early education brings us back to the holy mount of the Aventine, on which we have already seen so many interesting assemblies. The monastery of St. Mary has endured as little as the house of Marcella, though it is supposed that in the church of S. Maria Aventina there may still remain some portion of the original buildings. But the beautiful garden of the Priorato, so great a favourite with the lovers of the picturesque, guards for us, in that fidelity of nature which time cannot discompose, the very spot where that keen-eyed boy must have played, if he ever played, or at least must have dreamed the dreams of an ambitious young visionary, and perhaps, as he looked out musing to where the tombs of the Apostles gleamed afar on the other side of Tiber, have received the inheritance of that long hope and vision which had been slowly growing in the minds of Popes and priests—the hope of making the Church the mistress and arbiter of the nations, the supreme and active judge among all tumults of earthly politics and changes of power. He was nourished from his childhood in the house of St. Peter, says the biographer of the Acta Sanctorum. It would be more easy to realise the Apostle's sway, and that of his successors, on that mount of vision, where day and night, by sun and moon, the great temple of Christendom, the centre of spiritual life, shone before his eyes, than on any other spot. That wonderful visionary sovereignty, the great imagination of a central power raised above all the disturbances of worldly life, and judging austerely for right and against wrong all the world over—unbiassed, unaffected by meaner motives, the great tribunal from which justice and mercy should go forth over the whole earth—could there be a more splendid ideal to till the brain of an ardent boy? It is seldom that such an ideal is recognised, or such dreams as these believed in. We know how little the Papacy has carried it out, and how the faults and weaknesses even of great men have for many centuries taken all possibility from it. But it was while that wonderful institution was still fully possible, the devoutest of imaginations, a dream such as had never been surpassed in splendour and glory, that young Hildebrand looked out to Peter's prison on the Janiculum opposite, and from thence to Peter's tomb, and dreamt of Peter's white throne of justice dominating the darkness and the self-seeking of an uneasy world.

The monastery of St. Mary, a Benedictine house, must have been noted in its time. Among the teachers who instructed its neophytes was that same Giovanni Gratiano of whom we have just spoken, the arch-priest who devoted his wealth to the not ignoble purpose of getting rid of two false and immoral Popes: though perhaps his motives would have been less misconstrued had he not been elected in their place. And there was also much fine company at the monastery in those days—bishops with their suites travelling from south and north, seeking the culture and piety of Rome after long banishment from intellectual life—and at least one great abbot, more important than a bishop, Odilon of Cluny, at the head of one of the greatest of monastic communities. All of these great men would notice, no doubt, the young nephew of the superior, the favourite of the cloister, upon whom many hopes were already beginning to be founded, and in whose education every one loved to have a hand. One of these bishops was said afterwards to have taught him magical arts, which proves at least that they took a share in the training of the child of the convent. At what age it was that he was transferred to Cluny it is impossible to tell. Dates do not exist in Hildebrand's history until he becomes visible in the greater traffic of the world. He was born between 1015 and 1020—this is the nearest that we can approach to accuracy. He appears in full light of history at the deposition of Gratiano (Gregory VI.) in 1045. In the meantime he passed through a great many developments. Probably the youth—eager to see the world, eager too to fulfil his vocation, to enter upon the mortifications and self-abasement of a monk's career, and to "subdue the flesh" in true monkish fashion, as well as by the fatigues of travel and the acquirement of learning—followed Odilon and his train across i monti, a favourite and familiar, when the abbot returned from Rome to Cluny. It could not be permitted in the monkish chronicles, even to a character like that of the austere Hildebrand all brain and spirit, that he had no flesh to subdue. And we are not informed whether it was at his early home on the Aventine or in the great French monastery that he took the vows. The rule of Cluny was specially severe. One poor half hour a day was all that was permitted to the brothers for rest and conversation. But this would not matter much, we should imagine, to young Hildebrand, all on fire for work, and full of a thousand thoughts.

How a youth of his age got to court, and was heard and praised by the great Emperor Henry III., the head of Christendom, is not known. Perhaps he went in attendance on his abbot, perhaps as the humble clerk of some elder brethren bearing a complaint or an appeal; the legend goes that he became the tutor and playfellow of the little prince, Henry's son, until the Emperor had a dream in which he saw the stranger, with two horns on his head, with one of which he pushed his playfellow into the mud—significant and alarming vision which was a reasonable cause for the immediate banishment of Hildebrand. The dates, however, if nothing else, make this story impossible, for the fourth Henry was not born within the period named. At all events the young monk was sufficiently distinguished to be brought under the Emperor's notice and to preach before him, though we are not informed elsewhere that Hildebrand had any reputation as a preacher. He was no doubt full of earnestness and strong conviction, and that heat of youth which is often so attractive to the minds of sober men. Henry declared that he had heard no man who preached the word of God with so much faith: and the imperial opinion must have added much to his importance among his contemporaries. On the other hand, the great world of Germany and its conditions must have given the young man many and strange revelations. Nowhere were the prelates so great and powerful, nowhere was there so little distinction between the Church and the world. Many of the clergy were married, and left, sometimes their cures, often a fortune amassed by fees for spiritual offices, to their sons: and benefices were bought and sold like houses and lands, with as little disguise. A youth brought up in Rome would not be easily astonished by the lawlessness of the nobles and subject princes of the empire, but the importance of a central authority strong enough to restrain and influence so vast a sphere, and so many conflicting powers, must have impressed upon him still more forcibly the supreme ideal of a spiritual rule more powerful still, which should control the nations as a great Emperor controlled the electors who were all but kings. And we know that it was now that he was first moved to that great indignation, which never died in his mind, against simony and clerical license, which were universally tolerated, if not acknowledged as the ordinary rule of the age. It was high time that some reformer should arise.

It was not, however, till the year 1046, on the occasion of the deposition of Gregory VI. for simony, that Hildebrand first came into the full light of day. Curiously enough, the first introduction of this great reformer of the Church, the sworn enemy of everything simoniacal, was in the suite of this Pope deposed for that sin. But in all probability the simony of Gregory VI. was an innocent error, and resulted rather from a want of perception than evil intention, of which evidently there was none in his mind. He made up to the rivals who held Rome in fee, for the dues and tributes and offerings which were all they cared for, by the sacrifice of his own fortune. If he had not profited by it himself, if some one else had been elected Pope, no stain would have been left upon his name: and he seems to have laid down his dignities without a murmur: but his heart was broken by the shame and bitter conviction that what he had meant for good was in reality the very evil he most condemned. Henry proceeded on his march to Rome after deposing the Pope, apparently taking Gregory with him: and there without any protest from the silenced and terrified people, nominated a German bishop of his own to the papal dignity, from whose hands he himself afterwards received the imperial crown. He then returned to Germany, sweeping along with him the deposed and the newly-elected Popes, the former attended in silence and sorrow by Hildebrand, who never lost faith in him, and to the end of his life spoke of him as his master.

A stranger journey could scarcely have been. The triumphant German priests and prelates surrounding the new head of the Church, and the handful of crestfallen Italians following the fallen fortunes of the other, must have made a strange and not very peaceful conjunction. "Hildebrand desired to show reverence to his lord," says one of the chronicles. Thus his career began in the deepest mortification and humiliation, the forced subjection of the Church which it was his highest aim and hope to see triumphant, to the absolute force of the empire and the powers of this world.

Pope Gregory reached his place of exile on the banks of the Rhine, with his melancholy train, in deep humility; but that exile was not destined to be long. He died there within a few months: and his successor soon followed him to the grave. For a short and disastrous period Rome seems to have been left out of the calculations altogether, and the Emperor named another German bishop, whom he sent to Rome under charge of the Marquis, or Margrave, or Duke of Tuscany—for he is called by all these titles. This Pope, however, was still more short-lived, and died in three weeks after his proclamation, by poison it was supposed. It is not to be wondered at if the bishops of Germany began to be frightened of this magnificent nomination. Whether it was the judgment of God which was most to be feared, or the poison of the subtle and scheming Romans, the prospect was not encouraging. The third choice of Henry fell upon Bruno, the bishop of Toul, a relative of his own, and a saintly person of commanding presence and noble manners. Bruno, as was natural, shrank from the office, but after days of prayer and fasting yielded, and was presented to the ambassadors from Rome as their new Pope. Thus the head of the

Church was for the third time appointed by the Emperor, and the ancient privilege of his election by the Roman clergy and people swept away.

But Henry was not now to meet with complete submission and compliance, as he had done before. The young Hildebrand had shown no rebellious feeling when his master was set aside: he must have, like Gregory, felt the decision to be just. And after faithful service till the death of the exile, he had retired to Cluny, to his convent, pondering many things. We are not told what it was that brought him back to Germany at this crisis of affairs, whether he were sent to watch the proceedings, or upon some humbler mission, or by the mere restlessness of an able young man thirsting to be employed, and the instinct of knowing when and where he was wanted. He reappeared, however, suddenly at the imperial court during these proceedings; and no doubt watched the summary appointment of the new Pope with indignation, injured in his patriotism and in his churchmanship alike, by an election in which Rome had no hand, though otherwise not dissatisfied with the Teutonic bishop, who was renowned both for piety and learning. The chronicler pauses to describe Hildebrand in this his sudden reintroduction to the great world. "He was a youth of noble disposition, clear mind, and a holy monk," we are told. It was while Bishop Bruno was still full of perplexities and doubts that this unexpected counsellor appeared, a man, though young, already well known, who had been trained in Rome, and was an authority upon the customs and precedents of the Holy See. He had been one of the closest attendants upon a Pope, and knew everything about that high office—there could be no better adviser. The anxious bishop sent for the young monk, and Hildebrand so impressed him with his clear mind and high conception of the papal duties, that Bruno begged him to accompany him to Rome.

He answered boldly, "I cannot go with you." "Why?" said the Teuton prelate with amazement. "Because without canonical institution," said the daring monk, "by the sole power of the emperor, you are about to seize the Church of Rome."

Bruno was greatly startled by this bold speech. It is possible that he, in his distant provincial bishopric, had no very clear knowledge of the canonical modes of appointing a Pope. There were many conferences between the monk and the Pope-elect, the young man who was not born to hesitate but saw clear before him what to do, and his elder and superior, who was neither so well informed nor so gifted. Bruno, however, if less able and resolute, must have been a man of a generous and candid mind, anxious to do his duty, and ready to accept instruction as to the best method of doing so, which was at the same time the noblest way of getting over his difficulties. He appeared before the great diet or council assembled in Worms, and announced his acceptance of the pontificate, but only if he were elected to it according to their ancient privileges by the clergy and people of Rome. It does not appear whether there was any resistance to this condition, but it cannot have been of a serious character, for shortly after, having taken farewell of his own episcopate and chapter, he set out for Rome.

This is the account of the incident given by Hildebrand himself when he was the great Pope Gregory, towards the end of his career. It was his habit to tell his attendants the story of his life in all its varied scenes, during the troubled leisure of its end, as old men so often love to do. "Part I myself heard, and part of it was reported to me by many others," says one of the chroniclers. There is another account which has no such absolute authority, but is not unreasonable or unlikely, of the same episode, in which we are told that Bishop Bruno on his way to Rome turned aside to visit Cluny, of which Hildebrand was prior, and that the monk boldly assailed the Pope, upbraiding him with having accepted from the hand of a layman so great an office, and thus violently intruded into the government of the Church. In any case Hildebrand was the chief actor and inspirer of a course of conduct on the part of Bruno which was at once pious and politic. The papal robes which he had assumed at Worms on his first appointment were taken off, the humble dress of a pilgrim assumed, and with a reduced retinue and in modest guise the Pope-elect took his way to Rome. His episcopal council acquiesced in this change of demeanour, says another chronicler, which shows how general an impression Hildebrand's eloquence and the fervour of his convictions must have made. It was a slow journey across the mountains lasting nearly two months, with many lingerings on the way at hospitable monasteries, and towns where the Emperor's cousin could not but be a welcome guest. Hildebrand, who must have felt the great responsibility of the act which he had counselled, sent letter after letter, whenever they paused on their way, to Rome, describing, no doubt with all the skill at his command, how different was this German bishop from the others, how scrupulous he was that his election should be made freely if at all, in what humility he, a personage of so high a rank, and so many endowments, was approaching Rome, and how important it was that a proper reception should be given to a candidate so good, so learned, and so fit in every way for the papal throne. Meanwhile Bishop Bruno, anxious chiefly to conduct himself worthily, and to prepare for his great charge, beguiled the way with prayers and pious meditations, not without a certain timidity as it would appear about his reception. But this timidity turned out to be quite uncalled for. His humble aspect, joined to his high prestige as the kinsman of the emperor, and the anxious letters of Hildebrand had prepared everything for Bruno's reception. The population came out on all sides to greet his passage. Some of the Germans were perhaps a little indignant with this unnecessary humility, but the keen Benedictine pervaded and directed everything while the new Pope, as was befitting on the eve of assuming so great a responsibility, was absorbed in holy thought and prayer. The party had to wait on the further bank of the Tiber, which was in flood, for some days, a moment of anxious suspense in which the pilgrims watched the walls and towers of the great city in which lay their fate with impatience and not without alarm. But as soon as the water fell, which it did with miraculous rapidity, the whole town, with the clergy at its head, came out to meet the new-comers, and Leo IX., one of the finest names in the papal lists, entering barefooted and in all humility by the great doors of St. Peter's, was at once elected unanimously, and received the genuine homage of all Rome. One can imagine with what high satisfaction, yet with eyes ever turned to the future, content with no present achievement, Hildebrand must have watched the complete success of his plan.

This event took place, Villemain tells us (the early chroniclers, as has been said, are most sparing of dates), in 1046, a year full of events. Muratori in his annals gives it as two years later. Hildebrand could not yet have attained his thirtieth year in either case. He was so high in favour with the new Pope, to whom he had been so wise a guide, that he was appointed at once to the office of Economico, a sort of Chancellor of the Exchequer to the Court of Rome, and at the same time was created Cardinal-archdeacon, and abbot of St. Paul's, the great monastery outside the walls. Platina tells us that he received this charge as if the Pope had "divided with him the care of the keys, the one ruling the church of St. Peter and the other that of St. Paul."

That great church, though but a modern building now, after the fire which destroyed it seventy years ago, and standing on the edge of the desolate Campagna, is still a shrine universally visited. The Campagna was not desolate in Hildebrand's days, and the church was of the highest distinction, not only as built upon the spot of St. Paul's martyrdom, but for its own splendour and beauty. It is imposing still, though so modern, and with so few relics of the past. But the pilgrim of to-day, who may perhaps recollect that over its threshold Marcella dragged herself, already half dead, into that peace of God which the sanctuary afforded amid the sack and the tortures of Rome, may add another association if he is so minded in the thought of the great ecclesiastic who ruled here for many years, arriving, full of zeal and eager desire for universal reform, into the midst of an idle crew of depraved monks, who had allowed their noble church to fall into the state of a stable, while they themselves—a mysterious and awful description, yet not perhaps so alarming to us as to them—"were served in the refectory by women," the first and perhaps the only, instance of female servants in a monastery. Hildebrand made short work of these ministrants. He had a dream—which no doubt would have much effect on the monks, always overawed by spiritual intervention, however material they might be in mind or habits—in which St. Paul appeared to him, working hard to clear out and purify his desecrated church. The young abbot immediately set about the work indicated by the Apostle, "eliminating all uncleanness," says his chronicler: "and supplying a sufficient amount of temperate food, he gathered round him a multitude of honest monks faithful to their rule."

Hildebrand's great business powers, as we should say, enabled him very soon to put the affairs of the convent in order. The position of the monastery outside the city gates and defences, and its thoroughly disordered condition, had left it open to all the raids and attacks of neighbouring nobles, who had found the corrupt and undisciplined monks an easy prey; but they soon discovered that they had in the new abbot a very different antagonist. In these occupations Hildebrand passed several years, establishing his monastery on the strongest foundations of discipline, purity, and faith. Reform was what the Church demanded in almost every detail of its work. Amid the agitation and constant disturbance outside, it had not been possible to keep order within, nor was an abbot who had bought his post likely to attempt it: and a great proportion of the abbots, bishops, and great functionaries of the Church had bought their posts. In the previous generation it had been the rule. It had become natural, and disturbed apparently no man's conscience. A conviction, however, had evidently arisen in the Church, working by what influences we know not, but springing into flame by the action of Hildebrand, and by his Pope Leo, that this state of affairs was monstrous and must come to an end. The same awakening has taken place again and again in the Church as the necessity has unfortunately arisen: and never had it been more necessary than now. Every kind of immorality had been concealed under the austere folds of the monk's robe; the parish priests, especially in Germany, lived with their wives in a calm contempt of all the Church's laws in that respect. This, which to us seems the least of their offences, was not so in the eyes of the new race of Church reformers. They thought it worse than ordinary immoral relations, as counterfeiting and claiming the title of a lawful union; and to the remedy of this great declension from the rule of the Church, and of the still greater scandal of simony, the new Pope's utmost energies were now directed.

[PYRAMID OF CAIUS CESTIUS]

A very remarkable raid of reformation, which really seems the most appropriate term which could be used, took place accordingly in the first year of Leo IX.'s reign. We do not find Hildebrand mentioned as accompanying him in his travels—probably he was already too deeply occupied with the cleansing out of St. Paul's physically and morally, to leave Rome, of which, besides, he had the care, in all its external as well as spiritual interests, during the Pope's absence: but no doubt he was the chief inspiration of the scheme, and had helped to organise all its details. Something even of the subtle snare in which his own patron Gregory had been caught was in the plan with which Hildebrand, thus gleaning wisdom from suffering, sent forth his Pope. After holding various smaller councils in Italy, Leo crossed the mountains to France, where against the wish of the Emperor, he held a great assembly at Rheims. The nominal occasion of the visit was the consecration of that church of St. Remy, then newly built, which is still one of the glories of a city so rich in architectural wealth. The body of St. Remy was carried, with many wonderful processions, from the monastery where it lay, going round and round the walls of the mediæval town and through its streets with chants and psalms, with banner and cross, until at last it was deposited solemnly on an altar in the new building, now so old and venerable. Half of France had poured into Rheims for this great festival, and followed the steps of the Pope and hampered his progress—for he was again and again unable to proceed from the great throngs that blocked every street. This, however, though a splendid ceremony, and one which evidently made much impression on the multitude, was but the preliminary chapter. After the consecration came a wholly unexpected visitation, the council of Rheims, which was not concerned like most other councils with questions of doctrine, but of justice and discipline. The throne for the Pope was erected in the middle of the nave of the cathedral—not, it need scarcely be said, the late but splendid cathedral now existing—and surrounded in a circle by the seats of the bishops and archbishops. When all were assembled the object of the council was stated—the abolition of simony, and of the usurpation of the priesthood and the altar by laymen, and the various immoral practices which had crept into the shadow of the Church and been tolerated or authorised there. The Pope in his opening address adjured his assembled counsellors to help him to root out those tares which choked the divine grain, and implored them, if any among them had been guilty of the sin of simony, either by sale or purchase of benefices, that he should make a public confession of his sin.

Terrible moment for the bishops and other prelates, immersed in all the affairs of their times and no better than other men! The reader after all these centuries can scarcely fail to feel the thrill of alarm, or shame, or abject terror that must have run through that awful sitting as men looked into each other's faces and grew pale. The archbishop of Trèves got up first and declared his hands to be clean, so did the archbishop of Lyons and Besançon. Well for them! But he of Rheims in his own cathedral, he who must have been in the front of everything for these few triumphant days of festival, faltered when his turn came. He begged that the discussion might be adjourned till next day, and that he might be allowed to see the Pope in private before making his explanations. It must have been with a kind of grim benignancy, and awful toleration, that the delay was granted and the inquisition went on, while that great personage, one of the first magnates of the assembly, sat silent, pondering all there was against him and how little he had to say in his defence. The council became more lively after this with accusations and counter-accusations. The bishop of Langres procured the deposition of an abbot in his diocese for immoral conduct; but next day was assailed himself of simony, adultery, and the application of torture in order to extort money. After a day or two of discussion this prelate fled, and was finally excommunicated. Pope Leo was not a man to be trifled with. And so the long line of prelates was gone through with many disastrous consequences as the days ran on.

It is less satisfactory to find him easily excommunicating rebels and opponents of the Emperor, whose arms were too successful or their antagonism too important. Even the best of priests and Popes err sometimes—and to have such a weapon as excommunication at hand like a thunderbolt must have been very tempting. Leo at the same time excommunicated also the people of Benevento, who had rebelled against the Emperor, and the archbishop of Ravenna, who was in rebellion against himself.

The travels and activity of this Pope on his round of examination and punishment were extraordinary. He appears in one part of Italy after another: in the far south, in the midland plains, holding councils everywhere, deposing bishops, scourging the Church clean. Again he is over the hills in his own country, meeting the Emperor, as active as himself, and almost as earnest in his desire to cleanse the Church of simony—moving here and there, performing all kinds of sacred functions from the celebration of a feast to the excommunication of a city. His last, and as it proved fatal enterprise was an expedition against the Normans, who had got possession of a great part of Southern Italy, and against whom the Pope went, most inappropriately, at the head of an army, made up of the most heterogeneous elements, and which collapsed in face of the enemy. Leo himself either was made prisoner or took refuge in the town of Benevento, which had recently, by a bargain with the Emperor, become the property of the Holy See. Here he was detained for nearly a year, more or less voluntarily, and when, at length, he set out for Rome, with a strong escort of the Normans and every mark of honour, it was with broken health and failing strength. He died shortly after reaching his destination, in his own great church, having caused himself to be carried there as he grew worse; and nothing could be more imposing than the scene of his death, in St. Peter's, which was all hung with black and illuminated with thousands of funeral lights for this great and solemn event. All Rome witnessed his last hours and saw him die. He was one of the great Popes, though he did not fully succeed even in his own appropriate work of Church reform, and failed altogether when he took, unfortunately, sword in hand. Not a word, however, could be said against the purity of his life and motives, and these were universally acknowledged, especially among the Normans against whom he led his unfortunate army, and who worshipped, while probably holding captive, their rash invader.

During the eight years of Leo's popedom Hildebrand had been at the head of affairs in Rome, where erring priests and simoniacal bishops had been not less severely brought to book than in other places. He does not seem to have accompanied the Pope on any of his many expeditions; but with the aid of a new brother-in-arms, scarcely less powerful and able than himself, Peter Damian, then abbot of Fontavellona and afterwards bishop of Ostia, did his best under Leo to sweep clean the ecclesiastical world in general as he had swept clean his own church of St. Paul. When Leo died, Hildebrand was one of the three legates sent to consult the Emperor as to the choice of another Pope. This was a long and difficult business, since the susceptibilities of the Romans, anxious to preserve their own real or apparent privilege of election, had to be reconciled with the claims of Henry, who had no idea of yielding them in any way, and who had the power on his side. The selection seems to have been finally made by Hildebrand rather than Henry, and was that of Gebehard, bishop of Aichstadt, another wealthy German prelate, also related to the Emperor. Why he should have consented to accept this mission, however, he who had so strongly declined to follow Leo as the nominee of the Emperor, and made it a condition of his service that the new Pope should go humbly to Rome as a pilgrim to be elected there, is unexplained by any of the historians.

It was in the spring of 1055 that after long delays and much waiting, the Roman conclave came back, bringing their Pope with them. But Victor II. was like so many of his German predecessors, short-lived. His reign only lasted two years, the half of which he seems to have spent in Germany. "He was not one who loved the monks," and probably Hildebrand found that he would do but little with one whose heart would seem to have remained on the other side of i monti—as the Alps are continually called. No second ambassador was sent to the Imperial Court for a successor: for in the fateful year 1056 the

Emperor also died, preceding Victor to the grave by a few months. Without pausing to consult the German Court, with a haste which proves their great anxiety to reassert themselves, the Roman clergy and people elected Frederick, abbot of Monte Cassino and brother of the existing prince of Tuscany— Gottfried of Lorraine, the second husband of Beatrice of Tuscany and step-father of Matilda the actual heir to that powerful duchy. Perhaps a certain desire to cling to the only power in Italy which could at all protect them against an irritated Imperial Court mingled with this choice: but it was a perfectly natural and worthy one. Frederick, unfortunately, lived but a few months, disappointing many hopes. He had sent Hildebrand to the Imperial Court to explain and justify his election, but when he found his health beginning to give way, a sort of panic seems to have seized him, and collecting round him all the representatives of priests and people who could be gathered together, he made them swear on pain of excommunication to elect no successor until the return of Hildebrand. He died at Florence shortly after.

There is something monotonous in these brief records: a great turmoil almost reaching the length of a convulsion for the choice, and then a short and agitated span, a year or two, sometimes only a month or two, and all is over and the new Pope goes to rejoin the long line of his predecessors. It was not, either, that these were old men, such as have so often been chosen in later days, venerable fathers of the Church whose age brought them nearer to the grave than the throne:—they were all men in the flower of their age, likely according to all human probability to live long. It was not wonderful if the German bishops were afraid of that dangerous elevation which seemed to carry with it an unfailing fate.

Hildebrand was at the German Court when this sad news reached him. He was in the position, fascinating to most men—and he was not superior to others in this respect—of confidant and counsellor to a princess in the interesting position of a young widow, with a child, upon whose head future empire had already thrown its shadow. The position of the Empress Agnes was, no doubt, one of the most difficult which a woman could be called on to occupy, surrounded by powerful princes scarcely to be kept in subjection by the Emperor, who was so little more than their equal, though their sovereign—and altogether indisposed to accept the supremacy of a woman. There is nothing in which women have done so well in the world as in the great art of government, but the Empress Agnes was not one of that kind. She had to fall back upon the support of the clergy in the midst of the rude circle of potentates with whom she had to contend, and the visit of Hildebrand with his lofty views, his great hopes, his impetuous determination to vanquish evil with good, though not perhaps in the way recommended by the Apostles, was no doubt a wonderful refreshment and interest to her in the midst of all her struggles. But it was like a thunderbolt bursting at their feet to hear of the death of Frederick—(among the Popes Stephen IX.): and the swiftly following outburst in Rome when, in a moment, in the absence of any spirit strong enough to control them, the old methods were put into operation, and certain of the Roman nobles ever ready to take advantage of an opportunity—with such supporters within the city as terror or bribes could secure them, taking the people by surprise—procured the hurried election of a Pope without any qualifications for the office. Nothing could be more dramatic than the entire episode. A young Count of Tusculum, a stronghold seated amid the ruins of the old Roman city, above Frascati, one of a family who then seem to have occupied the position afterwards held by the Orsinis and Colonnas, was the leader of this conspiracy and the candidate was a certain Mincio, Bishop of Velletri, a member of the same family. The description in Muratori's Annals though brief is very characteristic.

"Gregorio, son of Albanio Count Tusculano, of Frascati, along with some other powerful Romans, having gained by bribes a good part of the clergy and people, rushed by night, with a party of armed followers, into the Church of St. Peter, and there, with much tumult, elected Pope, Giovanni, Bishop of Velletri, afterwards called Mincio (a word perhaps drawn from the French Mince and which probably was the original of the phrase now used Minciono, Minchione), who assumed the name of Benedict X. He was a man entirely devoid of letters."

The sudden raid in the night, all Rome silent and asleep, except the disturbed and hastily awakened streets by which the party had entered from across the Campagna and their robber fortress among the ruins of the classic Tusculum, makes a most curious and dramatic picture. The conspirators had among them certain so-called representatives of the people, with a few abbots who felt their seats insecure under a reforming Pope, and a few priests very desirous of shutting out all new and disturbing authority. They gathered hastily in the church which suddenly shone out into the darkness with flare of torch and twinkle of taper, while the intruder, Mincio, a lean and fantastic bishop, with affectations of pose and attitude such as his nickname implies, was hurried to the altar by his rude patrons and attendants. He was consecrated by the terrified archpriest of Ostia, upon whom the Frascati party had somewhere laid violent hands, and who faltered through the office half stupefied by fear. It was the privilege of the Bishop of Ostia to be the officiating prelate at the great solemnity of a Pope's consecration. When he could not be had the careless and profane barons no doubt thought his subordinate would do very well instead.

The news was received, however, though with horror, yet with a dignified self-restraint by the Imperial Court. Hildebrand set out at once for Florence to consult with the Sovereigns there, a royal family of great importance in the history of Italy, consisting of the widowed duchess Beatrice, her second husband Gottfried of Lorraine, and her young daughter Matilda, the actual heiress of the principality, all staunch supporters of the Church and friends of Hildebrand. That he should take the command of affairs at this sudden crisis seems to have been taken for granted on all sides. A council of many bishops "both German and Italian" was called together in Sienna, where it was met by a deputation from Rome, begging that fit steps might be taken to meet the emergency, and a legitimate Pope elected. The choice of this Council fell upon the Bishop of Florence, "who for wisdom and a good life was worthy of such a sublime dignity;" and the new Pope was escorted to Rome by a strong band of Tuscan soldiers powerful enough to put down all tumult or rebellion in the city. The expedition paused at Sutri, a little town, just within the bounds of the papal possessions, which had already on that account been the scene of the confusing and painful council which dethroned Gregory VI. to destroy the strongholds of the Counts of Tusculum near that spot, and make an end of their power. Mincio, however, poor fantastic shadow, had no heart to confront a duly elected Pope, or the keen eye of Hildebrand, and abdicated at once his ill-gotten power. His vague figure so sarcastically indicated has a certain half-comic, half-rueful effect, appearing amid all these more important forms and things, first in the dazzle of the midnight office, and afterwards in a hazy twilight of obscurity, stealing off, to be seen no more, except by the keen country folk and townsmen of his remote bishopric who, burlando—jesting as one is glad to hear they were able to do amid all their tumults and troubles—gave him his nickname, and thus sent down to posterity the fantastic vision of the momentary Pope with his mincing ways—no bad anti-pope though as Benedict X. he holds a faint footing in the papal roll—but a historical burla, a mediæval joke, not without its power to relieve the grave chronicle of the time.

The tumultuous public of Rome, which did not care very much either way, yet felt this election of the Pope to be its one remaining claim to importance, murmured and grumbled its best about the interference of Tuscany, a neighbour more insulting, when taking upon herself airs of mastery, than a distant and vaguely magnificent Emperor; and there was an outcry against Hildebrand, who had erected "a new idol" in concert with Beatrice and without the consent of the Romans. But it was in reality Hildebrand himself who now came to reign under the shadow of another insignificant and short-lived Pope. Nicolas II. and Alexander II. who followed were but the formal possessors of power; the true sway was henceforth in the hands of the ever-watchful monk, Cardinal-archdeacon, deputy and representative of the Holy See. It is one of the few instances to be found in the records of the world of that elevation of the man who can—so strongly preached by Carlyle—to the position which is his natural right. While Hildebrand had been scouring the world, an adventurous young monk, passing i monti recklessly as the young adventurer now crosses the Atlantic, more times than could be counted—while he was, with all the zeal of his first practical essay in reform, cleaning out his stable at St. Paul's, making his presence to be felt in the expenditure and revenues of Rome—there had been, as we have seen, Pope after Pope in the seat of the Apostle, most of them worthy enough, one at least, Leo IX., heroic in effort and devotion—but none of them born to guide the Church through a great crisis. The hour and the man had now come.

[TRINITA DE MONTI]

It was not long before the presence of a new and great legislator became clearly visible. One of the first acts of Hildebrand, acting under Nicolas, was to hold a council in Rome in 1059, at which many things of importance were decided. The reader will want no argument to prove that there was urgent need of an established and certain rule for the election of the Popes, a necessity constantly recurring and giving rise to a continual struggle. It had been the privilege of the Roman clergy and people; it had become a prerogative of the Emperors; it was exercised by both together, the one satisfying itself with a fictitious co-operation and assent to what the other did, but neither contented, and every vacancy the cause of a bitter and often disgraceful struggle. The nominal election by the clergy and people was a rule impossible, and meant only the temporary triumph of the party which was strongest or wealthiest for the moment, and could best pay for the most sweet voices of the crowd, or best overawe and cow their opponents. On the other hand, the action of the secular power, the selection or at least nomination of a

Pope—with armies behind, if necessary, to carry out his choice—by the Emperor across the Alps, was a transaction subject to those ordinary secular laws, which induce a superior in whatever region of affairs to choose the man who is likely to be most serviceable to himself and his interests—interests which were very different from those which are the objects of the Church. No man had seen the dangers and difficulties of this divided and inconsistent authority more than Hildebrand, and his determination to establish a steadfast and final method for the choice and election of the first great official of the Church was both wise and reasonable. Perhaps it was not without thought of the expediency of breaking away from all precedents, and thus preparing the way for a new method, that he had, apparently on his own authority, transferred in a manner, what we may call the patronage of the Holy See, to Tuscany. The moment was propitious for such a change, for there was no Emperor, the heir of Henry III. being still a child and his mother not powerful enough to interfere.

The new law introduced by Hildebrand and passed by the council was much the same in its general regulations as that which still exists. There was no solemn mysterious Conclave, and the details were more simple; but the rules of election were virtually the same. The Cardinal-bishops made their choice first, which they then submitted to the other Cardinals of lower rank. If both were agreed the name of the Pope-elect was submitted to the final judgment of the people, no doubt a mere formula. This, we believe, is nominally still the last step of the procedure. The name is submitted, i.e., announced to the eager crowd in St. Peter's who applaud, which is all that is required of them: and all is done. This decree was passed salvo debito honore et reverentia delecti filii nostri Henrici, a condition skilfully guarded by the promise to award the same honour (that is, of having a voice in the election) to those of his successors to whom the Holy See shall have personally accorded the same right. It was thus the Holy See which honoured the Emperors by according them a privilege, not the Emperors who had any right to nominate, much less elect, to the Holy See.

Other measures of great importance for the purification and internal discipline of the Church were made law by this council, which was held in April 1059, the year of the accession of Nicolas II.; but none of such fundamental importance as this, or so bold in their claim of spiritual independence. Hildebrand must by this time have been in the very height of life, a man of forty or so, already matured by much experience and beginning to systematise and regulate the dreams and plans of his youth. He must have known by this time fully what he wanted and what was, or at least ought to be, his mission in the world. It is very doubtful, however, we think, whether that mission appeared to him what it has appeared to all the historians since—a deep-laid and all-overwhelming plan for the establishment of the Papacy on such a pinnacle as never crowned head had attained. His purposes as understood by himself were first the cleansing of the Church—the clearing out of all the fleshly filth which had accumulated in it, as in his own noble Basilica, rendering it useless, hiding its beauty: and second the destruction of that system of buying and selling which went on in the Holy Temple—worse than money-changing and selling of doves, the sale of the very altars to any unworthy person who could pay for them. These were his first and greatest purposes—to make the Church pure and to make her free, as perhaps she never has been, as perhaps, alas, she never will wholly be: but yet the highest aim for every true churchman to pursue.

These purposes were elevated and enlarged in his mind by the noble and beautiful thought of thus preparing and developing the one great disinterested power in the world, with nothing to gain, which should arbitrate in every quarrel, and adjust contending claims and bring peace on earth, instead of the clashing of swords; the true work of the successor of Peter, Christ's Vicar in the world. This was not a dream of Hildebrand alone. Three hundred years later the great soul of Dante still dreamt of that Papa Angelico, the hope of ages, who might one day arise and set all things right. Hildebrand was not of the Angelical type. He was not that high priest made of benign charity, and love for all men—of whom the mediæval sages mused. But who will say that his dream, too, was not of the noblest or his ideal less magnanimous and great? Such an arbiter was wanted—what words could say how much?—in all those troubled and tumultuous kingdoms which were struggling against each other, overcoming and being overcome, always in disorder, carrying out their human fate with a constant accompaniment of human groans and sufferings and tears—one who would set all things right, who would judge the cause of the poor and friendless, who would have power to pull down a tyrant and erect with blessing and honour a new throne of justice in his dishonoured place. Have we less need of a Papa Angelico now? But unfortunately,[1] we have lost faith in the possibility of him, which is a fate which befalls so many high ideals from age to age.

[ARCH OF TITUS]

Did Hildebrand, a proud man and strong, a man full of ambition, full of the consciousness of great powers—did he long to grasp the reins of the universe in his own hand? to drive the chariots of the sun, to direct everything, to rule everything, to be more than a king, and hold Emperors trembling before him? It is very possible: in every great spirit, until fully disenchanted, something of this desire must exist. But that it was not a plan of ambition only, but a great ideal which it seemed to him well worth a man's life to carry out, there can, we think, be no reasonable doubt.

Thus he began his reign, in reality, though not by title, in Rome. The cloisters were cleansed and the integrity of the Church vindicated, though not by any permanent process, but one that had to be repeated again and again in every chapter of her history. The Popes were elected after a few stormy experiments in the manner he had decreed, and the liberty of election established and protected—even to some extent and by moments, his Papacy, that wonderful institution answered to his ideal, and promised to fulfil his dream: until the time came common to all men, when hope became failure, and he had to face the dust and mire of purpose overthrown. But in the meantime no such thoughts were in his mind as he laboured with all the exhilaration of capacity, and with immense zeal and pains, at his own affairs, which meant in those days to the Archdeacon of Rome the care of all the Churches. The letters of the Pope in Council which carried the addition of the name of that humblest of his sons and servants, Hildebrand, bore the commands of such a sovereign as Hildebrand dreamt of, to bishops and archbishops over all the world. Here is one of these epistles.

Although several unfavourable reports have reached the Apostolic See in respect to your Fraternity which cannot be rejected without inquiry—as, for example, that you have favoured our enemies, and have neglected pontifical ordinances: yet as you have defended yourself from these accusations by the testimony of a witness of weight and have professed fidelity to St. Peter, we are disposed to pass over these reports and to hope that the testimony in your favour is true. Therefore take care in future so to live, that your enemies shall have no occasion to sadden us on your account. Exert yourself to fulfil the hopes which the Apostolical See has formed of you: reprimand, entreat and warn your glorious king that he may not be corrupted by the counsels of the wicked, who hope under cover of our own troubles to elude Apostolic condemnation. Let him take care how he resists the sacred canons, or rather St. Peter himself, thereby rousing our wrath against him, who rather desire to love him as the apple of our eye.

These were high words to be said to a dubious, not well-assured archbishop, occupying a very high place in the Church and powerful for good or for evil: but Hildebrand did not mince matters, whatever he might have to say.

Meanwhile the good Pope, Nicolas, went on with his charities while his Cardinal Archdeacon thundered in his name. He went, in the end of his life, with his court on a visit to the Normans, who had now, for some time—since they defeated Pope Leo before the gates of Benevento and came under the charm of papal influence, though in the person of their prisoner—become the most devout and generous servants of the Papacy: which indeed granted them titles to the sovereignty of any chance principality they might pick up—which was a good equivalent. When the troops of Guiscard escorted his Holiness back to Rome they were so obliging as to destroy a castle or two of those robber nobles who infested all the roads and robbed the pilgrims, and were, in the midst of all greater affairs, like a nest of venomous wasps about the ears of the Roman statesmen and legislators—especially those of the ever turbulent family of Tusculum, the Counts of Frascati, who kept watch afar upon the northern gates and every pilgrim path. This Pope died soon after in 1061 in Florence, his former episcopal see, which he often revisited and loved.

And now came the opportunity for Hildebrand to carry out his own bold law, and elect at once, by the now legal methods, a new head to the Church. But his coadjutors probably had not his own courage: and though bold enough under his inspiration to pass that law, hesitated to carry it out. It is said, too, that in Rome itself there was the strong opposition of a German party really attached to the imperial order, or convinced that without the strong backing of the empire the Church could not stand. Reluctantly Hildebrand consented to send a messenger to consult the imperial court, where strong remonstrances and appeals were at once presented by the Germans and Lombards who were as little desirous of having an Italian Pope over them as the Romans were of a Teutonic one. The Empress Agnes had been alarmed probably by rumours in the air of her removal from the regency. She had been alienated from Hildebrand by the reports of his enemies, and no doubt made to believe that the rights of her son must suffer if any innovation was permitted. She forgot her usual piety in her panic, and would not so much as receive Hildebrand's messenger, who, alone of all the many deputations arriving on the same errand, was left five days (or seven) waiting at the gates of the Palace—"For seven days he waited in the antechamber of the king," says Muratori—while the others were admitted and listened to. This was too much for Hildebrand, to whom his envoy, Cardinal Stefano, returned full of exasperation, as was natural. The Cardinals with timidity, but sustained by Hildebrand's high courage and determination, then proceeded to the election, which was duly confirmed by the people assembled in St. Peter's, and therefore perfectly legal according to the latest law. We are told much, however, of the excited state of Rome during the election, and of the dislike of the people to the horde of monks, many of them mendicant, and even more or less vagabond, who were let loose upon the city, electioneering agents of the most violent kind, filling the streets and churches with clamour. This wild army, obnoxious to the citizens, was at Hildebrand's devotion, and prejudiced more than they promoted, his views among the crowd.

"Here returned to the Romans," says Muratori, whose right to speak on such a subject will not be doubted, "complete freedom in the election of the Popes, with the addition of not even awaiting the consent of the Emperors for their consecration; an independence ever maintained since, down to our own days." This daring act made a wonderful revolution in the politics of Rome: it was the first erection of her standard of independence. The Church had neither troops nor vassals upon whom she could rely, and to defy thus openly the forces of the Empire was a tremendous step to take. Nor was it only from Germany that danger threatened. Lombardy and all the north of Italy was, with the exception of Tuscany, in arms against the audacious monk. Only those chivalrous savages of Normans, who, however, were as good soldiers as any Germans, could be calculated on as faithful to the Holy See: and Godfried of Tuscany stood between Rome and her enemies fidelissimo, ready to ward off any blow.

The election passed over quietly, and Alexander II. (Anselm the Bishop of Lucca) took his place, every particular of his assumption of the new dignity being carefully carried through as though in times of deepest peace. In Germany, however, the news produced a great sensation and tumult. A Diet was held at Bâle, for the coronation in the first place of the young king Henry, now twelve years old—but still more for the immediate settlement of this unheard-of revolt. When that ceremonial was over the court proceeded to the choice of a Pope with a contemptuous indifference to the proceedings in Rome. This anti-pope has no respect from history. He is said by one authority to have been chosen because his evil life made him safe against any such fury of reform as that which made careless prelate and priest fall under the rod of Hildebrand on every side. Muratori, whose concise little sentences are always so refreshing after the redundancy of the monkish chronicles, is very contemptuous of this pretender, whose name was Cadalous or Cadulo, an undistinguished and ill-sounding name. "The anti-pope Cadaloo or Cadalo occupied himself all the winter of this year" (says Muratori) "in collecting troops and money, in order to proceed to Rome to drive out the legitimate successor of St. Peter and to have himself consecrated there. Some suppose that he had already been ordained Pope, and had assumed the name of Honorius II., but there is no proof of this. And if he did not change his name it is a sign that he had never been consecrated." Other authorities boldly give him the title of Honorius II.: but he is generally called the anti-pope Cadalous in history.

A conflict immediately arose between the two parties. Cadalous, at the head of an army appeared before Rome, but not till after Hildebrand had placed his Pope, who was for the moment less strong than the Emperor's Pope, in Tuscany under the protection of Beatrice and her husband Godfried. Then followed a stormy time of marches and countermarches round and about the city, in which sometimes the invaders were successful and sometimes the defenders. At length the Tuscans came to the rescue with the two Countesses in their midst who were always so faithful in their devotion to Hildebrand, Beatrice in the maturity of her beauty and influence, and the young Matilda, the real sovereign of the Tuscan states, fifteen years old, radiant in hope and enthusiasm and stirring up the spirits of the Florentines and Tuscan men at arms. Cadalous withdrew from that encounter making such terms as he could with Godfried, with many prayers and large presents, so that he was allowed to escape to Parma his bishopric, testa bassa. Yet the records are not very clear on these points, Muratori tells us. Doubts are thrown on the loyalty of Duke Godfried. He is said to have invited the Normans to come to the help of the Pope, and then invaded their territories, which was not a very knightly proceeding: but there is no appearance at this particular moment of the Normans, or any force but that of the Tuscan army with young Countess Matilda and her mother flashing light and courage into the ranks.

The anti-pope, if he deserved that title, did not trouble the legitimate authorities long. He was suddenly dropped by the Germans in the excitement of a revolution, originating in the theft of little Henry the boy-monarch, whom the Bishop of Cologne stole from his mother Agnes, as it became long afterwards a pleasant device of state to carry off from their mothers the young fatherless Jameses of Scots history. Young Henry was run away with in the same way, and Agnes humiliated and cast off by the Teutonic nobility, who forgot all about such a trifle as a Pope in the heat of their own affairs. It was only when this matter was settled that a council was held in Cologne by the archbishop who had been the chief agent in the abduction of Henry, and was now first in power. Of this council there seems no authoritative record. It is only by the answer to its deliberations published by Peter Damian in which, as is natural, that able controversialist has an easy victory over the other side—that anything is known of it. Whether Cadalous was formerly deposed by this council is not known: but he was dropped by the authorities of the Empire which had a similar result.

Notwithstanding, this rash pretender made one other vain attempt to seize the papal throne, being encouraged by various partisans in Rome itself, by whose means he got possession of St. Peter's, where the unfortunate man remained for one troubled night, making such appeals to God and to his supporters as may be imagined, and furtively performing the various offices of the nocturnal service, perhaps not without a sense of profanation in the minds of those who had stolen into the great darkness and silence of the Basilica to meet him, with a political rather than a devotional intention. Next day all Rome heard the news, and rising seized its arms and drove his handful of defenders out of the city. Cadalous was taken by one of his supporters, Cencio or Vincencio "son of the præfect" to St. Angelo, where he held out against the Romans for the space of two years, suffering many privations; and thence escaping on pain of his life after other adventures, disappears into the darkness to be seen no more.

This first distinct conflict between Rome and the Empire was the beginning of the long-continued struggle which tore Italy asunder for generations—the strife of the two parties called Guelfs and Ghibellines, the one for the Empire, the other for the Church, with all the ramifications of that great question.

The year in which Cadalous first appeared in Rome, which was the year 1062, was also distinguished by a very different visitor. The Empress Agnes deprived of her son, shorn of her power, had nothing more to do among the subject princes who had turned against her. She determined, as dethroned monarchs are apt to do, to cast off the world which had rejected her, and came to Rome, to beg pardon of the Pope and find a refuge for herself out of the noise and tumult. She had been in Rome once before, a young wife in all the pomp and pride of empire, conducted through its streets in the midst of a splendid procession, with her husband to be crowned. The strongest contrasts pleased the fancy of these days. She entered Rome the second time as a penitent in a black robe, and mounted upon the sorriest horse—"it was not to call a horse, but like a beast of burden, a donkey, no bigger than an ass." It is a curious sign of humiliation and accompanying elevation of mind, but this is not the first time that we have heard of a pilgrim entering Rome on a miserable hack, as if that were the highest sign of humility. She was received with enthusiasm, notwithstanding her late actions of hostility, and soon the walls of many churches were radiant with the spoils of her imperial toilettes, brocades of gold and silver encrusted with jewels, and wonders of rich stuffs which even Peter Damian with his accomplished pen finds it difficult to describe. "She laid down everything, destroyed everything, in order to become, in her deprivation yet freedom, the bride of Christ." We are not told if Agnes entered a convent or only lived the life of a religious person in her own house; but she had the frequent company of Hildebrand and Peter Damian, and of the Bishop of Como, who seems to have been devoted to her service; and perhaps like other penitents was not so badly off in her humility, thus delivered out of all the tumults against which she had so vainly attempted to make head for years.

[THE VILLA BORGHESE]

While these smaller affairs—for even the anti-pope never seems to have been really dangerous to Rome notwithstanding his many efforts to disturb the peace of the Church—the world of Christendom which surrounded that one steady though constantly contested throne of the papacy, was in commotion everywhere. It seems strange to speak in one breath of Hildebrand's great and noble ideal of a throne always standing for righteousness, and of a sacred monarch supreme and high above all worldly motives, dispensing justice and peace: and in the next to confess his perfect acquiescence in, and indeed encouragement of, the undertaking of William the Conqueror, so manifest an act of tyranny and robbery, and interference with the rights of an independent nation, an undertaking only different from those of the brigands from Tusculum and other robber castles who swept the roads to Rome, by the fact of its much higher importance and its complete success. The Popes had sanctioned the raids of the Normans in Italy, and confirmed to them by legal title the possessions which they had taken by the strong hand: with perhaps a conviction that one strong rule was better than the perpetual bloodshed of the frays between the existing races—the duke here, the marquis there, all seeking their own, and no man thinking of his neighbour's or his people's advantage. But the internal discords of England were too far off to secure the observation of the Pope, and the mere fact of Harold's renunciation in favour of William, though it seems so specious a pretence to us, was to the eyes of the priests by far the most important incident in the matter, a vow taken at the altar and which therefore the servants of the altar were bound to see carried out. These two reasons however were precisely such as show the disadvantage of that grand papal ideal which was burning in Hildebrand's brain; for a Pope, with a sacred authority to set up and pull down, should never be too far off to understand the full rights of any question were it in the remotest parts of the earth: and should be far above the possibility of having his judgment confused by a foregone ecclesiastical prejudice in favour of an unjust vow.

Hildebrand however not only gave William, in his great stroke for an empire, the tremendous support of the Pope's authority but backed him up in many of his most high-handed and arbitrary proceedings against the Saxon prelates and rich abbeys which the Conqueror spoiled at his pleasure. It must not be forgotten, in respect to these latter spoliations, that the internal war which was raging in the Church all over the world, between the new race of reformers and the mass of ordinary clergy—who had committed many ecclesiastical crimes, who sometimes even had married and were comfortable in the enjoyment of a sluggish toleration, or formed connections that were winked at by a contemptuously sympathetic world; or who had bought their benefices great and small, through an entangled system of gifts, graces, and indulgences, as well as by the boldest simony—made every kind of revolution within the Church possible, and produced endless depositions and substitutions on every side. When, as we have seen, the bishop of a great continental see in the centre of civilisation could be turned out remorselessly from his bishopric on conviction of any of these common crimes and forced into the Cloister to amend his ways and end his life, it is scarcely likely that more consideration would be shown for an unknown prelate far away across the Northern seas, though it would seem to be insubordination rather than any ecclesiastical vice with which the Saxon clergy were chiefly charged. This first instance however of the papal right to sanction revolution, and substitute one claimant for another as the selection of Heaven, is perhaps the strongest proof that could be found of the impossibility of that ideal, and of the tribunal thus set up over human thrones and human rights. The papal see was thus drawn in to approve and uphold one of the most bloody invasions and one of the most cruel conquests ever known—and did so with a confidence and certainty, in an ignorance, and with a bias, which makes an end of all those lofty pretensions to perfect impartiality and a judgment beyond all influences of passion which alone could justify its existence.

A great change had come over the firmament since the days when Leo IX. cleansed the Church at Rheims, and held that wonderful Council which set down so many of the mighty from their seats. Henry III., the enemy of simony, was dead, and the world had changed. As we shall often have occasion to remark, the papal rule of justice and purity was strong and succeeded—so long as the forces of the secular powers agreed with it. But when, as time went on, the Church found itself in conflict with these secular powers, a very different state of affairs ensued.

The action of Rome in opposition to the young Henry IV., was as legitimate as had been its general agreement with, and approval of, his predecessor. The youth of this monarch had developed into ways very different from those of his father, and under his long minority all the evils which Henry III. had honestly set his face against, reappeared in full force. Whether it was his removal from the natural and at least pure government of his mother, or from his native disposition which no authority or training had a chance in such circumstances of repressing, the young Henry grew up dissolute and vicious, and his court was the centre of a wild and disorganised society. Married at twenty, it was not very long before he tried by the most disreputable means to get rid of his young wife, and failing in that, called, or procured to be called by a complaisant archbishop, a council, in order to rid him of her. Rome lost no time in sending off to this council as legate, Peter Damian whose gift of speech was so unquestionable that he could even on occasion make the worse appear the better cause. But his cause in the present case was excellent, and his eloquence no less so, and he had all that was prudent as well as all that was wise and good in Germany on his side, notwithstanding the complaisance of the priests. The legate remonstrated, exhorted, threatened. The thing Henry desired was a thing unworthy of a Christian, it was a fatal example to the world; finally no power on earth would induce the Pope, whose hands alone could confer that consecration, to crown as Roman Emperor a man who had sinned so flagrantly against the laws of God. The great German nobles added practical arguments not less urgent in their way; and Henry surrounded on all sides with warnings was forced to give way. But this downfall for the moment had little effect on the behaviour of the young potentate, and his vices were such that his immediate vassals in his own country were on the point of universal rebellion, no man's castle or goods or wife or daughter being safe. The Church, which his father had given so much care and pains to cleanse and purify, sank again into the rankest simony, every stall in a cathedral, and cure in a bishopric selling like articles of merchandise. It was time in the natural course of affairs when the young monarch attained the full age of manhood that he should be promoted to the final dignity of emperor, and consecrated as such—a rite which only the Pope could perform: and no doubt it was with a full consciousness of the power thus resting with the Holy See, as well as in consequence of numerous informal but eager appeals to the Pope against the ever-increasing evils of his sway that Hildebrand proceeded to take such a step as had never been ventured on before by the boldest of Churchmen. He summoned Henry formally to appear before the papal court and defend himself against the accusations brought against him. "For the heresy of simony," says the papal letter, this being the great ecclesiastical crime which came immediately under the cognizance of the Pope.

This citation addressed to the greatest monarch then existing, and by a power but barely escaped from his authority and still owing to him a certain allegiance, was enough to thrill the world from end to end. Such a thing had never happened in the knowledge of man. But before we begin so much as to hear of the effect produced, the Pope who had, nominally at least, issued the summons, the good and saintly Alexander II., after holding the papacy for twelve years, died on the 21st of April, 1073. His reign for that time had been to a great degree the reign of Hildebrand, the ever watchful, ever laborious archdeacon, who, let the Pope travel as he liked—and his expeditions through Italy were many—was always vigilant at his post, always in the centre of affairs, with eyes and ears open to everything, and a mind always intent on its purpose. Hildebrand's great idea of the position and duties of the Holy See had developed much in those twelve years. It had begun to appear a fact, in the eyes of those especially who had need of its support. The Normans everywhere believed and trusted in it, with good secular reason for so doing, and they were at the moment a great power in the earth, especially in Italy. If it had not already acquired an importance and force in the thoughts of men, more subtle and less easy to obtain than external power, it would have been impossible for the boldest to launch forth a summons to the greatest king of Christendom the future Emperor. Already the first step towards that great visionary sway, of which poets and sages, as well as ecclesiastics, so long had dreamed, had been made.

Hildebrand had been virtually at the head of affairs since the year 1055, when he had brought across the Alps Victor II. chosen by himself, whose acts and policy were his. He might have attained the papacy in his own right on more than one occasion had he been so minded, but had persistently held back from the rank while keeping the power. But now humility would have been cowardice, and in the face of the tremendous contest which he had invited no other course was possible to him save to assume the full responsibility. Even before the ceremonies of the funeral of the Pope were completed, while Alexander lay in state, there was a rush of the people and priests to the church of the Lateran, where Hildebrand was watching by the bier, shouting "Hildebrand! The blessed St. Peter has elected Hildebrand." A strange scene of mingled enthusiasm and excitement broke the funereal silence in the great solemn church, amid its forest of columns all hung with black, and glittering with the silver ornaments which are appropriate to mourning, while still the catafalque upon which the dead Pope lay rose imposing before the altar. Hildebrand, startled, was about to ascend the pulpit to address the people, but was forestalled by an eager bishop who hurried into it before him, to make solemn announcement of the event. "The Archdeacon is the man who, since the time of the holy Pope Leo, has by his wisdom and experience contributed most to the exaltation of the Church, and has delivered this town from great danger," he cried. The people responded by shouts of "St. Peter has chosen Hildebrand!" We all know how entirely fallacious is this manner of testing the sentiment of a people; but yet it was the ancient way, the method adopted in those earlier times when every Christian was a tried and tested man, having himself gone through many sufferings for the faith.

It appears that Hildebrand hesitated, which seems strange in such a man; one who, if ever man there was, had the courage of his opinions and was not likely to shrink from the position he himself had created; and it is almost incredible that he should have sent a sort of appeal, as Muratori states, to Henry himself—the very person whom he had so boldly summoned before the tribunal of the Church—requesting him to withhold his sanction from the election. Muratori considers the evidence dubious, we are glad to see, for this strange statement. At all events, after a momentary hesitation Hildebrand yielded to the entreaties of the people. The decree in which his election is recorded is absolutely simple in its narrative.

"The day of the burial of our lord, the Pope Alexander II. (22nd April, 1073), we being assembled in the Basilica of San Pietro in Vincoli,[2] members of the holy Roman Church catholic and apostolic, cardinals, bishops, clerks, acolytes, sub-deacons, deacons, priests—in presence of the venerable bishops and abbots, by consent of the monks, and accompanied by the acclamations of a numerous crowd of both sexes and of divers orders, we elect as pastor and sovereign pontiff a man of religion, strong in the double knowledge of things human and divine, the love of justice and equity, brave in misfortune, moderate in good fortune, and following the words of the apostle, a good man, chaste, modest, temperate, hospitable, ruling well his own house, nobly trained and instructed from his childhood in the bosom of the Church, promoted by the merit of his life to the highest rank in the Church, the Archdeacon Hildebrand, whom, for the future and for ever, we choose; and we name him Gregory, Pope. Will you have him? Yes, we will have him. Do you approve our act? Yes, we approve."

Nothing can be more graphic than this straightforward document, and nothing could give a clearer or more picturesque view of the primitive popular election. The wide-reaching crowd behind, women as well as men, a most remarkable detail, filled to its very doors the long length of the Basilica. The little group of cardinals and their followers made a glow of colour in the midst: the mass of clergy in the centre of the great nave lighted up by bishops and abbots in their distinctive dresses and darkening into the surrounding background of almost innumerable monks: while the whole assembly listened breathless to this simple yet stately declaration, few understanding the words, though all knew the meaning, the large Latin phrases rolling over their heads: until it came to that well-known name of Hildebrand—Ildebrando—which woke a sudden storm of shouts and outcries. Will you have this man? Yes, we will have him! Do you approve? Approviamo! Approviamo! shouted and shrieked the crowd. So were the elections made in Venice long years after, under the dim arches of St. Marco; but Venice was still a straggling village, fringing a lagoon, when this great scene took place.

[WHERE THE GHETTO STOOD]

Hildebrand was at this time a man between fifty and sixty, having spent the last eighteen years of his life in the control and management of the affairs of Rome. He was a small, spare man of the most abstemious habits, allowing himself as few indulgences in the halls of the Lateran as in a monastic cell. His fare was vegetables, although he was no vegetarian in our modern sense of the word, but ate that food to mortify the flesh and for no better reason. Not long before he made the rueful, and to us comic, confession that he had "ended by giving up leeks and onions, having scruples on account of their flavour, which was agreeable to him." Scruple could scarcely go further in respect to the delights of this world. We are glad however that he who was now the great Pope Gregory denied himself that onion. It was a dignified act and sacrifice to the necessities of his great position.

FOOTNOTES:

[1] It is touching and pathetic to divine, in the present Pope, something of that visionary and disinterested ambition, that longing to bless and help the universe, which was in those dreams of the mediæval mind, prompted by a great pity, and a love that is half divine. Leo XIII. is too wise a man to

dream of temporal power restored, though he is a martyr to the theory of it: but there would seem to be in his old age which makes it impossible if nothing else did, a trembling consciousness of capacity to be in himself a Papa Angelico, and gather us all under his wings.

[2] It is supposed by some from this that the election took place in this church and not in the Lateran; but that is contradicted by Gregory himself, who says it took place in Ecclesia S. Salvatoris, a name frequently used for the Lateran. Bowden suggests that "at the close of the tumultuous proceedings in the Lateran the cardinal clergy" may have "adjourned to St. Peter ad Vincula formally to ratify and register the election."

[FROM SAN GREGORIO MAGNO]

CHAPTER III

THE POPE GREGORY VII

The career of Hildebrand up to the moment in which he ascended the papal throne could scarcely be called other than a successful one. He had attained many of his aims. He had awakened the better part of the Church to a sense of the vices that had grown up in her midst, purified in many quarters the lives of her priests, and elevated the mind and ideal of Christendom. But bad as the vices of the clergy were, the ruling curse of simony was worse, to a man whose prevailing dream and hope was that of a great power holding up over all the world the standards of truth and righteousness in the midst of the wrongs and contentions of men. A poor German priest holding fast in his distant corner by the humble wife or half-permitted female companion at whose presence law and charity winked, was indeed a dreadful thought, meaning dishonour and sacrilege to the austere monk; but the bishops and archbishops over him who were so little different from the fierce barons, their kin and compeers, who had procured their benefices by the same intrigues, the same tributes and subserviences, the same violence, by which these barons in many cases held their fiefs, how was it possible that such men could hold the balance of justice, and promote peace and purity and the reign of God over the world? That they should help in any way in that great mission which the new Pope felt himself to have received from the Head of the Church was almost beyond hope. They vexed his soul wherever he turned, men with no motive, no inspiration beyond that of their fellows, ready to scheme and struggle for the aggrandisement of the Church, if you will—for the increase of their own greatness and power and those of the corporations subject to them: but as little conscious of that other and holier ambition, that hope and dream of a reign of righteousness, as were their fellows and brethren, the dukes and counts, the fighting men, the ambitious princes of Germany and Lombardy. Until the order of chiefs and princes of the Church could be purified, Hildebrand had known, and Gregory felt to the bottom of his heart, that nothing effectual could be done.

The Cardinal Archdeacon of Rome, under Popes less inspired than himself—who were, however, if not strong enough to originate, at least acquiescent, and willing to adopt and sanction what he did—had carried on a holy war against simony wherever found. He had condemned it by means of repeated councils, he had poured forth every kind of appeal to men's consciences, and exhortations to repentance, without making very much impression. The greatest offices were still sold in spite of him. They were given to tonsured ruffians and debauchees who had no claim but their wealth to ascend into the high places of the Church, and who, in short, were but secular nobles with a difference, and the fatal addition of a cynicism almost beyond belief, though singularly mingled at times with superstitious terrors. Hildebrand had struggled against these men and their influence desperately, by every means in his power: and Pope Gregory, with stronger methods at command, was bound, if possible, to extirpate the evil. This had raised him up a phalanx of enemies on every side, wherever there was a dignitary of the Church whose title was not clear, or a prince who derived a portion of his revenue from the traffic in ecclesiastical appointments. The degenerate young King not yet Emperor, who supported his every scheme of rapine and conquest by the gold of the ambitious priests whom he made into prelates at his will, was naturally the first of these enemies: Guibert of Ravenna, more near and readily offensive, one of the most powerful ecclesiastical nobles in Italy, sat watchful if he might catch the new Pope tripping, or find any opportunity of accusing him: Robert Guiscard, the greatest of the Normans, who had been so much the servant and partisan of the late Popes, remained sullen and apart, giving no allegiance to this: Rome itself was surrounded by a fierce and audacious nobility, who had always been the natural enemies of the Pope, unless when he happened to be their nominee, and more objectionable than themselves. Thus the world was full of dark and scowling faces. A circle of hostility both at his gates and in the distance frowned unkindly about him, when the age of Hildebrand was over, and that of Gregory began. All his great troubles and sufferings were in this latter part of his life. Nothing in the shape of failure had befallen him up to this point. He had met with great respect and honour, his merit and power had been recognised almost from his earliest years. Great princes and great men—Henry himself, the father of the present degenerate Henry, a noble Emperor, honouring the Church and eager for its purification—had felt themselves honoured by the friendship of the monk who had neither family nor wealth to recommend him. But when Pope Gregory issued from his long probation and took into his hand the papal sceptre, all these things had changed. Whether he was aware by any premonition of the darker days upon which he had now fallen who can say? It is certain that confronting them he bated no jot of heart or hope.

He appears to us at first as very cautious, very desirous of giving the adversary no occasion to blaspheme. The summons issued in the name of the late Pope to Henry requiring him to appear and answer in Rome the charges made against him, seems to have been dropped at Alexander's death: and when his messengers came over the Alps demanding by what right a Pope had been consecrated without his consent, Gregory made mild reply that he was not consecrated, but was awaiting not the nomination but the consent of the Emperor, and that not till that had been received would he carry out the final rites. These were eventually performed with some sort of acquiescence from Henry, given through his wise and prudent ambassador, on the Feast of St. Peter, the 29th June, 1073. Gregory did what he could, as appears, to continue this mild treatment of Henry with all regard to his great position and power. He attempted to call together a very intimate council to discuss the state of affairs between the King and himself: a council of singular construction, which, but that the questions as to the influence and place of women are questions as old as history, and have been decided by every age according to no formal law but the character of the individuals before them, might be taken for an example of enlightenment before his time in Gregory's mind. He invited Duke Rudolf of Suabia, one of Henry's greatest subjects, a man of religious character and much reverence for the Holy See, to come to Rome, and in common with himself, the Empress Agnes, the two Countesses of Tuscany, the Bishop of Como (who was the confessor of Agnes), and other God-fearing persons, to consider the crisis at which the Church had arrived, and to hear and give advice upon the Pope's intentions and projects. The French historian Villemain throws discredit upon this projected consultation of "an ambitious vassal of the King of Germany and three women, one of whom had once been a prisoner in the camp of Henry III., the other had been brought up from infancy in the hate of the empire and the love of the Church, and the last was a fallen empress who was more the penitent of Rome than the mother of Henry." This seems, however, a futile enumeration. There could surely be no better defender found for a son accused than his mother, who we have no reason to suppose was ever estranged from him personally, and who shortly after went upon an embassy to him, and was received with every honour. Beatrice, on the other hand, had been the prisoner of his father the great Emperor, and not of young Henry of whom she was the relative and friend, and between whom and the Pope, as all good statesmen must have seen, it was of the greatest importance to Europe that there should be peace; while any strong personal feeling which might exist would be modified by Gregory himself, by Raymond of Como, and the wisest heads of Rome.

But this board of advice and conciliation never sat, so we need not comment upon its possible concomitants. In every act of his first year, however, Gregory showed a desire to conciliate Henry rather than to defy him. The young king had his hands very full, and his great struggle with the Saxon nobles and people was not at the moment turning in his favour. And he had various natural defenders and partisans about the Roman Court. The Abbot Hugo of Cluny, who was one of Gregory's dearest friends, had been the young king's preceptor, and bore him a strong affection. We have no reason to believe that the influence of Agnes was not all on the side of her son, if not to support his acts, at least to palliate and excuse them. With one of these in his most intimate council, and one an anxious watcher outside, both in command of his ear and attention, it would have been strange if Gregory had been unwilling to hear anything that was in Henry's favour.

And in fact something almost more than a full reconciliation seems to have been effected between the new Pope and the young king, so desirous of winning the imperial crown, and conscious that Gregory's help was of the utmost importance to him. Henry on his side wrote a letter to his "most loving lord and father," his "most desired lord," breathing such an exemplary mind, so much penitence and submission, that Gregory describes it as "full of sweetness and obedience:" while the Pope, if not altogether removing the sword that hung suspended over Henry's head, at least received his communications graciously, and gave him full time and encouragement to change his mind and become the most trusted lieutenant of the Holy See. The King was accordingly left free to pursue his own affairs and his great struggle with the Saxons without any further question of ecclesiastical interference: while Gregory spent the whole ensuing year in a visitation of Italy, and much correspondence and conference on the subject of simony and other abuses in the Church. When he returned to Rome he endeavoured, but in vain, to act as peacemaker between Henry and the Saxons. And it was not till June in the year 1074, when he called together the first of the Lateran Councils, an assembly afterwards renewed yearly, a sort of potential Convocation, that further steps were taken. With this the first note of the great warfare to follow was struck. The seriousness of the letters by which he summoned its members sufficiently shows the importance attached to it.

"The princes and governors of this world, seeking their own interest and not that of Jesus Christ, trample under foot all the veneration they owe to the Church, and oppress her like a slave. The priests and those charged with the conduct of the Church sacrifice, the law of God, renounce their obligations towards God and their flocks, seeking in ecclesiastical dignities only the glory of this world, and consuming in pomp and pride what ought to serve for the salvation of many. The people, without prelates or sage counsellors to lead them in the way of virtue, and who are instructed by the example of their chiefs in all pernicious things, go astray into every evil way, and bear the name of Christian without its works, without even preserving the principle of the faith. For these reasons, confident in the mercies of God, we have resolved to assemble a Synod in order to seek with the aid of our brethren for a remedy to these evils, and that we may not see in our time the irreparable ruin and destruction of the Church. Wherefore we pray you as a brother, and warn you in the name of the blessed Peter, prince of apostles, to appear at the day fixed, convoking by this letter, and by your own, your suffragan bishops; for we can vindicate the freedom of religion and of ecclesiastical authority with much more surety and strength according as we find ourselves surrounded by the counsels of your prudence, and by the presence of our brethren."

A few Italian princes, Gisulfo of Salerno, Azzo d'Este, Beatrice and Matilda of Tuscany, were convoked to the council and held seats in it. The measures passed were very explicit and clear. They condemned the simoniacal clergy in every rank, deposing them from their positions and commanding them to withdraw from the ministrations of the altar. The same judgment was passed upon those who lived with wives or concubines. Both classes were put beyond the pale of the Church, and the people were forbidden, on pain of sharing their doom, to receive the sacraments from them, or to yield them obedience. Nothing more thorough and far-reaching could be. Hitherto the Popes had proceeded by courts of investigation, by examination of individuals, in which the alternative of repentance and renunciation was always open to the prelate who had perhaps inadvertently fallen into these crimes. But such gentle dealings had been but very partially successful. Here and there an archbishop or great abbot had been convicted by his peers, and made to descend from his high estate—here and there a great personage had risen in his place and made confession. Some had retired to the cloister, putting all their pomps and glories aside, and made a good end. But as is usual after every religious revival, life had risen up again and gone upon its usual course, and the bishoprics thus vacated had probably been sold to the highest bidder or yielded to the most violent assailant, as if no such reformation had ever been.

The matter had gone too far now for any such occasional alleviations; and Gregory struck at the whole body of proud prelates, lords of secular as well as ecclesiastical greatness, men whose position was as powerful in politics and the affairs of the empire as was that of the princes and margraves who were their kin, and whom they naturally supported—as the others had supported them by money and influence in their rise to power: but who had very little time for the affairs of the Church, and less still for the preservation of peace and the redress of wrong.

The other measures passed at this council were more searching still; they were aimed against the disorders into which the clergy had fallen, and chiefly what was to Gregory and his followers the great criminality, of married priests, who abounded in the Church. In this the lower orders of the clergy were chiefly assailed, for the more important members of the hierarchy did not marry though they might be vicious otherwise. But the rural priests, the little-educated and but little-esteemed clerks who abounded in every town and village, were very generally affected by the vice—if vice it was—of marriage, which was half legal and widely tolerated: and their determination not to abandon it was furious. Meetings of the clergy to oppose this condemnation were held in all quarters, and often ended in riot, the priests declaring that none of the good things of the Church fell to their lot, but that rather than give up their wives, their sole compensation, they would die. This was not likely to make Gregory's proceedings less determined: but it may easily be imagined what a prodigious convulsion such an edict was likely to make in the ecclesiastical world.

It is said by the later historians that the Empress Agnes was made use of, with her attendant bishop and confessor, to carry these decrees to Henry's court: though this does not seem to be sanctioned by the elder authorities, who place the mission of Agnes in the previous year, and reckon it altogether one of peace and conciliation. But Henry still continued in a conciliatory frame of mind. His own affairs were not going well, and he was anxious to retain the Pope's support in the midst of his conflicts with his subjects. Neither do the great dignitaries appear to have made any public protest or resistance: it was the poor priests upon whom individually this edict pressed heavily, who were roused almost to the point of insurrection.

One of the most curious effects of the decree was the spirit roused among the laity thus encouraged to judge and even to refuse the ministrations of an unworthy priest. Not only was their immediate conduct affected to acts of spiritual insubordination, but a fundamental change seems to have taken place in their conception of the priest's character. No doubt Gregory's legislation must have originated that determined though illogical opposition to a married priesthood, and disgust with the idea, which has had so singular a sway in Catholic countries ever since, and which would at the present moment we believe make any change in the celibate character of the priesthood impossible even were all other difficulties overcome. We are not aware that it had existed in any force before. The thing had been almost too common for remark: and there seems to have been no fierce opposition to the principle. It arose now gradually yet with a force beyond control: there were many cases of laymen baptizing their children themselves, rather then give them into the hands of a polluted priest—until there arose almost a risk of general indifference to this sacrament because of the rising conviction that the hands which administered it were unworthy: and other religious observances were neglected in the same way, an effect which must have been the reverse of anything intended by the Pope. To this hour in all Catholic countries an inexpressible disgust with the thought, mingles even with the theory that perhaps society might be improved were the priest a married man, and so far forced to content himself with the affairs of his own house. Probably it was Gregory's strong denunciation, and his charge to the people not to reverence, not to obey men so soiled: as well as the conviction long cultivated by the Church, and by this time become a dogma, that the ascetic life was in all cases the holiest—which originated this powerful general sentiment, more potent in deciding the fact of a celibate clergy than all the ecclesiastical decrees in the world.

In the second Lateran Council held in the next year, at the beginning of Lent, along with the reiteration of the laws in respect to simony and the priesthood, a solemn decree against lay investiture was passed by the Church. This law transferred the struggle to a higher ground. It was no longer bishops and prelates of all classes, no longer simple priests, but the greatest sovereigns, all of whom had as a matter of course given ecclesiastical benefices as they gave feudals fiefs, who were now involved. The law was as follows:

"Whosoever shall receive from the hands of a layman a bishopric, or an abbey, shall not be counted among the bishops and abbots, nor share their privileges. We interdict him from entrance into the Church and from the grace of St. Peter until he shall have resigned the dignity thus acquired by ambition and disobedience, which are equal to idolatry. Also, if any emperor, duke, marquis, count, or other secular authority shall presume to give investiture of a bishopric or other dignity of the Church, let him understand that the same penalty shall be exacted from him."

The position of affairs between Pope and Emperor was thus fundamentally altered. The father of Henry, a much more faithful son of the Church, had almost without opposition made Popes by his own will where now his son was interdicted from appointing a single bishop. The evil was great enough perhaps for this great remedy, and Gregory, who had gone so far, was restrained now by no prudent precautions from proceeding to the utmost length possible. The day of prudence was over; he had entered upon a path in which there was no drawing back. That it was not done lightly or without profound and painful thought, and a deep sense of danger and impending trouble, is apparent from the following letter in which the Pope unbosoms himself to the head of his former convent, the great Hugo of Cluny, his own warm friend, and at the same time Henry's tutor and constant defender.

"I am overwhelmed (he writes) with great sorrow and trouble. Wherever I look, south, north, or west, I see not a single bishop whose promotion and conduct are legal, and who governs the Christian people for the love of Christ, and not by temporal ambition. As for secular princes, there is not one who prefers the glory of God to his own, or justice to interest. Those among whom I live—the Romans, the Lombards, the Normans—are, as I tell them to their faces, worse than Jews and Pagans. And when I return within myself, I am so overwhelmed by the weight of life that I feel no longer hope in anything but the mercy of Christ."

Notwithstanding the supreme importance of this question, and Gregory's deep sense of the tremendous character of the struggle on which he had thus engaged, matters of public morality in other ways were not sacrificed to these great proceedings for the honour of the Church. He not only himself assumed, but pressed upon all spiritual authorities under him, the duty and need of prompt interference in the cause of justice and public honesty. The letters which follow were called forth by a remarkable breach of these laws of honesty and the protection due to strangers and travellers which were fundamental rules of society. This was the spoliation of certain merchants robbed in their passage through France, and from whom the Pope accuses the young King Philip I. to have taken, "like a brigand, an immense sum of money." Gregory addresses himself to the bishops of France in warning and entreaty as follows:

"As it is not possible that such crimes should escape the sentence of the Supreme Judge, we pray you and we warn you with true charity to be careful and not to draw upon yourself the prophet's curse: 'Woe to him who turns back his sword from blood'—that is to say, as you well understand, who does not use the sword of the Word for the correction of worldly men; for you are in fault, my brethren, you who, instead of opposing these vile proceedings with all the rigour of the priesthood, encourage wickedness by your silence. It is useless to speak of fear. United and armed to defend the just, your force will be such that you will be able to quench evil passions in penitence. And even if there were danger, that is no reason for giving up the freedom of your priesthood. We pray you, then, and we warn you by the authority of the Apostles, to unite in the interest of your country, of your glory and salvation, in a common and unanimous counsel. Go to the king, tell him of his shame, of his danger and that of his kingdom. Show him to his face how criminal are his acts and motives, endeavour to move him by every inducement that he may undo the harm which he has done.

"But if he will not listen to you, and if, scorning the wrath of God, and indifferent to his own royal dignity, to his own salvation and that of his people, he is obstinate in the hardness of his heart, let him hear as from our mouth that he cannot escape much longer the sword of apostolic punishment."

These are not such words as Peter was ever commissioned in Holy Writ to give forth; but granting all the pretensions of Peter's successors, as so many good Christians do, it is no ignoble voice which thus raises itself in warning, which thus denounces the vengeance of the Church against the evil-doer, be he bishop, clown, or king. Gregory had neither armies nor great wealth to support his interference with the course of the world—he had only right and justice, and a profound faith in his mission. He risked everything—his life (so small a matter!), his position, even the safety of the Church itself, which these potentates could have crushed under their mailed shoes; but that there should be one voice which would not lie, one champion who would not be turned aside, one witness for good, always and everywhere, against evil, was surely as noble a pretension as ever was lifted under heaven. It was to extend the power of Rome, all the historians say; which no doubt he wished to do. But whether to extend the power of Rome was his first object, or to pursue guilt and cruelty and falsehood out of the very boundaries of the world if one man could drive them forth, God only can judge. When there are two evident motives, however, it is not always wise to believe that the worst is the one to choose.

In most curious contrast to these great and daring utterances is the incident, quite temporary and of no real importance, in his life, which occurred to Pope Gregory at the very moment when he was thus threatening a world lying in wickedness with the thunderbolts of Rome. The city which had gone through so many convulsions, and was now the centre of the pilgrimages of the world, was still in its form and construction the ancient Rome, and more or less a city of ruins. The vast open spaces, forums, circuses, great squares, and amphitheatres, which made old Rome so spacious and magnificent, still existed as they still to a certain extent exist. But no great builder had as yet arisen among the Popes, no one wealthy enough or with leisure enough to order the city upon new lines, to give it a modern shape, or reduce it to the dimensions necessary for its limited population. It was still a great quarry for the world, full of treasures that could be carried away, a reservoir and storehouse of relics to which every man might help himself. Professor Lanciani, the accomplished and learned savant to whom we owe so much information concerning the ancient city, has shown us how much mediæval covetousness in this way had to do with the actual disappearance of ancient buildings, stone by stone. But this was not the only offence committed against the monuments of the past. The great edifices of the classic age were often turned, not without advantage in the sense of the picturesque, into strongholds of the nobles, sometimes almost as much isolated amid the great gaps of ruins as in the Campagna outside. The only buildings belonging to the time were monasteries, generally surrounded by strong walls, capable of affording protection to a powerful community, and in which the humble and poor could find refuge in time of trouble. These establishments, and the mediæval fortresses and towers built into the midst of the ruins, occupied with many wild spaces between, where the luxuriant herbage buried fallen pillars and broken foundations, the wastes of desolation which filled up half the area of the town. The population seems to have clustered about the eastern end of the city; all the life of which one reads, except an occasional tumult around St. Peter's and north of St. Angelo, seems to have passed on the slopes or under the shadow of the Aventine and Coelian hills, from thence to the Latin gate, and the Pope's palace there, the centre of government and state—and on the hill of the Capitol, where still the people gathered when there was a motive for a popular assembly. The ordinary populace must have swarmed in whatsoever half-ruined barracks of old palaces, or squalid huts of new erection hanging on to their skirts, might be attainable in these quarters, clustering together for warmth and safety, while the rest of the city lay waste, sprinkled with ruins and desolate paths, with great houses here and there in which the strangely mixed race bearing the names, often self-appropriated, of ancient Roman patrician families, lived and robbed and made petty war, and besieged each other within their strong walls.

One of these fortified houses or towers, built at or on the bridge of St. Angelo—in which the noble owner sat like a spider, drawing in flies to his web, taking toll of every stranger who entered Rome by that way—belonged to a certain Cencio[3] or Cencius of the family of Tusculum, the son of the Præfect of Rome. The Præfect, unlike his family, was one of the most devoted adherents of the Popes; he is, indeed, in the curious glimpse afforded to us by history, one of the most singular figures that occur in that crowded foreground. A mediæval noble and high official, he was at the same time a lay-preacher, delighted to exercise his gift when the more legitimate sermon failed from any cause, and only too proud, it would appear, of hearing his own voice in the pulpit. That his son should be of a very different disposition was perhaps not to be wondered at. Cencius was as turbulent as his father was pious; but he must have been a soldier of some note, as he held the post of Captain of St. Angelo, and in that capacity had maintained during a long siege the anti-pope Cadalous, or Honorius II., from whom, brigand as he was, he exacted a heavy ransom before permitting the unfortunate and too ambitious prelate to steal away like a thief in the night when his chance was evidently over. Cencius would seem to have lost his post in St. Angelo, but he maintained his robber's tower on the other end of the bridge, and was one of the most dangerous and turbulent of these internal enemies of Rome. During an interval of banishment, following a more than usually cruel murder, he had visited Germany, and had met at young Henry's court with many people to whom Pope Gregory was obnoxious, from Gottfried the Hunchback, the husband of the Countess Matilda, to the young king himself. Whether what followed was the result of any conspiracy, however, or if it was an outburst of mad vengeance on the part of Cencius himself, or the mere calculating impulse of a freebooter to secure a good ransom, is not known. A conspiracy, with Godfrey at the head of it, not without support from Henry, and the knowledge at least of the Archbishop of Ravenna and Robert Guiscard, all deeply irritated by the Pope's recent proceedings, was of course the favourite idea at the time. But no clear explanation of motives has ever been attained, and only the facts are known.

On Christmas-eve it was the habit of the Popes to celebrate a midnight mass in the great basilica of Sta. Maria Maggiore in what was then a lonely and dangerous neighbourhood, though not very far from the Lateran Church and palace. It was usually the occasion of a great concourse from all parts of the city, attracted by the always popular midnight celebration. But on Christmas-eve of the year 1076 (Muratori says 1075) a great storm burst over the city as the hour approached for the ceremony. Torrents of rain, almost tropical in violence, as rain so often is in Rome, poured down from the blackness of the skies, extinguishing even the torches by which the Pope and his diminished procession made their way to the great church, blazing out cheerfully with all its lighted windows into the night. Besides the priests only a very small number of the people followed, and there was no such murmur and rustle of sympathy and warmth of heart as such an assembly generally calls forth. But the great altar was decorated for Christmas, and the Pope attired in his robes, and everything shining with light and brightness within, though the storm raged without. The mass was almost over, Gregory and the priests had communicated, the faithful company assembled were receiving their humbler share of the sacred feast, and in a few minutes the office would have been completed, when suddenly the church was filled with noise and clamour and armed men. There was no one to defend the priests at the altar, even had it been possible in the suddenness of the assault to do so. Cencius's band was composed of ruffians from every region, united only in their lawlessness and crime; they seized the Pope at the altar, one of them wounding him slightly in the forehead. It is said that he neither asked for mercy nor uttered a complaint, nor even an expostulation, but permitted himself without a word to be dragged out of the church, stripped of his robes, placed on a horse behind one of the troopers, and carried off into the night not knowing where.

All this happened before the terrified priests and people—many of the latter probably poor women from the hovels round about—recovered their surprise. The wild band, with the Pope in the midst, galloped out into the blackness and the rain, passing under garden walls and the towers of silent monasteries, where the monks, too much accustomed to such sounds to take much notice, would hear the rush of the horses and the rude voices in the night with thankfulness that no thundering at the convent gates called upon them to give the free lances shelter. It appears that it was not to Cencius's stronghold on the bridge but to the house of one of his retainers that this great prize was conveyed. Here Gregory, in the cassock which he had worn under his gorgeous papal dress, wet and bleeding from the wound in his forehead, was flung without ceremony into an empty room. The story is that some devout man in the crowd and a Roman lady, by some chance witnessing the arrival of the band, stole in with them, and found their way to the place in which the Pope lay, covering him with their own furs and mantles and attending to his wound. And thus passed the Christmas morning in the misery of that cruel cold which, though rare, is nowhere more bitter than in Rome.

[SANTA MARIA MAGGIORE]

In the meantime the terrified congregation in Sta. Maria Maggiore had recovered its senses, and messengers hurried out in all directions to trace the way by which the freebooters had gone, and to spread the news of the Pope's abduction. The storm had by this time passed over, and the people were easily roused on the eve of the great festival. Torches began to gleam by all the darkling ways, and the population poured forth in the excitement of a great event. It would seem that in all the tumultuous and factious city there was but one thought of horror at the sacrilege, and determination to save the Pope if it were still possible. Gregory was not, like his great predecessor the first of that name, the idol of his people. He had not the wealth with which many great ecclesiastics had secured the homage of the often famished crowd; and a stern man, with no special geniality of nature, and views that went so far beyond the local interests of Rome, he does not seem the kind of ruler to have secured popular favour. Yet the city had never been more unanimous, more determined in its resolution. The tocsin was sounded in all the quarters of Rome during that night of excitement; every soldier was called forth, guards were set at all the gates, lest the Pope should be conveyed out of the city; and the agitated crowd flocked to the Capitol, the only one of the seven hills of Rome where some kind of repair and restoration had been attempted, to consult, rich and poor together, people and nobles, what was to be done. To this spot came the scouts sent out in search of information, to report their discoveries. They had found that the Pope was still in Rome, and where he was—a prisoner, but as yet unharmed.

With one impulse the people of Rome, forming themselves into an undignified but enthusiastic army, rushed down from their place of meeting towards the robber's castle. We hear of engines of war, and all the cumbrous adjuncts of a siege and means of breaching the walls, as if those articles had been all ready in preparation for any emergency. The palace, though strong, could not stand the assault of the whole population, and soon it was necessary to bring the Pope from his prison and show him at a window to pacify the assailants. Cencius did all that a ruffian in such circumstances would naturally do. He first tried to extract money and lands from the Pope's terrors, and then flung himself on his knees before Gregory, imploring forgiveness and protection. The first attempt was useless, for Gregory was not afraid; the second was more successful, for remorseless to the criminals whose evil acts or example injured the Church, the Pope was merciful enough to ordinary sinners, and had never condemned any man to death. "What you have done to me I pardon you as a father; but what you have done against God and the Church must be atoned for," said Gregory, still at the mercy of any rude companion in that band of ruffians: and he commanded his captor to make a pilgrimage to Jerusalem, to cleanse himself from this sin. The Pope was conveyed out of his prison by the excited and enthusiastic crowd, shouting and weeping, half for joy, and half at sight of the still bleeding scar on his forehead. But weak and exhausted as he was, without food, after a night and almost a day of such excitement, in which he had not known from one hour to another what might happen, helpless in the hands of his enemies, Gregory had but one thought—to conclude his mass which he had not finished when he was interrupted at the altar. He went back in his cassock, covered by the stranger's furred cloak, along the same wild way over which he had been hurried in the darkness; and followed by the entire population, which swarmed into every corner and blocked every entrance, returned to the great basilica, where he once more ascended the altar steps, completed the mass, offered his thanksgivings to God, and blessed and thanked his deliverers, before he sought in the quick falling twilight of the winter day the rest of his own house.

It is common to increase the effect of this most picturesque scene by describing Gregory as an aged man, old and worn out, in the midst of his fierce foes; but he was barely sixty and still in the fulness of his strength, though spare and shrunken by many fasts and still more anxieties. That he had lost nothing of his vigour is evident, and in fact the incident, though never forgotten as a dramatic and telling episode by the historians, was a mere incident of no importance whatever in his life.

In the meantime the Emperor Henry, who had been disposed to humility and penitence by the efforts of his mother, and by the distresses of his own position during a doubtful and dangerous intestine war, in which all at the time seemed to be going against him, had subdued the Saxons and recovered the upper hand: and, thus victorious in his own country, was no longer disposed to bow his neck under any spiritual yoke. He had paid no attention to Gregory's commands in respect to simony nor to the ordinance against lay investiture which had proceeded from the Council of 1075; but had, on the contrary, filled up several bishoprics in the old way, continued to receive the excommunicated nobles, and treated Gregory's decrees as if they had never been. His indignation at the Pope's interference— that indignation which every secular prince has always shown when interfered with by the Holy See, and which so easily translates the august titles of the successor of St. Peter, the Vicar of Christ, into a fierce denunciation of the "Italian priest" whom mediæval princes feared and hated—was only intensified by his supreme pretensions as Emperor, and grew in virulence as Gregory's undaunted front and continued exercise, so far as anathemas would do it, of the weapons of church discipline, stood steadily before him. It is very possible that the complete discomfiture of Cencius's attempt upon the Pope's liberty or life, to which Henry is believed to have been accessory, and the disgrace and ridicule of that failure, irritated and exasperated the young monarch, and that he felt henceforward that no terms could be kept with the man whom he had failed to destroy.

Gregory, on the other hand, finding all his efforts unsuccessful to gain the submission of Henry, had again taken the strong step of summoning him to appear before the yearly council held in Rome at the beginning of Lent, there to answer for his indifference to its previous decisions. The following letter sent to Henry a short time after the attempt of Cencius, but in which not a word of that attempt is said, is a remarkable example of Gregory's dignified and unyielding attitude:

"Gregory, servant of the servants of God.

"To Henry, king, salutation and the blessing of the apostles, if he obeys the apostolic see, as becomes a Christian king.

"Considering with anxiety, within ourselves, to what tribunal we have to give an account of the dispensation of the ministry which has been extended to us by the Prince of the apostles, we send you with doubt our apostolic blessing, since we are assured that you live in close union with men excommunicated by the judgment of the Apostolic See and the censure of the synod. If this is true, you will yourself perceive that you cannot receive the grace of blessing either divine or apostolic, until you have dismissed from your society these excommunicated persons, or in forcing them to express their repentance have yourself obtained absolution by penitence and expiation. We counsel your highness, if you are guilty in this respect, to have recourse, without delay, to the advice of some pious bishop, who, under our authority, will direct you what to do, and absolve you, informing us with your consent of your penitence."

The Pope goes on to point out, recalling to Henry's mind the promises he had made, and the assurances given—how different his conduct has been from his professions.

"In respect to the church of Milan, how you have kept the engagements made with your mother, and with the bishops our colleagues, and with what intention you made these promises, the event itself shows. And now to add wound to wound, you have disposed of the churches of Spoleto and of Fermo. Is it possible that a man dares to transfer or give a church to persons unknown to us, while the imposition of hands is not permitted, except on those who are well known and approved? Your own dignity demands, since you call yourself the son of the Church, that you should honour him who is at her head, that is the blessed Peter, the prince of the apostles, to whom, if you are of the flock of the Lord, you have been formally confided by the voice and authority of the Lord—him to whom Christ said 'Feed my sheep.' So long as we, sinful and unworthy as we are, hold his place in his seat and apostolical government, it is he who receives all that you address to us either by writing or speech; and while we read your letters or listen to your words, it is he who beholds with a penetrating eye what manner of heart it is from which they come."

In this dignified and serious remonstrance there is not a word of the personal insult and injury which the Pope himself had suffered. He passes over Cencius and his foiled villainy as if it had never been; but while Gregory could forget, Henry could not: and historians have traced to the failure of this desperate attempt to subdue or extinguish the too daring, too steadfast Pontiff, the new spirit—the impulse of equally desperate rage and vengeance—which took possession of the monarch, finding, after all his victories, that here was one opponent whom he could not overcome, whose voice could reach over all

Christendom, and who bore penalties in his unarmed hand at which no crowned head could afford to smile. To crush the audacious priest to the earth, if not by the base ministry of Roman bravos, then by the scarcely more clean hands of German barons and excommunicated bishops, was the impulse which now filled Henry's mind. He invoked a council in Worms, a month after the failure in Rome, which was attended by a large number, not only of the German nobility, but of the great ecclesiastics who nowhere had greater power, wealth, and influence than in Teutonic countries. Half of them had been condemned by Gregory for simony or other vices, many of them were aware that they were liable to similar penalties. The reformer Pope, who after the many tentatives and half-measures of his predecessors, was now supreme, and would shrink from nothing in his great mission of purifying the Church, was a constant danger and fear to these great mediæval nobles varnished over with the names of churchmen. One stroke had failed: but another was quite possible which great Henry the king, triumphant over all his enemies, might surely with their help and sanction bring to pass.

The peers spiritual and temporal, the princes who scorned the interference of a priest, and the priests who feared the loss of all their honours and the disgrace and humiliation with which the Pope threatened them, came together in crowds to pull down their enemy from his throne. Nothing so bold had ever been attempted since Christendom had grown into the comity of nations it now was. Cencius had pulled the Pope from the altar steps in the night and dark: Henry and his court assembled in broad day, with every circumstance of pomp and publicity, to drag him from his spiritual throne. It would be difficult to say whether the palm of fierceness and brutality should be given to the brigand of the Tusculan hills, or to the great king, princes, archbishops, and bishops of the Teutonic empire. Cencius swore in his beard, unheard of after generations; the others, less fortunate, have left on record what were the manner of words they said. This is the solemn act signed by all the members of the assembly, by which the Pope was to learn his doom. It is a long and furious scold from beginning to end.

"Hildebrand, taking the name of Gregory, is the first who, without our knowledge, against the will of the emperor chosen by God, contrary to the habit of our ancestors, contrary to the laws, has, by his ambition alone, invaded the papacy. He does whatever pleases him, right or wrong, good or evil. An apostate monk, he degrades theology by new doctrines and false interpretations, alters the holy books to suit his personal interests, mixes the sacred and profane, opens his ears to demons and to calumny, and makes himself at once judge, witness, accuser, and defender. He separates husbands from wives, prefers immodest women to chaste wives, and adulterous and debauched and incestuous connections to legitimate unions; he raises the people against their bishops and priests. He recognises those only as legally ordained who have begged the priesthood from his hands, or who have bought it from the instruments of his extortions; he deceives the vulgar by a feigned religion, fabricated in a womanish senate: it is there that he discusses the sacred mysteries of religion, ruins the papacy, and attacks at once the holy see and the empire. He is guilty of lèse-majesté both divine and human, desiring to deprive of life and rank our consecrated emperor and gracious sovereign.

"For these reasons, the emperor, the bishops, the senate, and the Christian people declare him deposed, and will no longer leave the sheep of Christ to the keeping of this devouring wolf."

Among the papers sent to Rome this insolent act is repeated at greater length, accompanied by various addresses to the bishops and people, and two letters to the Pope himself, from one of which, the least insolent, we quote a few sentences.

"Henry, king by the grace of God, to Hildebrand.

"While I expected from you the treatment of a father, and deferred to you in everything, to the great indignation of my faithful subjects, I have experienced on your part in return the treatment which I might have looked for from the most pernicious enemy of my life and kingdom.

"First having robbed me by an insolent procedure of the hereditary dignity which was my right in Rome, you have gone further—you have attempted by detestable artifices to alienate from me the kingdom of Italy. Not content with this, you have put forth your hand on venerable bishops who are united to me as the most precious members of my body, and have worn them out with affronts and injustice against all laws human and divine. Judging that this unheard-of insolence ought to be met by acts, not by words, I have called together a general assembly of all the greatest in my kingdom, at their own request, and when there had been publicly produced before them things hidden up to that moment, from fear or respect, their declarations have made manifest the impossibility of retaining you in the Holy See. Therefore adhering to their sentence, which seems to me just and praiseworthy before God and men, I forbid to you the jurisdiction of Pope which you have exercised, and I command you to come down from the Apostolic See of Rome, the superiority of which belongs to me by the gift of God, and the assent and oath of the Romans."

The other letter ends with the following adjuration, which the king prefaces by quoting the words of St. Paul: "If an angel from heaven preach any other doctrine to you than that we have preached unto you, let him be accursed":

"You who are struck by this curse and condemned by the judgment of the bishops and by our own, come down, leave the apostolic chair; let another assume the throne of St. Peter, not to cover violence with the mantle of religion, but to teach the doctrine of the blessed apostle. I, Henry, king by the grace of God, and all my bishops, we command you, come down, come down!"

These letters were sent to Rome by Count Eberhard, the same who had come to inquire into the election of Gregory two years before, and had confirmed and consented to it in the name of his master. He was himself one of the excommunicated barons whom Gregory had struck for simoniacal grants of benefices; but he had not the courage to carry fire and flame into the very household of the Pope. He did, however, all the harm he could, publishing the contents of the letters he carried in the great Italian cities, where every guilty priest rejoiced to think that he had thus escaped the hands of the terrible Gregory. But when he came within reach of Rome the great German baron lost heart. He found a substitute in a priest of Parma, a hot-headed partisan, one of those instruments of malice who are insensible to the peril of burning fuse or sudden explosion. The conspirators calculated with a sense of the dramatic which could scarcely have been expected from their nationality, and which looks more like the inspiration of the Italian himself—that he should arrive in Rome on the eve of the yearly council held in the Lateran at the beginning of Lent. This yearly synod was a more than usually important one; for already the news of the decision at Worms was known in Italy, and a great number of the clergy, both small and great, had crowded to Rome. A hundred and ten prelates are reckoned as present, besides many other dignitaries. Among them sat, as usual on such occasions, Beatrice and Matilda of Tuscany, the only secular protectors of Gregory, the greatest and nearest of Italian sovereigns. It was their presence that was aimed at in the strangely abusive edict of Worms as making the Council a womanish senate: and it was also Matilda's case which was referred to in the accusation that the Pope separated husbands from their wives. The excitement of expectation was in the air as all the strangers in Rome, and the people, ever stirred like the Athenians by the desire to hear some new thing, thronged the corridors and ante-chapels of the Lateran, the great portico and square which were for the moment the centre of Rome. Again the vast basilica, the rustling mediæval crowd in all its glow of colour and picturesqueness of grouping, rises before us. Few scenes more startling and dramatic have ever occurred even in that place of many histories.

The Pope had seated himself in the chair of St. Peter, the long half-circular line of the great prelates extending down the long basilica on either side, the princes in a tribune apart with their attendants, and the crowd of priests filling up every corner and crevice: the Veni Creator had been sung: and the proceedings were about to begin—when Roland of Parma was introduced, no doubt with much courtesy and ceremony, as the bearer of letters from the Emperor. When these letters were taken from him, however, the envoy, instead of withdrawing, as became him, stood still at the foot of the Pope's chair, and to the consternation, as may be supposed, of the assembly, addressed Gregory. "The king, my master," he cried, "and all the bishops, foreign and Italian, command you to quit instantly the Church of Rome, and the chair of Peter." Then turning quickly to the astonished assembly, "My brethren," he cried, "you are hereby warned to appear at Pentecost in the presence of the king to receive your Pope from him; for this is no Pope but a devouring wolf."

The intensity of the surprise alone can account for the possibility of the most rapid speaker delivering himself of so many words before the assembly rose upon him to shut his insolent mouth. The Bishop of Porto was the first to spring up, to cry "Seize him!" but no doubt a hundred hands were at his throat before the Prætorian guard, with their naked swords making a keen line of steel through the shadows of the crowded basilica, now full of shouts and tumult, came in from the gates. The wretch threw himself at the feet of the Pope whom he had that moment insulted, and who seems to have come down hurriedly to rescue him from the fury of the crowd: and was with difficulty placed under the protection of the soldiers. It is not difficult to imagine the supreme excitement which must have filled the church as they disappeared with their prisoner, and the agitated assembly turned again towards their head, the insulted pontiff. Gregory was not the man to fail in such an emergency. He entreated the assembly to retain its composure and calm. "My children," he said, "let not the peace of the Church be broken by you. Perilous times, the gospel itself tells us, shall come: times in which men shall be lovers of their own selves, covetous, boasters, disobedient to parents. It must needs be that offences come, and the Lord has sent us as sheep into the midst of wolves. We have long lived in peace, but it may be that God would now water his growing corn with the blood of martyrs. We behold the devil's force at length displaying itself against us in the open field. Now, therefore, as it behoves the disciples of Christ with hands trained to the war, let us meet him and bravely contend with him until the holy faith which through his practices appears to be throughout the world abandoned and despised shall, the Lord fighting through us, be restored."

It seems a strange descent from the dignity of this address, that the Pope should have gone on to comment upon a marvellous egg which it was said had been found near the church of St. Peter, with a strange design raised upon its surface—a buckler with the figure of a serpent underneath, struggling with bent head and wriggling body to get free. This had seemed, however, a wonderful portent to all Rome, and though his modern historians censure Gregory for having no doubt prepared the prodigy and taken a despicable advantage of it, there does not seem the slightest reason to suppose either that Gregory was guilty of this, or that he was so little a man of his time as not to be himself as much impressed by it as any one else there. Appearances of the kind, which an age on the lookout for portents can define, and make others see, are not wanting in any period. The crowd responded with cries that it was he, the father of the Church, who was supreme, and that the blasphemer should be cut off from the Church and from his throne.

The sensation was not lessened when the full text[4] of Henry's letters, parts of which we have already quoted, was read out to the reassembled council next day. The words which named their Pope—their head who had been the providence and the guide of Rome for so many years—with contemptuous abuse as "the monk Hildebrand," must have stirred that assembly to its depths. The council with one voice demanded from Gregory the excommunication of the Emperor, and of the impious bishops, false to every vow, who had ventured to launch an anathema against the lawful head of the Church. The solemn sentence of excommunication was accordingly pronounced against Henry: his subjects were freed from their oath of allegiance, and his soul cut off from the Church which he had attempted to rend in twain. Excommunications had become so common in these days that the awe of the extraordinary ceremonial was much lessened: but it was no mere spiritual deprivation, as all were aware, but the most tremendous sentence which could be launched against a man not yet assured in his victories over his own rebellious tributaries, and whose throne depended upon the fidelity of powerful vassals, many of whom were much more impressed by the attitude of the Pope than by that of the king.

Thus after so many preliminaries, treaties of peace and declarations of war, the great conflict between Pope and Emperor, between the Church and the State, began. The long feud which ran into every local channel, and rent every mediæval town asunder with the struggles of Guelfs and Ghibellines, thus originated amid events that shook the world. The Synod of Worms and the Council of Rome, with their sudden and extraordinary climax in the conference of Canossa, formed the first act in a drama played upon a larger stage and with more remarkable accompaniments than almost any other in the world.

The effect of Henry's excommunication was extraordinary. The world of Christendom, looking on beyond the sphere of Henry's immediate surroundings and partisans, evidently felt with an impulse almost unanimous that the anathema launched by a partly lay assembly and a secular King against a reigning Pope unassailable in virtue, a man of power and genius equal to his position, was a sort of grim jest, the issue of which was to be watched for with much excitement, but not much doubt as to the result, the horror of the profanity being the gravest point in the matter. But no one doubted the power of Gregory on his part, amid his lawful council, to excommunicate and cut off from the Church the offending king. Already, before the facts were known, many bishops and other ecclesiastics in Germany had sent timid protests against the act to which in some cases they had been forced to append their names: and the public opinion of the world, if such an expression can be used, was undoubtedly on Gregory's side. Henry's triumphant career came to a pause. Not only the judgment of the Church and the opinion of his peers, but the powers of Heaven seemed to be against him. One of his greatest allies and supporters, Gottfried, surnamed Il Gobbo, the son of that Gottfried of Lorraine who married Beatrice of Tuscany, and who had imposed his hunchback son as her husband upon the young Matilda, the daughter of Beatrice—was murdered immediately after. The Bishop of Utrecht, who had been one of the king's chief advisers and confidants in his war with Gregory, died in misery and despair, declaring with his last breath that he saw his bed surrounded by demons, and that it was useless to offer prayers for him. On the other hand, the great Dukes of Suabia, Bavaria, and Carinthia, all faithful to the Church, abandoned the excommunicated king. Some of the greater bishops, trembling before the just ire of the Pope whom they had bearded, took the same part. The half-assuaged rebellion of the Saxon provinces broke forth with greater force than ever. Henry had neither arms nor supporters left to secure further victories, and the very air of the empire was full of the letters of Gregory, in which all his attempts to win the young king to better ways, and all the insults which that king had poured forth against the Holy See, were set forth. The punishment, as it appeared on all sides, was prompt as thunderbolts from heaven to follow the offence.

While Henry hesitated in dismay and alarm, not knowing what step to take, seeing his friends, both lay and clerical, abandon him on every side, consequences more decisive still followed. The great princes met together in an assembly of their own in Ulm without any reference to Henry, whom they named in their proceedings the ex-king, and decided upon another more formal meeting later to choose a new sovereign. These potentates became doubly religious, doubly Catholic, in their sudden revulsion. They surrounded Gregory's legates with reverence, they avoided all communion with simoniacal prelates, and even—carrying the Pope's new influence to the furthest extent—with the married priests against whom he had long fulminated in vain. A reformation of all evils seemed to be about to follow. They formally condemned the excommunicated Henry on every point moral and political, and though they hesitated over the great step of the threatened election of a king in his place, they announced to him that unless he could clear himself of the interdict before the beginning of the following year, when they had decided to call a diet in Augsburg to settle the question, his fall would be complete and without remedy. At the same time they formally and solemnly invited the presence of the Pope at Augsburg to preside over and confirm their conclusions. This invitation Gregory accepted at once, and Henry, with no alternative before him, consented also to appear before the tribunal of his subjects, and to receive from their hands, and those of the Pope whom he had so insulted and outraged, the sentence of his fate. His humiliation was complete.

The assembly which was to make this tremendous decision was convoked for the 2nd February, 1077, the feast of the Purification, at Augsburg. Gregory had accepted the invitation of the German potentates without fear; but there was much alarm in Rome at the thought of such a journey—of the passage through rebellious Lombardy, of the terrible Alps and their dangers, and at the end of all the fierce German princes, who did not always keep faith, and whose minds before this time might have turned again towards their native prince. The Pope set out, however, under the guard of Matilda of Tuscany and her army, to meet the escort promised him from beyond the Alps. On the other hand, Henry was surrounded by dangers on every side. He had been compelled to give up his own special friends, excommunicated like himself; he had no arms, no troops, no money; the term which had been allowed him to make his peace with the Pope was fast passing, and the dreadful moment when it would be his fate to stand before his revolted subjects and learn their decision, appeared before him in all its humiliation and dishonour. Already various offenders had stolen across the mountains privately, to make their submission to Gregory. It seemed the only course for the desperate king to take. At length, after much wavering, he made up his mind, and escaping like a fugitive from the town of Spires to which he had retired, he made his way in the midst of a rigorous winter, and with incredible difficulty, across the Alps, with the help and under the guardianship of Adelaide of Susa, his mother-in-law, who, however, it is said, made him pay a high price for her help. He had begged of the Pope to give him audience at Rome, but this was refused: and in partial despair and confusion he set out to accomplish his hated mission somehow, he did not know where or by what means. A gleam of comfort, however, came to Henry on his travels. He was received with open arms in Lombardy where the revolted bishops eagerly welcomed him as their deliverer from Gregory and his austerities: but there was too much at stake for such an easy solution of the matter as this.

In the meantime Gregory travelled northwards surrounded by all the strength of Tuscany, accompanied by the brilliant and devoted Matilda, a daughter in love and in years, the pupil and youthful friend, no doubt the favourite and beloved companion, of a man whose age and profession and character alike would seem to have made any other idea impossible even to the slanderers of the middle ages. Matilda of Tuscany has had a great fate: not only was she the idol of her own people and the admired of her own age—such an impossible and absurd piece of slander as that which linked the name of a beautiful young woman with that of the austere and aged Gregory being apparently the only one which had ever been breathed against her:—but the great poets of her country have placed her, one in the sweeter aspect of a ministering angel of heaven, the other in that of the most heroic of feminine warriors, on the heights of poetic fame. Matilda on the banks of that sacred river of Lethe where all that is unhappy is forgotten, who is but one degree less sacred to Dante than his own Beatrice in Paradise: and Clorinda, the warrior maiden of Tasso, have carried the image of this noble princess to the hearts of many an after age. The hunchback husband imposed upon her in her extreme youth, the close union between her and her mother Beatrice, the independent court held by these two ladies, their prominent place among all the great minds of their time—and not least the faithful friendship of both with the great Gregory, combine to make this young princess one of the most interesting figures of her day. The usual solaces of life had been cut off from her at the beginning by her loveless marriage. She had no children. She was at this period of her career alone in the world, her mother having recently died, following Il Gobbo very closely to the grave. Henceforward Matilda had more to do in the field and council chamber than with the ordinary delights of life.

The Pope had left Rome with many anxieties on his mind, fully appreciating the dangers of the journey before him, and not knowing if he might ever see the beloved city again. While he was on the way the news reached him that Henry, whom he had refused to receive in Rome, was on his way across the Alps, and as probably the details of that painful journey were unknown, and the first idea would be that the king was coming with an army in full force—still greater anxieties, if not alarms, must have been awakened among the Pope's supporters. It was still more alarming to find that the German escort which was to have met him at Mantua had not been sent, the hearts of the princes having failed them, and their plans having fallen into confusion at the news of the king's escape. Henry had been received with enthusiasm in Lombardy, always rebellious, and might make his appearance any day to overpower the chivalry of Tuscany, and put the lives of both Pope and Princess in danger. They were on the road to Mantua when this news reached them, and in the anxious council of war immediately held, it was resolved that the strong castle of Canossa, supposed to be impregnable, should be, for the moment at least, the Pope's shelter and resting-place. One of the great strongholds of Italy, built like so many on a formidable point of rock, of itself almost inaccessible, and surrounded by three lines of fortified walls, among which no doubt clustered the rude little dwellings of a host of retainers—the situation of this formidable place was one which promised complete protection: and the name of the Tuscan castle has since become one of the best-known names in history, as the incident which followed contains some of the most picturesque and remarkable scenes on record. The castle had already a romantic story; it had sheltered many a fugitive; forlorn princesses had taken refuge within its walls from the pursuit of suitors or of enemies, the one as dangerous as the other. Painfully carried up in his litter by those steep and dangerous ways, from one narrow platform of the cliff to another, with the great stretch of the landscape ever widening as he gained a higher point, and the vast vault of heaven rounding to a vaster horizon, the Pope gained this eyrie of safety, this eagle's nest among the clouds.

We hear of no luxuries, not even those of intellectual and spiritual discourse, which to many an ascetic have represented, and represented well, the happiness of life, in this retreat of Gregory with his beautiful hostess, amid his and her friends. By his side, indeed, was Hugo, Abbot of Cluny, one of his most cherished and life-long companions; but the Pope spent his days of seclusion in prayer and anxious thought. The great plain that lay at his feet, should it be deluged with Christian blood once more, should brother stand against brother in arms, and Italy be crushed under the remorseless foot which even the more patient Teuton had not been able to bear? Many melancholy thoughts were no doubt in Gregory's mind in that great fastness surrounded by all the ramparts of nature and of art. He had dreamed—before the name of Crusade had yet been heard or thought of—of an expedition to Jerusalem at the head of all who loved the Lord, himself in his age and weakness the leader of an army composed of valiant and generous hearts from every quarter of the world, to redeem the Sepulchre of the Lord, and crush the rising power of the Saracens. This had been the favourite imagination of his mind—though as yet it called forth little sympathy from those about him—for some years past. Instead of that noble expedition was it possible that, perhaps partly by his fault, Christians were about to fly at each other's throats and the world to be again torn asunder by intestine warfare? But such thoughts as these were not the thoughts of the eleventh century. Gregory might shed tears before his God at the thought of bloodshed: but that his position in the presence of the Highest was the only right one, and his opponent's that of the most dangerous wrong, was no doubt his assured conviction. He awaited the progress of events, knowing as little as the humblest man-at-arms what was going to happen, with a troubled heart.

Nevertheless the retirement of these first days was broken by many hurried arrivals which were more or less of good omen. One by one the proud German bishops specially designated in Gregory's acts of excommunication, and nobles more haughty still, under the same burden, climbed the steep paths of Canossa, and penetrated from gate to gate, barefooted pilgrims denuding themselves of every vestige of power. "Cursed be he who turns back his sword from the blood," that is, who weakly pauses in the execution of a divine sentence—was one of Gregory's maxims. He received these successive suppliants with more sternness than sweetness. "Mercy," he said, "can never be refused to those who acknowledge and deplore their sins; but long disobedience, like rust on a sword, can be burned out only by the fire of a long repentance;" and he sent them one by one to solitary chambers in which, with the sparest of nourishment, they might reflect upon their sins. After a sufficient seclusion, however, they were liberated and sent away, reprimanded yet blessed—at least the laymen among them. It remained now to see what Henry would do.

[ARCH OF DRUSUS (1860)]

Henry was no longer at the lowest ebb of his fortunes. The princes of Germany had come to a pause: they had not sent the promised escort for the Pope; they were irresolute, not knowing what step to take next: and all Lombardy had risen to welcome the king; he had the support of every schismatic bishop, every censured priest, and of the excited people who were hostile to the pretensions of Rome, or rather to the severe purity of Gregory which was so uncompromising and determined. But by some unaccountable check upon his high spirit Henry, for the moment, was not moved to further rebellion either by the support of a Lombard army at his back, or by the hopes of his reviving followers at home. He was accompanied by his wife and by her mother, Adelaide of Susa, and perhaps the veneration of the women for the authority of the Church and dread of its penalties, affected him, although he had no love for the wife of whom he had tried so hard to get rid. Whatever was the explanation it is very evident, at least, that his spirit was cowed and that he saw nothing before him but submission. He went on probably to Parma, with a small and unarmed retinue, leaving his turbulent Lombard followers behind. On the way he sent various messengers before him, asking for an interview with Matilda, who was supposed likely to move the Pope in his favour. We are not told where the meeting took place, but probably it was in some wondering village at the foot of the hill, where the princely train from the castle, the great Contessa, the still greater abbot, Hugo of Cluny, and "many of the principal Italian princes," met the wandering pilgrim party, without sign or evidence of royalty—Henry and his Queen, the Marchesa Adelaide of Este, her son Amadeo, and other great persons in the same disguise of humility. The ladies on either side were related to each other, and all belonged to that close circle of the reigning class, in which every man calls his neighbour brother or cousin. Hugo of Cluny was the godfather of the king and loved him, and Adelaide, though on the side of her son-in-law, and now his eager champion, was a true and faithful daughter of the Church. Henry declared on the other side to his anxious friends that the accusations of the Germans were not true, that he was not as they had painted him: and implored their intercession with the Pope, not for any temporal advantage, but solely to be delivered from the anathema which weighed upon his soul. And Matilda and the others were but too anxious to make peace and put faith in all he said.

It is very likely that Gregory believed none of these protestations, but now or never, certainly he was bound to fulfil his own maxim, and not to turn back his sword from the blood. All the arguments of Henry's friends could not induce him to grant an easy absolution at the king's first word. Finally he consented to receive him as a penitent, but in no other character. Probably it was while the prayers and entreaties of Matilda and of Abbot Hugo were still going on in the castle that Henry came day by day, barefooted, in a humble tunic of woollen cloth, and waited at the gates to know the result. It was "an atrocious winter," such as had never been seen before, with continual snowstorms, and the rugged paths and stairs up the cliff, never easy, were coated with frost. Twice over the king climbed with naked feet as far as the second circle of the walls, but only to be turned away. It seems little short of a miracle that such a man, in such circumstances, should have so persevered. On the third day the pleaders within had been successful, and Henry was admitted, on the generous guarantee of Matilda, who took upon her to answer for him that his repentance was genuine. At last the culprit was led into the Pope's presence. He was made to give various promises of amendment, which were accepted, not on his oath, a last and supreme humiliation, but on the undertaking of various of his friends who swore, rashly one cannot but think, on the relics of the saints that the king would keep his promises. This is the document to which these generous friends set their seals.

"I, Henry, King, in respect to the complaints of the archbishops, bishops, dukes, counts and other princes of the Teutonic kingdom, and of all those who follow them, within the time fixed by the Lord Pope will do justice according to his sentence, or make peace according to his advice if no unavoidable hindrance occurs; and in that case, the moment the hindrance is taken away I will be ready to fulfil my promise. In addition, if the Lord Pope Gregory desires to cross the Alps, or go into other countries, he shall be held safe on my part, and on the part of those whom I command, from all danger of death, mutilation, or captivity, himself and those who form his escort, both during the journey, as long as he remains, and on the return; nothing shall be done by me contrary to his dignity, and if anything is done by others, I will lend him my help in good faith according to my power."

This does not seem a very large bond.

Next day, the 25th January, 1077, Henry came again in the same penitential dress, but this time according to formal appointment. He came into the room where the Pope awaited him, followed by all the excommunicated princes in his train, barefooted and half frozen with the painful climb up the rocky paths; and throwing himself on the floor before Gregory, asked his pardon, which Gregory gave, shedding many tears over the penitents. They were then received back into the Church with all the due ceremonials, the Pope in his vestments, the penitents naked to the waist, despoiled of all ornaments and dignities. In the castle church, of which now nothing but the foundations remain, Gregory solemnly absolved the miserable party, and offered them the Communion. At this act a very strange scene took place. The Pope, the great assailant of Simony, had himself been accused of it, ridiculous as was the accusation in a case like his, of which every circumstance was so perfectly known, and formally by Henry himself in the insolent command already quoted to abandon the papal see. At the moment of communion, in the most solemn part of the service, the Pope turned to Henry, standing before the altar, with the host in his hands. He appealed to God in the most impressive manner according to the usage of the time.

"You have long and often accused me," said the Pope, "of having usurped the Apostolical chair by Simony.... I now hold the body of the Saviour in my hands, which I am about to take. Let Him be the witness of my innocence: let God Himself all powerful absolve me to-day of the crime imputed to me if I am innocent, or strike me with sudden death if I am guilty." Then after a solemn pause he added: "My son, do as I have done: if you are certain of your innocence, if your reputation is falsely attacked by the lies of your rivals, deliver the Church of God from a scandal and yourself from suspicion; take the body of Our Lord, that your innocence may have God for witness, that the mouth of your enemies may be stopped, and that I—henceforward, your advocate and the most faithful defender of your cause—may reconcile you with your nobles, give you back your kingdom, and that the tempest of civil war which has so long afflicted the State may henceforth be laid at rest."

Would a guilty king in these unbelieving days venture upon such a pledge? Henry at least was incapable of it. He dared not call God to witness against the truth, and refused, trembling, murmuring confused excuses to take this supreme test. The mass was accomplished without the communion of the king; but not the less he was absolved and the anathema taken from his head.

In a letter written immediately after, Gregory informed the German princes of what he had done, adding that he still desired to cross the Alps and assist them in the settlement of the great question remaining, Henry having been avowedly received by him as a penitent, but not in any way as a restored king.

This great historical event, which has been the subject of so much commentary and discussion, and has been supposed to mark so great a step in the power and pretensions of the Popes, was in fact without any immediate effect in history. Henry went forth wroth and sore, humiliated but not humbled, and thinking of nothing so much as how to return to Gregory the shame he had himself suffered. And Gregory remained in his stronghold as little convinced of any advantage attained, as he had been of Henry's repentance. He is said to have answered the Saxon envoys who reproached him with his leniency, by a grim reassurance which is almost cynical. "He goes back worse than he came," said the Pope. It was indeed impossible that the eye of a man so conversant with men as Gregory should not have perceived how entirely his penitent's action was diplomatic and assumed for a purpose, and what a solemn farce Henry was playing as he stood barefooted in the snow, to obtain the absolution which was his only chance for Germany. It is perfectly permissible to believe that not only the determination not "to turn back his sword from the blood" or to fail in exacting every punctilio of penance, but a natural impulse of scorn for the histrionic exhibition made for the benefit of the great audience across the Alps, induced the Pope to keep the king dangling at those icy gates. That there should have been in Gregory's mind, along with this conviction, momentary relentings of hope that the penitent's heart might really be touched, was equally natural, and that it was one of these sudden impulses which moved him to the startling and solemn appeal to God over the sacramental host which formed so remarkable an incident in the ceremonial, may be taken for granted. In that age miracles were more than common, they were looked for and expected; and in all ages the miracle which we call conversion, the sudden and inexplainable movement of a heart, touched and turned in an instant from evil to good, has been known and proved. That a priest at the altar should hope that it might be his, by some burning word or act, to convey that inexpressible touch was a very human and natural hope: and yet Gregory knew well in his after survey of what had passed that the false penitent went away worse than he came. He wrote, however, an account of the matter to the German princes, who looked on trembling for the consequences, and probably blaming the Pope for an action that might destroy all their combinations— in which he described to them Henry's penitence and promise, without implying a doubt of the sincerity of either, but with a full statement of the fact that the absolution awarded to the man made no difference in respect to the king.

"Things being thus arranged [writes the Pope] in order to secure, by the help of God, the peace of the Church and the union of the Kingdom, which we have so long desired, we are anxious to pursue our journey into your countries on the first occasion possible; for we desire you to know, as you may perceive from the written engagements, that everything is still in suspense, so that our arrival among you and the unanimity of your council is absolutely necessary to settle matters. Therefore be very attentive to continue as you have begun in faith and the love of justice, and understand that we have done nothing for the king, except to tell him that he might trust to us to help him in such things as may touch his salvation and his honour, with justice and with mercy, without putting our soul and his in peril."

In the meantime Henry had enough to do in winning back again to his side the rebellious Lombards, who considered his submission to the Pope, however artificial, a desertion of their cause, and shut upon him the gates of their cities, which before his visit to Canossa had been thrown wide open. He had apparently, though only for a moment, lost them, while he had not regained the sympathies of Germany. There was nothing for it but a new apostasy, throwing over of his promises, and reassumption of the leadership of the schismatic party, which made the position of Gregory, surrounded by that angry sea of Lombard rebellion which beat against the base of his rocky stronghold, a very dangerous one. Through the whole spring of 1077 the Pope was more or less confined to the Castle of Canossa or other similar fortresses, under the vigilant care of Matilda; and it was from these strong places that he wrote a succession of remarkable letters to the nobles of Germany, who, strongly set upon the Diet in which the affairs of the kingdom were to be placed on a permanent footing, were proceeding to carry out their intention without waiting either for the presence of Gregory which they had invited, or Henry whose interests were at stake. Gregory did everything that was possible to delay the Diet until he could be present at it. He was anxious also to delay whatever great step might be in contemplation until the mind of the country was a little less anxious and disturbed: and he desired to be present, not only in the position of Arbitrator, but also to moderate with his counsels the excited spirits, and prevent if possible any great catastrophe.

We may allow, as it is one of the conventionalities of history to assert, that Gregory's intention was to establish in such matters the jurisdiction of the Popes and make it apparent to the world that thrones and principalities were at the disposition of the Church. But at the same time Gregory was, like all men, chiefly moved by the immediate question before him, and he was a man sincerely occupied with what was best for both Church and State, fearing the rashness of an angry and excited assembly, and remembering his promise to do what he could for his most unworthy penitent; and we see no reason to believe that his purposes were not, according to his perception of his duty, honest and noble. He retained his hope of proceeding to Germany as long as that was possible, asking again and again for the guide and escort promised, even asking from Henry a safe conduct through the territory now held by him. Even after the election at Forchheim of Rudolf of Suabia as king in the place of Henry, he continued to urge upon the legates whom he had sent to that assembly the necessity for his presence. And he undoubtedly did this on the highest ground possible, putting forth his right to judge in the matter in the very clearest words. He bids his messengers in the name of St. Peter to summon the heads of both parties, Henry and Rudolf, to make his journey possible.

"With the advice of the clergy and laymen fearing God, we desire to judge between the two kings, by the grace of God, and point out which of the two parties is most justly to be entrusted with the government of the State. You are aware that it is our duty, and that it appertains to the providential wisdom of the Apostolic See, to judge the governments of the great Christian kingdoms and to regulate them under the inspiration of justice. The question between these two princes is so grave, and the consequences may be so dangerous, that if it was for any reason neglected by us, it would bring not only upon us and upon them, but on the Church entire, great and lamentable misfortune. Therefore, if one or other of these kings refuses to yield to our decision and conform to our counsels, and if, lighting the torch of pride and human covetousness against the honour of God, he aspires in his fury to the desolation of the Roman Empire, resist him in every way, by every means, to the death if necessary, in our name and by the authority of the blessed Peter."

The Pope in another letter makes his appeal no longer to the ruling class but to the entire people. He informs "all the faithful of Christ in the Teutonic empire" that he has sent his legates to both kings to demand of them both "either in their own persons or by sufficient messengers" to open the way for his journey to Germany in order with the help of God to judge the question between them.

"Our heart is full of sadness and sorrow to think that for the pride of one man so many thousands of Christians may be delivered over to death both temporal and eternal, the Christian religion shaken to its foundations, and the Roman Empire precipitated into ruin. Both of these kings seek aid from us, or rather from the Apostolic See, which we occupy, though unworthy; and we, trusting in the mercy of Almighty God, and the help of the blessed Peter, with the aid of your advice, you who fear God and love the Church, are ready to examine with care the right on either side and to help him whom justice notoriously calls to the administration of the kingdom....

"You know, dear brethren, that since our departure from Rome we have lived in the midst of dangers among the enemies of the faith; but neither from fear nor from love have we promised any help, but justice to one or other of these kings. We prefer to die, if necessary, rather than to consent by our own will that the Church of God should be put from her place; for we know that we have been ordained and set upon the apostolic chair in order to seek in our life not our own interests but those of Christ, and to follow through a thousand labours in the steps of the fathers to the future and eternal repose, by the mercy of God."

The reader must remember that Gregory had very good reason for all that he said, and that irrespective of the claims of the Church a wise and impartial umpire at such a moment might have been of the last importance to Germany; also that his services had been asked for in this capacity, and that therefore he had a right to insist upon being heard. The position which he claimed had been offered to him; and he was entitled to ask that such an important matter should not be settled in his absence.

The remonstrances which the Pope continued to make by his own voice and those of his legates as long as any remonstrance was possible, were however regarded by neither party. Neither the authority of Rome nor the visible wisdom of settling a question which must convulse the world and tear Germany in pieces, peacefully and on the foundation of justice if that were possible, as urged by Gregory—could prevail, nor ever has prevailed on any similar occasion against the passions and ambitions of men. It was a devout imagination, appealing to certain minds here and there by the highest motives, and naturally by very different ones to all the interested souls likely to be advantaged by it, which always form the reverse of the medal; but men with arms in their hands and all the excitements of faction and party, of imperial loss and gain around them, were little like to await a severe and impartial judgment. The German bishops made a curious remonstrance in their turn against the reception by Gregory of Henry's professions of penitence, and on either side there was a band of ecclesiastics, presumably not all good or all bad perplexing every judgment.

We have fortunately nothing to do with the bloody struggles of Rudolf and Henry. When the latter made his way again over the Alps, to defend his rights, carrying with him the Iron Crown which Gregory's refusal had prevented him from assuming—he carried it away however, though he did not dare to put it on, a curious mixture of timidity and furtive daring—the Pope, up to that moment virtually confined within the circle of the mountain strongholds of Tuscany, returned to Rome: where he continued to be assailed by constant and repeated entreaties to take up one or the other side, his own council of the Lateran inclining towards Henry. But nothing moved him from his determination that this question should be decided by a Diet under his own presidence, and by that alone. This question runs through the entire story of the period from year to year. No council—and in addition to the usual yearly council held always in the beginning of Lent, at the Lateran, there seem to have been various others between whiles, made compulsory by the agitation of the time—could take place without the arrival of the two bands of German ambassadors, one from Henry and the other from Rudolf, to plead the cause of their respective masters, both professing all obedience, and inviting a decision in their favour by every argument: but neither taking a single step to bring about the one thing which the Pope demanded—a lawful assembly to settle the question.

There is no pretence that Gregory treated them with anything but the severest impartiality, or that he at any time departed from the condition he had proposed from the first—the only preference given to one above the other being that he is said to have sent his apostolical blessing to Rudolf, a virtuous prince and his friend, and not to Henry the apostate and false penitent, which is scarcely wonderful. But it is easy to understand the agitation in which the constant arrival of these ambassadors must have kept Rome, a city so prone to agitation, and with so many parties within its own walls, seditious nobles and undisciplined priests, and the ever-restless, ever-factious populace, struggling continually for some new thing. The envoys of Henry would seem to have had more or less the popular favour: they were probably a more showy band than the heavier Saxons: and Henry's name and the prestige of his great father, and all those royal shows which must still have been remembered in the city, the coronation of the former Henry in St. Peter's, and all its attendant ceremonials and expenses, must have attached a certain interest to his name. Agnes too, the empress, who had died so recently in the odour of sanctity among them, must have left behind her, whether she loved him or not, a certain prepossession in favour of her son. And the crowd took sides no doubt, and in its crushing and pressing to see the strangers, in the great Lateran square or by the gates of their lodging, formed itself into parties attracted by a glance or a smile, made into enemies by a hasty word, and preparing for the greater troubles and conflicts which were about to come.

In the midst of these continual arrivals and departures and while the trumpets of the Saxon or the German party were still tingling in the air, and the velvet and jewels of the ambassadors had scarcely ceased to gleam among the dark robes of the clergy, there came up other matters of a nature more suitable to the sacred courts and the interests of the Church. Berengarius of Tours, a mild and speculative thinker, as often convincing himself that he was wrong as proving himself to be right, appeared before the council of 1079 to answer for certain heresies respecting the Eucharist, of which there had often already been question. His opinions were those of Luther, of whom he is constantly called the precursor: but there was little of Luther's strength in this gentle heretic, who had already recanted publicly, and then resumed his peculiar teachings, with a simplicity that for a time disarmed criticism. Gregory had always been his friend and protector, tolerating if not sharing his opinions, which were not such as moved or interested deeply the Church at the moment: for the age was not heretical, and the example of such a candid offender, who did not attempt to resist the arguments brought against him, was rather edifying than otherwise. At least there were no theological arguments of fire and sword, no rack or stake for the heretic in Gregory's day. The pressure of theological judgment, however, became too strong for the Pope to resist, preoccupied as he was with other matters, and Berengarius was once more compelled to recant, which he did cordially, with the same result as before.

It was a more congenial occupation for the vigilant head of the Church to watch over the extension of the faith than to promote the internal discipline of the fold of Christ by prosecutions for heresy. His gaze penetrated the mists of the far north, and we find Gregory forestalling (as indeed his great predecessor the first Gregory had done before him) the missionaries of our own day in the expedient of training young natives to preach the faith among their countrymen, over which there was so much modern rejoicing when it was first adopted in recent days, as an entirely new and altogether wise thing. Gregory the Great had already practised it with his Anglo-Saxon boys: and Gregory VII. recommended it to Olaf, king of Norway, to whom he wrote that he would fain have sent a sufficient number of priests to his distant country: "But as this is very difficult because of the great distance and difference of language, we pray you, as we have also asked from the king of Denmark, to send to our apostolical court some young nobles of your country in order that being nourished with care in divine knowledge under the wings of St. Peter and St. Paul, they may carry back to you the counsels of the Apostolical See, arriving among you, not as men unknown, but as brothers—and preaching to you the duties of Christianity, not as strangers and ignorant, but as men whose language is yours, and who are yet trained and powerful in knowledge and morals." Thus, while the toils were gathering round his feet at home, and the most ancient centre of Christianity was ready to cast him out as a fugitive, the great Pope was extending the invisible links of Christian fealty to the ends of the earth.

It was in the year 1080, three years after the events of Canossa, that the next step was taken by Gregory. In that long interval he had never ceased to insist upon the only lawful mode of settling the quarrel, i.e., the assembly in Germany of all the persons most concerned, to take the whole matter into solemn consideration and come to a permanent conclusion upon grounds more solid than the appeal to arms which ravaged the empire, and which, constantly fluctuating, gave the temporary victory now to one side, now to the other. The age was far from being ripe for any such expedient as arbitration, and the ordeal of arms was its most natural method: yet the proposal had proceeded in the first place from the Teutonic princes themselves, and it was entirely in accordance with German laws and primitive procedure. And except the Pope, or some other great churchman, there was no possible president of such a Diet, or any one who could have had even a pretence of impartiality. He was the only man who could maintain the balance and see justice done, even in theory: for the awe of his presence and of his spiritual powers might have restrained these fierce princes and barons and made some sort of reasonable discussion possible. For all these reasons, and also no doubt to assert practically the claim he had made for himself and his successors to be the judges of the earth and settle all such disputes as representatives of God, he was very unwilling to give up the project. It had come to be evident, however, in the spring of 1080 when Lent began and the usual Council of the Lateran assembled, that Henry would never consent to this Diet, the very reason for which was the discussion of claims which he held as divine and infallible. Rudolf, his rival, was, or professed to be, as anxious for it as the Pope, though he never had taken any step to make Gregory's journey across the Alps possible. But at last it would seem that all parties gave up the thought of any such means of making peace. The state of affairs in Germany was daily becoming more serious, and when the envoys of Rudolf, after many fruitless visits to Rome, appeared at last with a sort of ultimatum, demanding that some decisive step should be taken to put an end to the suspense, there was no longer any possibility of further delay. Henry also sent ambassadors on the same occasion: but they came late, and were not received. The Council of the Lateran met, no doubt with many searchings of heart and a great excitement pervading the assembly where matters of such importance were about to be settled, and such a decision as had never been asked from any Pope before, was about to be given from the chair of St. Peter to a half-believing, half-rebellious world. Whether any one really believed that a question involving the succession to the empire could be solved in this way, it is impossible to tell: but the envoys of Rudolf, whose arms had been for the moment victorious, and who had just driven Henry a fugitive before him, made their appeal to the Pope with a vehemence almost tragic, as to one whose power and responsibility in the matter were beyond doubt. The statement of their case before the Council was as follows:

"We delegates of our lord the King, Rudolf, and of the princes, we complain before God, and before St. Peter to you our father and this holy Council, that Henry, set aside by your Apostolic authority from the kingdom, has notwithstanding your prohibition invaded the said kingdom, and has devastated everything around by sword and fire and pillage; he has with impious cruelty, driven bishops and archbishops out of their sees, and has distributed their dignities as fiefs among his partisans. Werner of holy memory, archbishop of Magdeburg, has perished by his tyranny; Aldebert, bishop of Worms, is still held in prison contrary to the Apostolic order; many thousands of men have been slaughtered by his faction, many churches pillaged, burned and destroyed. The assaults of Henry upon our princes because they withdrew their obedience from him according to the command of the Apostolic See, are numberless. And the assembly which you have desired to call together, Holy Father, for the establishment of the truth and of peace, has not been held, solely by the fault of Henry and his adherents. For these reasons we supplicate your clemency in our own name and that of the Holy Church of God to do justice upon the sacrilegious violator of the Church."

It will be remarked that the whole blame of the struggle is here thrown upon the Church:—as in the remonstrance of the Saxon bishops, who say not a word of their national grievances against Henry, which nevertheless were many and great, and the real foundation of the war—but entirely attribute it to the action of Gregory in excommunicating and authorising them to withdraw their homage from the king. Nobody, we think, can read the chaotic and perplexing history of the time without perceiving how mere a pretext this was, and how little in reality the grievances of the Church had to do with the internecine struggle. The curious thing however, is that Gregory, either in policy or self-deception, accepts the whole responsibility and is willing to be considered the cause and maker of these deadly wars, as if the struggle had been one between the Church and the King alone. A sense of responsibility was evidently strong in his mind as he rose from his presiding chair on this great occasion, in the breathless silence that followed the complaint and appeal of Rudolf's emissaries. Not a voice in defence of Henry had been raised in the Council, which, as many voices were in his favour in preceding assemblies, shows the consciousness of the conclave that another and more desperate phase of the quarrel had been reached.

Gregory himself had sat silent for a moment, overwhelmed with the awe of the great crisis. When he rose it was with a breaking voice and tears in his eyes: and the form of the deliverance was as remarkable as its tenor. Gregory addressed—not the Council: but, with an extraordinary outburst of emotion, the Apostle in whose name he pronounced judgment and in whose chair he sat. Nothing could have been more impressive than this sudden and evidently spontaneous change from the speech expected from him by the awed and excited assembly, to the personal statement and explanation given forth in trembling accents but with uplifted head and eyes raised to the unseen, to the great potentate in heavenly places whose representative he believed himself to be. However vague might be the image of the apostle in other eyes, to Gregory St. Peter was his living captain, the superior officer of the Church, to whom his second in command had to render an account of his procedure in face of the enemy. The amazement of that great assembly, the awe suddenly imposed even on the great body of priests, too familiar perhaps with holy things to be easily impressed—much more on the startled laymen, Rudolf's envoys and their attendants, by this abstract address, suddenly rising out of the midst of the rapt assembly to a listener unseen, must have been extraordinary. It marked, as nothing else could have done, the realisation in Gregory's mind of a situation of extraordinary importance, such an emergency as since the Church came into being had seldom or never occurred in her history before. He stood before the trembling world, himself a solitary man shaken to the depths, calling upon his great predecessor to remember that it was not with his own will that he had ascended that throne or accepted that responsibility—that it was Peter, or rather the two great leaders of the Church together, Peter the Prince of the Apostles, Paul the Doctor and instructor of the nations, who had chosen him, not he who had thrust himself into their place. To these august listeners he recounted everything, the whole story of the struggle, the sins of Henry, his submission and absolution, his renewed rebellion, always against the Church, against the Apostles, against the Ecclesiastical authority: while the breathless assembly around, left out in this solemn colloquy, sat eager, drinking in every word, overcome by the wonder of the situation, the strange attitude of the shining figure in the midst, who was not even praying, but reporting, explaining every detail to his unseen general above. Henry had been a bad king, a cruel oppressor, an invader of every right: and it would have been the best policy of the Churchman to put forth these effective arguments for his overthrow. But of this there is not a word. He was a rebel against the Church, and by the hand of the Church it was just and right that he should fall.

One cannot but feel a descent from this high and visionary ground in the diction of the sentence that followed, a sentence not now heard for the first time, and which perhaps no one there felt, tremendous as its utterance was, to be the last word in this great quarrel.

"Therefore trusting to the judgment and to the mercy of God, and of the Holy Mother of God, and armed with your authority, I place under excommunication and I bind with the chains of anathema, Henry called King, and all his fellow sinners; and on the part of Almighty God, and of You, shutting him out henceforward from the kingdoms of Germany and of Italy, I take from him all royal power and dignity; I forbid any Christian to obey him as king; and I absolve from their sworn promises all those who have made, or may make, oaths of allegiance to him. May this Henry with his fellow sinners have no force in fight and obtain no victory in life!"

Having with like solemnity bestowed upon Rudolf the kingdom of Germany (Italy is not named) with all royal rights, the Pope thus concludes his address to the spiritual Heads in heaven of the Church on earth:

"Holy Fathers and Lords! let the whole world now know and understand that as you can bind and loose in heaven, you can also upon earth give and take away from each according to his merits, empires, kingdoms, principalities, duchies, marquisates, counties, and all possessions. You have often already taken from the perverse and the unworthy, patriarchal sees, primacies, archbishoprics, and bishoprics, in order to bestow them upon religious men. If you thus judge in things spiritual, with how much more power ought you not to do so in things secular! And if you judge the angels who are the masters of the proudest princes, what may you not do with the princes, their slaves! Let the kings and great ones of the earth know to-day how great you are, and what your power is; let them fear to neglect the ordinances of the Church! Accomplish quickly your judgment on Henry so that to the eyes of all it may be apparent that it falls upon him not by chance but by your power. Yet may his confusion turn to repentance, that his soul may be saved in the day of the Lord."

[ISLAND ON TIBER]

Whether the ecstasy of his own rapt and abstract communion with the unseen, that subtle inspiration of an Invisible too clearly conceived for human weakness to sustain, had gone to Gregory's head and drawn him into fuller expression of this extraordinary assertion and claim beyond all reason: or whether the long-determined theory of his life thus found complete development it is difficult to tell. These assumptions were, indeed, the simple and practical outcome of claims already made and responsibilities assumed: claims which had been already put feebly into operation by other Popes before. But they had never before been put into words so living or so solemn. Gregory himself had, hitherto, claimed only the right to judge, to arbitrate at the head of a National Diet. He had not himself, so far as we can see, assumed up to this moment the supposed rights of Peter, alone and uncontrolled. He had given England to William, but only on the warrant of the bond of Harold solemnly sworn before the altar. He had made legitimate the claims already established by conquest of Robert Guiscard and others of the Norman conquerors. But the standard set up in the Lateran Council of 1080 was of a far more imperative kind, and asserted finally through Peter and Paul, his holy fathers and lords, an authority absolute and uncompromising such as made the brain reel. This extraordinary address must have sent a multitude, many of them no doubt ordinary men with no lofty ideal like his own, back to their bishoprics and charges, swelling with a sense of spiritual grandeur and power such as no promotion could give, an inspiration which if it made here and there a high spirit thrill to the necessities of a great position, was at least as likely to make petty tyrants and oppressors of meaner men. The only saving clause in a charge so full of the elements of mischief, is that to the majority of ordinary minds it would contain very little personal meaning at all.

From this time nothing was possible but war to the death between Gregory and Henry, the deposed king, who was as little disposed to accept his deposition as any anathema was able to enforce it. We have already remarked on various occasions, and it is a dreadful coming down from the height of so striking a scene, and so many great words, to be obliged to repeat it: yet it is very evident that notwithstanding the terrible pictures we have had of the force of these anathemas, they made very little difference in the life of the world. There were always schismatic or rebellious priests enough to carry on, in defiance of the Pope, those visible ceremonies and offices of religion which are indispensable to the common order of life. There were, no doubt, great individual sufferings among the faithful, but the habits of ordinary existence could only have been interfered with had every bishop and every priest been loyal to the Pope, which was far from being the case.

It was at the conclusion of this Council that Gregory is said to have sent to Rudolf the famous imperial crown bearing the inscription

Petra dedit Petro, Petrus diadema Rodolpho,

of which Villemain makes the shabby remark that, "After having held the balance as uncertain, and denied the share he had in the election of Rudolf, now that it was confirmed by success Gregory VII. claimed it for himself and the Church."—a conclusion neither in consonance with the facts nor with the character of the man.

That Henry should receive this decision meekly was of course impossible. Once more he attempted to make reprisals in an assembly held at Brixen in the following June, when by means of the small number of thirty bishops, chiefly excommunicated persons, and, of course, in any case without any right to judge their superior, Gregory himself was once more deposed, excommunicated, and cut off from the communion of these ecclesiastics and their followings. In the sentence given by this paltry company, Gregory is accused of following the heresy of Berengarius, whose recantation had the year before been received at the Lateran: and also of being a necromancer and magician, and possessed by an evil spirit. These exquisite reasons are the chief of the allegations against him, and the principal ground upon which his deposition was justified. Guibert of Ravenna, long his enemy, and one of the excommunicated, was elected by the same incompetent tribunal as Pope in his place, naturally without any of the canonical requirements for such an election; though we are told that Henry laid violent hands on the bishop of Ostia whose privilege it was to officiate at the consecration of the Popes, and who was then in foreign parts acting as legate, in order to give some show of legality to the election. Guibert however, less scrupulous than the former intruder Cadalous, took at once the title of Clement III. The great advantage of such a step, beside the sweetness of revenge, no doubt was that it practically annulled the papal interdict so far as the knowledge of the vulgar was concerned: for so long as there were priests to officiate, a bishop to preside, and a Pope to bless and to curse, how should the uninstructed people know that their country was under any fatal ban? To make such a universal excommunication possible the whole priesthood must have been subject and faithful to the one sole authority in the Church.

Unfortunately for the prestige of Gregory, Henry was much more successful in the following year in all his enterprises, and it was Rudolf, the friend and elected of the Pope, and not his adversary, who died after a battle which was not otherwise decisive. This event must have been a great blow and disappointment as well as an immediate and imminent danger. For some time, however, the ordinary course of life went on in Rome, and Gregory, by means of various negotiations, and also no doubt by reason of his own consciousness of the pressing need for a champion and supporter, made friends again with Robert Guiscard, exerting himself to settle the quarrels between him and his neighbours, and to win him thus by good offices to the papal side. To complete this renewal of friendship Gregory, though ailing, and amid all these tumults beginning to feel the weight of years, made a journey to Benevento, which belonged to the Holy See, and there met his former penitent and adversary, the brave and wily Norman. The interview between them took place in sight of a great crowd of the followers of both and the inhabitants of the whole region, assembled in mingled curiosity and reverence, to see so great a scene. The Norman, relieved of the excommunications under which he had lain for past offences, and endowed with the Pope's approval and blessing, swore fealty and obedience to Gregory, promising henceforward to be the champion of Holy Church, protecting her property and her servants, keeping her counsel and acknowledging her authority.

"From this hour and for the future I will be faithful to the Holy Roman Church, and to the Apostolic See, and to you, my lord Gregory, the universal Pope. I will be your defender, and that of the Roman Church, aiding you according to my power to maintain, to occupy, and to defend the domains of St. Peter and his possessions, against all comers, reserving only the March of Fermo, of Salerno, and of Amalfi, concerning which no definite arrangement has yet been made."

These last, and especially the town of Salerno, one of the cities la piu bella e piu deliziosa of Italy, says old Muratori, had been recently taken by Guiscard from their Prince Gisolfo, a protégé and friend of the Pope, who excepts them in the same cautious manner from the sanction given to Robert's other conquests. Gregory's act of investiture is altogether a very cautious document:

I Gregory, Pope, invest you Duke Robert, with all the lands given you by my predecessors of holy memory, Nicolas and Alexander. As for the lands of Salerno, Amalfi and a portion of the March of Fermo, held by you unjustly, I suffer it patiently for the present, having confidence in God and in your honesty, and that you will conduct yourself in future for the honour of God and St. Peter in such a manner as becomes you, and as I may tolerate, without risking your soul or mine.

It is not likely that Gregory hoped so much from Guiscard's probity as that he would give up that citta deliziosa, won by his bow and his spear. Nor was he then aware how his own name and all its associations would remain in Salerno, its chief distinction throughout all the ages to come.

The life of Gregory had never been one of peace or tranquillity. He had been a fighting man all his days, but during a great part of them a successful one: the years which remained to him, however, were one long course of agitations, of turmoil, and of revolution. In 1081 Henry, scarcely successful by arms, but confident in the great discouragement of the rival party through the death of Rudolf, crossed the Alps again, and after defeating Matilda, ravaging her duchy and driving her to the shelter of Canossa, marched upon Rome. Guibert of Ravenna, the Anti-Pope, accompanied him with many bishops and priests of his party. On his first appearance before Rome, the energy of Gregory, and his expectation of some such event, had for once inspired the city to resistance, so that the royal army got no further than the "fields of Nero," outside the walls of the Leonine city to the north of St. Peter's, by which side they had approached Rome. Henry had himself crowned emperor by his anti-pope in his tent, an act performed by the advice of his schismatic bishops, and to the great wonder, excitement, and interest of the surrounding people, overawed by that great title which he had not as yet ventured to assume. This futile coronation was indeed an act with which he amused himself periodically during the following years from time to time. But the heats of summer and the fever of Rome soon drove the invaders back. In 1082 Henry returned to the attack, but still in vain. In 1083 he was more successful, and seized that portion of Rome called the Leonine city, which included St. Peter's and the tombs of the Apostles, the great shrine which gave sanctity to the whole. The Pope, up to this time free, though continually threatened by his enemies, and still carrying on as best he could the universal affairs of the Church, was now forced to retire to St. Angelo. He was at this moment without defender or champion on any side. The brave Matilda, ever faithful, was shut up in impregnable Canossa. Guiscard, after having secured all that he wanted from Gregory, had gone off upon his own concerns, and was now struggling to make for himself a footing in Greece, indifferent to the Pope's danger. The Romans, after the brief interval of inspiration which gave them courage to make a stand for the Pope and the integrity of their city, had fallen back into their usual weakness, dazzled by Henry's title of Emperor, and cowed by the presence of his Germans at their gates. They had never had any spirit of resistance, and it was scarcely to be expected of a corrupt and fickle population, accustomed for ages to be the toys of circumstance, that they should begin a nobler career now. And there the Pope remained, shut up in that lonely stronghold, overlooking the noisy and busy streets which overflowed with foreign soldiers and the noise of arms, while in the Church of St. Peter close by, Guibert the mock Pope assembled a mock council to absolve the new Emperor from all the anathemas that had followed one another upon his head.

There was much discussion and debate in that strange assembly, in which every second man at least must have had in his secret heart a sense of sacrilege, over this subject. They did not apparently deny the legal weight of these anathemas, which they recognised as the root and origin of all the misfortunes that had followed; but they maintained a feeble contention that the proceedings of Gregory had been irregular, seeing that Henry had never had the opportunity of defending himself. Another of the pretensions attributed to the Roman Church by her enemies, and this time with truth, as it has indeed become part of her code—was, as appears, set up on this occasion for the first time, and by the schismatics. Gregory had forbidden the people to accept the sacraments from the hands of vicious or simoniacal priests. Guibert, called Clement III., and his fictitious council declared with many learned quotations that the sacraments in themselves were all in all, and the administrators nothing; and that though given by a drunkard, an adulterer, or a murderer, the rites of the Church were equally effectual. It was however still more strange that in this assembly, made up of schismatics, many of them guilty of these very practices, a timid remonstrance should have been made against the very sins which had separated them from the rest of the Church and which Gregory had spent his life in combating. The Pope had not been successful either in abolishing simony or in maintaining celibacy and continence among the clergy, but he had roused a universal public opinion, a sentiment stronger than himself, which found a place even in the mind of his antagonist and rival in arms.

Thus the usurper timidly attacked with arguments either insignificant or morally dangerous the acts of the Pope—yet timidly echoed his doctrine: with the air throughout all of a pretender alarmed by the mere vicinity of an unfortunate but rightful monarch. Guibert had been bold enough before; he had the air now of a furtive intruder trembling lest in every chance sound he might hear the step of the true master returning to his desecrated house.

The next event in this curious struggle is more extraordinary still. Henry himself, it is evident, must have been struck with the feeble character of this unauthorised assembly, notwithstanding that the new Pope was of his own making and the council held under his auspices; or perhaps he hoped to gain something by an appearance of candour and impartiality though so late in the day. At all events he proposed, immediately after the close of the fictitious council, to the citizens and officials who still held the other portions of the city, in the name of Gregory—to withdraw his troops, to leave all roads to Rome free, and to submit his cause to another council presided over by Gregory and to which, as in ordinary cases, all the higher ranks of the clergy should be invited. It is impossible to conceive a more extraordinary contradiction of all that had gone before. The proposal, however, strange as it seems, was accepted and carried out. In November, 1083, this assembly was called together. Henry withdrew with his army towards Lombardy, the peaceful roads were all reopened, and bishops and abbots from all parts of Christendom hastened, no doubt trembling, yet excited, to Rome. Henry, notwithstanding his liberality of kind offers, exercised a considerable supervision over these travellers, for we hear that he stopped the deputies whom the German princes had sent to represent them, and also many distinguished prelates, two of whom had been specially attached to his mother Agnes, along with one of the legates of the Pope. The attempt to pack the assembly, or at least to weed it of its most remarkable members in this way was not, however, successful, and a large number of ecclesiastics were got together notwithstanding all the perils of the journey.

The meeting was a melancholy one, overshadowed by the hopelessness of a position in which all the right was on one side and all the power on the other. After three days' deliberation, which came to nothing, the Pope addressed—it was for the last time in Rome—his faithful counsellors. "He spoke with the tongue of an angel rather than of a man," bidding them to be firm and patient, to hold fast to the faith, and to quit themselves like men, however dark might be the days on which they had fallen. The entire convocation broke forth into tears as the old man concluded.

But Gregory would not be moved to any clemency towards his persecutor. He yielded so far as not to repeat his anathema against him, excommunicating only those who by force or stratagem had turned back and detained any who were on their way to the Council. But he would not consent to crown Henry as emperor, which—notwithstanding his previous coronation in his tent by Guibert, and a still earlier one, it is said, at Brixen immediately after the appointment of the anti-pope—was what the rebellious monarch still desired; nor would he yield to the apparent compulsion of circumstances and make peace, without repentance on the part of Henry. No circumstances could coerce such a man. The fruitless council lasted but three days, and separated without making any change in the situation. The Romans, roused again perhaps by the brief snatch of freedom they had thus seemed to have, rose against Henry's garrison and regained possession of the Leonine city which he had held: and thus every particular of the struggle was begun and repeated over again.

This extraordinary attempt, after all that had happened—after the council in which Henry had deposed Gregory, the council in St. Peter's itself, held by the anti-pope, and all the abuse he had poured upon "the monk Hildebrand," as he had again and again styled the Pope—by permitting an assembly in which the insulted pontiff should be restored to all his authority and honours, to move Gregory to accept and crown him, is one of the most wonderful things in history. But the attempt was the last he ever made, as it was the most futile. After the one flash of energy with which Rome renewed the struggle, and another period of renewed attacks and withdrawals, Henry became master of the city, though never of the castle of St. Angelo where Gregory sat indomitable, relaxing not a jot of his determination and strong as ever in his refusal to withdraw, unless after full repentance, his curse from Henry. Various castles and fortified places continued to be held in the name of the Pope, both within and without the walls of the city: which fact throws a curious light upon its existing aspect: but these remnants of defence had little power to restrain the conqueror and his great army.

And then again Rome saw one of those sights which from age to age had become familiar to her, the triumph of arms and overwhelming force under the very eyes of the imprisoned ruler of the city. The Lateran Palace, so long deserted, awoke to receive a royal guest. The sober courts of the papal house blazed with splendid costumes and resounded with all the tumult of rejoicing and triumph. The first of the great ceremonies was the coronation of the Archbishop Guibert as Clement III., which took place in Passion Week in the year 1084. Four months before Gregory had descended from his stronghold to hold the council in which Henry had still hoped to persuade or force him to complaisance, flinging Guibert lightly away; but the king's hopes had failed and Guibert was again the temporary symbol of that spiritual power without which he could not maintain himself. On Easter Sunday following, three great processions again streamed over the bridge of St. Angelo under the eyes, it may be, of Gregory high on the battlements of his fortress, or at least penetrating to his seclusion with the shouts and cheers that marked their progress—the procession of the false Pope, that of the king, that of Bertha the king's wife, whom it had required all the efforts of Gregory and his faithful bishops to preserve from a cruel divorce: she who had set her maids with baton and staff to beat the life half out of that false spouse and caitiff knight in his attempt to betray her. The world had triumphed over the Church, the powers of darkness over those of light, a false and treacherous despot, whose word even his own followers held as nothing, over the steadfast, pure, and high-minded priest, who, whatever we may think of his motives—and no judgment upon Gregory can ever be unanimous—had devoted his life to one high purpose and held by it through triumph and humiliation, unmoved and immovable. Gregory was as certain of his great position now, the Vicar of Christ commissioned to bind and to loose, to judge with impartiality and justice all men's claims, to hold the balance of right and wrong all over the world, as he watched the gay processions pass, and heard the heralds sounding their trumpets and the anti-pope, the creature of Henry's will, passing by to give his master (for the third time) the much-longed-for imperial crown, as when he himself stood master within the battlements of Canossa and raised that suppliant king to the possibilities of empire from his feet.

It is a curious detail adding a touch to the irony which mingles with so many human triumphs and downfalls, that the actual imperial crown seems at one time at least to have been in Gregory's keeping. During the abortive council, for which, for three days he had returned to the Lateran, he offered, though he refused to place it on his head, to give it up to Henry's hands, letting it down with a cord from a window of St. Angelo. This offer, which could scarcely be other than ironical, seems to have been refused; but whether Gregory retained it in St. Angelo, or left it to be found in the Lateran treasury by the returning king, there is no information. If it was a fictitious crown which was placed upon Henry's head by the fictitious Pope, the curious travesty would be complete. And history does not say even why the ceremony performed before by the same hands on the banks of the Tiber, should have dropped out of recollection as a thing that had not been.

During all this time nothing had been heard of Robert Guiscard who had so solemnly taken upon him the office of champion of the Holy See and knight of St. Peter. He had been about his own business, pursuing his conquests, eager to carve out new kingdoms for himself and his sons: but at last the Pope's appeals became too strong to be resisted. Henry, whose armies had doubtless not improved in force during the desultory warfare which must have affected more or less the consciences of many, and the hot summers, unwholesome for northerners, did not await the coming of this new and formidable foe. Matilda's Tuscans were more easily overcome than Guiscard's veterans of northern race. He called in his men from all the petty sieges which were wearing them out, and from that wall which he had forced the Romans with their own pitiful hands to build as a base of attacks against St. Angelo, and withdrew in haste, leaving the terrified citizens whom he had won over to his party, as little apt to arms as their forefathers had been, and in the midst of a half-ruined city—the strong positions in which were still held by the friends of the Pope—to do what they could against the most dreaded troops of Christendom. The catastrophe was certain before it occurred. The resistance of the Romans to Robert Guiscard was little more than nominal, only enough to inflame the Normans and give the dreadful freedom of besiegers to their armed hordes. They delivered the Pontiff, but sacked the town which lay helpless in its ruins at their feet; not even the churches were spared, nor their right of sanctuary acknowledged as six hundred years before Attila had acknowledged it. And all the fault of the Pope, as who could wonder if the sufferers cried? It was he who had brought these savages upon them, as it was he who had exposed them before to the hostility of Henry. Gregory had scarcely come forth from his citadel and returned to his palace when Rome was filled with scenes of blood and carnage, such as recalled the invasions of Huns and Vandals. The flames of the burning city lighted up the skies as he came forth in sorrow, delivered from his bondage, but a sad and burdened man. The chroniclers tell us that he flung himself at the feet of Guiscard to beg him to spare the city, crying out that he was Pope for edification and not for ruin. And though his prayer was to some extent granted, there is little doubt that here at the last the heart of Gregory and his courage were broken, and that though his resolution was never shaken, his strength could bear little more. This was the greatest, as it was the most uncalled for, misfortune of his life.

He held a strange council in desolate Rome in the few days that followed, in which he repeated his anathema against Henry, Guibert, and all the clergy who were living in rebellion or in sin. But it would seem that even at such a moment the council was not unanimous and that the spirit of his followers was broken and cowed, and few could follow him in the steadfastness of his own unchangeable mind. And when this tremulous and disturbed assembly was over, held in such extraordinary circumstances, fierce Normans, wild Saracens forming the guard of the Pontiff, fire and ruin, and the shrieks of victims still disturbing the once peaceful air—Gregory, sick at heart, turned his back upon the beloved city which he had laboured so hard to make once more mistress of the world. Perhaps he was not aware that he left Rome for ever; but the conditions of that last restoration had broken his heart. He to bring bloodshed and rapine! he who was Pope to build up and not to destroy! It was more than the man who had borne all things else could endure. No doubt it was a crowning triumph for Guiscard to lead away with him the rescued Pontiff, and pose before all the world as Gregory's deliverer. The journey itself, however, was not without perils. The Campagna and all the wilder country beyond, about the Pontine marshes, was full of freebooting bands, Henry's partisans, or calling themselves so, who harassed the march with guerilla attacks. In one such flying combat a monk of Gregory's own retinue was killed, and the Pope had to ride like the men-at-arms, now starting at daybreak, now travelling deep into the night. At Monte Cassino, in the great convent where his friend Desiderius, who was to be his successor reigned, there was a welcome pause, and he had time to refresh himself among his old friends, the true brethren and companions of his soul. The legends of the monks—or was it the pity of the ages beginning already to awaken and rising to a great height of human compunction by the time the early historians began to write his story?—accord to him here that compensation of divine acknowledgment which the heart recognises as the only healing for such wounds. Some one among the monks of Monte Cassino saw a dove hovering over his head as he said mass. Perhaps this was merely a confusion with the legend of Gregory the Great, his predecessor, to whom that attribute belongs; perhaps some gentle brother whose heart ached with sympathy for the suffering Pope had glamour in his eyes and saw.

Gregory continued his journey, drawn along in the army of Robert Guiscard as in a chariot, which began now to be, as he reached the south Italian shores, a chariot of triumph. All the towns and villages on the way came out to greet the Pope, to ask his blessing. The bishop of Salerno, with his clergy, came forth in solemn procession with shining robes and sacred standards to meet him. Neither Pope nor prince could have found a more exquisite retreat from the troubles of an evil world. The beautiful little city, half Saracenic, in all the glory of its cathedral still new and white and blooming with colour like a flower, sat on the edge of that loveliest coast, the sea like sapphire surging up in many lines of foam, the waves clapping their hands as in the Psalms, and above, the olive-mantled hills rising soft towards the bluest sky, with on every point a white village, a little church tower, the convent walls shining in the sun. It is still a region as near Paradise as human imagination can grasp, more fair than any scene we know. One wonders if the Pope's heart had sufficient spring left in it to take some faint delight in that wonderful conjunction of earth and sea and sky. But such delights were not much thought of in his day, and it is very possible he might have felt it something like a sin to suffer his heart to go forth in any such carnal pleasure.

But at least something of his old energy came back when he was settled in this wonderful place of exile. He sent out his legates to the world, charged with letters to the faithful everywhere, to explain the position of affairs and to assert, as if now with his last breath, that it was because of his determination to purify the Church that all these conspiracies had risen against him—which was indeed, notwithstanding all the developments taken by the question, the absolute truth. For it was Gregory's strongly conceived and faithfully held resolution to cleanse the Church from simony, to have its ministers and officers chosen for their worth and virtue, and power to guide and influence their flocks for good, and not because they had wealth to pay for their dignity and to maintain it, which was the beginning of the conflict. Henry who refused obedience and made a traffic of the holiest offices, and those degenerate and rebellious priests who continued to buy themselves into rich bishoprics and abbacies in defiance of every ecclesiastical law and penalty, were the original offenders, and ought before posterity at least to bear the brunt.

It is perhaps indiscreet to speak of an event largely affecting modern life in such words, but there is a whimsical resemblance which is apt to call forth a smile between the action of a large portion of the Church of Scotland fifty years ago, and the life struggle of Gregory. In the former case it was the putting in of ministers to ecclesiastical benefices by lay authority, however veiled by supposed popular assent, which was believed to be an infringement of the divine rights of the Church, and of the headship of Christ, by a religious body perhaps more scornful and condemnatory than any other of everything connected with a Pope. It was not supposed in Scotland that the humble candidates for poor Scotch livings bought their advancement; but the principle was the same.

In the case of Gregory the positions thus bought and sold were of very great secular importance, carrying with them much wealth, power, and outward importance, which was not the case in the other; but in neither case were the candidates chosen canonically or for their suitableness to the charge, but from extraneous motives and in spite of the decisions of the Church. This was to destroy the headship of Peter, the authority of his representative, the rights of the sacred Spouse of Christ. Both claims were perfectly honest and true. But Gregory, as in opposition to a far greater grievance, and one which overspread all Christendom, was by far the more distinguished confessor, as he was the greater martyr of the Holy Cause.

For this was undoubtedly the first cause of all the sufferings of the Pontiff, the insults showered upon him, the wrongs he had to bear, the exile in which he died. The question has been settled against him, we believe, in every country, even the most deeply Christian. Scotland indeed has prevailed in having her own way, but that is because she has no important benefices, involving secular rank and privilege. No voice in England has ever been raised in defence of simony, but the congé d'élire would have been as great an offence to Pope Gregory, and as much of a sin to Dr. Chalmers, as the purchase of an archbishopric in one case, or the placing of an unpopular preacher in another. The Pope's claim of authority over both Church and world, though originally and fundamentally based upon his rights as the successor of Peter, developed out of this as the fruit out of the flower. From a religious point of view, and if we could secure that all Popes, candidates for ecclesiastical offices, and electors to the same, should be wise and good men, the position would be unassailable; but as it is not so, the question seems scarcely worth risking a man's living for, much less his life. But perhaps no man since, if it were not his successors in the popedom, had such strenuous reasons to spend his life for it as Gregory, as none has ever had a severer struggle.

This smaller question, however, though it is the fundamental one, has been almost forgotten in the struggle between the Pope and the Emperor—the sacred and the secular powers—which developed out of it. The claim to decide not only who was to be archbishop but who was to be king, rose into an importance which dwarfed every other. This was not originated by Gregory, but it was by his means that it became the great question of the age, and rent the world in twain. The two great institutions of the Papacy and the Empire had been or seemed to be an ideal method of governing the world, the one at the head of all spiritual concerns, the other commanding every secular power and all the progress of Christendom. Circumstances indeed, and the growth of independence and power in other nations, had circumscribed the sphere of the Empire, while the Papacy had grown in influence by the same means. But still the Empire was the head of the Christian world of nations, as the Pope was the head of those spiritual princedoms which had developed into so much importance. When the interests were so curiously mingled, it was certain that a collision must occur one time or another. There had been frequent jars, in days when the power of the Empire was too great for anything but a momentary resistance on the part of the Pope. But when the decisive moment came and the struggle became inevitable, Gregory—a man fully equal to the occasion—was there to meet it. His success, such as it was, was for later generations. To himself personally it brought the crown of tragedy only, without even any consciousness of victory gained.

The Pope lived not quite a year in Salerno. He died in that world of delight in the sweetness of the May, when all is doubly sweet by those flowery hills and along that radiant shore. Among his last words were these:—"My brethren, I make no account of my good works: my only confidence is that I have always loved justice and hated iniquity:—and for that I die in exile," he added before his end. In the silence and the gathering gloom one of his attendants cried out, "How can you say in exile, my lord, you who, the Vicar of Christ and of the apostles, have received all the nations for your inheritance, and the world for your domain?" With these words in his ears the Pope departed to that country which is the hope of every soul, where iniquity is not and justice reigns.

He died on the 25th May, 1085, not having yet attained his seventieth year. He had been Pope for twelve years only, and during that time had lived in continual danger, fighting always for the Church against the world. A suffering and a melancholy man, his life had none of those solaces which are given to the commonest and the poorest. His dearest friends were far from him: the hope of his life was lost: he thought no doubt that his standard fell with him, and that the labours of his life were lost also, and had come to nothing. But it was not so; Gregory VII. is still after these centuries one of the greatest Popes of Rome: and though time has wrought havoc with that great ideal of the Arbiter and universal Judge which never could have been made into practical reality, unless the world and the Church had been assured of a succession of the wisest and holiest of men—he yet secured for a time something like that tremendous position for a number of his successors, and created an opinion and sentiment throughout Christendom that the reforms on which he insisted ought to be, which is almost the nearest that humanity can come to universal reformation. The Church which he left seemed shattered into a hundred fragments, and he died exiled and powerless; but yet he opened the greatest era of her existence to what has always been one of the wisest, and still remains one of the strongest institutions in the world, against which, in spite of many errors and much tribulations, it has never been in the power of the gates of hell to prevail.

[IN THE VILLA BORGHESE]

FOOTNOTES:

[3] This personage is always called Cencio in the Italian records. He is supposed by some to have been of the family of the Crescenzi, of which name, as well as of Vincenzo, this is the diminutive.

[4] On this subject the records differ, some asserting these letters to have been read at once on Roland's removal, some that the sitting was adjourned after that wonderful incident.

[THE FOUNTAIN OF THE TORTOISE]

It is not our object, the reader is aware, to give here a history of Rome, or of its pontiffs, or of the tumultuous world of the Middle Ages in which a few figures of Popes and Princes stand out upon the ever-crowded, ever-changing background, helping us to hear among the wild confusion of clanging swords and shattering lances, of war cries and shouts of rage and triumph—and to see amidst the mist and smoke, the fire and flame, the dust of breached walls and falling houses. Our intention is solely to indicate those among the chiefs of the Church who are of the most importance to the great city, which, ever rebelling against them, ever carrying on a scarcely broken line of opposition and resistance, was still passive in their hands so far as posterity is concerned, dragged into light, or left lying in darkness, according as its rulers were. It is usual to say that the great time of the Church, the age of its utmost ascendency, was during the period between Gregory VII. and Innocent III., the first of whom put forth its claim as Universal Arbiter and Judge as no one had ever done before, while the second carried that claim to its climax in his remarkable reign—a reign all-influencing, almost all-potent, something more like a universal supremacy and rule over the whole earth than has ever been known either before or since. The reader has seen what was the effect upon his world of the great Hildebrand: how he laboured, how he proclaimed his great mission, with what overwhelming faith he believed in it, and, it must be added, with how little success he was permitted to carry it out. This great Pope, asserting his right as the successor of Peter to something very like a universal dominion and the power of setting down and raising up all manner of thrones, principalities, and powers, lived fighting for the very ground he stood on, in an incessant struggle not only with the empire, but with every illiterate and ignoble petty court of his neighbourhood, with the robber barons of the surrounding hills, with the citizens in his streets, with the villagers on his land—and, after having had more than once his independent realm restricted to the strong walls of St. Angelo, had at last to abandon his city for mere safety's sake, and die in exile far from the Rome he loved.

The life of the other we have now to trace, as far as it is possible to keep the thread of it amid the tremendous disorders, disastrous wars and commotions of his time, in all of which his name is so mingled that in order to distinguish his story the student must be prepared to struggle through what is really the history of the world, there being scarcely a corner of that world—none at least with which history was then acquainted—which was not pervaded by Innocent, although few we think in which his influence had any such power as is generally believed.

This Pope was not like Hildebrand a man of the people. He had a surname and already a distinguished one. Lothario Conti, son of Trasimondo, lord of Ferentino, of the family of the Dukes of Spoleto, was born in the year 1161 in the little town of Anagni, where his family resided, a place always dear to him, and to which in the days of his greatness he loved to retire, to take refuge from the summer heats of Rome or other more tangible dangers. He was thus a member of the very nobility with which afterwards he had so much trouble, the unruly neighbours who made every road to Rome dangerous, and the suzerainty of the Pope in many cases a simple fiction. The young Lothario had three uncles in the Church in high places, all of them eventually Cardinals, and was destined to the ecclesiastical profession, in which he was so certain of advancement, from his birth; he was educated partly at Rome, at the school of St. John Lateran, specially destined for the training of the clergy, and therefore spent his boyhood under the shadow of the palace which was to be his home in later years. From Rome he went to the

University of Paris, one of the greatest of existing schools, and studied canon law so as to make himself an authority on that subject, then one of the most engrossing and important branches of learning. He loved the "beneficial tasks," and perhaps also the freedom and freshness of university life, where probably the bonds of the clerical condition were less felt than in other places, though Innocent never seems to have required indulgence in that respect. Besides his readings in canon law, he studied with great devotion the Scriptures, and their interpretation, after the elaborate and highly artificial fashion of the day, dividing each text into a myriad of heads, and building up the most recondite argument on a single phrase with meanings spiritual, temporal, scholastic, and imaginary. There he made several warm friends, among others Robert Curzon, an Englishman who served him afterwards in various high offices, not so much to the credit of their honour in later times as of the faithfulness of their friendship.

Young Conti proceeded afterwards to Bologna, then growing into great reputation as a centre of instruction. He had, in short, the best education that his age was acquainted with, and returned to his ecclesiastical home at Rome and the protection of his Cardinal-uncles a perfectly well-trained and able young man, learned in all the learning of his day, acquainted more or less with the world, and ready for any service which the Church to which he was wholly devoted might require of him. He was a young man certain of promotion in any case. He had no sooner taken the first orders than he was made a canon of St. Peter's, of itself an important position, and his name very soon appears as acting in various causes brought on appeal to Rome—claims of convents, complaints among others of the monks of Canterbury in some forgotten question, where he was the champion of the complainants who were afterwards to bring him into so much trouble. These appeals were constantly occurring, and occupied a great deal of the time and thoughts of that learned and busy court of Rome, the Consistory, which became afterwards, under Innocent himself, the one great court of appeal for the world.

About a hundred years had passed between the death of the great Pope Gregory, the monk Hildebrand, and the entrance of Lothario Conti upon public life; but when the reader surveys the condition of that surging sea of society—the crowded, struggling, fighting, unresting world, which gives an impression of being more crowded, more teeming with wild life and force, with constant movement and turmoil, than in our calmer days, though no doubt the facts are quite the reverse—he will find but little change apparent in the tremendous scene. As Gregory left the nations in endless war and fighting, so his great successor found them—king warring against king, prince against prince, count against count, city against city, nay, village against village, with a wide margin of personal struggle around, and a general war with the Church maintained by all. A panorama of the kingdoms of the world and the glory of them, could it have been furnished to any onlooker, would have showed its minutest lines of division by illuminations of devastating fire and flame, by the clangour of armies in collision, by wild freebooters in roaming bands, and little feudal wars in every district: every man in pursuit of something that was his neighbour's, perhaps only his life, a small affair—perhaps his wife, perhaps his lands, possibly the mere satisfaction of a feud which was always on hand to fill up the crevices of more important fighting.

With more desperate hostility still the cities in pairs set themselves against each other, all flourishing, busy places, full of industry, full of invention, but fuller still of rage against the brother close by, of the same tongue and race, Milan against Parma, Pisa against Genoa, Florence against all comers. Bigger wars devastated other regions, Germany in particular in all its many subdivisions, where it seems impossible to believe there could ever be a loaf of bread or a cup of wine of native growth, so perpetually was every dukedom ravaged and every principality brought to ruin. Two Emperors claiming the allegiance of that vast impossible holy Empire which extended from the northern sea to the soft Sicilian shores, two Popes calling themselves heads of the Church, were matters of every day. The Emperors had generally each a show of right; but the anti-popes, though they had each a party, were altogether false functionaries with no show of law in their favour, generally mere creatures of the empire, though often triumphant for a moment. In Gregory's day Henry IV. and Rudolf were the contending Emperors. In those of Innocent they were Philip and Otho. There were no doubt different principles involved, but the effect was the same; in both cases the Popes were deeply concerned, each asserting a prerogative, a right to choose between the contending candidates and terminate the strife. That prerogative had been boldly claimed and asserted by Gregory; in the century that followed every Pope had reasserted and attempted with all his might to enforce it; but though Innocent is universally set forth as the greatest and most powerful of all who did so, and as in part responsible for almost every evil thing that resulted, I do not myself see that his interference was much more potential than that of Gregory, of which also so much is said, but which was so constantly baulked, thwarted, and contradicted in his day. So far as the Empire was concerned the Popes certainly possessed a right and privilege which gave a certain countenance to their claim, for until crowned by the ruling Pontiff no Emperor had full possession of his crown: but this did not affect the other Christian kingdoms over which Innocent claimed and attempted to exercise the same prerogative. The state of things, however, to the spectator is very much the same in the one century as the other. The age of storm and stress for the world of Christendom extended from one to another; no doubt progress was being made, foundations laid, and possibilities slowly coming into operation, of which the beginnings may be detected even among all the noise and dust of the wars; but outwardly the state of Europe was very much the same under Innocent as under Gregory: they had the same difficulties to encounter and the same ordeals to go through.

Several short-lived Popes succeeded each other on the papal throne after Innocent began to ascend the steps of ecclesiastical dignity, which were so easy to the nephew of three Cardinals. He became a canon of St. Peter's while little more than twenty-one. Pope Lucius III. employed him about his court, Pope Gregory VIII. made him a sub-deacon of Rome. Pope Clement III. was his uncle Octavian, and made him Cardinal of "St. Sergius and St. Bacchus," a curious combination, and one which would better have become a more jovial priest. Then there came a faint and momentary chill over the prospects of the most rising and prosperous young ecclesiastic in Rome. His uncle was succeeded in the papal chair by a certain Cardinal, old and pious but little known to history, a member of the Orsini family and hostile to the Conti, so that our young Cardinal relapsed a little into the cold shade. It is supposed to be during this period that he turned his thoughts to literature, and wrote his first book, a singular one for his age and position—and yet perhaps not so unlike the utterance of triumphant youth under its first check as might be supposed—De contemptu mundi, sive de miseriis humanæ conditionis, is its title. It was indeed the view of the world which every superior mind was supposed to take in his time, as it has again become the last juvenile fashion in our own; but the young Cardinal Conti had greater justification than our young prophets of evil. His work is full, as it always continues to be in his matured years, of the artificial constructions which Paris and Bologna taught, and which characterise the age of the schoolmen: and it is not to be supposed that he had much that was new to say of that everlasting topic which was as hackneyed in the twelfth century as it is in the nineteenth. After he has explained that "every male child on his birth cries A and every female E; and when you say A with E it makes Eva, and what is Eva if not heu! ha!—alas!"—he adds a description of the troubles of life which is not quite so fanciful.

"We enter life amid pains and cries, presenting no agreeable aspect, lower even than plants and vegetables, which give forth at least a pleasant odour. The duration of life becomes shorter every day; few men reach their fortieth year, a very small number attain the sixtieth.... And how painful is life! Death threatens us constantly, dreams frighten us, apparitions disturb us, we tremble for our friends, for our relations; before we are prepared for it misfortune has come: sickness surprises us, death cuts the thread of our life. All the centuries have not been enough to teach even to the science of medicine the different kind of sufferings to which man's fragility exposes him. Human nature is more corrupt from day to day; the world and our bodies grow old. Often the guilty is acquitted and the innocent is punished.... Every thought, every act, all the arts and devices are employed for no other end but to secure the glory and favour of men. To gain honour he uses flattery, he prays, he promises, he tries every underground way if he cannot get what he wants by direct measures; or he takes it by force if he can depend on the support of friends or of relations. And what a burden are those high dignities! When the ambitious man has attained the height of his desires his pride knows no bounds, his arrogance is without restraint; he believes himself so much a better man as he is more elevated in position; he disdains his friends, recognises no one, despises his oldest connections, walking proudly with his head high, insolent in words, the enemy of his superiors and the tyrant of his dependents."

The young Cardinal spares no class in his animadversions, but the rich are held up as warnings rather than the poor, and the vainglory of the miserable sons of Adam is what disgusts him most. Here is a passage which carries us into the inner life of that much devastated, often ruined Rome, which nevertheless at its most distracted moment was never quite devoid of the splendours and luxuries it loved.

"Has not the prophet declared his anathema against luxury in dress? Yet the face is coloured with artificial colours as if the art of man could improve the work of God. What can be more vain than to curl the hair, to paint the cheeks, to perfume the person? And what need is there for a table ornamented with a rich cover, and laid with knives mounted in ivory, and vases of gold and silver? What more vain again than to paint the rooms, to cover the doors with fine carvings, to lay down carpets in the ante-chambers, to repose one's self on a bed of down, covered with silken stuffs and surrounded with curtains?"

Some historical commentators take exception to this picture as imaginary, and too luxurious for the age; but after all a man of the time must have known better than even Muratori our invaluable guide: and we find again and again in the descriptions of booty taken in the wars, accounts of the furniture of the tents of the conquered, silver and gold vases, and costly ornaments of the table which if carried about to embellish the wandering and brief life of a campaign would surely be more likely still to appear among the riches of a settled dwelling-place. Cardinal Lothario however did not confine himself altogether to things he had intimate knowledge of, for one of his illustrations is that of a discontented wife, a character of which he could have no personal experience: the picture is whimsically correct to conventional precedent; it is the established piece which we are so well acquainted with in every age.

"She desires fine jewels and dresses, and beautiful furniture without regard to the means of her husband; if she does not get them she complains, she weeps, she grumbles and murmurs all night through. Then she says, 'So-and-so is much more expensive than I am, and everybody respects her; while I, because I am poor, they look at me disdainfully over their shoulders.' Nobody must be praised or loved but herself; if any other is beloved she thinks herself hated; if any one is praised she thinks herself injured. She insists that everybody should love what she loves, and hate what she hates; she will submit to nothing but dominates all; everything ought to be permitted to her, and nothing forbidden. And after all (adds the future pope) whatever she may be, ugly, sick, mad, imperious, ill-tempered, whatever may be her faults, she must be kept if she is not unchaste; and even then though the man may separate from her, he may not take another."

This sounds as if the young Cardinal would have been less severe on the question of divorce than his clerical successors. The book however is quite conventional, and gives us little insight into the manner of man he was. Nevertheless there are some actual thoughts in the perennial and often repeated argument, as when he maintains the sombre doctrine of eternal punishment with the words: "Deliverance will not be possible in hell, for sin will remain as an inclination even when it cannot be carried out." He also wrote a book upon the Mass in the quiet of these early days; and was diligent in performing his duties and visiting the poor, to whom he was always full of charity.

[THE CAPITOL]

When the old Pope died, however, there seems not to have been a moment's doubt as to who should succeed him. The Cardinal Lothario was but thirty-seven, his ability and learning were known indeed, but had as yet produced no great result: his family was distinguished but not of force enough to overawe the Conclave, and nothing but the impression produced upon the minds of his contemporaries by his character and acquirements could account for his early advancement. Pope Celestine in dying had recommended with great insistence the Cardinal John Colonna as his successor; but this seems scarcely to have been taken into consideration by the electors, who now, according to Hildebrand's institution, somewhat modified by succeeding Popes, performed their office without any pretence of consulting either priests or people, and still less with any reference to the Emperor. The election was held, not in the usual place, but in a church now untraceable, "Ad Septa Solis," situated somewhere near the Colosseum. The object of the Cardinals in making the election there, was safety, the German troops of the Emperor being at the time in possession of the entire surrounding country up to the very gates of Rome, and quite capable of making a raid upon the Lateran to stop any proceedings which might be disagreeable to their master; for the imperial authorities on their part had never ceased to assert their right to be consulted in the election of a Pope. Lothario made the orthodox resistance without which perhaps no early Pope ever ascended the papal throne, protesting his own incapacity for so great an office; but the Cardinals insisted, not granting him even a day's delay to think over it. The first of the Cardinal-deacons, Gratiano, an old man, invested him with the pluvial and greeted him as Innocent, apparently leaving him no choice even as to his name. Thus the grave young man, so learned and so austere, in the fulness of his manhood ascended St. Peter's chair. There is no need to suppose that there was any hypocrisy in his momentary resistance; the papal crown was very far from being one of roses, and a young man, even if he had looked forward to that position and knew himself qualified for it, might well have a moment's hesitation when it was about to be placed on his head.

When the announcement of the election was made to the crowd outside, it was received with cries of joy: and the entire throng—consisting no doubt in a large degree of the clergy, mingled with the ever-abundant masses of the common people,—accompanied the Cardinals and the Pope-elect to the Lateran, though that church, one would suppose, must still have been occupied by the old Pope on his bier, and hung with the emblems of mourning: for it was on the very day of Celestine's death that the election took place. Muratori suggests a mistake of dates. "Either Pope Celestine must have died a day sooner, or Innocent have been elected a day later," he says. After the account, more full than usual, of the ceremonies of the election, the brilliant procession, and the rejoicing crowd, sweep away into the silence, and no more is heard of them for six weeks, during which time Lothario waited for the Rogation days, the proper time for ordinations; for though he had already risen so high in the Church, he was not yet a priest, but only in deacon's orders, which seems to have been the case in so many instances. The two ordinations took place on two successive days, the 22nd and 23rd of February, 1198.

When he had received the final consecration, and had been invested with all the symbols of his high office—the highest in the world to his own profound consciousness, and to the belief of all who surrounded him—Pope Innocent III. rose from the papal chair, of which he had just taken possession, and addressed the immense assembly. Whether it had become the custom to do so we are not informed. Innocent, so far as can be made out from his writings, was no heaven-born preacher, yet he would seem to have been very ready to exercise his gift, such as it was; it appears to have been his habit to explain himself in all the most important steps in life, and there could be no greater occasion than this. He stood on the steps of his throne in all the glory of his shining robes, over the dark and eager crowd, and there addressed to them a discourse in which the highest pretensions, yet the most humble faith, are conjoined, and which shows very clearly with what intentions and ideas he took upon himself the charge of Christendom, and supreme authority not only in the Church but in the world. He had been deeply agitated during the ceremonies of his consecration, shedding many tears; but now he had recovered his composure and calm.

There are four sermons existing among his works which bear the title In consecratione Romani Pontificis. Whether they were all written for this occasion, in repeated essays before he satisfied himself with what he had to say, is unknown. Perhaps some of them were used on the occasion of the consecration of other great dignitaries of the Church; but this is merely conjecture. We have at all events under his own hand the thoughts which arose in the mind of such a man at the moment of such an elevation: the conception of his new and great dignity which he had formed and held with the faith of absolute conviction: and the purposes with which he began his work. His text, if text was necessary for so personal a discourse, was the words of our Lord: "Who then is that faithful and wise steward whom his lord shall make ruler over his household, to give them their portion of meat in due season?" We quote of course from our own authorised version: the words of the Vulgate, used by Innocent, do not put this sentence in the form of a question. His examination of the meaning of the word "house" is the first portion of the argument.

"He has constituted in the fulness of his power the pre-eminence of the Holy See that no one may be so bold as to resist the order which He has established, as He has Himself said: 'Thou art Peter, and upon this stone I will build my Church; and the gates of hell shall not prevail against it.' For as it is He who has laid the foundations of the Church, and is himself that foundation, the gates of hell could in nothing prevail against it. And this foundation is immovable: as says the Apostle, no man can lay another foundation than that which is laid, which is Jesus Christ.... This is the building set upon a rock of which eternal truth has said: 'The rain fell and the wind blew and beat upon that house; but it stood fast, for it was built upon a rock,' that is to say, upon the rock of which the Apostle said: 'And this Rock was Christ.' It is evident that the Holy See, far from being weakened by adversity, is fortified by the divine promise, saying with the prophet: 'Thou hast led me by the way of affliction.' It throws itself with confidence on that promise which the Lord has made to the Apostles: 'Behold I am with you always, even unto the end of the world.' Yes, God is with us, who then can be against us? for this house is not of man but of God, and still more of God made man: the heretic and the dissident, the evil-minded wolf endeavours in vain to waste the vineyard, to tear the robe, to smother the lamp, to extinguish the light. But as was said by Gamaliel: 'If the work is of man it will come to naught; if it is of God ye cannot overthrow it: lest haply ye should find that you are fighting against God.' The Lord is my trust. I fear nothing that men can do to me. I am the servant whom God has placed over His house; may I be prudent and faithful so as to give the meat in due season!"

He then goes on to describe the position of the faithful steward.

"I am placed over this house. God grant that I were as eminent by my merit as by my position. But it is all the more to the honour of the mighty Lord when He fulfils His will by a feeble servant; for then all is to His glory, not by human strength but by force divine. Who am I, and what is my father's house, that I should be set over kings, that I should occupy the seat of honour? for it is of me that the prophet has said, 'I have set thee over people and kingdoms, to tear and to destroy, to build and to plant.' It is of me that the Apostle has said, 'I have given thee the keys of the kingdom of heaven; whatsoever thou bindest on earth is bound in heaven.' And again it is to me (though it is said by the Lord to all the Apostles in common), 'The sins which you remit on earth shall be remitted; and those you retain shall be retained.' But speaking to Peter alone He said: 'That which thou bindest on earth shall be bound in heaven.' Peter may bind others but he cannot be bound himself.

"You see now who is the servant placed over the house; it is no other than the Vicar of Jesus Christ, the Successor of Peter. He is the intermediary between God and men, beneath God, yet above men, much lower than God but more than men; he judges all but is judged by none as the Apostle says: 'It is God who is my judge.' But he who is raised to the highest degree of consideration is brought down again by the functions of a servant that the humble may be raised up and greatness may be humiliated—for God resists the proud but gives grace to the humble. O greatest of wise counsels—the greater you are the more profoundly must you humble yourself before them all! You are there as a light on a candlestick that all in the house may see; when that light becomes dark, how thick then is the darkness? You are the salt of the earth: when that salt becomes without savour, with what will you be seasoned? It is good for nothing but to be thrown out and trodden under foot of men. For this reason much is demanded from him to whom much is given."

Thus Innocent began his career, solemnly conscious of the greatness of his position. But the reader will perceive that nothing could be more evangelical than his doctrine. Exalting as he does the high claims of Peter, he never falls into the error of supposing him to be the Rock on which the foundations of the Church are laid. On the other hand his idea of the Pope as beneath God but above men, lower than God but greater than men, is startling. The angel who stopped St. John in his act of worship proclaiming himself one of the Apostles' brethren the prophets, made no such pretension. But Innocent was strong in the consciousness that he himself, the arbiter on earth of all reward and punishment, was the judge of angels as well as men, and held a higher position than any of them in the hierarchy of heaven.

The first act of Innocent's papacy was the very legitimate attempt to establish his own authority and independence at home. The long subsistence of the idea that only a Pope-king with enough of secure temporal ascendency to keep him free at least from the influence of other sovereigns, could be safe in the exercise of his spiritual functions—is curious when we think of the always doubtful position of the Popes, who up to this time and indeed for long after retained the most unsteady footing in their own metropolis, the city which derived all its importance from them. The Roman citizens took many centuries to learn—if they were ever taught—that the seat of a great institution like the Church, the court of a monarch who claimed authority in every quarter of the world, was a much more important thing than a mere Italian city, however distinguished by the memories and relics of the past. We doubt much whether the great Innocent, the most powerful of the Popes, had more real control over the home and centre of his supposed dominions at the outset of his career than Pope Leo XIII., dispossessed and self-imprisoned, has now, or might have if he chose. No one can doubt that Innocent chose—and that with all the strength and will of an unusually powerful character—to be master in his own house: and he succeeded by times in the effort; but, like other Popes, he was at no time more than temporarily successful. Twice or oftener he was driven by the necessity of circumstances, if not by actual violence, out of the city: and though he never altogether lost his hold upon it, as several of his predecessors had done, it was at the cost of much trouble and exertion, and at the point of the sword, that he kept his place in Rome.

He was, however, in the first flush of his power, almost triumphant. He succeeded in changing the fluctuating constitution of the Roman commonwealth, which had been hitherto presided over by a Præfect, responsible to the Emperor and bound to his service, along with a vague body of senators, sometimes larger, sometimes smaller in number, and swayed by every popular demonstration or riot—the very best machinery possible for the series of small revolutions and changes of policy in which Rome delighted. It was in every way the best thing for the interests of the city that it should have learnt to accept the distinction, all others having perished, of being the seat of the Church. For Rome was by this time, as may be said, the general court of appeal for Europe; every kind of cause was tried over again before the Consistory or its delegates; and a crowd of appellants, persons of all classes and countries, were always in Rome, many of them completely without acquaintance in the place, and dependent only upon such help and guidance as money could procure, money which has always been the great object of desire to most communities, the means of grandeur and greatness, if also of much degradation. It must not be supposed, however, that the Pope took advantage of any such mean motive to bind the city to himself. He guarded against the dangers of such a situation indeed by a strenuous endeavour to clear his court, his palace, his surroundings, of all that was superfluous in the way of luxury, all that was merely ostentatious in point of attendants and services, and all that was mercenary among the officials. When he succeeded in transferring the allegiance of the Præfect from the Emperor to himself, he made at the same time the most stringent laws against the reception of any present or fee by that Præfect and his subordinate officers, thus securing, so far as was possible, the integrity of the city and its rulers as well as their obedience. And whether in the surprise of the community to be so summarily dealt with, or in its satisfaction with the amount of the present, which Innocent, like all the other Popes, bestowed on the city on his consecration, he succeeded in carrying out these changes without opposition, and so secured before he went further a certain shelter and security within the walls of Rome.

He then turned his eyes to the States of the Church, the famous patrimony of St. Peter, which at that period of history St. Peter was very far from possessing. Certain German adventurers, to whom the Emperor had granted the fiefs which Innocent claimed as belonging to the Holy See, were first summoned to do homage to the Pope as their suzerain, then threatened with excommunication, then laid under anathema: and finally—Markwald and the rest remaining unconvinced and unsubdued—were driven out of their ill-gotten lands by force of arms, which proved the most effectual way. The existence of these German lords was the strongest argument in favour of the Papal sway, and was efficacious everywhere. The towns little and great, scattered over the March of Ancona, the duchy of Spoleto, and the wealthy district of Umbria, received the Pope and his envoys as their deliverers. The Tedeschi were as fiercely hated in Italy in the twelfth century as they were in recent times; and with greater reason, for their cruelty and exactions were indescribable. And the civic spirit which in the absence of any larger patriotism kept the Italian race in energetic life, and produced in every little centre of existence a longing for at least municipal liberty and independence, hailed with acclamations the advent of the head of the Church, a suzerain at least more honourable and more splendid than the rude Teuton nobles who despised the race over which they ruled.

[PORTA MAGGIORE]

That spirit had already risen very high in the more important cities of Northern Italy. The Lombard league had been already in existence for a number of years, and a similar league was now formed by the Tuscan towns which Innocent also claimed, in right of the legacy made to the Church more than a hundred years before by the great Countess Matilda, the friend of Hildebrand, but which had never yet been secured to the Holy See. The Tuscans had not been very obedient vassals to Matilda herself in her day; and they were not likely perhaps to have afforded much support to the Popes had the Church ever entered into full enjoyment of Matilda's splendid legacy. But in the common spirit of hatred against the Tedeschi, the cruel and fierce German chiefs to whom the Emperor had freely disposed of the great estates and castles and rich towns of that wonderful country, the supremacy of the Church was accepted joyfully for the moment, and all kinds of oaths taken and promises made of fidelity and support to the new Pope. When Innocent appeared, as in the duchy of Spoleto, in Perugia, and other great towns, he was received with joy as the saviour of the people. We are not told whether he visited Assisi, where at this period Francis of that city was drawing crowds of followers to his side, and the idea of a great monastic order was rising out of the little church, the Portiuncula, at the bottom of the hill: but wherever he went he was received with joy. At Perugia, when the papal procession streamed through the crowded gates, and reached the old palazzo appropriated for its lodging, there suddenly sprang up a well which had been greatly wanted in the place, a spring of fresh water henceforward and for ever known as the Fontana di Papa. These cities all joined the Tuscan league against the Germans with the exception of Pisa, always arrogant and self-willed, which stood for those same Germans perhaps because their rivals on every side were against them. It was at this period, some say, and that excellent authority Muratori among them, that the titles of Guelf and Ghibelline first came into common use, the party of the Pope being Guelf, and that of the empire Ghibelline—the one derived from the house of Este, which was descended from the old Teutonic race of Guelf on the female side, the other, Waiblingen, from that of Hohenstaufen, also descended by the female side from a traditionary German hero. It is curious that these distant ancestors should have been chosen as godfathers of a struggle with which they had nothing to do, and which arose so long after their time.

Innocent, however, was not so good a Guelf as his party, for the Pope was the guardian and chief defender, during his troubled royal childhood, of Frederic of Sicily, afterwards the Emperor Frederic II., but at the beginning of Pope Innocent's reign a very helpless baby prince, fatherless, and soon, also, motherless, and surrounded by rapacious Germans, each man fighting for a scheme of his own, by which to transfer the insecure crown to his own head, or at least to rob it of both power and revenue. The Pope stood by his helpless ward with much steadfastness through the very brief years of his minority—for Frederic seems to have been a married man and ambitious autocrat at an age when ordinary boys are but beginning their studies—and had a large share eventually in his elevation to the imperial throne: notwithstanding that he belonged to the great house which had steadily opposed the claims of the Papacy for generations. It must be added, however, that the great enterprises of Innocent's first years could not have been taken up, or at least could not have been carried to so easy and summary a conclusion—whole countries recovered, the Emperor's nominees cast out, the cities leagued against their constant invaders and oppressors—had there been a fierce Emperor across i monti ready to descend upon the always struggling, yet continually conquered, Italy. Henry VI., the son of Barbarossa, had died in the preceding year, 1198, in the flower of his age, leaving only the infant Frederic, heir to the kingdom of Sicily in right of his mother, behind him to succeed to his vast possessions. But the crown of Germany was, at least nominally, elective not hereditary; and notwithstanding that the Emperor had procured from his princes a delusive oath of allegiance to his child, that was a thing which in those days no one so much as thought of keeping. The inactivity of the forces of the Empire was thus accounted for; the holders of imperial fiefs in Italy were left to fight their own battles, and thus the Pope with very moderate forces, and the cities of Tuscany and Umbria, each for its own hand, were able to assert themselves, and drive out the oppressors. And there was a period of hopefulness and comparative peace.

Innocent, however, who had the affairs of the world on his hands, and could not long confine himself to those of St. Peter's patrimony, was soon plunged into the midst of those ever-recurring struggles in Germany, too important in every way not to call for his closest attention. The situation was very much, the same as that in which Gregory VII. had found himself involved: with this great difference, however, that both competitors for the German crown were new men, and had neither any burden of crime against the Church nor previous excommunications on their head. Philip of Suabia, the brother of Henry VI., had been by him entrusted—with that curious confidence in the possibility of self-devotion on the part of others, which dying men, though never capable of it themselves, so often show—with the care and guardianship of his child and its interests, and the impossible task of establishing Frederic, as yet scarcely able to speak, upon a throne so important and so difficult. Philip did, it is said, his best to fulfil his trust and hurried from Sicily to the heart of Germany as soon as his brother was dead, with that object; but the princes of his party feared an infant monarch, and he was himself elected in the year 1199 to the vacant seat. There seems no criminality in this in the circumstances, for the little Frederic was in any case impossible; but Philip had inherited a hatred which he had not done anything personally to deserve. "So exasperated were the Italians against the Germans by the barbarous government of Frederic I. and Henry VI. his son, that wherever Philip passed, whether through Tuscany or any other district, he was ill-used and in danger of his life, and many of his companions were killed," says Muratori. He had thus a strong feeling against him in Italy independent of any demerit of his own.

It is a little difficult, however, to understand why Pope Innocent, so careful of the interests of the little king in Sicily, should have so strongly and persistently opposed his uncle. Philip had been granted possession of the duchy of Tuscany, which the Pope claimed as his own, and some offence on this account, as well as the shadow of an anathema launched against him for the same reason by one of Innocent's predecessors, may have prepossessed the Pope against him; but it is scarcely possible to accept this as reason enough for his determined opposition.

The rival emperor Otho, elected by the Guelf party, was the son of Henry the Lion, the nephew of Richard Plantagenet of England the Coeur de Lion of our national story, and of a family always devoted to the Church. The two men were both young and full of promise, equally noble and of great descent, related to each other in a distant degree, trained in a similar manner, each of them quite fit for the place which they were called to occupy. It seems to the spectator now as if there was scarcely a pin to choose between them. Nor was it any conflict of personal ambition which set them up against each other. They were the choice of their respective parties, and the question was as clearly one of faction against faction as in an Irish village fight.

These were circumstances, above all others, in which the arbitration of such an impartial judge as a Pope might have been of the greatest advantage to the world. There never was perhaps such an ideal opportunity for testing the advantage and the possibility of the power claimed by the Papacy. Otho was a young gallant at Richard's court expecting nothing of the kind, open to all kinds of other promotions, Earl of Yorkshire, Count of Poitou—the first not successful because he could not conciliate the Yorkshiremen, perhaps difficult in that way then as now: but without, so far as appears, any thought of the empire in his mind. And Philip had the right of possession, and was the choice of the majority, and had done no harm in accepting his election, even if he had no right to it. The case was quite different from that of the similar struggle in which Gregory VII. took part. At the earlier period the whole world, that was not crushed under his iron foot, had risen against Henry IV. His falsehood, his cruelty, his vices, had alienated every one, and nobody believed his word or put the smallest faith even in his most solemn vows. The struggle between such an Emperor and the head of the Church was naturally a struggle to death. One might almost say they were the impersonations of good and evil, notwithstanding that the good might be often alloyed, and the evil perhaps by times showed gleams of better meaning. But the case of Philip and Otho was completely different. Neither of them were bad men nor gave any augury of evil. The one perhaps by training and inclination was slightly a better Churchman than the other at the beginning of his career; but, on the other hand, Philip had various practical advantages over Otho which could not be gainsaid.

Had Pope Innocent been the wholly wise man and inspired judge he claimed by right of his office to be, without prejudice or bias, nobly impartial, holding the balance in a steady hand, was not this the very case to test his powers? Had he helped the establishment of Philip in the empire and deprecated the introduction of a rival, a great deal of bloodshed might have been avoided, and a satisfactory result, without any injustice, if not an ideal selection, might have been obtained. All this was problematical, and depended upon his power of getting himself obeyed, which, as it turned out, he did not possess. But in this way, in all human probability, he might have promoted peace and secured a peaceful decision; for Philip's election was a fait accompli, while Otho was not as yet more than a candidate. The men were so equal otherwise, and there was so little exclusive right on one side or the other, that such facts as these would naturally have been taken into the most serious consideration by the great, impartial, and unbiassed mind which alone could have justified the interference of the Pope, or qualified him to assume the part of arbitrator in such a quarrel. He did not attempt this, however, but took his place with his own faction as if he had been no heaven-sent arbiter at all, but a man like any other. He has himself set forth the motives and reasons for his interference, with the fulness of explanation which he loved. The bull in which he begins by setting aside the claims of his own infant ward, Frederic, to whom his father Henry had caused the German princes to swear fealty, as inadmissible—the said princes being freed of their oath by the death of the Emperor, a curious conclusion—is in great part an indictment of Philip, couched in the strongest and most energetic terms. In this document it is stated in the first place that Philip had been excommunicated by the previous Pope, as having occupied by violence the patrimony of St. Peter, an excommunication taken off by the legate, but not effectually; again he was involved in the excommunication of Markwald and the other invaders of Sicily whom he had upheld; in the next place he had been false to the little Frederic, whose right he had vowed to defend, and was thus perjured, though the princes who had sworn allegiance to the child were not so. Then follows a tremendous description of Philip's family and predecessors, of their dreadful acts against the Popes and Church, of the feuds of Barbarossa with the Holy See, of the insults and injuries of which all had been equally guilty. A persecutor himself and the son of persecutors, how could the Pope support the cause of Philip? The argument is full of force and strengthened by many illustrations, but it proves above all things that Innocent was no impartial judge, but a man holding almost with passion to his own side.

The pleas in favour of Otho are much weaker. It is true, the Pope admits, that he had been elected by a minority, but then the number of notable and important electors were as great on his side as on Philip's: his house had a purer record than that of Philip: and finally he was weaker than Philip and more in need of support; therefore the Holy See threw all its influence upon his side. Nothing could be feebler than this conclusion after the force of the hostile judgments. We fear it must be allowed that Innocent being merely a man (which is the one unsurmountable argument against papal infallibility) went the way his prepossessions and inclinations—and also, we have no doubt, his conviction of what was best—led him, and was no more certain to be right in doing so than any other man.

Having come to this conclusion, Innocent took his stand with all the power and influence he possessed upon Otho's side—a support which probably kept that prince afloat and made the long struggle possible, but was quite inadequate to set him effectually on the throne, or injure his rival in any serious way. In this partisan warfare, excommunication was the readiest of weapons; but excommunications, as we have already said, were very ineffectual in the greater number of cases; for Germany especially was full of great prelates as great as the princes, in most cases of as high race and as much territorial power, and they by no means always agreed with the Pope, and made no pretence of obeying him; and how was the people to find out that they lay under anathema when they saw the offices of the Church carried on with all the splendour of the highest ritual, its services unbroken, however the Pope might thunder behind? Some of these prelates—such as Leopold of Mainz, appointed by the Emperor, to whom Innocent refused his sanction, electing on his own part another archbishop, Siegfried, in his stead, who was not for many years permitted even to enter the diocese of which he was the titular head—

maintained with Rome a struggle as obstinate as any secular prince. They were as powerful as the princes among whom they sat and reigned, and elected emperors. Most of the German bishops, we are told, were on Philip's side notwithstanding the decision of the Pope against him. In such circumstances the anathema was little more than a farce. The Archbishop of Mainz was excommunicated as much as the emperor, but being all the same in full possession of his see and its privileges, naturally acted as though nothing had happened, and found plenty of clergy to support him, who carried on the services of the Church as usual and administered the sacraments to Philip as much as if he had been in the full sunshine of Papal favour.

Such a chance had surely never been foreseen when the expedient of excommunication was first thought of, for it is apt to turn every claim of authority into foolishness—threats which cannot be carried out being by their nature the most derogatory things possible to the person from whom they proceed. The great prelates of Germany were in their way as important as the Pope, their position was more steadily powerful than his, they had vassals and armies to defend them, and a strong and settled seat, from which it was as difficult, or indeed even dangerous, to displace them as to overthrow a throne. And what could the Pontiff do when they disobeyed and defied him? Nothing but excommunicate, excommunicate, for which they cared not a straw—or depose, which was equally unimportant, when, as happened in the case of Mainz, the burghers of the cathedral city vowed that the substituted bishop should never enter their gates.

Thus the ten years' struggle produced nothing but humiliation for Innocent. The Pope did not relax in his determined opposition, nor cease to threaten penalties which he could not inflict until nearly the end of the struggle; and then when the logic of events began, it would appear, to have a little effect upon his mind, and he extended with reluctance a sort of feeble olive-branch towards the all-victorious Philip—a larger fate came in, and changed everything with the sweeping fulness of irresistible power. It is not said anywhere, so far as we know, that the overtures of Innocent brought the Emperor ill-luck; but it would certainly have been so said had such an accident occurred under Pio Nono, for example, who, it is well known, had the evil eye. For no sooner had Innocent taken this step than Philip's life came to a disastrous end. The Count Palatine of Wittelsbach, a great potentate of Germany, who had some personal grievance to avenge, demanded a private audience and murdered him in his temporary dwelling, in the moment of his highest prosperity. Thus in the twinkling of an eye everything was changed. The House of Hohenstaufen went down in a moment without an attempt made to prop it up. And Otho, who was at hand, already a crowned king, and demanding no further trouble, at once took the vacant place. This occurred in the year 1208—ten years after the beginning of the struggle. But in this extraordinary and sudden transformation of affairs Innocent counted for nothing; he had not done it nor even contributed to the doing of it: though he had kept the air thunderous with anathemas, and the roads dusty with the coming and going of his legates for all these unhappy years.

Otho, however, did not at first forget the devotion which the Pope had shown him in his evil days, when triumph so unexpected and accidental (as it seemed) came to him. After taking full possession of the position which now there was no one to contest with him, he made a triumphal progress across the Alps, and was crowned Emperor at Rome, the last and crowning dignity which Philip had never been able to attain: where he behaved himself with much show of affection and humility to Innocent, whose stirrup he held like the most devoted son of the Church as he professed to be. There was much swearing of oaths at the same time. Otho vowed to preserve all the rights of the Church, and, with reservations, to restore the Tuscan fiefs of Matilda, and all the presents with which from time to time the former Emperors had endowed the Holy See, to the Pope's undisturbed possession. Rome was a scene of the utmost display and splendour during this imperial visit. Otho had come at the head of his army, and lay encamped at the foot of Monte Mario, where now the little group of pines stand up against the sky in the west, dark against the setting sun. It was October when all the summer glow and heat is mellowed by autumnal airs, and the white tents shone outside the city gates with every kind of splendid cognisance of princes and noble houses, and magnificence of mediæval luxury. The ancient St. Peter's, near the camp, was then planted, we are told, in the midst of a great number of convents, churches, and chapels, "Like a majestic mother surrounded by beautiful daughters"—though there was no Vatican as yet to add to its greatness: but the line of the walls on the opposite side of the river and the ancient splendour of Rome, more square and massive in its lingering classicism than the mediæval towns to which the German forces were more accustomed, shone in the mid-day sun: while towards the left the great round of St. Angelo dominated the bridge and the river, and all the crowds which poured forth towards the great church and shrine of the Apostles. There was, however, one shadow in this brilliant picture, and that was the fact that Rome within her gates lay not much unlike a couching lion, half terrified, half excited by the army outside, and not sure that the abhorred Tedeschi might not at any moment steal a march upon her, and show underneath those splendid velvet gloves, all heavy with embroideries of gold, the claws of that northern wolf which Italy had so often felt at her very heart. It is a curious sign of this state of agitated feeling that Otho published in Rome before his coronation a solemn engagement in his own name and that of his army that no harm should be done to the city, to the Pope and Cardinals, or to the people and their property, while he remained there. He had strong guards of honour at all the adjacent gates as a precautionary measure while the great ceremonies of his consecration went on.

It was not the present St. Peter's, it need not be said, which, hung with splendid tapestries and lit with innumerable candles, glistening with precious marbles and gilding, and decorated with all the splendour of the church in silver and gold, received this great German potentate for that final act which was to make his authority sacred, and establish him beyond all question Emperor of the Holy Roman Empire, a dignity which only the Pope could complete, which was nothing, bringing no additional dominion with it, yet of the utmost importance in the estimation of the world. It cannot but have been that a sense of elation, perhaps chequered with doubt, but certainly sanctioned by many noble feelings—convictions that God had favoured his side in the long run, and that a better age was about to begin—must have been in Innocent's mind as he went through the various ceremonies of the imposing ritual, and received the vows of the monarch and placed the imperial crown on his head. We are not told, however, whether there was any alarm in the air as the two gorgeous processions conjoined, sweeping forth from the gates of St. Peter's, and across the bridge and by all the crowded ways, to the other side of the city, to the Lateran palace, where the great banquet was held. Otho with his crown on his head held the stirrup of the Pope at the great steps of St. Peter's as Innocent mounted; and the two greatest potentates of earth, the head of the secular and the head of the spiritual, dividing, with the most confusing elasticity of boundary between them, the sway of the world, rode alone together, followed by all that was most magnificent in Germany and Italy, the great princes, the great prelates vying with each other in pomp and splendour. The air was full of the ringing of bells and the chanting of the priests; and as they went along through the dark masses of the people on every side, the officers of Otho scattered largesse through all the crowded streets, and everything was festivity and general joy.

But when the great people disappeared into the papal palace, and the banquet was spread, the German men-at-arms began to swagger about the streets as if they were masters of all they surveyed. There is no difference of opinion as to the brutality and insolence of the German soldiers in those days, and the Romans were excited and in no humour to accept any insult at such a moment. How they came to blows at last was never discovered, but after the great spectacle was over, most probably when night was coming on, and the excitement of the day had risen to irritability and ready passion, a fray arose in the streets no one knowing how. The strangers had the worst of it, Muratori says. "Many of the Teutons were killed," says one of the older chronicles, "and eleven hundred horses;" which would seem to imply that the dregs of the procession had been vapouring about Rome on their charges, riding the inhabitants down. Nor was it only men-at-arms: for a number of Otho's more distinguished followers were killed in the streets. How long it was before it came to the ears of the Emperor we are not informed, nor whether the banquet was interrupted. Probably Otho had returned to his tent (Muratori says he did so at once, leaving out all mention of any banquet) before the "calda baruffa" broke out: but at all events it was a startling change of scene. The Emperor struck his tents next morning, and departed from the neighbourhood of Rome in great rage and indignation:—and this, so far as Pope Innocent was concerned, was the last good that was ever heard of Otho. He broke all his vows one by one, took back the Tuscan States, seized the duchy of Spoleto and every city he passed on his way, and defied the Pope, to whom he had been so servile, having now got all from him that Innocent could give.

The plea by which Otho defended himself for his seizure of the States of Tuscany was worthy of that scholastic age. He had vowed, he said, it was true, to preserve St. Peter's patrimony and all the ecclesiastical possessions: but he had vowed at the same time to preserve and to recover all imperial rights and possessions, and it was in discharge of this obligation that he robbed the Pope. Thus ended Innocent's long and faithful support of Otho; he had pledged the faith of heaven for his success, which was assured only by accident and crime; but no sooner had that success been secured, than the Emperor deserted and betrayed the Pope who had so firmly stood by him. It is said that Innocent redoubled from that moment his care of the young Frederic, the King of Sicily, the head of the Hohenstaufen house and party, and prepared him to revenge Otho's broken oaths by a downfall as complete as his elevation had been; but this is an assumption which has no more proof than any other uncharitable judgment of motives unrevealed. At all events it is very apparent that in this long conflict, which occupied so much of his life, the Pope played no powerful or triumphant part.

In France the action of Innocent was more successful. The story of Philip Augustus and his wives, which is full of romantic incidents, is better known to the general reader than the tragedy of the Emperors. Philip Augustus had married a wife, a Danish princess, who did not please him. Her story, in its first chapter at least, is like that of Anne of Cleves, the fortunate princess who had the good luck not to please Henry VIII. (or perhaps still more completely resembles a comparatively recent catastrophe in our own royal house, the relations of George IV. and his unlucky wife). But the French king did not treat Ingelburga with the same politeness which Henry Tudor exhibited, neither had she the discretion to hold her tongue like the lady of Flanders. The complaints of the injured queen filled the world, and she made a direct appeal to the Pope, who was not slow to reply. When Philip procured a divorce from his wife from the complacent bishops of his own kingdom on one of those absurd allegations of too close relationship (it might be that of third or fourth cousin), which were of so much use to discontented husbands of sufficient rank, and married the beautiful Agnes of Meran, with whom he was in love, Innocent at once interfered. He began by commands, by entreaties, by attempts at settling the question by legal measures, commissioning his legates to hold a solemn inquiry into the matter, examining into Ingelburga's complaints, and using every endeavour to bring the king back to a sense of his duty. There could be no doubt on which side justice lay, and the legates were not, as in the case of Henry and Catherine, on the side of the monarch. It was the rejected queen who had the Pope's protection and not her powerful husband.

Philip Augustus, however, was summoned in vain to obey. The litigation and the appeals went on for a long time, and several years elapsed before Innocent, after much preparation and many warnings, determined not merely as on former occasions to excommunicate the offender, but to pronounce an interdict upon the kingdom. Perhaps Innocent had learned the lesson which had been taught him on such a great scale, that excommunication was not a fortunate weapon, and that only the perfect subordination of the higher clergy could make it successful at all. The interdict was a much greater and more dreadful thing; it was dependent not upon the obedience of a great prelate, but upon every priest who had taken the sacred vows. Had he excommunicated the king as on former occasions, no doubt there would always have been some lawless bishop in France who would have enabled his sovereign to laugh at the Pope and his sentence. But an interdict could not thus be evaded, the mass of the clergy being obedient to the Pope whatever important individual exceptions there might be. The interdict was proclaimed accordingly with all the accessories of ritualistic solemnity. After a Council which had lasted seven days, and which was attended by a great number of the clergy, the bells of the cathedral—it was that of Dijon—began to toll as for a dying man: and all the great bishops with their trains, and the legate at their head, went solemnly from their council chamber to the church. It was midnight, and the long procession went through the streets and into the great cathedral by the wavering and gloomy light of torches. For the last time divine service was celebrated, and the canons sang the Kyrie Eleison amid the silence, faintly broken by sobs and sounds of weeping, of the immense crowds who had followed them. The images of Christ and the saints were covered with crape, the relics of the saints, worshipped in those days with such strange devotion, were solemnly taken away out of the shrines and consecrated places to vaults and crypts underground where they were deposited until better times; the remains of the consecrated bread which had sustained the miracle of transubstantiation were burned upon the altar. All these details of the awful act of cutting off France from the community of the faithful were performed before a trembling and dismayed crowd, which looked on with a sense of the seriousness of the proceedings which was overwhelming.

"Then the legate, dressed in a violet stole, as on the day of the passion of our Lord, advanced to the altar steps, and in the name of Jesus Christ pronounced the interdict upon all the realm of France. Sobs and groans echoed through the great aisles of the cathedral; it was as if the day of judgment had come."

Once more after this tremendous scene there was a breathing space, a place of repentance left for the royal sinner, and then through all the churches of France the midnight ceremonial was repeated. The voice of prayer was silenced in the land, no more was psalm sung or mass said; a few convents were permitted by special grace, in the night, with closed doors and whispering voices, to celebrate the holy mysteries. For all besides the public worship of God and all the consolations of religion were cut off. We have seen how lightly personal excommunication was treated in Germany; but before so terrible a chastisement as this no king could hold out. Neither was the cause one of disobedience to the Holy See, or usurpation of the Church's lands, or any other offence against ecclesiastical supremacy: it was one into which every peasant, every clown could enter, and which revolted the moral sense of the nation. Matrimonial infidelities of all kinds have always been winked at in a monarch, but the strong step of putting away a guiltless queen and setting another in her place is a different matter. The nation was on the side of the Church: the clergy, except in very rare cases, were unanimous: and for once Innocent in his severity and supremacy was successful. After seven months of this terrible régime the king yielded. It had been a time of threatening rebellion, of feuds and dissensions of all kinds, of diminished revenues and failing prosperity. Philip Augustus could not stand against these consequences. He sent away the fictitious wife whom he loved—and who died, as the world, and even history at its sternest, loves to believe, of a broken heart, the one victim whom no one could save, a short time after—and the interdict was removed. One is almost glad to hear that even then the king would have none of Ingelburga, the woman who had filled the world with her cries and complaints, and brought this tremendous anathema on France. She continued to cry and appeal to the Pope that her captivity was unchanged or even made harder than ever, but Innocent was too wise to risk his great expedient a second time. He piously advised her to have recourse to prayer and to have confidence in God, and promised not to abandon her. But the poor lady gained little by all the misery that had been inflicted to right her wrongs. Many years after, when no one thought any more of Ingelburga, the king suddenly took her out of her prison and restored her to her share, such as it was, of the throne, for what reason no man can tell.

This, however, was the only great success of Innocent in the exercise of his papal power. It was an honourable and a just employment of that power, very different from the claim to decide between contending Emperors, or to nominate to the imperial crown; but it was in reality, as we think, the only triumphant achievement of the Pope, in whom all the power and all the pretensions of the papacy are said to have culminated. He had his hand in every broil, and interfered with everything that was going on in every quarter. Space fails us to tell of his endless negotiations, censures, recommendations and commands, sent by legates continually in motion or by letters of endless frequency and force, to regions in which Christianity itself was as yet scarcely established. Every little kingdom from the utmost limits of the north to the east were under this constant supervision and interference: and no doubt there were instances, especially among the more recent converts of the Church, and in respect to ecclesiastical matters, in which it was highly important; but so far as concerned the general tenor of the world's history, it can never be said to have had any important result.

In England, Innocent had the evil fortune to have to do with the worst of the Plantagenet kings, the false and cowardly John, who got himself a little miserable reputation for a time by the temporary determination of his resolve that "no Italian priest, should tithe or toll in our dominions," and who struggled fiercely against Innocent on the question of the Archbishopric of Canterbury and other great ecclesiastical offices, as well as in matters more personal, such as the dower of Berengaria, the widow of Coeur de Lion, which the Pope had called upon him to pay. John drove the greater part of the clergy out of England in his fury at the interdict which Innocent pronounced, and took possession, glad of an occasion of acquiring so much wealth, of the estates and properties of the Church throughout the realm. But the interdict which had been so efficacious in France failed altogether of its effect in England. It was too early for any Protestant sentiment, and it is extraordinary that a people by no means without piety should have shown so singular an indifference to the judgment of the Church. Perhaps the fact that so many of the superior clergy were of the conquering Norman race, and, therefore, still sullenly resisted by the passive obstinacy of the humiliated Saxons, had something to do with it: while at the same time the banishment of many prelates would probably leave a large portion of the humbler priests in comparative ignorance of the Pope's decree.

But whatever were the operative causes this is plain, that whereas in France the effect of the interdict was tremendous in England it produced scarcely any result at all. The banished bishops and archbishops, and at their head Stephen Langton, the patriotic Englishman of whom the Pope had made wise choice for the Archbishopric of Canterbury, stood on the opposite shore in consternation, and watched the contempt of their flocks for this greatest exercise of the power of Rome; and with still greater amazement perceived the success that followed the king in his enterprises, and the obedience of the people, with whom he had never been so popular before.

We are not told what Innocent felt at the sight of this unexpected failure. He proceeded to strike King John with special excommunication, going from the greater to the smaller curse, in a reversal of the usual method; but this being still ineffectual, Innocent turned to practical measures. He proceeded to free King John's subjects from their oath of allegiance and to depose the rebellious monarch; and not only so, for these ordinances would probably have been as little regarded as the other—but he gave permission and authority to the King of France, the ever-watchful enemy of the Plantagenets, to invade

England and to place his son Louis upon the vacant throne. Great preparations were made in France for this congenial Crusade—for it was in their quality as Crusaders that the Pope authorised the invasion. Then and not till then John paused in his career. He had laughed at spiritual dangers, but he no longer laughed when the French king gathered his forces at Boulogne, and the banished and robbed bishops prepared to return, not penitent and humiliated, but surrounded by French spears.

Then at last the terrified king submitted to the authority of the Pope; he received the legates of Innocent in a changed spirit, with the servility of a coward. He vowed with his hand on the Gospels to redress all ecclesiastical wrongs, to restore the bishops, and to submit in every way to the judgment of the Church. Then in his craven terror, without, it is said, any demand of the kind on the part of the ecclesiastical ambassadors, John took a step unparalleled in the annals of the nations.

"In order to obtain the mercy of God for the sins we have done against His holy Church, and having nothing more precious to offer than our person and our kingdom, and in order to humiliate ourself before Him who humbled Himself for us even to death: by an inspiration of the Holy Spirit, neither formed by violence nor by fear, but in virtue of our own good and free will we give, with the consent of our barons, to God, to His holy apostles, Peter and Paul, to our mother the Holy Roman Church, to our Lord the Pope Innocent and to his Catholic successors, in expiation of our sins and those of our family, living and dead, our kingdoms of England and Ireland with all their accompaniments and rights, in order that we may receive them again in the quality of vassal of God and of Holy Church: in faith of which we take the oath of vassal, in the presence of Pandulphus, putting ourselves at the disposition of the Pope and his successors, as if we were actually in the presence of the Pope; and our heirs and successors shall be obliged to take the same oath."

[IN THE CAMPAGNA (1860)]

So John swore, but not because of the thunders and curses of Innocent—because of Philip Augustus of France hurrying on his preparations on the other side of the Channel, while angry barons and a people worn out with constant exactions gave him promise of but poor support at home. The Pope became now the only hope of the humiliated monarch. He had flouted the sentences and disdained the curses of the Holy See; but if there was any power in the world which could restore the fealty of his vassals, and stop the invader on his way, it was Innocent: or so at least in this last emergency it might be possible to hope.

Innocent on his part did not despise the unworthy bargain. Notwithstanding his powerful intellect and just mind, and the perception he must have had of the miserable motives underneath, he did not hesitate. He received the oath, though he must have well known that it would be so much waste paper if John had ever power to cast it off. Of all men Innocent must have been most clearly aware what was the worth of the oaths of kings. He accepted it, however, apparently with a faith in the possibility of establishing the suzerainty thus bestowed upon him, which is as curious as any other of the facts of the case, whether flattered by this apparent triumph after his long unsuccess, or believing against all evidence—as men, even Popes, can always believe what they wish—that so shameful a surrender was genuine, and that here at last was a just acknowledgment of the rights of the Holy See. Henceforward the Pope put himself on John's side. He risked the alienation of the French king by forbidding the enterprise which had been undertaken at his command: he rejected the appeal of the barons, disapproved Magna Charta, transferred the excommunication to its authors with an ease which surely must have helped these unlikely penitents to despise both the anathema and its source. It is impossible either to explain or excuse this strange conduct. The easiest solution is that he did not fully understand either the facts or the characters of those with whom he had to deal: but how then could he be considered fit to judge and arbitrate between them?

The death of John liberated the Pope from what might have been a deliberate breach of his recommendations on the part of France. And altogether in this part of his conduct the imaginary success of Innocent was worse than a defeat. It was a failure from the high dignity he claimed, more conspicuous even than that failure in Germany which had already proved the inefficacy of spiritual weapons to affect the business of the world: for not only had all his efforts failed of success, until the rude logic of a threatened invasion came in to convince the mind of John—but the Pope himself was led into unworthy acts by a bargain which was in every way ignoble and unworthy. If the Church was to be the high and generous umpire, the impartial judge of all imperial affairs which she claimed to be—and who can say that had mortal powers been able to carry it out, this was not a noble and splendid ideal?— it was not surely by becoming the last resort against just punishment of a traitor and caitiff, whose oath made one day was as easily revoked the next, as the putting on or pulling off of a glove. It is almost inconceivable that a man like Innocent should have received with joy and with a semblance of faith such a submission on the part of such a man as John. But it is evident that he did so, and that probably the Roman court and community took it as a great event and overwhelming proof of the progress of the authority of the Church.

But perhaps an Italian and a Churchman in these days was the last person in the world to form a just idea of what we call patriotism, or to understand the principle of independence which made a nation, even when divided within itself, unite in fierce opposition to interference from without. Italy was not a country, but a number of constantly warring states and cities, and to Innocent the Church was the one sole institution in the world qualified and entitled to legislate for others. He accepted the gift of England almost with elation, notwithstanding all he had learned of that distant and strange country which cared not for an interdict, and if it could in any circumstances have loved its unworthy king, would have done so on account of his resistance to the Pope. And it would appear that the Pontiff believed in something serious coming of that suzerainty, all traditions and evidence to the contrary notwithstanding. Thus Innocent's part in the bloody and terrible drama that was then being played in England was neither noble nor dignified, but a poor part unworthy of his character and genius. His interference counted for nothing until France interfered with practical armies which had to be reckoned with—when the hand which had launched so many ineffectual thunderbolts was gripped at by an expedient of cowardly despair which in reality meant and produced nothing. Both sides were in their turn excommunicated, given over to every religious penalty; but unconcerned fought the matter out their own way and so settled it, unanimous only in resisting the jurisdiction of Rome. The vehement letters of the Pope as the struggle grew more and more bitter sound through the clang of arms like the impotent scoldings of a woman:

"Let women ... war with words,
With curses priests, but men with swords."

Let Pope or prelate do what they might, the cold steel carried the day.

Not less complete in failure, though with a flattering promise in it of prosperity and advantage, was the great crusade of Innocent's day—that which is called the Venetian Crusade, the immense expedition which seemed likely to produce such splendid results but ended so disastrously, and never set foot at all in the Holy Land which was its object. The Crusades were, of all other things, the dearest object to the hearts of the Popes, small and great. The first conception of them had risen, as the reader will remember, in the mind of Gregory VII., who would fain have set out himself at the head of the first, to recover out of the hands of the infidel the sacred soil which enshrined so many memories. The idea had been pursued by every worthy Pope between Hildebrand and Innocent, with fluctuations of success and failure—at first in noble and pious triumph, but latterly with all the dissensions, jealousies, and internal struggles, which armies, made up of many differing and antagonistic nationalities, could with difficulty avoid. Before Innocent's accession to the papacy there had been a great and terrible reverse, which was supposed to have broken the heart of the old Pope under whom it occurred, and which filled Christendom with horror, woe, and shame. The sacred territory for which so much blood had been shed fell again entirely into the hands of the Saracens. In consequence of this, one of the first acts of Innocent was to send out letters over all the world, calling for a new Crusade, exhorting princes and priests alike to use every means for the raising of a sufficient expedition, and promising every kind of spiritual advantage, indulgence, and remission to those who took the cross.

The first result of these impassioned appeals was to fire the spirits of certain priests in France to preach the Crusade, with all the fiery enthusiasm which had first roused Christendom: and a very large expedition was got together, chiefly from France, whose preliminary negotiations with the doge and government of Venice to convey them to Palestine furnishes one of the most picturesque scenes in the history of that great and astute republic. It was in the beginning of the thirteenth century, the opening of the year 1201, when the bargain, which was a very hard one, was made: and in the following July the expedition was to set sail. But when the pilgrims assembled at Venice it was found that with all their exertions they had not more than half the sum agreed upon as passage money. Perhaps the Venetians had anticipated this and taken their measures accordingly. At all events, after much wrangling and many delays, they agreed to convey the Crusaders on condition only of obtaining their assistance to take the town of Zara on the Dalmatian coast, which had once been under Venetian rule, but which now belonged to the King of Hungary, and was a nest of pirates hampering the trade of Venice and holding her merchants and seamen in perpetual agitation. Whether Innocent had surmised that some such design was possible we are not told, but if not his instructions to the Crusaders were strangely prophetic. He besought them on no account whatever to go to war with any Christian people. If their passage were opposed by any, they were permitted to force their way through that like any other obstacle, but even in such a case were only to act with the sanction of the legate who accompanied them. The Pope added a word of sorrowful comment upon the "very different aims" which so often mingled in the minds of the Crusaders with that great and only one, the deliverance of the Holy Land, which was the true object of their expedition; and complained sadly that if the heads of the Christian Church had possessed as much power as they had goodwill, the power of Mahomet would have been long since broken, and much Christian blood remained unshed.

He could not have spoken with more truth had he been prophetically aware of the issues to which that expedition was to come. The Crusaders set out, in 1202, covering the sea with their sails, dazzling every fishing boat and curious merchantman with reflections from their shining bucklers and shields, and met with such a course of adventure as never had befallen any pilgrims of the Cross before. The story is told in the most picturesque and dramatic pages of Gibbon; and many a historian more has repeated the tale. They took Zara, and embroiled themselves, as the Pope had feared, with the Hungarians, themselves a chivalrous nation full of enthusiasm for the Cross, but not likely to allow themselves to be invaded with impunity; then, professedly in the cause of the young Alexis, the boy-king of the Greek Empire, went to Constantinople—which they took after a wonderful siege, and in which they found such booty as turned the heads of the great penniless lords who had mortgaged every acre and spent every coin for the hire of the Venetian ships, and of the rude soldiers who followed them, who had never possessed a gold piece probably in their lives, and there found wealth undreamt of to be had for the taking. There is no need for us to enter into that extraordinary chapter in the history of the Greek Empire, of which these hordes of northern invaders, all Christian as they were, and with so different an object to start with, possessed themselves—with no less cruelty and as great rapacity as was shown by the barbarians of an elder age in the sack and destruction of Rome.

Meantime the Pope did not cease to protest against this turning aside of the expedition from its lawful object. The legate had forbidden the assault of Zara, but in vain; the Pope forbade the attack upon Constantinople also in vain, and vainly pressed upon the Crusaders, by every argument, the necessity of proceeding to the Holy Land without delay. Innocent, it is true, did not refuse his share of the splendid stuffs and ornaments which fell into their hands, for ecclesiastical uses: and he was silenced by the fictitious submission of the Greek Church, and the supposed healing of the schism which had rent the East and the West from each other. Nevertheless he looked on upon the progress of affairs in Constantinople with unquiet eyes. But what could the Pope do in his distant seat, armed with those spiritual powers alone which even at home these fierce warriors held so lightly, against the rage of acquisition, the excitement of conquest, even the sweep and current of affairs, which carried the chiefs of the armies in the East so much further and in so changed a direction from that which even they themselves desired? He entreated, he commanded, he threatened: but when all was said he was but the Pope, far off and powerless, who could excommunicate indeed, but do no more. The only thing possible for Innocent was to look on, sometimes with a gleam of high hope as when the Greek Church came over to him, as appeared, to be received again into full communion with the rest of Christendom: sometimes with a half unwilling pleasure as when Baldwin's presents arrived, cloth of gold and wonderful embroideries to decorate the great arches of St. Peter's and the Lateran: and again with a more substantial confidence when Constantinople itself had become a Latin empire under the same Baldwin—that it might henceforward become a basis of operations in the holy war against the Saracens and promote the objects of the Crusade more effectually than could be done from a distance. Amid all his disappointments and the impatient sense of futility and helplessness which must have many a time invaded his soul, it is comfortable to know that Innocent died in this last belief, and never found out how equally futile it was.

There was, however, one other great undertaking of his time in which it would seem that the Pontiff was more directly influential, even though, for any reader who respects the character and ideal of

Innocent, it is sickening to the heart to realise what it was. It was that other Crusade, so miserable and so bloody, against the Albigenses, which was the only successful enterprise which with any show of justice could be set down to the account of the Church. Nobody seems even now to know very well what the heresies were, against which, in the failure of other schemes, the arms of the defenders of religion were directed. They were, as Dissent generally is, manifold, while the Church regarded them as one. Among them were humble little sects who desired only to lead a purer and truer life than the rude religionists among whom they dwelt; while there were also others who held in various strange formulas all kinds of wild doctrine: but between the Poor Men of Lyons, the Scripture-Readers whose aim was to serve God in humility, apart from all pomps of religion and splendour of hierarchies—and the strange Manichean sects with their elaborate and confused philosophical doctrine—the thirteenth century knew no difference. It ranked them all under the same name of heretic, and attributed to all of them the errors of the worst and smallest section. Even so late as the eighteenth century, Muratori, a scholar without prejudice, makes one sweeping assertion that they were Manicheans, without a doubt or question. It is needless to say that whatever they were, fire and sword was not the way to mend them of their errors; for that also was an idea wholly beyond the understanding of the time.

When Innocent came first to the Papacy his keen perception of the many vices of the Church was increased by a conviction that error of doctrine accompanied in certain portions of Christendom the general corruption of life. In some of his letters he comments severely, always with a reference to the special evils against which he struggled, on the causes and widening propagation of heresy. "If the shepherd is a hireling," he says, "and thinks not of the flock, but solely of himself: if he cares only for the wool and the milk, without defending them from the wolves that attack them, or making himself a wall of defence against their enemies: and if he takes flight at the first sound of danger: the ruin and loss must be laid to his charge. The keeper of the sheep must not be like a dumb dog that cannot bark. When the priesthood show that they do not know how to separate holy things from common, they resemble those vile wine-sellers who mingle water with their wine. The name of God is blasphemed because of those who love money, who seek presents, who justify the wicked by allowing themselves to be corrupted by them. The vigilance of the ministers of religion can do much to arrest the progress of evil. The league of heretics should be dissolved by faithful instruction: for the Lord desires not the death of a sinner, but rather that he should be converted and live."

It may be curious also to quote here the cautious utterance of Innocent upon the pretension of the more pious sectarians to found everything on Scripture and to make the study of the Bible their chief distinction. The same arguments are still used in the Catholic Church, sometimes even in the same terms.

"The desire to know the Holy Scriptures and to profit by their teaching is praiseworthy, but this desire must not be satisfied in secret, nor should it degenerate into the wish to preach, or to despise the ministers of religion. It is not the will of God that His word should be proclaimed in secret places as is done by these heretics, but publicly in the Church. The mysteries of the faith cannot be explained by every comer, for not every intellect is capable of understanding them. The Holy Scriptures are so profound that not only the simple and ignorant but even intelligent and learned men are unqualified to interpret them."

At no time however, though he spoke so mildly and so candidly, acknowledging that the best way to overcome the heretics was to convert and to convince them, did Innocent conceal his intention and desire to carry proceedings against them to the sternest of conclusions. If it were possible by any exertions to bring them back to the bosom of the Church, he charged all ecclesiastical authorities, all preachers, priests, and monastic establishments to do everything that was possible to accomplish this great work; but failing that, he called upon all princes, lords, and civil rulers to take stringent measures and cut them off from the land—recommendations that ended in the tremendous and appalling expedient of a new Crusade, a Crusade with no double motive, no object of restoration and deliverance combined with that of destruction, but bound to the sole agency of sheer massacre, bloodshed, and ruin, an internecine warfare of the most horrible kind.

It must be added, however, that the preachers who at Innocent's command set out, more or less in state, high officials, ecclesiastics of name and rank, to convince the heretics, by their preaching and teaching, took the first part in the conflict. According to his lights he spared no pains to give the doomed sects the opportunity of conversion, though with very little success. Among his envoys were two Spaniards, one a bishop, one that great Dominic, the founder of the Dominican order, who filled so great a part in the history of his time. Amid the ineffectual legates these two were missionaries born: they represented to the other preachers that demonstrations against heresy in the cathedrals was no way of reaching the people, but that the true evangelists must go forth into the country, humble and poor as were the adversaries whom they had to overcome. They themselves set out on their mission barefoot, without scrip or purse, after the manner of the Apostles. Strange to think that it was in Provence, the country of the Troubadours, the land of song, where poetry and love were supreme according to all and every tradition of history, that the grimmest heresy abounded, and that this stern pair carried on their mission! but so it was. Toulouse, where Courts of Love sate yearly, and the trouvères held their tournaments of song, was the centre of the tragedy. But not even those devoted preachers, nor the crowd of eager priests and monks who followed in their steps, succeeded in their mission. The priesthood and the religion it taught had fallen very low in Provence, and no one heeded the new missionaries, neither the heretics nor the heedless population around.

No doubt the Pope, the man of so many disappointments, had set his heart on this as a thing in which for once he must not fail, and watched with a sore and angry heart the unsuccess of all these legitimate efforts. But it was not until one of the legates, a man most trusted and honoured, Pierre de Castelnau, was treacherously killed in the midst of his mission, that Innocent was fully roused. Heretofore he had rained excommunications over all the world, and his curses had come back to him without avail. But on this occasion at least he had a sure weapon in hand. The Pope proclaimed a Crusade against the heretics. He proclaimed throughout Europe that whoever undertook this holy enterprise it should be counted to him as if he had fought for Jerusalem: all the indulgences, blessings, hopes for heaven and exemptions for earth, which had been promised to those who were to deliver the Holy Sepulchre, were equally bestowed on those who went no further than the south of France, one of the richest districts in Christendom, where fair lands and noble castles were to be had for the conquest without risking a stormy voyage or a dangerous climate. The goods of unrepentant heretics were confiscated, and every one was free to help himself as if they had been Turks and infidels. In none of his undertakings was the Pope so hotly in earnest. There is something of the shrillness of a man who has found himself impotent in many undertakings in the passion which Innocent throws into this. "Rise, soldier of Christ!" he cries to the king of France; "up, most Christian prince! The groans of the Church rise to your ears, the blood of the just cries out: up, then, and judge my cause: gird on your sword; think of the unity of the cross and the altar, that unity taught us by Moses, by Peter, by all the fathers. Let not the bark of the Church make shipwreck. Up, for her help! Strike strongly against the heretics, who are more dangerous than the Saracens!"

The appeal came to a host of eager ears. Many good and true men were no doubt among the army which gathered upon the gentle hill of Hyères in the blazing midsummer of the year 1209, cross on breast and sword in hand, sworn to exterminate heresy, and bring back the country to the sway of the true religion; but an overwhelming number besides, who were hungry for booty however obtained, and eager to win advancement for themselves, filled up the ranks. Such motives were not absent even from the bosom of Simon de Montfort, their general, otherwise a good man and true. The sovereignty of Toulouse glimmered before him over seas of blood, which was as the blood of the Saracen, no better, though it flowed in the veins of Frenchmen; but the Provençaux could scarcely be called Frenchmen in those early days. They were no more beloved of their northern neighbours than the English were by the Scots, and the expedition against them was as much justified by distinctions of race as was the conflict of Bannockburn.

The chapter of history that followed we would fain on all sides obliterate, if we could, from the records of humanity, and we doubt not that the strictest Catholic as much as the most indignant Protestant would share this wish; but that, alas, cannot be done. And no such feeling was in any mind of the time. The remedy was not thought to be too terrible for the disease, for centuries after: and the most Christian souls rejoiced in the victories of the Crusade, the towns destroyed, the nests of heretics broken up. The very heretics themselves, who suffered fiercely and made reprisals when they could, had no doctrine of toleration among themselves, and would have extirpated a wicked hierarchy, and put down the mass with a high hand, as four hundred years later their more enlightened successors did, when the power came to them. There are many shuddering spectators who now try to represent to themselves that Innocent so far off was but half, or not at all, acquainted with the atrocities committed in his name; that his legates over-stepped their authority, as frequently happened, and were carried away by the excitement of carnage and the terrible impulse of destruction common to wild beasts and men when that fatal passion is aroused; and that his generals soon converted their Crusade, as Crusades more or less were converted everywhere, into a raid of fierce acquisition, a war for booty and personal enrichment. And all this is true for as much as it is worth in reducing the guilt of Innocent; but that is not much, for he was a man very well acquainted with human nature, and knew that such things must be.

As for Simon de Montfort and his noble companions, they were not, much less were the men-at-arms under their orders, superior to all that noble chivalry of France which had started from Venice with so fine a purpose, but had been drawn aside to crush and rob Constantinople on their way, only some seven years before. Baldwin of Flanders became Emperor of the great eastern city in 1204. Simon de Montfort named himself Count de Toulouse in 1215. Both had been sent forth with the Pope's blessing on quite a different mission, both had succumbed to the temptation of their own aggrandisement. But of the two, at the end Simon was the more faithful. If he committed or permitted to be committed the most abominable cruelties, he nevertheless did stamp out heresy. Provence regained her gaiety, her courts of love, her gift of song. Innocent, for once in his life, with all the dreadful drawbacks accompanying it, was successful in the object for which he had striven.

It is a dreadful thing to have to say of the most powerful of Popes, in whose time the Papacy, we are told, reached its highest climax of power in the affairs of men: he was successful once: in devastating a country and slaughtering by thousands its inhabitants in the name of God and the Church. All his attempts to set right the affairs of the world failed. He neither nominated an emperor, nor saved a servile king from ruin, nor struck a generous blow for that object of the enthusiasm of his age, the deliverance of Jerusalem. All of these he attempted with the utmost strain and effort of his powers, and many more, but failed. Impossible to say that it was not truth and justice which he set before him at all times; he was an honest man and loved not bloodshed; he had a great intelligence, and there is no proof that his heart was cold or his sympathies dull. But his career, which is so often quoted as an example of the supremacy of the Papacy, seems to us the greatest and most perfect demonstration that such a supremacy was impossible. Could it have been done, Innocent would have done it; but it could not be done, and in the plenitude of his power he failed over and over again. What credit he might have had in promoting Otho to the empire fades away when we find that it was the accident of Philip's death and not the support of the Pope that did it. In England his assumed suzerainty was a farce, and all his efforts ineffectual to move one way or the other the destinies of the nation. At Constantinople his prayers and commands and entreaties had about as much power as the outcries of a woman upon his own special envoys and soldiers. In France he had one brief triumph indeed, and broke a poor woman's heart, a thing which is accomplished every day by much easier methods; though his action then was the only moral triumph of his reign, being at least in the cause of the weak against the strong. And he filled Provence with blood and misery, and if he crushed heresy, crushed along with it that noble and beautiful country, and its royal house, and its liberties. Did he ever feel the contrast between his attempts and his successes? Was he sore at heart with the long and terrible failure of his efforts? or was he comforted by such small consolations as fell to him, the final vindication of Ingelburga, the fictitious submission of the Greek Church, the murderous extinction of heresy? Was it worth while for a great man to have endured and struggled, to have lived sleepless, restless, ever vigilant, watching every corner of the earth, keeping up a thousand espionages and secret intelligences all for this, and nothing more?

He was the greatest of the Popes and attained the climax of papal power. He carried out the principles which Hildebrand had established, and asserted to their fullest all the claims which that great Pontiff, also a deeply disappointed man, had made. Gregory and Innocent are the two most prominent names in the lists of the Papacy; they are the greatest generals of that army which, in its way, is an army invincible, against which the gates of hell cannot prevail. Let us hope that the merciful illusions which keep human nature going prevented them from seeing how little all their great claims had come to. Gregory indeed, dying sad and in exile, felt it more or less, but was able to set it down to the wickedness of the world in which truth and justice did not reign. And there is a profound sadness in the last discourse of Innocent; but perhaps they were neither of them aware what a deep stamp of failure remains, visible for all the world to see, upon those great undertakings of theirs which were not for the Church but for the world. God had not made them judges and dividers among men, though they believed so to the bottom of their hearts.

It is perhaps overbold in a writer without authority to set forth an individual opinion in the face of much more powerful judgments. But this book pretends to nothing except, so far as it is possible to form it, a glance of individual opinion and impression in respect to matters which are otherwise too great for any but the most learned and weighty historian. The statement of Dean Milman that "He (Innocent) succeeded in imposing an Emperor on Germany" appears to us quite inconsistent with the facts of the case. But we would not for a moment pretend that Milman does not know a hundred times better than the present writer, whose rapid glance at the exterior aspects of history will naturally go for what it is worth and no more. The aspect of a pageant however to one who watches it go by from a window, is sometimes an entertaining variety upon its fullest authoritative description.

It will be understood that we have no idea of representing the reign of these great Popes as without power in many other matters. They strengthened greatly the authority and control exercised by the Holy See over its special and legitimate empire, the Church. They drew to the court of Rome so many appeals and references of disputed cases in law and in morals as to shed an increased influence over the world like an unseen irrigation swelling through all the roots and veins of Christendom. They even gave so much additional prestige and importance to Church dignitaries as to increase the power which the great Prelates often exercised against themselves. But the highest pretensions of the Successors of Peter, the

Vicars of God, to be judges and arbiters of the world, setters up and pullers down of thrones, came to no fulfilment. The Popes were flattered by appeals, by mock submissions on the weaker side, even by petitions for the ever ready interference which they seem to have attempted in good faith, always believing in their own authority. But in the end their decisions and decrees in Imperial questions were swept away like chaff before the strong wind of secular power and policy, and history cannot point to one important revolution[5] in the affairs of the world or any separate kingdom made by their unaided power.

The last great act of Innocent's life was the council held in the year 1215 in Rome, known as the fourth Lateran Council. It was perhaps the greatest council that had ever been held there, not only because of the large number of ecclesiastics present, but because for the first time East and West sat together, the Patriarch of Constantinople (or rather two patriarchs, for the election was contested) taking their place in it, in subordination to the Pope, as if the great schism had never been. From all the corners of the earth came the bishops and archbishops, the not less important abbots, prelates who were nobles as well as priests, counting among them the greatest lords in their respective districts as well as the greatest ecclesiastics. Innocent himself was a man of fifty-five, of most temperate life, vigorous in mind and body, likely to survive for years, and to do better than he had ever yet done—and he was so far triumphant for the moment that all the kings of Christendom had envoys at this council, and everything united to make it magnificent and important. Why he should have taken for his text the ominous words he chose when addressing that great and splendid assembly in his own special church and temple, surrounded with all the emblems of power and supremacy, it is impossible to tell; and one can imagine the thrill of strange awe and astonishment which must have run through that vast synod, when the Pope rose, and from his regal chair pronounced these words, first uttered in the depths of the mysterious passion and anguish of the greatest sufferer on earth. "With desire I have desired to eat this passover with you before I suffer." What was it that Innocent anticipated or feared? There was no suffering before him that any one knew, no trouble that could reach the chief of Christendom, heavy-hearted and depressed, amid all his guards, spiritual and temporal, as he may have been. What could they think, all those great prelates looking, no doubt, often askance at each other, brethren in the church, but enemies at home? Nor were the first words of his discourse less solemn.

"As to me, to live is Christ and to die is gain, I should not refuse to drink the cup of suffering, were it presented to me, for the defence of the Catholic Church, for the deliverance of the Holy Land, or for the freedom of the Church, even although my desire had been to live in the flesh until the work that has been begun should be accomplished. Notwithstanding not my will, but the will of God be done! This is why I say, 'With desire I have desired to eat this passover with you before I suffer.'"

These words sound in our ears as if the preacher who uttered them was on the verge, if not of martyrdom, at least of death and the premature end of his work. And so he was: although there was as yet no sign in heaven or earth, or so far as appears in his own consciousness, that this end was near.

The discourse which followed was remarkable in its way, the way of the schoolmen and dialecticians so far as its form went. He began by explaining the word Passover, which in Hebrew he said meant passage—in which sense of the word he declared himself to desire to celebrate a triple Passover, corporal, spiritual, and eternal, with the Church around him.

"A corporal Passover, the passage from one place to another to deliver Jerusalem oppressed: a spiritual Passover, a passage from one situation to another for the sanctification of the universal Church; an eternal Passover, a passage from one life to another, to eternal glory." For the first, the deliverance of the Holy Land and the Holy Sepulchre, after a solemn description of the miseries of Jerusalem enslaved, he declares that he places himself in the hands of the brethren.

"There can be no doubt that it ought to be the first object of the Church. What ought we now to do, dear brethren? I place myself in your hands. I open my heart entirely to you, I desire your advice. I am ready, if it seems good to you, to go forth on a personal mission to all the kings, princes, and peoples, or even to the Holy Land—and if I can to awaken them all with a strong voice that they may arise to fight the battle of the Lord, to avenge the insult done to Jesus Christ, who has been expelled by reason of our sins from the country and dwelling which He bought with His blood, and in which He accomplished all things necessary for our salvation. We, the priests of the Lord, ought to attach a special importance to the redemption of the Holy Land by our blood and our wealth; no one should draw back from such a great work. In former times the Lord seeing a similar humiliation of Israel saved it by means of the priests; for he delivered Jerusalem and the Temple from the infidels by Matthias the son of the priest Maccabæus."

[ST. PETER'S AND THE CASTLE OF ST. ANGELO]

He goes on to describe the spiritual passage by the singular emblem to be found in the prophecies of Ezekiel, of the man clothed in white linen who inscribed a Tau upon the foreheads of all those who mourned over the iniquities committed around them, the profanations of the temple and the universal idol worship—while the executors of God's will went after him, to slay the rest. There could be no doubt of the application of this image. It had already been seen in full fulfilment in the streets of Beziers, Carcassone, and Toulouse, and many of those present had taken part in the carnage. It is true that the rumour went that the men marked with a mark had not even been looked for, and one of the wonderful sayings which seem to spring up somehow in the air, at great moments, had been fathered upon a legate—Tuez les tous. Dieu reconnaîtra les siens—a phrase which, like the "Up, Guards, and at them!" of Waterloo, is said to have no historical foundation whatever. Innocent was, however, clear not only that every good Catholic should be marked with the Tau—but that the armed men whom he identifies with the priests, his own great army, seated there round him, men who had already seen the blood flow and the flames arise, should strike and spare not.

"You are commanded then to go through the city; obey him who is your supreme Pontiff, as your guide and your master—and strike by interdict, by suspension, by excommunication, by deprivation, according to the weight of the fault. But do no harm to those who bear the mark, for the Lord says: 'Hurt not the earth, neither the sea, neither the trees till we have sealed on their foreheads the servants of God.' It is said in other places, 'Let your eye spare no man, and let there be no acceptance of persons among you,' and in another passage, 'Strike in order to heal, kill in order to give life.'"

These were the Pope's sentiments, and they were those of his age; how many centuries it took to modify them we are all aware; four hundred years at least, to moderate the practical ardour of persecution—for the theory never dies. But there is at the same time something savage in the fervour of such an address to all these men of peace. It is perhaps a slight modification that like Ezekiel it is the priests themselves, the dwellers in the Temple, who fill it with false gods and abominations, that he specially threatens. There were, however, so far as appears, few priests among the slaughtered townsfolk of those unhappy cities of Provence.

The Council responded to the uncompromising directions of their head by placing among the laws of the Church many stringent ordinances against heretics; their goods were to be confiscated, they were to be turned out of their houses and possessions; every prince who refused to act against them was to be excommunicated, his people freed from their vow of allegiance. If any one ventured to preach without the permission of the Pope he also was subject to excommunication. A great many laws for the better regulation of the Church itself followed, for Innocent had always acknowledged the fact that the worldliness of the Church, and the failure of the clergy to maintain a high ideal of Christian life, was the great cause of heresy. The Council was also very distinct in refusing temporal authority to the priests. The clergy had their sphere and laymen theirs; those spheres were separate, they were inviolable each by the other. It is true that this principle was established chiefly with the intention of freeing the clergy from the necessity of answering before civil tribunals; but logically it cuts both ways. The Jews, to whom Innocent had been just and even merciful, were also dealt with and placed under new and stringent disabilities, chiefly on account, it seems, of the extortions they practised on needy Crusaders, eager at any price to procure advances for their equipment. Various doctrinal points were also decided, as well as many questions of rank and precedence in the hierarchy, and the establishment of the two new monastic orders of St. Francis and of St. Dominic. It is needless to add a list of who was excommunicated and who censured throughout the world. Among the former were the barons of Magna Charta and Louis of France, the son of Philip Augustus, who had gone to England on their call and to their relief, a movement set on foot by Innocent himself before the submission of King John. As usual, neither of them took any notice of the anathema, though other combinations shortly arose which broke their alliance.

The great event of the Council, however, was the appeal of the forfeited lords of Provence against the leaders of the late Crusade. Raymond of Toulouse, accompanied by the Counts of Foix and of Comminges, appeared before the Pontiff and the high court of the Church to make their plaint against Simon de Montfort, who had deprived all three of their lands and sovereignties. A great recrimination arose between the two sides, both so strongly represented. The dethroned princes accused their conquerors with all the vehemence of men wronged and robbed; and such a bloodstained prelate as Bishop Fulk of Toulouse was put forth as the advocate on the other side. "You are the cause of the death of a multitude of Catholic soldiers," cried the bishop, "six thousand of whom were killed at Montjoye alone." "Nay, rather," replied the Comte de Foix, "it is by your fault that Toulouse was sacked and 10,000 of the inhabitants slain." Such pleas are strange in any court of justice; they were altogether new in a Council of the Church. The princes themselves, who thus laid their wrongs before the Pope, were not proved to be heretics, or if they had ever wavered in the faith were now quite ready to obey; and

Innocent himself was forced to allow that: "Since the Counts and their companions have promised at all times to submit to the Church, they cannot without injustice be despoiled of their principalities." But the utterance, it may well be understood, was weak, and choked by the impossibility of denouncing Simon de Montfort, the leader of a Crusade set on foot by the Church, the Captain of the Christian army. It might be that he had exceeded his commission, that the legates had misunderstood their instructions, and that all the leaders, both secular and spiritual, had been carried away by the horrible excitement and passion of bloodshed: but yet it was impossible to disown the Captain who had taken up this enterprise as a true son of the Church, although he had ended in the spirit (not unusual among sons of the Church) of an insatiable raider and conqueror. The love of gain had warped the noble aims even of the first Crusade: what wonder that it became a fiery thirst in the invaders of lands so rich and tempting as those of the fertile and sunny Provence. And the Pope could not pronounce against his own champion. He would fain have preserved Raymond of Toulouse and Simon de Montfort too—but that was impossible. And the Council decreed by a great majority that Raymond had been justly deprived of his lands, and that Simon, the new Count, was their rightful possessor. The defender of Innocent can only say that the Pope yielded to and sanctioned this judgment in order that the bishops of France might not be alienated and rendered indifferent to the great Crusade upon which his heart was set, which he would fain have led himself had Providence permitted it so to be.

There is a most curious postscript to this bloody and terrible history. Young Raymond of Toulouse, whose fate seemed a sad one even to the members of the Council who finally confirmed his deprivation, attracted the special regard—it is not said how, probably by some youthful grace of simplicity or gallant mien—of Innocent, who bade him take heart, and promised to give him certain lands that he might still live as a prince. "If another council should be held," said the Pope with a curious casuistry, "the pleas against Montfort may be listened to." "Holy Father," said the youth, "bear me no malice if I can win back again my principalities from the Count de Montfort, or from those others who hold them." "Whatever thou dost," said the Pope piously, "may God give thee grace to begin it well, and to finish it still better." Innocent is scarcely a man to tolerate a smile. We dare not even imagine a touch of humour in that austere countenance; but the pious hope that this fair youth might perhaps overcome his conqueror, who was the very champion and captain of the army of the Lord as directed by the Pope, is remarkable indeed.

The great event of the Council was over, the rumour of the new Crusade which the Pope desired to head himself, and for which in the meantime he was moving heaven and earth, began to stir Europe. If, perhaps, he had accomplished little hitherto of all that he had hoped, here remained a great thing which Innocent might still accomplish. He set out on a tour through the great Italian towns to rouse their enthusiasm, and, if possible, induce them, in the first place, to sacrifice their mutual animosities, and then to supply the necessary ships, and help with the necessary money for the great undertaking. The first check was received from Pisa, which would do whatever the Pope wished except forego its hatred against Genoa or give up its revenge. Innocent was in Perugia, on his way towards the north, when this news arrived to vex him: but it was not unexpected, nor was there anything in it to overwhelm his spirit. It was July, and he was safer and better on that hillside than he would have been in his house at the Lateran in the heats of summer: and an attack of fever at that season is a simple matter, which the ordinary Roman anticipates without any particular alarm. He had, we are told, a great love for oranges, and continued to eat them, notwithstanding his illness, though it is difficult to imagine what harm the oranges could do. However, the hour was come which Innocent had perhaps dimly foreseen when he rose up among all his bishops and princes in the great Lateran church, and, knowing nothing, gave forth from his high presiding chair the dying words of our Lord, "With desire I have desired to eat this passover with you before I suffer." One wonders if his text came back to him, if he asked himself in his heart why his lips should have uttered those fateful words unawares, and if the bitterness of that withdrawal, while still full of force and life, from all the hopes and projects to which he had set his hand, was heavy upon him? He had proclaimed them in the hush and breathless silence of that splendid crowd in the ruddy days of the late autumn, St. Martin's festival at Rome: and the year had not gone its round when, in the summer weather at Perugia, he "suffered"—as he had—yet had not, perhaps foreseen.

Thus ended a life of great effort and power, a life of disappointment and failure, full of toil, full of ambition, the highest aims, and the most consistent purpose—but ending in nothing, fulfilling no lofty aim, and, except in the horrible episode of bloodshed and destruction from which his name can never be dissociated, accomplishing no change in the world which he had attempted, in every quarter, to transform or to renew. Never was so much attempted with so little result. He claimed the power to bind and loose, to set up and to pull down, to decide every disputed cause and settle every controversy. But he succeeded in doing only one good deed, which was to force the king of France to retain an unloved wife, and one ill one, to print the name of Holy Church in blood across a ruined province, to the profit of many bloody partisans, but never to his own, nor to any cause which could be considered that of justice or truth. This, people say, was the age of history in which the power of the Church was highest, and Innocent was its strongest ruler; but this was all which, with his great powers, his unyielding character and all the forces at his command, he was able to achieve. He was in his way a great man, and his purpose was never ignoble; but this was all: and history does not contain a sadder page than that which records one of the greatest of all the pontificates, and the strongest Pope that history has known.

During the whole of Innocent's Popedom he had been more or less at war with his citizens notwithstanding his success at first. Rome murmured round him never content, occasionally bursting out into fits of rage, which, if not absolute revolt, were so near it as to suggest the withdrawal of the Pope to his native place Anagni, or some other quiet residence, till the tumult calmed down. The greatest of these commotions occurred on the acquisition of certain properties in Rome, by the unpopular way of foreclosure on mortgages, by the Pope's brother Richard, against whom no doubt some story of usury or oppression was brought forth, either real or invented, to awaken the popular emotion: and in this case Innocent's withdrawal had very much the character of an escape. The Papa-Re was certainly not a popular institution in the thirteenth century. This same brother Richard had many gifts bestowed upon him to the great anger and suspicion of the people, and it was he who built, with money given him, it is said, from "the treasury of the Church," the great Torre dei Conti, which for many generations stood strong and sullen near the Baths of Titus, and within easy reach of the Lateran, "for the defence of the family," a defence for which it was not always adequate. Innocent afterwards granted a valuable fief in the Romagna to his brother, and he was generally far from unmindful of his kindred. All that his warmest defenders can say for him indeed in this respect is that he made up for his devotion to the interests of the Conti by great liberality towards Rome. On one occasion of distress and famine he fed eight thousand people daily, and at all times the poor had a right to the remnants left from his own table—which however was not perhaps any great thing as his living was of the simplest.

What was still more important, he built or perhaps rather rebuilt and enlarged, the great hospital, still one of the greatest charitable institutions of the world, of the Santo Spirito, which had been first founded several centuries before by the English king Ina for the pilgrims of his country. The Ecclesia in Saxia, probably forsaken in these days when England had become Norman, formed the germ of the great building, afterwards enlarged by various succeeding Popes. It is said now to have 1,600 beds, and to be capable, on an emergency, of accommodating almost double that number of patients, and is, or was, a sort of providence for the poor population of Rome. It was Innocent also who began the construction, or rather reconstruction, for in that case too there was an ancient building, of the Vatican, now the seat and title of the papal court—thinking it expedient that there should be a house capable of receiving the Popes near the church of St. Peter and St. Paul the tomb and shrine of the Apostles. It is not supposed that the present building retains any of the work of that early time, but Innocent must have superintended both these great edifices, and in this way, as also by many churches which he built or rebuilt, and some which he decorated with paintings and architectural ornament, he had his part in the reconstruction and embellishment of that mediæval Rome which after long decay and much neglect, and the wholesale robbery of the very stones of the older city, was already beginning to lift up its head out of the ashes of antiquity.

[ALL THAT IS LEFT OF THE GHETTO]

Thus if he took with one hand—not dishonestly, in the interest of his family, appropriating fiefs and favours which probably could not have been better bestowed, for the safety at least of the reigning Pope—he gave liberally and intelligently with the other, consulting the needs of the people, and studying their best interests. Yet he would not seem ever to have been popular. His spirit probably lacked the bonhomie which conciliates the crowd: though we are told that he loved public celebrations, and did not frown upon private gaiety. His heart, it is evident, was touched for young Raymond of Toulouse, whom he was instrumental in despoiling of his lands, but whom he blessed in his effort to despoil in his turn the orthodox and righteous spoiler. He was neither unkind, nor niggardly, nor luxurious. "The glory of his actions filled the great city and the whole world," said his epitaph. At least he had the credit of being the greatest of all the Popes, and the one under whom, as is universally allowed, the papal power attained its climax. The reader must judge how far this climax of power justified what has been said.

FOOTNOTE:

[5] The Vice-Provost of Eton who has kindly read these pages in the gentle criticism which can say no harsh word, here remarks: "If success is measured less by immediate results than by guiding the way in which men think, I should say that Innocent was successful. 'What will the Pope say?' was the question asked in every corner of the world—though he was not always obeyed."

[ON THE TIBER]

BOOK III

LO POPOLO: AND THE TRIBUNE OF THE PEOPLE

CHAPTER I

ROME IN THE FOURTEENTH CENTURY

When the Papal Seat was transferred to Avignon, and Rome was left to its own devices and that fluctuating popular government which meant little beyond a wavering balance of power between two great families, the state of the ancient imperial city became more disorderly, tumultuous and anarchical than that of almost any other town in Italy, which is saying much. All the others had at least the traditions of an established government, or a sturdy tyranny: Rome alone had never been at peace and scarcely knew how to compose herself under any sway. She had fought her Popes, sometimes desperately, sometimes only captiously with the half-subdued rebelliousness of ill-temper, almost from the beginning of their power; and her sons had long been divided into a multiplicity of parties, each holding by one of the nobles who built their fortresses among the classic ruins, and defied the world from within the indestructible remnants of walls built by the Cæsars. One great family after another entrenched itself within those monuments of the ancient ages. The Colosseum was at one time the stronghold of the great Colonna: Stefano, the head of that name, inhabited the great building known as the Theatre of Marcellus at another period, and filled with his retainers an entire quarter. The castle of St. Angelo, with various flanking towers, was the home of the Orsini; and these two houses more or less divided the power between them, the other nobles adhering to one or the other party. Even amid the tumults of Florence there was always a shadow of a principle, a supposed or real cause in the name of which one party drove another fuori, out of the city. But in Rome even the great quarrel of Guelf and Ghibelline took an almost entirely personal character to increase the perpetual tumult. The vassals of the Pope were not on the Pope's side nor were they against him,

—non furon rebelli Nè fur fedeli a Dio, mà per sé foro.

The community was distracted by mere personal quarrels, by the feuds of the great houses who were their lords but only tore asunder, and neither protected nor promoted the prosperity of that greatest of Italian cities, which in its miserable incompetence and tumult was for a long time the least among them.

The anonymous historian who has left to us the story of Cola di Rienzi affords us the most lively picture of the city in which, in his terse and vivid record, there is the perpetual sound of a rushing, half-armed crowd, of blows that seem to fall at random, and trumpets that sound, and bells that ring, calling out the People—a word so much misused—upon a hundred trifling occasions, with little bloodshed one would imagine but a continual rushing to and fro and disturbance of all the ordinary habits of life. We need not enter into any discussion of who this anonymous writer was. He is the only contemporary historian of Rienzi, and his narrative has every appearance of truth. He narrates the things he saw with a straightforwardness and simplicity which are very convincing. "I will begin," he says, "with the time when these two barons (the heads of the houses of Colonna and Orsini) were made knights by the people of Rome. Yet," he adds, with an afterthought, "I will not begin with an account of that, because I was then at too tender an age to have had clear knowledge of it." Thus our historian is nothing if not an eye-witness, very keenly aware of every incident, and viewing the events, and the streams of people as they pass, with the never-failing interest of a true chronicler. We may quote the incident with which he does begin as an example of his method: his language is the Italian of Rome, a local version, yet scarcely to be called a patois: it presents little difficulty after the first moment to the moderately instructed reader, who however, I trust, will kindly understand that the eccentricities are the chronicler's and not errors of the press.

"With what new thing shall I begin? I will begin with the time of Jacopo di Saviello. Being made Senator solely by the authority of King Robert, he was driven out of the Capitol by the Syndics, who were Stefano de la Colonna, Lord of Palestrina, and Poncello, and Messer Orso, lord of the Castle of St. Angelo. These two went to the Aracoeli, and ringing the bell collected the people, half cavalry and half on foot. All Rome was under arms. I recollect it well as in a dream. I was in Sta. Maria del Popolo (di lo Piubbico). And I saw the line of horsemen passing, going towards the Capitol: strongly they went and proudly. Half of them were well mounted, half were on foot. The last of them (If I recollect rightly) wore a tunic of red silk, and a cap of yellow silk on his head, and carried a bunch of keys in his hand. They passed along the road by the well where dwell the Ferrari, at the corner of the house of Paolo Jovenale. The line was long. The bell was ringing and the people arming themselves. I was in Santa Maria di lo Piubbico. To these things I put my seal (as witness). Jacopo di Saviello, Senator, was in the Capitol. He was surrounded on all sides with fortifications: but it did him no good to entrench himself, for Stefano, his uncle, went up, and Poncello the Syndic of Rome, and took him gently by the hand and set him on his horse that there might be no risk to his person. There was one who thought and said, 'Stefano, how can you bring your nephew thus to shame?' The proud answer of Stefano was: 'For two pennyworth of wax I will set him free,—but the two pence were not forthcoming."

Jacopo di Saviello, thus described as a nominee of the King of Naples, is a person without much importance, touching whose individuality it would take too much space to inquire. He appears afterwards as the right hand man of his cousin, Sciarra Colonna, and the incident has no doubt some connection with the story that follows: but we quote it merely as an illustration of the condition of Rome at the beginning of the fourteenth century. In the month of September in the year 1327 there occurred an episode in the history of the city which affords many notable scenes. The city of Rome had in one of its many caprices taken the part of Louis of Bavaria, who had been elected Emperor to the great displeasure of John XXII., the Pope then reigning in Avignon. According to the chronicler, though the fact is not mentioned in other histories, the Pope sent his legate to Rome, accompanied by the "Principe de la Morea" and a considerable army, in order to prevent the reception there of Il Bavaro as he is called, who was then making his way through Italy with much success and triumph. By this time there would seem to have been a complete revolution in the opinions of Rome, and the day when two-pennyworth of wax could not be got for the ransom of Saviello was forgotten under the temporary rule of Sciarra Colonna, the only one of his family who was a Ghibelline, and who held strongly for Louis of Bavaria, rejecting all the traditions of his house. Our chronicler, who is very impartial, and gives us no clue to his own opinions, by no means despised the party of the Pope. There arrived before Rome, he tells us, "seven hundred horsemen and foot soldiers without end. All the barons of the house of Orsini," and many other notable persons: and the whole army was molto bella e bene acconcia, well equipped and beautiful to behold. This force gained possession of the Leonine city, entering not by the gates which were guarded, but by the ruined wall: and occupied the space between that point and St. Peter's, making granne festa, and filling the air with the sound of their trumpets and all kinds of music.

"But when Sciarra the bold captain (franco Capitano) heard of it, it troubled him not at all. Immediately he armed himself and caused the bell to be rung. It was midnight and men were in their first sleep. A messenger with a trumpet was sent through the town, proclaiming that every one should arm himself, that the enemy had entered the gates (in Puortica) and that all must assemble on the Capitol. The people who slept, quickly awakened, each took up his arms. Cossia was the name of the crier. The bell was ringing violently (terribilmente). The people went to the Capitol, both the barons and the populace: and the good Capitano addressed them and said that the enemy had come to outrage the women of Rome. The people were much excited. They were then divided into parties, of one of which he was captain himself. Jacopo Saviello was at the head of the other which was sent to the gate of San Giovanni, then called Puorta Maggiore. And this was done because they knew that the enemy was divided in two parties. But it did not happen so. When Jacopo reached the gate he found no one. On the other hand Sciarra rode with his barons. Great was the company of horsemen. Seven Rioni had risen to arms and innumerable were the people. They reached the gate of San Pietro. I remember that on that night a Roman knight who had ridden to the bridge heard a trumpet of the enemy, and desiring to fly jumped from his horse, and leaving it came on on foot. I know that there was no lack of fear (non habe carestia di paura). When the people reached the bridge it was already day, the dawn had come. Then Sciarra commanded that the gate should be opened. The crowd was great, and the enemy were much troubled to see on the bridge the number of pennons, for they knew that with each pennon there were twenty-five men. Then the gate was opened. The Rione of li Monti went first: the people filled the Piazza of the Castello: they were all ranged in order, both soldiers and people.

"Now were seen the rushing of the horses, one on the top of another. One gave, another took (che dao, che tolle), great was the noise, great was the encounter. Trumpets sounded on this side and that. One gave, and another took. Sciarra and Messer Andrea di Campo di Fiore confronted each other and abused each other loudly. Then they broke their lances upon each other: then struck with their swords: neither would have less than the life of the other. Presently they separated and came back each to his people. There was great striking of swords and lances and some fell. It could be seen that it was a cruel fight. The people of Rome wavered back and forward like waves of the sea. But it was the enemy that gave way, the people gained the middle of the Piazza. Then was done a strange thing. One whose name was Giovanni Manno, of the Colonna, carried the banner of the people of Rome. When he came to the great well, which is in that Piazza, in front of the Incarcerate, where was the broken wall, he took the banner and threw it into the well. And this he did to discourage the people of Rome. The traitor well deserved to lose his life. The Romans however did not lose courage, and already the Prince of the Morea began to give way. He had either to fly or to be killed. Then Sciarra de la Colonna, like a good mother with her son, comforted the people and made everything go well, such great sense did he show. Also another novel thing was done. A great man of Rome (Cola de Madonna Martorni de li Anniballi was his name) was a very bold person and young. He was seized with desire to take prisoner the Prince himself. He spurred his horse, and breaking through the band of strong men who encircled the Prince put out his hand to take him. So he had hoped to do at least, but was not successful, for the Prince with an iron club wounded his horse. The strength of the Prince's charger was such that Cola was driven back: but the horse of Cola had not sufficient space to move, and its hind feet slipping, it fell into the ditch which is in front of the gate of the Hospital of Santo Spirito, to defend the garden. In the ditch both his horse and he, trying to escape, fell, pressed by the soldiers of the Prince: and there was he killed. Great was the mourning which Rome made over so distinguished a baron—and all the people were fired with indignation.

"The Prince now retired, his troops yielded. They began to fly. The flight was great. Greater was the slaughter. They were killed like sheep. Much resistance was made, many people were killed, and the Romans gained much prey. Among those taken was Bertollo the chief of the Orsini, Captain of the army of the Church, and of the Guelf party: and if it had not been that Sciarra caught him up on the croup of his horse, he would have been murdered by the people."

[APPROACH TO THE CAPITOL (1860)]

Then follows a horrible account of the number of dead who lay mutilated and naked on every roadside, and even among the vineyards: and the story ends with Sciarra's return to the Capitol with great triumph, and of a beautiful pallium which was sent to the Church of Sant'Angelo in Pescheria, along with a chalice, "in honour of this Roman victory."

Curiously enough our chronicler takes no notice of the episode of which this attack and repulse evidently form part, the reception of Il Bavaro in Rome, which is one of the unique incidents in Roman history. It took place in May of the following year, and afforded a very striking scene to the eager townsfolk, never quite sure that they could tolerate the Tedeschi, though pleased with them for a novelty and willing enough to fight their legitimate lord the Pope on behalf of the strangers. It was in January 1328 that Louis of Bavaria made his entrance into Rome—Sciarra Colonna above named being still Senator, head of the Ghibelline party, and the friend of the new-made Emperor. After being met at Viterbo by the Roman officials and questioned as to his intentions, Louis marched with his men into the Leonine city and established himself for some days in what is called the palace of St. Peter, the beginning of the Vatican, where, though there was still a party not much disposed to receive him, he was hailed with acclamations by the people, always eager for a new event, and not unmindful of the liberal largesse which an Emperor on his promotion, and especially when about to receive the much coveted coronation in St. Peter's, scattered around him. Louis proposed to restore the city to its ancient grandeur, and to promote its interests in every way, and flattered the people by receiving their vote of approval on the Capitol. "Going up to the Capitol," says Muratori, "he caused an oration to be made to the Roman people with many expressions of gratitude and praise, and with promises that Rome should be raised up to the stars." These honeyed words so pleased the people that he was declared Senator and Captain of Rome, and in a few days was crowned Emperor with every appearance of solemnity and grandeur.

This would seem to be the first practical revival of the strange principle that Rome, as a city, not by its Emperor nor by its Pope, but in its own right, was the fountain of honour, the arbiter of the world—everything in short which in classical times its government was, and in the mediæval ages, the Papacy wished to be. It is curious to account for such an article of belief; for the populace of Rome had never in modern times possessed any of the characteristics of a great people, and was a mixed and debased race according to all authorities. This theory, however, was now for a time to affect the whole story of the city, and put a spasmodic life into her worn-out veins. It was the only thing which could have made such a story as that of Rienzi possible, and it was strongly upheld by Petrarch and other eager and philosophic observers. The Bavarian Louis was, however, the first who frankly sought the confirmation of his election from the hands of the Roman people. One cannot, however, but find certain features of a farce in this solemn ceremony.

The coronation processions which passed through the streets from Sta. Maria Maggiore, according to Sismondi, to St. Peter's, were splendid, the barons and counsellors, or buon-homini of Rome leading the cortège, and clothed in cloth of gold. "Behind the monarch marched four thousand men whom he had brought with him; all the streets which he traversed were hung with rich tapestries." He was accompanied by a lawyer eminent in his profession, to watch over the perfect legality of every point in the ceremonial. The well-known Castruccio Castracani, who had followed him to Rome, was appointed by the Emperor to be his deputy as Senator, and to watch over the city; and in this capacity he took his place in the procession in a tunic of crimson silk, embroidered with the words in gold on the breast, "He is what God wills"; on the back, "He will be what God pleases." There was no Pope, it need not be said, to consecrate the new Emperor. The Pope was in Avignon, and his bitter enemy. There was not even a Bishop of Ostia to present the great monarch before St. Peter and the powers of heaven. Nevertheless the Church was not left out, though it was placed in a secondary position. Some kind of ceremony was gone through by the Bishop of Venice, or rather of Castello, the old name of that restless diocese, and the Bishop of Alecia, both of them deposed and under excommunication at the moment: but it was Sciarra Colonna who put the crown on Louis's head. The whole ceremonial was secular, almost pagan in its meaning, if meaning at all further than a general throwing of dust in the eyes of the world it could be said to have. But there is a fictitious gravity in the proceedings which seems almost to infer a sense of the prodigious folly of the assumption that these quite incompetent persons were qualified to confer, without any warrant for their deed, the greatest honour in Christendom upon the Bavarian. John XXII. was not a very noble Pope, but his sanction was a very different matter from that of Sciarra Colonna. No doubt however the people of Rome—Lo Popolo, the blind mob so pulled about by its leaders, and made to assume one ridiculous attitude after another at their fancy—was flattered by the idea that it was from itself, as the imperial city, that the Emperor took the confirmation of his election and his crown.

Immediately afterwards a still more unjustifiable act was performed by the Emperor thus settled in his imperial seat. Assisted by his excommunicated bishops and his rebellious laymen, Louis held, Muratori tells us, in the Piazza of St. Peter a gran parlamento, calling upon any one who would take upon him the defence of Jacques de Cahors, calling himself Pope John XXII., to appear and answer the accusations against him.

"No one replied: and then there rose up the Syndic of that part of the Roman clergy who loved gold better than religion, and begged Louis to take proceedings against the said Jacques de Cahors. Various articles were then produced accusing the Pope of heresy and treason, and of having raised the cross (i.e. sent a crusade, probably the expedition of the Prince of the Morea in the chronicle) against the Romans. For which reasons the Bavarian declared Pope John to be deposed from the pontificate and to be guilty of heresy and treason, with various penalties which I leave without mention. On the 23rd of April, with the consent of the Roman people, a law was published that every Pope in the future ought to hold his court in Rome, and not to be absent more than three months in the year on pain of being deposed from the Papacy. Finally on the twelfth day of May, in the Piazza of San Pietro, Louis with his crown on his head, proposed to the multitude that they should elect a new Pope. Pietro de Corvara, a native of the Abbruzzi, of the order of the Friars Minor, a great hypocrite, was proposed: and the people, the greater part of whom hated Pope John because he was permanently on the other side of the Alps (dè la dai monti), accepted the nomination. He assumed the name of Nicolas V. Before his consecration there was a promotion of seven false cardinals: and on the 22nd of May he was consecrated bishop by one of these, and afterwards received the Papal crown from the hands of the said Louis, who caused himself to be once more crowned Emperor by this his idol.

"The brutality of Louis the Bavarian in arrogating to himself (adds Muratori) the authority of deposing a Pope lawfully elected, who had never fallen into heresy as was pretended: and to elect another, contrary to the rites and canons of the Catholic Church, sickened all who had any conscience or light of reason, and pleased only the heretics and schismatics, both religious and secular, who filled the court of the Bavarian, and by whose counsels he was ruled. Monstrosity and impiety could not be better declared and detested. And this was the step which completed the ruin of his interests in Italy."

The apparition of this German court in Rome, with its curious ceremonials following one upon another: the coronation in St. Peter's, so soon to be annulled by its repetition at the hands of the puppet Pope whom Louis had himself created, in the vain hope that a crown bestowed by hands nominally consecrated would be more real than that given by those of Sciarra Colonna—makes the most wonderful episode in the turbulent story. In the same way Henry IV. was crowned again and again—first in his tent, afterwards by his false Pope in St. Peter's, while Gregory VII. looked grimly on from St. Angelo, a besieged and helpless refugee, yet in the secret consciousness of all parties—the Emperor's supporters as well as his own—the only real fountain of honour, the sole man living from whom that crown could be received with full sanction of law and right. Perhaps when all is said, and we have fully acknowledged the failure of all the greater claims of the Papacy, we read its importance in these scenes more than in the loftiest pretensions of Gregory or of Innocent. Il Bavaro felt to the bottom of his heart that he was no Emperor without the touch of those consecrated hands. A fine bravado of triumphant citizens delighting to imagine that Rome could still confer all honours as the mother city of the world, was well enough for the populace, though even for them the excommunicated bishops had to be brought in to lend a show of authenticity to the unjustifiable proceedings; but the uneasy Teuton himself could not be contented even by this, and it is to be supposed felt that even an anti-pope was better than nothing. It is tempting to inquire how Sciarra Colonna felt when the crown he had put on with such pride and triumph was placed again by the Neapolitan monk, false Pope among false cardinals, articles d'occasion, as the French say—on the head of the Bavarian. One cannot but feel that it must have been a humiliation for Colonna and for the city at this summit of vainglory and temporary power.

The rest of the story of Sciarra and his emperor is quickly told, so far as Rome is concerned. Louis of Bavaria left the city in August of the same year. He had entered Rome in January amid the acclamations of the populace: he left it seven months later amid the hisses and abusive cries of the same people, carrying with him his anti-pope and probably Sciarra, who at all events took flight, his day being over, and died shortly after. Next day Stefano della Colonna, the true head of the house, arrived in Rome with Bartoldo Orsini, and took possession in the name of Pope John, no doubt with equal applause from the crowd which so short a time before had witnessed breathless his deposition, and accepted the false Nicolas in his place. Such was popular government in those days. The legate so valiantly defeated by Sciarra, and driven out of the gates according to the chronicle, returned in state with eight hundred knights at his back.

We do not attempt to follow the history further than in those scenes which show how Rome lived, struggled, followed the impulse of its masters, and was flung from one side to the other at their pleasure, during this period of its history. The wonderful episode in that history which was about to open is better understood by the light of the events which roused Lo Popolo into wild excitement at one moment, and plunged them into disgust and discouragement the next.

The following scene, however, has nothing to do with tumults of arms. It is a mere vignette from the much illustrated story of the city. It relates the visit of what we should now call a Revivalist to Rome, a missionary friar, one of those startling preachers who abounded in the Middle Ages, and roused, as almost always in the history of human nature, tempests of short-lived penitence and reformation, with but little general effect even on the religious story of the time. Fra Venturino was a Dominican monk of Bergamo, who had already when he came to Rome the fame of a great preacher, and was attended by a multitude of his penitents, dressed in white with the sacred monogram I.H.S. on the red and white caps or hoods which they wore on their heads, and a dove with an olive branch on their breasts. They came chiefly from the north of Italy and were, according to the chronicle, honest and pious persons of good and gentle manners. They were well received in Florence, where many great families took them in, gave them good food, good beds, washed their feet, and showed them much charity. Then, with a still larger contingent of Florentines following his steps, the preacher came on to Rome.

"It was said in Rome that he was coming to convert the Romans. When he arrived he was received in San Sisto. There he preached to his own people, of whom there were many orderly and good. In the evening they sang Lauds. They had a standard of silk which was afterwards given to La Minerva (Sta. Maria sopra Minerva). At the present day it may still be seen there in the Chapel of Messer Latino. It was of green silk, long and large. Upon it was painted the figure of Sta. Maria, with angels on each side, playing upon viols; and St. Dominic and St. Peter Martyr and other prophets. Afterwards he preached in the Capitol, and all Rome went to hear him. The Romans were very attentive to hear him, quiet, and following carefully if he went wrong in his bad Latin. Then he preached and said that they ought to take off their shoes, for the place on which they stood was holy ground. And he said that Rome was a place of much holiness from the bodies of the saints who lay there, but that the Romans were wicked people: at which the Romans laughed. Then he asked a favour and a gift from the Romans. Fra Venturino said, 'Sirs, you are going to have one of your holidays which costs much money. It is not either for God or the saints: therefore you celebrate this idolatry for the service of the Demon. Give the money to me. I will spend it for God to men in need, who cannot provide for themselves.' Then the Romans began to mock at him, and to say that he was mad: thus they said and that they would stay no longer: and rising up went away leaving him alone. Afterwards he preached in San Giovanni, but the Romans would not hear him, and would have driven him away. He then became angry and cursed them, and said that he had never seen people so perverse. He appeared no more, but departed secretly and went to Avignon, where the Pope forbade him to preach."

We may conclude these scraps of familiar contemporary information with a companion picture which does not give a reassuring view of the state of the Church in Rome. It is the story of a priest elected to a great place and dignity who sought the confirmation of his election from the Pope at Avignon.

"A monk of St. Paolo in Rome, Fra Monozello by name, who at the death of the Abbot had been elected to fill his place, appeared before Pope Benedict. This monk was a man who delighted in society, running about everywhere, seeing the dawn come in, playing the lute, a great musician and singer. He spent his life in a whirl, at the court, at all the weddings, and parties to the vineyards. So at least said the Romans. How sad it must have been for Pope Benedict to hear that a monk of his did nothing but sing and dance. When this man was chosen for Abbot, he appeared before the sanctity of the Pope and said, 'Holy Father, I have been elected to San Paolo in Rome.' The Pope, who knew the condition of all who came to him, said, 'Can you sing?' The Abbot-elect replied, 'I can sing.' The Pope, 'I mean songs' (la cantilena). The Abbot-elect answered, 'I know concerted songs' (il canzone sacro). The Pope asked again, 'Can you play instruments' (sonare)? He answered, 'I can.' The Pope, 'I ask can you play (tonare) the organ and the lute?' The other answered, 'Too well.' Then the Pope changed his tone and said, 'Do you think it is a suitable thing for the Abbot of the venerable monastery of San Paolo to be a buffoon? Go about your business.'"

Thus it would appear that, careless as they might be and full of other thoughts, the Popes in Avignon still kept a watchful eye upon the Church at Rome. These are but anecdotes with which the historian of Rienzi prepares his tragic story. They throw a little familiar light, the lanthorn of a bystander, upon the town, so great yet so petty, always clinging to the pretensions of a greatness which it could not forget, but wholly unworthy of that place in the world which its remote fathers of antiquity had won, and incapable even when a momentary power fell into its hands of using it, or of perceiving in the midst of its greedy rush at temporary advantage what its true interests were—insubordinate, reckless, unthinking, ready to rush to arms when the great bell rang from the Capitol a stuormo, without pausing to ask which side they were on, with the Guelfs one day and the Ghibellines the next, shouting for the

Emperor, yet terror-stricken at the name of the Pope—obeying with surly reluctance their masters the barons, but as ready as a handful of tow to take flame, and always rebellious whatever might be the occasion. This is how the Roman Popolo of the fourteenth century appear through the eyes of the spectators of its strange ways. Fierce to fight, but completely without object except a local one for their fighting, ready to rebel but always disgusted when made to obey, entertaining a wonderful idea of their own claims by right of their classic descent and connection with the great names of antiquity, while on the other hand they allowed the noblest relics of those times to crumble into irremediable ruin.

The other Rome, the patrician side, with all its glitter and splendour of the picturesque, is on the surface a much finer picture. The romance of the time lay altogether with the noble houses which had grown up in mediæval Rome, sometimes seizing a dubious title from an ancient Roman potentate, but most often springing from some stronghold in the adjacent country or the mountains, races which had developed and grown upon highway robbery and the oppression of those weaker than themselves, yet always with a surface of chivalry which deceived the world. The family which was greatest and strongest is fortunately the one we know most about. The house of Colonna had the good luck to discover in his youth and extend a warm, if condescending, friendship to the poet Petrarch, who was on his side the most fortunate poet who has lived in modern ages among men. He was in the midst of everything that went on, to use our familiar phraseology, in his day: he was the friend and correspondent of every notable person from the Pope and the Emperor downward: only a poor ecclesiastic, but the best known and most celebrated man of his time. The very first of all his contemporaries to appreciate and divine what was in him was Giacomo Colonna, one of the sons of old Stefano, whom we have already seen in Rome. He was Bishop of Lombez in Gascony, and his elder brother Giovanni was a Cardinal. They were in the way of every preferment and advantage, as became the sons of so powerful a house, but no promotion they attained has done so much for them with posterity as their friendship with this smooth-faced young priest of Vaucluse, to whom they were the kindest patrons and most faithful friends.

Petrarch was but twenty-two, a student at Bologna when young Colonna, a boy himself, took, as we say, a fancy for him, "not knowing who I was or whence I came, and only by my dress perceiving that what he was I also was, a scholar." It was in his old age that Petrarch gave to another friend a description of this early patron, younger apparently than himself, who opened to him the doors of that higher social life which were not always open to a poet, even in those days when the patronage of the great was everything. "I think there never was a man in the world greater than he or more gracious, more kind, more able, more wise, more good, more moderate in good fortune, more constant and strong against adversity," he writes in the calm of his age, some forty years after the beginning of this friendship and long after the death of Giacomo Colonna. When the young bishop first went to his diocese Petrarch accompanied him. "Oh flying time, oh hurrying life!" he cries. "Forty-four years have passed since then, but never have I spent so happy a summer." On his return from this visit the bishop made his friend acquainted with his brother Giovanni, the Cardinal, a man "good and innocent more than Cardinals are wont to be." "And the same may be said," Petrarch adds, "of the other brothers, and of the magnanimous Stefano, their father, of whom, as Crispus says of Carthage, it is better to be silent than to say little." This is a description too good, perhaps, to be true of an entire family, especially of Roman nobles and ecclesiastics in the middle of the fourteenth century, between the disorderly and oppressed city of Rome, and the corrupt court of Avignon: but at least it shows the other point of view, the different aspect which the same man bears in different eyes: though Petrarch's enthusiasm for his matchless friends is perhaps as much too exalted as the denunciations of the populace and the popular orator are excessive on the other side.

It was under this distinguished patronage that Petrarch received the great honour of his life, the laurel crown of the Altissimo Poeta, and furnished another splendid scene to the many which had taken place in Rome in the midst of all her troubles and distractions. The offer of this honour came to him at the same time from Paris and Rome, and it was to Cardinal Giovanni that he referred the question which he should accept: and he was surrounded by the Colonnas when he appeared at the Capitol to receive his crown. The Senator of the year was Orso, Conte d'Anquillara, who was the son-in-law of old Stefano Colonna, the husband of his daughter Agnes. The ceremony took place on Easter Sunday in the year 1341, the last day of Anquillara's office, and so settled by him in order that he might himself have the privilege of placing the laurel on the poet's head. Petrarch gives an account of the ceremony to his other patron King Robert of Naples, attributing this honour to the approbation and friendship of that monarch—which perhaps is a thing necessary when any personage so great as a king interests himself in the glory of a poet. "Rome and the deserted palace of the Capitol were adorned with unusual delight," he says: "a small thing in itself one might say, but conspicuous by its novelty, and by the applause and pleasure of the Roman people, the custom of bestowing the laurel having not only been laid aside for many ages, but even forgotten, while the republic turned its thoughts to very different things—until now under thy auspices it was renewed in my person." "On the Capitol of Rome," the poet wrote to another correspondent, "with a great concourse of people and immense joy, that which the king in Naples had decreed for me was executed. Orso Count d'Anquillara, Senator, a person of the highest intelligence, decorated me with the laurel: all went better than could have been believed or hoped," he adds, notwithstanding the absence of the King and of various great persons named—though among these Petrarch, with a policy and knowledge of the world which never failed him, does not name to his Neapolitan friends Cardinal Giovanni and Bishop Giacomo, the dearest of his companions, and his first and most faithful patrons, neither of whom were able to be present. Their family, however, evidently took the lead on this great occasion. Their brother Stefano pronounced an oration in honour of the laureate: he was crowned by their brother-in-law: and the great celebration culminated in a banquet in the Colonna palace, at which, no doubt, the father of all presided, with Colonnas young and old filling every corner. For they were a most abundant family—sons and grandsons, Stefanos and Jannis without end, young ones of all the united families, enough to fill almost a whole quarter of Rome themselves and their retainers. "Their houses extended from the square of San Marcello to the Santi Apostoli," says Papencordt, the modern biographer of Rienzi. The ancient Mausoleum of Augustus, which has been put to so many uses, which was a theatre not very long ago, and is now, we believe a museum, was once the headquarters and stronghold of the house.

This ceremonial of the crowning of the poet was conducted with immense joy of the people, endless applause, a great concourse, and every splendour that was possible. So was the reception of Il Bavaro a few years before; so were the other strange scenes about to come. The populace was always ready to form a great concourse, to shout and applaud, notwithstanding its own often miserable condition, exposed to every outrage, and finding justice nowhere. But the reverse of the medal was not so attractive. Petrarch himself, departing from Rome with still the intoxicating applause of the city ringing in his ears, was scarcely outside the walls before he and his party fell into the hands of armed robbers. It would be too long to tell, he says, how he got free; but he was driven back to Rome, whence he set out again next day, "surrounded by a good escort of armed men." The ladroni armati who stopped the way might, for all one knows, wear the badge of the Colonnas somewhere under their armour, or at least find refuge in some of their strongholds. Such were the manners of the time, and such was specially the condition of Rome. It gave the crown of fame to the poet, but could not secure him a safe passage for a mile outside its gates. It still put forth pretensions, as on this, so in more important cases, to exercise an authority over all the nations, by which right it had pleased the city to give Louis of Bavaria the imperial crown; but no citizen was safe unless he could protect himself with his sword, and justice and the redress of wrong were things unknown.

[ON THE PINCIO]

CHAPTER II

THE DELIVERER

It was in this age of disorder and anarchy that a child was born, of the humblest parentage, on the bank of the Tiber, in an out-of-the-way suburb, who was destined to become the hero of one of the strangest episodes of modern history. His father kept a little tavern to which the Roman burghers, pushing their walk a little beyond the walls, would naturally resort; his mother, a laundress and water-carrier—one of those women who, with the port of a classical princess, balance on their heads in perfect poise and certainty the great copper vases which are still used for that purpose. It was the gossip of the time that Maddalena, the wife of Lorenzo, had not been without adventures in her youth. No less a person than Henry VII. had found shelter, it was said, in her little public-house when her husband was absent. He was in the dress of a pilgrim, but no doubt bore the mien of a gallant gentleman and dazzled the eyes of the young landlady, who had no one to protect her. When her son was a man it pleased him to suppose that from this meeting resulted the strange mixture of democratic enthusiasm and love of pomp and power which was in his own nature. It was not much to be proud of, and yet he was proud of it. For all the world he was the son of the poor innkeeper, but within himself he felt the blood of an Emperor in his veins. Maddalena died young, and when her son began to weave the visions which helped to shape his life, was no longer there to clear her own reputation or to confirm him in his dream.

These poor people had not so much as a surname to distinguish them. The boy Niccola was Cola di Rienzo, Nicolas the son of Laurence, as he is called in the Latin chronicles, according to that simplest of all rules of nomenclature which has originated so many modern names. "He was from his youth nourished on the milk of eloquence; a good grammarian, a better rhetorician, a fine writer," says his biographer. "Heavens, what a rapid reader he was! He made great use of Livy, Seneca, Tully, and Valerius Maximus, and delighted much to tell forth the magnificence of Julius Cæsar. All day long he studied the sculptured marbles that lie around Rome. There was no one like him for reading the ancient inscriptions. All the ancient writings he put in choice Italian; the marbles he interpreted. How often did he cry out, 'Where are these good Romans? where is their high justice? might I but have been born in their time?' He was a handsome man, and he adopted the profession of a notary."

We are not told how or where Cola attained this knowledge. His father was a vassal of the Colonna, and it is possible that some of the barons coming and going may have been struck by the brilliant, eager countenance of the innkeeper's son, and helped him to the not extravagant amount of learning thus recorded. His own character, and the energy and ambition so strangely mingled with imagination and the visionary temperament of a poet, would seem to have at once separated him from the humble world in which he was born. It is said by some that his youth was spent out of Rome, and that he only returned when about twenty, at the death of his father—a legend which would lend some show of evidence to the suggestion of his doubtful birth: but his biographer says nothing of this. It is also said that it was the death of his brother, killed in some scuffle between the ever-contending parties of Colonna and Orsini, which gave his mind the first impulse towards the revolution which he accomplished in so remarkable a way. "He pondered long," says his biographer, "of revenging the blood of his brother; and long he pondered over the ill-governed city of Rome, and how to set it right." But there is no definite record of his early life until it suddenly flashes into light in the public service of the city, and on an occasion of the greatest importance as well for himself as for Rome.

This first public employment which discloses him at once to us was a mission from the thirteen Buoni homini, sometimes called Caporoni, the heads of the different districts of the city, to Pope Clement VI. at Avignon, on the occasion of one of those temporary overturns of government which occurred from time to time, always of the briefest duration, but carrying on the traditions of the power of the people from age to age. He was apparently what we should call the spokesman of the deputation sent to explain the matter to the Pope, and to secure, if possible, some attention on the part of the Curia to the condition of the abandoned city.

"His eloquence was so great that Pope Clement was much attracted towards him: the Pope much admired the fine style of Cola, and desired to see him every day. Upon which Cola spoke very freely and said that the Barons of Rome were highway robbers, that they were consenting to murder, robbery, adultery, and every evil. He said that the city lay desolate, and the Pope began to entertain a very bad opinion of the Barons."

"But," adds the chronicler, "by means of Messer Giovanni of the Colonna, Cardinal, great misfortunes happened to him, and he was reduced to such poverty and sickness that he might as well have been sent to the hospital. He lay like a snake in the sun. But he who had cast him down, the very same person raised him up again. Messer Giovanni brought him again before the Pope and had him restored to favour. And having thus been restored to grace he was made notary of the Cammora in Rome, so that he returned with great joy to the city."

This succinct narrative will perhaps be a little more clear if slightly expanded: the chief object of the Roman envoy was to disclose the crimes of the "barons," whose true character Cola thus described to the Pope, on the part of the leaders of a sudden revolt, a sort of prophetical anticipation of his own, which had seized the power out of the hands of the two Senators and conferred it upon thirteen Buoni homini, heads of the people, who took the charge in the name of the Pope and professed, as was usual in its absence, an almost extravagant devotion to the Papal authority. The embassy was specially charged with the prayers and entreaties of the people that the Pope would return and resume the government of the city: and also that he would proclaim another jubilee—the great festival, accompanied by every kind of indulgence and pious promise to the pilgrims, attracted by it from all the ends of the earth to Rome—which had been first instituted by Pope Boniface VIII. in 1300 with the intention of being repeated once every century only. But a century is a long time; and the jubilee was most profitable, bringing much money and many gifts both to the State and the Church. The citizens were therefore very anxious to secure its repetition in 1350, and its future celebration every fifty years. The Pope graciously accorded the jubilee to the prayers of the Romans, and accepted their homage and desire for his return, promising vaguely that he would do so in the jubilee year if not before. So that whatever afterwards happened to the secretary or spokesman, the object of the mission was attained.

Elated by this fulfilment of their wishes, and evidently at the moment of his highest favour with the Pope, Cola sent a letter announcing this success to the authorities in Rome, which is the first word we hear from his own mouth. It is dated from Avignon, in the year 1343. He was then about thirty, in the full ardour of young manhood, full of visionary hopes and schemes for the restoration of the glories of Rome. The style of the letter, which was so much admired in those days, is too florid and ornate for the taste of a severer period, notwithstanding that his composition received the applause of Petrarch, and was much admired by all his contemporaries. He begins by describing himself as the "consul of orphans, widows and the poor, and the humble messenger of the people."

[THEATRE OF MARCELLUS]

"Let your mountains tremble with happiness, let your hills clothe themselves with joy, and peace and gladness fill the valleys. Let the city arise from her long course of misfortunes, let her re-ascend the throne of her ancient magnificence, let her throw aside the weeds of widowhood and clothe herself with the garments of a bride. For the heavens have been opened to us and from the glory of the Heavenly Father has issued the light of Jesus Christ, from which shines forth that of the Holy Spirit. Now that the Lord has done this miracle, brethren beloved, see that you clear out of your city the thorns and the roots of vice, to receive with the perfume of new virtue the Bridegroom who is coming. We exhort you with burning tears, with tears of joy, to put aside the sword, to extinguish the flames of battle, to receive these divine gifts with a heart full of purity and gratitude, to glorify with songs and thanksgiving the name of our Lord Jesus Christ, and also to give humble thanks to His Vicar, and to raise to that supreme Pontiff, in the Capitol or in the amphitheatre, a statue adorned with purple and gold that the joyous and glorious recollection may endure for ever. Who indeed has adorned his country with such glory among the Ciceros, the Cæsars, Metullus, or Fabius, who are celebrated as liberators in our old annals and whose statues we adorn with precious stones because of their virtues? These men have obtained passing triumphs by war, by the calamities of the world, by the shedding of blood: but he, by our prayers and for the life, the salvation and the joy of all, has won in our eyes and in those of posterity an immortal triumph."

It is like enough that these extravagant phrases expressed an exultation which was sufficiently genuine and sincere, for while he was absent the city of Rome desired and longed for its Pope, although when present it might do everything in its power to shake off his yoke. And Cola the ambassador, in whose mind as yet his own great scheme had not taken shape, might well believe that the gracious Pope who flattered him by such attention, who admitted him so freely to his august presence, and to whom he was as one who playeth very sweetly upon an instrument, was the man of all men to bring back again from anarchy and tumult the imperial city. He had even given up, it would seem, his enthusiasm for the classic heroes in this moment of hope from a more living and present source of help.

This elation however did not last. The Cardinal Giovanni Colonna, son of old Stefano, the head of that great house, of whose magnificent old age Petrarch speaks with so much enthusiasm, himself a man of many accomplishments, a scholar and patron of the arts—and to crown all, as has been said, the dear friend and patron of the poet—was one of the most important members of the court at Avignon, when the deputation from Rome, with that eloquent young plebeian as its interpreter, appeared before the Pope. We may imagine that its first great success, and the pleasure which the Pope took in the conversation of Cola, must have happened during some temporary absence of the Cardinal, whose interest in the affairs of his native city would be undoubted. And it was natural that he should be a little scornful of the ambassadors of the people, and of the orator who was the son of Rienzo of the wine-shop, and very indignant at the account given by the advocate of lo Popolo, of the barons and their behaviour. The Colonna were, in fact, the least tyrannical of the tyrants; they were the noblest of all the Roman houses, and no doubt the public sentiment against the nobles in general might sometimes do a more enlightened family wrong. Certainly it is hard to reconcile the pictures of this house as given by Petrarch with the cruel tyranny of which all the nobles were accused. This no doubt was the reason why, after the triumph of that letter, the consent of the Pope to the prayer of the citizens, and his interest in Cola's tale and descriptions, the young orator fell under the shadow of courtly displeasure, and after that intoxication of victory suffered all those pangs of neglect which so often end the temporary triumph of a success at court. The story is all vague, and we have no explanation why he should have lingered on in Avignon, unless perhaps with hopes of advancement founded on that evanescent favour, or perhaps in consequence of his illness. There is a forlorn touch in the description of the chronicler that "he lay like a snake in the sun," which is full of suggestion. The reader seems to see him hanging about the precincts of the court under the stately walls of the vast Papal palace, which now stands in gloomy greatness, absorbing all the light out of the landscape. It was new then, and glorious like a heavenly palace; and sick and sad, disappointed and discouraged, the young envoy, lately so dazzled by the sunshine of favour, would no doubt haunt the great doorway, seeking a sunny spot to keep himself warm, and waiting upon Providence. Probably the Cardinal, sweeping out and in, in his state, might perceive the young Roman fallen from his temporary triumph, and be touched by pity for the orator who after all had done no harm with his pleading; for was not Stefano Colonna again, in spite of all, Senator of Rome? Let us hope that the companion at his elbow, the poet who formed part of his household, and who probably had heard, too, and admired, like Pope Clement, the parole ornate of the speaker, who, though so foolish as to assail with his eloquent tongue the nobles of the land, need not after all be left to perish on that account—was the person who pointed out to his patron the poor fellow in his cloak, shivering in the mistral, that chill wind unknown in the midlands of Italy. It is certain that Petrarch here made Cola's acquaintance, and that Cardinal Colonna, remorseful to see the misery he had caused, took trouble to have his young countryman restored to favour, and procured him the appointment of Notary of the city, with which Cola returned to Rome—"fra i denti minacciava," says his biographer, swearing between his teeth.

It was in 1344 that his promotion took place, and for some years after Cola performed the duties of his office cortesemente, with courtesy, the highest praise an Italian of his time could give. In this occupation he had boundless opportunities of studying more closely the system of government which had resumed its full sway under the old familiar succession of Senators, generally a Colonna and an Orsini. "He saw and knew," says the chronicler, himself growing vehement in the excitement of the subject, "the robbery of those dogs of the Capitol, the cruelty and injustice of those in power. In all the commune he did not find one good citizen who would render help." It would seem, though there is here little aid of dates, that he did not act precipitately, but, probably with the hope of being able himself to do something to remedy matters, kept silence while his heart burned, as long as silence was possible. But the moment came when he could do so no longer, and the little scene at the meeting of the Cammora, the City Council, stands out as clearly before us as if it had been a municipal assembly of the present day. We are not told what special question was before the meeting which proved the last straw of the burden of indignation and impatience which Cola at his table, writing with the silver pen which he thought more worthy than a goose quill for the dignity of his office, had to bear. (One wonders if he was the inventor, without knowing it, of that little instrument, the artificial pen of metal with which, chiefly, literature is manufactured in our days? But silver is too soft and ductile to have ever become popular, and though very suitable to pour forth those mellifluous sentences in which the young spokesman of the Romans wrote to his chiefs from Avignon, would scarcely answer for the sterner purposes of the council to inscribe punishments or calculate fines withal.) One day, however, sitting in his place, writing down the decrees for those fines and penalties, sudden wrath seized upon the young scribe who already had called himself the consul of widows and orphans, and of the poor.

"One day during a discussion on the subject of the taxes of Rome, he rose to his feet among all the Councillors and said, 'You are not good citizens, you who suck the blood of the poor and will not give them any help.' Then he admonished the officials and the Rectors that they ought rather to provide for the good government, lo buono stato, of their city of Rome. When the impetuous address of Cola di Rienzi was ended, one of the Colonna, who was called Andreozzo di Normanno, the Camarlengo, got up and struck him a ringing blow on the cheek: and another who was the Secretary of the Senate, Tomma de Fortifiocca, mocked him with an insulting sign. This was the end of their talking."

We hear of no more remonstrances in the council. It is said that Cola was not a brave man, though we have so many proofs of courage afterwards that it is difficult to believe him to have been lacking in this particular. At all events he went out from that selfish and mocking assembly with his cheek tingling from the blow, and his heart burning more and more, to ponder over other means of moving the community and helping Rome.

The next incident opens up to us a curious world of surmise, and suggests to the imagination much that is unknown, in the lower regions of art, a crowd of secondary performers in that arena, the unknown painters, the half-workmen, half-artists, who form a background wherever a school of art exists. Cola perhaps may have had relations with some of these half-developed artists, not sufficiently advanced to paint an altar-piece, the scholars or lesser brethren of some local bottega. There was little native art at any time in Rome. The ancient and but dimly recorded work of the Cosimati, the only Roman school, is lost in the mists, and was over and ended in the fourteenth century. But there must have been some humble survival of trained workmen capable at least of mural decorations if no more. Pondering long how to reach the public, Cola seems to have bethought himself of this humble instrument of art. As we do not hear before of any such method of instructing the people, we may be allowed to suppose it was his invention as well as the silver pen. His active brain was buzzing with new things in every way, both great and small, and this was the first device he hit upon. Even the poorest art must have been of use in the absence of books for the illustration of sacred story and the instruction of the ignorant, and it was at this kind of instantaneous effect that Cola aimed. He had the confidence of the visionary that the evil state of affairs needed only to be known to produce instant reformation. The grievance over and over again insisted upon by his biographer, and which was the burden of his outburst in the council, was that "no one would help"—non si trovava uno buon Cittatino, che lo volesse adjutare. Did they but know, the common people, how they were oppressed, and the nobles what oppressors they were, it was surely certain that every one would help, and that all would go right, and the buono stato be established once more.

Here is the strange way in which Cola for the first time publicly "admonished the rectors and the people to do well, by a similitude."

"A similitude," says his biographer, "which he caused to be painted on the palace of the Capitol in front of the market, on the wall above the Cammora (Council Chamber). Here was painted an allegory in the following form—namely, a great sea with horrible waves, and much disturbed. In the midst of this sea was a ship, almost wrecked, without helm or sails. In this ship, in great peril, was a woman, a widow, clothed in black, bound with a girdle of sadness, her face disfigured, her hair floating wildly, as if she would have wept. She was kneeling, her hands crossed, beating her breast and ready to perish. The superscription over her was This is Rome. Round this ship were four other ships wrecked: their sails torn away, their oars broken, their rudders lost. In each one was a woman smothered and dead. The first was called Babylon; the second Carthage; the third Troy; the fourth Jerusalem. Written above was: These cities by injustice perished and came to nothing. A label proceeding from the women dead bore the lines:

'Once were we raised o'er lords and rulers all,
And now we wait, Oh Rome, to see thee fall.'

"On the left hand were two islands: on one of these was a woman sitting shamefaced with an inscription over her This is Italy. And she spoke and said:

'Once had'st thou power o'er every land, I only now, thy sister, hold thy hand.'

"On the other island were four women, with their hands at their throats, kneeling on their knees, in great sadness, and speaking thus:

'By many virtues once accompanied
Thou on the sea goest now abandonëd.'

"These were the four Cardinal virtues, Temperance, Justice, Prudence and Fortitude. On the other side was another little isle, and on this islet was a woman kneeling, her hands stretched out to heaven as if she prayed. She was clothed in white and her name was Christian Faith: and this is what her verse said:

'Oh noblest Father, lord and leader mine,
Where shall I be if Rome sink and decline?'

"Above on the right of the picture were four kinds of winged creatures who breathed and blew upon the sea, creating a storm and driving the sinking ship that it might perish. The first order were Lions, Wolves, and Bears, and were thus labelled: These are the powerful Barons and the wicked Officials. The second order were Dogs, Pigs, and Goats, and over them was written: These are the evil counsellors, the followers of the nobles. The third order were Sheep, Goats, and Foxes, and the label: These are the false officials, Judges and Notaries. The fourth order were Hares, Cats, and Monkeys, and their label: These are the People, Thieves, Murderers, Adulterers, and Spoilers of Men. Above was the sky: in the midst the Majesty Divine as though coming to Judgment, two swords coming from His mouth. On one side stood St. Peter, and on the other St. Paul praying. When the people saw this similitude with these figures every one marvelled."

Who painted this strange allegory, and how the work could be done in secret, in such a public place, so as to be suddenly revealed as a surprise to the astonished crowd, we have no means of knowing. It would be, no doubt, of the rudest art, probably such a scroll as might be printed off in a hundred examples and pasted on the walls by our readier methods, not much above the original drawings of our pavements. We can imagine the simplicity of the symbolism, the agitated sea in curved lines, the galleys dropping out of the picture, the symbolical figures with their mottoes. The painting must have been executed by the light of early dawn, or under cover of some license to which Cola himself as an official had a right, perhaps behind the veil of a scaffolding—put up on some pretence of necessary repairs: and suddenly blazing forth upon the people in the brightness of the morning, when the early life of Rome began again, and suitors and litigants began to cluster on the great steps, each with his private grievance, his lawsuit or complaint. What a sensation must that have occasioned as gazer after gazer caught sight of the fresh colours glowing on what was a blank wall the day before! The strange inscriptions in their doggerel lines, mystic enough to pique every intelligence, simple enough to be comprehensible by the crowd, would be read by one and another to show their learning over the heads of the multitude. How strange a thing, catching every eye! No doubt the plan of it, so unusual an appeal to the popular understanding, was Cola's; but who could the artist be who painted that "similitude"? Not any one, we should suppose, who lived to make a name for himself—as indeed, so far as we know, there were none such in Rome.

This pictorial instruction was for the poor: it placed before them Rome, their city, for love of which they were always capable of being roused to at least a temporary enthusiasm—struggling and unhappy, cheated by those she most trusted, ravaged by small and great, in danger of final and hopeless shipwreck. In all her ancient greatness, the peer and sister of the splendid cities of the antique world, and like them falling into a ruin which in her case might yet be avoided, the suggestion was one which was admirably fitted to stir and move the spectators, all of them proud of the name of Roman, and deeply conscious of ill-government and suffering. This, however, was but one side of the work which he had set himself to do. A short time after, when his picture had become the subject of all tongues in Rome, Cola the notary invited the nobles and notables of the city to meet in the Church of St. John Lateran to hear him expound a certain inscription there which had hitherto (we are told) baffled all interpreters. It must be supposed that he stood high in the favour of the Church, and of Raymond the Bishop of Orvieto, the Pope's representative, or he would scarcely have been permitted to use the great basilica for such a purpose.

The Church of the Lateran, however, as we know from various sources, was in an almost ruined state, nearly roofless and probably, in consequence, open to invasions of such a kind. Cola must have already secured the attention of Rome in all circles, notwithstanding that box on the ear with which Andreozzo of the Colonna had tried to silence him. He was taken by some for a burlatore, a man who was a great jest and out of whom much amusement could be got; and this was the aspect in which he appeared to one portion of society, to the young barons and gilded youth of Rome—a delusion to which he would seem to have temporarily lent himself, in order to diffuse his doctrine; while the more serious part of the aristocracy seem to have become curious at least to hear what he had to say, and prescient of meanings in him which it would be well to keep in order by better means than the simple method of Andreozzo. The working of Cola's own mind it is less easy to trace. His picture had been such an allegory as the age loved, broad enough and simple enough at the same time to reach the common level of understanding. When he addressed himself to the higher class, it was with an instinctive sense of the difference, but without perhaps a very clear perception what that difference was, or how to bear himself before this novel audience. Perhaps he was right in believing that a striking spectacle was the best thing to startle the aristocrats into attention: perhaps he thought it well to take advantage of the notion that Cola of Rienzo was more or less a buffoon, and that a speech of his was likely to be amusing whatever else it might be. The dress which his biographer describes minutely, and which had evidently been very carefully prepared, seems to favour this idea.

"Not much time passed (after the exhibition of the picture) before he admonished the people by a fine sermon in the vulgar tongue, which he made in St. John Lateran. On the wall behind the choir, he had fixed a great and magnificent plate of metal inscribed with ancient letters, which none could read or interpret except he alone. Round this tablet he had caused several figures to be painted which represented the Senate of Rome conceding the authority over the city to the Emperor Vespasian. In the midst of the Church was erected a platform (un parlatorio) with seats upon it, covered with carpets and curtains—and upon this were gathered many great personages, among whom were Stefano Colonna, and Giovanni Colonna his son, who were the greatest and most magnificent in the city. There were also many wise and learned men, Judges and Decretalists, and many persons of authority. Cola di Rienzo came upon the stage among these great people. He was dressed in a tunic and cape after the German fashion, with a hood up to his throat in fine white cloth, and a little white cap on his head. On the round of his cap were crowns of gold, the one in the front being divided by a sword made in silver, the point of which was stuck through the crown. He came out very boldly, and when silence was procured he made a fine sermon with many beautiful words, and said that Rome was beaten down and lay on the ground, and could not see where she lay, for her eyes were torn out of her head. Her eyes were the Pope and the Emperor, both of whom Rome had lost by the wickedness of her citizens. Then he said (pointing to the pictured figures), 'Behold, what was the magnificence of the Senate when it gave the authority to the Emperor.' He then read a paper in which was written the interpretation of the inscription, which was the act by which the imperial power was given by the people of Rome to Vespasian. Firstly that Vespasian should have the power to make good laws, and to make alliances with any whom he pleased, and that he should be entitled to increase or diminish the garden of Rome, that is Italy: and that he should give accounts less or more as he would. He might also raise men to be dukes and kings, put them up or pull them down, destroy or rebuild cities, divert rivers out of their beds to flow in another channel, put on taxes or abolish them at his pleasure. All these things the Romans gave to Vespasian according to their Charter to which Tiberius Cæsar consented. He then put aside that paper and said, 'Sirs, such was the majesty of the people of Rome that it was they who conferred this authority upon the Emperor. Now they have lost it altogether.' Then he entered more fully into the question and said, 'Romans, you do not live in peace: your lands are not cultivated. The Jubilee is approaching and you have no provision of grain or food for the people who are coming, who will find themselves unprovided for, and who will take up stones in the rage of their hunger: but neither will the stones be enough for such a multitude.' Then concluding he added: 'I pray you keep the peace.' Then he said this parable: 'Sirs, I know that many people make a mock at me for what I do and say. And why? For envy. But I thank God there are three things which consume the slanderers. The first luxury, the second jealousy, the third envy.' When he had ended the sermon and come down, he was much lauded by the people."

The inscription thus set before the people was the bronze table, called the Lex Regia. Why it was that no one had been able to interpret it up to that moment we are not told. Learning was at a very low ebb, and the importance of such great documents whether in metal or parchment was as yet but little recognised. This was evidently one of the results of Cola's studies of the old inscriptions of which we are told in the earliest chapter of his career. It had formed part of an altar in the Lateran Church, being placed there as a handy thing for the purpose in apparent ignorance of any better use for it, by Pope Boniface VIII. when he restored the church. No doubt some of the feeble reparations that were going on had brought the storied stone under Cola's notice, and he had interest enough to have it removed from so inappropriate a place. It is now let into the wall in the Hall of the Faun on the Capitol.

We have here an instance not only of the exaltation of Cola's mind and thoughts, imaginative and ardent, and his possession by the one idea of Roman greatness, but also of his privileges and power at this moment, before he had as yet struck a blow or made a step towards his future position. That he should have been allowed to displace the tablet from the altar (which however may have been done in the course of the repairs) to set it up in that conspicuous position, and to use the church, he a layman and a plebeian, for his own objects, testifies to very strong support and privilege. The influence of the Pope must have been at his back, and the resources of the Church thrown open to him. Neither his audacious speech nor his constant denunciation of barons and officials seem to have been attended by the risks we should have expected. Either the authorities must have been very magnanimous, or he was well protected by some power they did not choose to encounter. Some doubt as to his sanity or his seriousness seems to have existed among them. Giovanni Colonna, familiarly Janni, grandson of old Stefano, a brilliant young gallant likely to grow into a fine soldier, the hope of the house, invited him constantly to entertainments where all the gilded youth of Rome gathered as to a play to hear him talk. When he said, "I shall be a great lord, perhaps even emperor," the youths gave vent to shouts of laughter. "All the barons were full of it, some encouraging him, some disposed to cut off his head. But nothing was done to him. How many things he prophesied about the state of the city, and the generous rule it required!" Rome listened and was excited or amused according to its mood, but nothing was done either to conform that rule to his demands or to stop the bold reformer.

By this time it had become the passion of his life, and the occupation of all his leisure. He could think of nothing but how to persuade the people, how to make their condition clear to them. Once more his painter friends, the journeymen of the bottega, whoever they were, came to his aid and painted him again a picture, this time on the wall of St. Angelo in Pescheria, which we may suppose to have been Cola's parish church, as it continually appears in the narrative—where once more they set forth in ever bolder symbolism the condition of Rome. Again she was represented as an aged woman, this time in the midst of a great conflagration, half consumed, but watched over by an angel in all the glories of white attire and flaming sword, ready to rescue her from the flames, under the superintendence of St. Peter and St. Paul who looked on from a tower, calling to the angel to "succour her who gave shelter to us"; while a white dove fluttered down from the skies with a crown of myrtle to be placed upon the head of the woman, and the legend bore "I see the time of the great justice—and thou, wait for it." Once more the crowd collected, the picture was discussed and what it meant questioned and expounded. There were some who shook their heads and said that more was wanted than pictures to amend the state of affairs; but it may easily be supposed that as these successive allegories were represented before them, in a language which every one could understand, the feeling grew, and that there would be little else talked about in Rome but those strange writings on the walls and what their meanings were. The picture given by Lord Lytton in his novel of Rienzi, of this agitated moment of history, is very faithful to the facts, and gives a most animated description of the scenes; though in the latter part of his story he prefers romance to history.

All these incidents however open to our eyes side glimpses of the other Rome underneath the surface, which was occupied by contending nobles and magnificent houses, and all the little events and picturesque episodes with which a predominant aristocracy amused the world. If Mr. Browning had expounded Rome once more on a graver subject, as he did once in The Ring and the Book, what groups he might have set before us! The painters who had as yet produced no one known to fame, but who, always impressionable, would be agitated through all the depths of their workshops by the breath of revolution, the hope of something fine to come, would have taken up a portion of the foreground: for with the withdrawal of the Pope and the court, the occupation of a body of artist workmen, good for little more than decoration, ecclesiastical or domestic, must have suffered greatly: and none can be more easily touched by the agitation of new and aspiring thought than men whose very trade requires a certain touch of inspiration, a stimulus of fancy. No doubt in the studios there were many young men who had grown up with Cola, who had hung upon his impassioned talk before it was known to the world, and heard his vague and exalted schemes for Rome, for the renovation of all her ancient glories, not forgetting new magnificences of sculpture and of painting worthy of the renovated city, the mistress of the world. Their eager talk and discussions, their knowledge of his ways and thoughts, the old inscriptions he had shown them, the new hopes which he had described in his glowing language, must have filled with excitement all those bottegas, perched among the ruins, those workshops planned out of abandoned palaces, the haunt of the Roman youth who were not gentlemen but workmen, and to whom Janni Colonna and his laughing companions, who thought Cola so great a jest in his mad brilliancy, were magnificent young patrons half admired, half abhorred. How great a pride it must have been to be taken into Cola's confidence, to reduce to the laws of possible representation those "similitudes" of his, the stormy sea with its galleys and its islets, the blaze of the fatal fire: and to hurry out by dawn, a whole band of them, in all the delight of conspiracy, to dash forth the joint conception on the wall, and help him to read his lesson to the people!

And Browning would have found another Rome still to illustrate in the priests, the humbler clergy, the curé of St. Angelo in the Fishmarket, and so many more, of the people yet over the people, the humble churchmen with their little learning, just enough to understand a classical name or allusion, some of whom must have helped Cola himself to his Latin, and pored with him over his inscriptions, and taken fire from his enthusiasm as a mind half trained, without the limitations that come with completer knowledge, is apt to do—feeling everything to be possible and ignoring the difficulties and inevitable disasters of revolution. The great ideal of the Church always hovering in the air before the visionary priest, and the evident and simple reason why it failed in this case from the absence of the Pope, and the widowhood of the city, must have so tempered the classical symbolism of the leader as to make his dreams seem possible to men so little knowing the reality of things, and so confident that with the strength of their devotion and the purity of their aims everything could be accomplished. To such minds the possible and impossible have no existence, the world itself is such a thing as dreams are made of, and the complete reformation of all things, the heavens and the earth in which shall dwell righteousness, are always attainable and near at hand, if only the effort to reach them were strong enough, and the minds of the oppressed properly enlightened. No one has sufficiently set forth, though many have essayed to do so, this loftiness of human futility, this wild faith of inexperience and partial ignorance, which indeed sometimes does for a moment at least carry everything before it in the frenzy of enthusiasm and faith.

On the other side were Janni Colonna and his comrades, the young Savelli, Gaetani, all the gallant band, careless of all things, secure in their nobility, in that easy confidence of rank and birth which is perhaps the most picturesque of all circumstances, and one of the most exhilarating, making its possessor certain above all logic that for him the sun shines and the world goes round. There were all varieties among these young nobles as among other classes of men; some were bons princes, careless but not unthoughtful in any cruel way of others, if only they could be made to understand that their triumphant career was anyhow hurtful of others—a difficult thing always to realise. The Colonnas apart from their feuds and conflicts were generally bons princes. They were not a race of oppressors; they loved the arts and petted their special poet, who happened at that moment to be the great poet of Italy, and no doubt admired the eloquent Cola and were delighted with his discourses and sallies, though they might find a spice of ridicule in them, as when he said he was to be a great seigneur or even emperor. That was his jest, could not one see the twinkle in his eye? And probably old Stefano, the noble grandsire, would smile too as he heard the laughter of the boys, and think not unkindly of the mad notary with his enthusiasms, which would no doubt soon enough be quenched out of him, as was the case with most men when experience came with years to correct those not ungenerous follies of youth. The great churchmen would seem to have been still more tolerant to Cola—glad to find this unexpected auxiliary who helped to hold the balance in favour of the Pope, and keep the nobles in check.

In the meantime Cola proceeded with his warnings, and by and by with more strenuous preparation. We come to a date fortunately when we read of a sudden issue of potent words which came forth like the handwriting on the wall one morning, on February 15th, 1347. "In a short time the Romans shall return to their ancient good government." In brievo tempo—the actual sonorous words sounding forth large and noble like flute and trumpet in our ear, are worth quoting for the sound if no more: In brievo tempo I Romani tornaraco a lo loro antico buono stato. What a thrill of excitement to turn round a sudden corner and find this facing you on the church wall, words that were not there yesterday! Lo antico buono stato! the most skilful watchword, which thereafter became the special symbol of the new reformation. It is after this that we hear of the gathering of a little secret assembly in some quiet spot on the Aventine, "a secret place"—where on some privately arranged occasion there came serious men from all parts of the city, "many Romans of importance and buoni homini," which was the title, as we have seen, given to the popular leaders. "And among them were some of the gentry (cavalerotti) and rich merchants"—to consider what could be done to restore the good government (lo buono stato) of the city of Rome.

"Among whom Cola rose to his feet, and narrated, weeping, the misery, servitude and peril in which lay the city. And also what once was the great and lordly state which the Romans were wont to enjoy. He also spoke of the loss of all the surrounding country which had once been in subjection to Rome. And all this he related with tears, the whole assembly weeping with him. Then he concluded and said that it behoved them to serve the cause of peace and justice, and consoled them adding: 'Be not afraid in respect to money, for the Roman Cammora has much and inestimable returns.' In the first place the fires: each smoke paying four soldi, from Cepranno to the Porta della Paglia. This amounts to a hundred thousand florins. From the salt tax a hundred thousand florins. Then come the gates of Rome and the castles, and the dues there amount to a hundred thousand florins which is sent to his Holiness the Pope, and that his Vicar knows. Then he said, 'Sirs, do not believe that it is by the consent or will of the Pope that so many of the citizens lay violent hands on the goods of the Church.' By these parables the souls of the assembly were kindled. And many other things he said weeping. Then they deliberated how to restore the Buono Stato. And every one swore this upon the Holy Gospels—(in the Italian 'in the letter,' by a recorded act)."

It appears very probable by the allusion to the Pope's Vicar that he was present at this secret assembly. At all events he was informed of all that was done, and took part in the first overt act of the revolution. To give fuller warrant for these secret plans and conspiracies, the state of the city went on growing worse every day. The two parties, that of Colonna, and that of Orsini, so balanced each other, the one availing itself of every incident which could discredit and put at a disadvantage the other, that justice and law were brought to a standstill, every criminal finding a protector on one side or the other, and every kind of rapine and violence going unpunished. "The city was in great travail," our chronicler says, "it had no lord, murder and robbery went on on every side. Women were not safe either in convents or in their own houses. The labourer was robbed as he came back from his work, and even children were outraged; and all this within the gates of Rome. The pilgrims making their way to the shrines of the Apostles were robbed and often murdered. The priests themselves were ready for every evil. Every wickedness flourished: there was no justice, no restraint: and neither was there any remedy for this state of things. He only was in the right who could prove himself so with the sword." All that the unfortunate people could do was to band themselves together and fight, each for his own cause.

In the month of April of the year 1347 this state of anarchy was at its height. Stefano Colonna had gone to Corneto for provisions, taking with him all the milice, the Garde Nationale or municipal police of Rome. Deprived even of this feeble support and without any means of keeping order, the Senators, Agapito Colonna and Robert Orsini, remained as helpless to subdue any rising as they were to regulate the internal affairs of the city. The conspirators naturally took advantage of this opportunity. They sent a town crier with sound of trumpet to call all men to prepare to come without arms to the Capitol, to the Buono Stato at the sound of the great bell. During the night Cola would seem to have kept vigil—it was the eve of Pentecost—in the Church of St. Angelo in Pescheria hearing "thirty masses of the Holy Ghost," says the chronicler, spending the night in devotion as we should say. At the hour of tierce, in the early morning, he came out of Church, having thus invoked with the greatest solemnity the aid of God. It was the 20th of May, a summer festival, when all Rome is glorious with sunshine, and the orange blossoms and the roses from every garden fill the air with sweetness. He was fully armed except his head, which was bare. A multitude of youths encircled him with sudden shouts and cheering, breaking the morning quiet, and startling the churchgoers hastening to an early mass, who must have stood gaping to see one banner after another roll out between them and the sky, issuing from the church doors. The first was red with letters of gold, painted with a figure of Rome seated on two lions, carrying an orb, and a palm in her hands—"un Mundo e una Palma"—signs of her universal sovereignty. "This was the Gonfalon of Liberty"—and it was carried by Cola Guallato distinguished as "Lo buon dicitore"—another orator like

Rienzi himself. The second was white with an image of St. Paul, on the third was St. Peter and his keys. This last was carried by an old knight who, because he was a veteran, was conveyed in a carriage. By this time the great bell of the Capitol was ringing and the men who had been invited were hurrying there through all the streets. "Then Cola di Rienzo took all his courage, though not without fear, and went on alone with the Vicar of the Pope and went up to the Palace of the Capitol." There he addressed the crowd, making a bellissima diceria upon the misery and anarchy in Rome, saying that he risked his life for the love of the Pope and the salvation of the people. The reader can almost hear the suppressed quiver of excitement "not without fear" in his voice. And then the rules of the Buono Stato were read. They were very simple but very thorough. The first was that whoever murdered a man should die for it, without any exception. The second that every case heard before the judges should be concluded within fifteen days; the third that no house should be destroyed for any reason, except by order of the authorities. The fourth that every rione or district of the city should have its force of defenders, twenty-four horsemen and a hundred on foot, paid by and under the order of the State. Further, that a ship should be kept for the special protection of the merchants on the coast; that taxes were necessary and should be spent by the officers of the Buono Stato; that the bridges, castles, gates and fortresses should be held by no man except the rector of the people, and should never be allowed to pass into the hands of a baron: that the barons should be set to secure the safety of the roads to Rome and should not protect robbers, under a penalty of a thousand marks of silver:—that the Commune should give help in money to the convents; that each rione should have its granary and provide a reserve there for evil times; that the kin of every man slain in battle in the cause of the Commune should have a recompense according to their degree:—that the ancient States subject to Rome should be restored; and that whoever brought an accusation against a man which could not be proved should suffer the penalty belonging to the offence if it had been proved. This and various other regulations which pleased the people much were read, and passed unanimously by a show of hands and great rejoicing. "And it was also ordained that Cola should remain there as lord, but in conjunction with the Vicar of the Pope. And authority was given to him to punish, slay, pardon, to make laws and alliances, determine boundaries; and full and free imperia, absolute power, was given him in everything that concerned the people of Rome."

Thus was Cola's brag which so much amused the young lords made true over all their heads before many weeks were past. He had said that he would be a great lord, as powerful as an emperor. And so he was.

[THE LUNGARA]

The first incident in this new reign, so suddenly inaugurated, was a startling one. Stefano Colonna was the father of all the band—he of whom Petrarch speaks with such enthusiasm: "Dio immortale! what majesty in his aspect, what a voice, what a look, what nobility in his air, what vigour of soul and body at that age of his! I seemed to stand before Julius Cæsar or Africanus, if not that he was older than either. Wonderful to say, this man never grows old, while Rome is older and older every day." He was absent from Rome, as has been said, on the occasion of the wonderful overthrow of all previous rule, and establishment of the Buono Stato; but as soon as he heard what had happened, he hastened back, with but few followers, never doubting that he would soon make an end of that mountebank revolution. Early in the following morning he received from Cola a copy of the edict made on the Capitol and an order to leave Rome at once. Stefano took the paper and tore it in a thousand pieces. "If this fool makes me angry," he said, "I will fling him from the windows of the Capitol." When this was reported to Cola, he caused the bell of the Capitol to be sounded a stuormo, and the people rushed from all quarters to the call. Everything went rapidly at this moment of fate, and even the brave Colonna seems to have changed his mind in the twinkling of an eye. The aspect of affairs was so threatening that Stefano took the better part of valour and rode off at once with a single attendant, stopping only at San Lorenzo to eat, and pushing on to Palestrina, which was his chief seat and possession. Cola took instant advantage of this occurrence: with the sanction of the excited people, he sent a similar order to that which Stefano had received, to all the other barons, ordering them to leave the city. Strange to say the order of the popular leader was at once obeyed. Perhaps no one ventured to stand after the head of the Roman chivalry had fled. These gallant cavaliers yielded to the Pazzo, the madman, with whom the head of the Colonnas had expected to make such short work, without striking a blow, in a panic sudden and complete. Next day all the bridges were given up and officials of the people set over them. "One was served in one way, another in another—these were banished and those had their heads cut off without mercy. The wicked were all judged cruelly." Afterwards another Parlamento was held on the Capitol, and all that had been done approved and confirmed—and the people with one voice declared Cola, and with him the Pope's Vicar, who had a share in all these wonderful proceedings, Tribunes of the People and Liberators.

There would seem after this alarmed dispersion of the nobles to have been some attempt on their part to regain the upper hand, which failed as they could not agree among themselves: upon which they received another call from Cola to appear in the Capitol and swear to uphold the Buono Stato. One by one the alarmed nobles came in. The first was Stefanello Colonna, the son of the old man, the first of his children after the two ecclesiastics, and heir of his influence and lands. Then came Ranello degli Orsini, then Janni Colonna, he who had invited Cola to dinner and laughed loud and long with his comrades over the buffoonery of the orator. What Cola said was no longer a merry jest. Then came Giordano of the same name, then Messer Stefano himself, the fine old man, the magnanimous—bewildered by his own unexpected submission yet perhaps touched with some sense of the justice there was in it, swearing upon the Evangels to be faithful to the Commune, and to busy himself with his own share of the work: how to clear the roads, and turn away the robbers, to protect the orphans and the poor. The nobles gazed around them at the gathering crowd; they were daunted by all they saw, and one by one they took the oaths. One of the last was Francesco Savelli, who was the proper lord of Cola di Rienzo, his master—yet took the oath of allegiance to him, his own retainer. It was such a wonder as had never been seen. But everything was wonderful—the determination of the people, the Pope's Vicar by the side of that mad Tribune, the authority in Cola's eyes, and in his eloquent voice.

There must, however, have been a strong sense of the theatrical in the man. As he had at first appealed to the people by visible allegories, by pictures and similitudes, he kept up their interest now by continual spectacles. He studied his dress, as we have already seen, on all occasions, always aiming at something which would strike the eye. His robe of office was "of a fiery colour as if it had been scarlet." "His face and his aspect were terrible." He showed mercy to no criminal, but exercised freely his privilege of life and death without respect of persons. A monk of San Anastasio, who was a person of infamous conduct, was beheaded like any other offender; and a still greater, Martino di Porto, head of one of the great houses, met the same fate. Sometimes, his biographers allow, Cola was cruel. He would seem to have been a man of nervous courage "not without fear"; very keenly alive to the risk he was running and not incapable, as was afterwards proved, of a sudden panic, as quickly roused as his flash of excessive valour. In one mood he was pushed by the passion of the absolute to rash proceedings, sudden vengeance, which suited well enough with the instincts of his followers; in another his courage was apt to sink and his composure to fail at the first frown of fortune. The beginning of his career is like that of a man inspired—what he determined on was carried out as if by magic. He seemed to have only to ordain and it was accomplished. Within a very short time the courts of law, the markets, the public life in Rome were all transformed. The barons, unwilling as they were, must have done their appointed work, for the roads all at once became safe, and the disused processes of lawful life were resumed. "The woods rejoiced, for there were no longer robbers in them. The oxen began to plough. The pilgrims began again to make their circuits to the Sanctuaries, the merchants to come and go, to pursue their business. Fear and terror fell on the tyrants, and all good people, as freed from bondage, were full of joy." The bravos, the highwaymen, all the ill-doers who had kept the city and its environs in terror fled in their turn, finding no protectors, nor any shelter that could save them from the prompt and ready sword of justice. Refinements even of theoretical benevolence were in Cola's courts of law. There were Peacemakers to hear the pleas of men injured by their neighbours and bring them, if possible, into accord. Here is one very curious scene: the law of compensations, by which an injury done should be repaid in kind, being in full force.

"It happened that one man had blinded the eye of another; the prosecutors came and their case was tried on the steps of the Capitol. The culprit was kneeling there, weeping, and praying God to forgive him when the injured person came forward. The malefactor then raised his face that his eye might be blinded, if so it was ordained. But the other was moved with pity, and would not touch his eye, but forgave him the injury."

No doubt the ancient doctrine of an eye for an eye, has in all times been thus tempered with mercy.

It would appear that Cola now lived in the Capitol as his palace; and he gradually began to surround himself with all the insignia of rank. This was part of his plan from the beginning, for, as has been said, he lost no opportunity of an effective appearance, either from a natural inclination that way, or from a wise appreciation of the tastes of the crowd, which he had such perfect acquaintance with. But there was nothing histrionic in the immediate results of his new reign. That he should have styled himself in all his public documents, letters and laws, "Nicholas, severe and clement, Tribune of peace, freedom, and justice, illustrious Liberator of the holy Roman Republic," may have too much resembled the braggadocio which is so displeasing to our colder temperaments; but Cola was no Englishman, neither was he of the nineteenth century: and there was something large and harmonious, a swing of words such as the Italian loves, a combination of the Brutus and the Christian, in the conjunction of these qualities which recommends itself to the imaginative ear. But however his scarlet robes and his inflated self-description may be objected to, nothing could mar the greatness of the moral revolution he effected in a city restored to peace and all the innocent habits of life, and a country tranquillised and made safe, where men came and went unmolested. Six years before, as we have noted, Petrarch, the hero of the moment, was stopped by robbers just outside the walls of Rome, and had to fly back to the city to get an armed escort before he could pursue his way. "The shepherd armed," he says, "watches his sheep, afraid of robbers more than of wolves; the ploughman wears a shirt of mail and goads his oxen with a lance. There is no safety, no peace, no humanity among the inhabitants, but only war, hate, and the work of devils."

Such was the condition of affairs when Cola came to power. In a month or two after that sudden overturn his messengers, unarmed, clothed, some say, in white with the scarcella at their girdle embroidered with the arms of Rome, and bearing for all defence a white wand, travelled freely by all the roads from Rome, unmolested, received everywhere with joy. "I have carried this wand," says one of them, "over all the country and through the forests. Thousands have knelt before it and kissed it with tears of joy for the safety of the roads and the banishment of the robbers." The effect is still as picturesque as eye of artist could desire; the white figures with their wands of peace traversing everywhere those long levels of the Campagna, where every knot of brushwood, all the coverts of the macchia and every fortification by the way, had swarmed with robber bands—unharmed, unafraid, like angels of safety in the perturbed country. But it was none the less real, an immense and extraordinary revolution. The Buono Stato was proclaimed on the day of Pentecost, Whit Sunday, May 20th, 1347: and in the month of June following, Cola was able to inform the world—that is to say, all Italy and the Pope and the Emperor—that the roads were safe and everything going well. Clement VI. received this report at Avignon and replied to it, giving his sanction to what had been done, "seeing that the new constitution had been established without violence or bloodshed," and confirming the authority of Cola and of his bishop and co-tribune, in letters dated the 27th of June.

Nor was the change within the city less great. The dues levied by their previous holders on every bridge, on all merchandise and every passer-by, were either turned into a modest octroi, or abolished altogether; every man's goods were safe in his house; the women were free to go about their various occupations, the wife safe in the solitude of her home, in her husband's absence at his work, the girls at their sewing—in itself a revolution past counting. Rome began to breathe again and realise that her evil times were over, and that the Buono Stato meant comfort as well as justice. The new Tribune made glorious sights, too, for all bystanders in these June days. He rode to Church, for example, in state on the feast of Santo Janni di Jugnio, St. John the Baptist, the great Midsummer festa, a splendid sight to behold.

"The first to come was a militia of armed men on horseback, well dressed and adorned, to make way before the Præfect. Then followed the officials, judges, notaries, peacemakers, syndics, and others; followed by the four marshals with their mounted escort. Then came Janni d'Allo carrying the cup of silver gilt in which was the offering, after the fashion of the Senators: who was followed by more soldiers on horseback and the trumpeters, sounding their silver trumpets, the silver mouths making an honest and magnificent sound. Then came the public criers. All these passed in silence. After came one man alone, bearing a naked sword in sign of justice. Baccio, the son of Jubileo, was he. Then followed a man scattering money on each side all along the way, according to the custom of the Emperors: Liello Magliari was his name—he was accompanied by two persons carrying a sack of money. After this came the Tribune, alone. He rode on a great charger, dressed in silk, that is velvet, half green and half yellow, furred with minever. In his right hand he carried a wand of steel, polished and shining, surmounted by an apple of silver gilt, and above the apple a cross of gold in which was a fragment of the Holy Cross. On one side of this were letters in enamel, 'Deus,' and on the other 'Spiritus Sanctus.' Immediately after him came Cecco di Alasso, carrying a banner after the mode of kings. The standard was white with a sun of gold set round with silver stars on a field of blue: and it was surmounted by a white dove, bearing in its beak a crown of olive. On the right and left came fifty vassals of Vetorchiano on foot with clubs in their hands, like bears clothed and armed. Then followed a crowd of people unarmed, the rich and the powerful, counsellors, and many honest people. With such triumph and glory came he to the bridge of San Pietro, where every one saluted, the gates were thrown wide, and the road left spacious and free. When he had reached the steps of San Pietro all the clergy came forth to meet him in their vestments and ornaments. With white robes, with crosses and with great order, they came chanting Veni Creator Spiritus, and so received him with much joy."

This is how Cola rode from the Capitol to St. Peter's, traversing almost the whole of the existing city: his offering borne before him after the manner of the Senators: money scattered among the people after the manner of the Emperors: his banner carried as before kings: united every great rank in one. Panem et circenses were all the old Roman populace had cared for. He gave them peace and safety and beautiful processions and allegories to their hearts' content. There were not signs wanting for those who divined them afterwards, that with all this triumph and glory the Tribune began a little to lose his self-restraint. He began to make feasts and great entertainments at the Capitol. The palaces of the forfeited nobles were emptied of their beautiful tapestries, and hangings, and furniture, to make the long disused rooms there splendid; and the nobles were fined a hundred florins each for repairs to this half-royal, half-ruinous abode, making it glorious once more.

But in the meantime everything went well. One of the Colonnas, Pietro of Agapito[6]—who ought to have been Senator for the year—was taken and sent to prison, whether for that offence merely or some other we are not told; while the rest of the house, with old Stefano at their head, kept a stormy quiet at Palestrina, saying nothing as yet. Answers to Cola's letters came from all the states around, in congratulation and friendship, the Pope himself, as we have seen, at the head of all. "All Italy was roused," says Petrarch. "The terror of the Roman name extended even to countries far away. I was then in France and I know what was expressed in the words and on the faces of the most important personages there. Now that the needle has ceased to prick, they may deny it; but then all were full of alarm, so great still was the name of Rome. No one could tell how soon a movement so remarkable, taking place in the first city of the world, might penetrate into other places." The Soldan of Babylon himself, that great potentate, hearing that a man of great justice had arisen in Rome, called aloud upon Mahomet and Saint Elimason (whoever that might be) to help Jerusalem, meaning Saracinia, our chronicler tells us. Thus the sensation produced by Cola's revolution ran through the world: and if after a while his mind lost something of its balance, it is scarcely to be wondered at when we read the long and flattering letters, some of which have been preserved, which Petrarch talks of writing to him "every day": and in which he is proclaimed greater than Romulus, whose city was small and surrounded with stakes only, while that of Cola was great and defended by invincible walls: and than Brutus who withstood one tyrant only, while Cola overthrew many: and than Camillus, who repaired ruins still smoking and recent, while Cola restored those which were ancient and inveterate almost beyond hope. For one wonderful moment both friends and foes seem to have believed that Rome had at one step recovered the empire of the world.

Cola had thus triumphed everywhere by peaceful methods, but he had yet to prove what he could do in arms; and the opportunity soon occurred. The only one of the nobles who had not yielded at least a pretence of submission was Giovanni di Vico, of the family of the Gaetani, who had held the office of Præfect of Rome, and was Lord of Viterbo. Against him the Tribune sent an expedition under one of the Orsini, which defeated and crushed the rebel, who, on hearing that Cola himself was coming to join his forces, gave himself up and was brought into Rome to make his submission: so that in this way also the triumph of the popular leader was complete. All the surrounding castles fell into his hands, Civita Vecchia on one hand and Viterbo on the other; and he employed a captain of one family against the rebels of another with such skill and force that all were kept within control.

Up to the end of July this state of affairs continued unbroken; success on every side, and apparently a new hope for Italy, possibly deliverance for the world. The Tribune seemed safe as any monarch on his seat, and still bore himself with something of the simplicity and steadfastness of his beginning. But this began to modify by degrees. Especially after his easy victory over Giovanni di Vico, he seems to have treated the nobles whom he had crushed under his heel with contemptuous incivility, which is the less wonderful when we see how Petrarch, courtly as he was, speaks of the same class, acknowledging even his beloved Colonnas to be unworthy of the Roman name. The Tribune sat in his chair of state, while the barons were required to stand in his presence, with their arms folded on their breasts and their heads uncovered. His wife, who was beautiful and young, was escorted by a guard of honour wherever she went and attended by the noblest ladies of Rome. The old palace of the Campidoglio was gay with feasts; its dilapidated walls were adorned with the rich hangings taken from the confiscated houses of the potenti. And then the Tribune's poor relations began to be separated from the crowd, to ride about on fine horses and dwell in fine houses. And the sights and spectacles provided for the people, as well as the steps taken by Cola himself to enhance his dignity and to occupy the attention of everybody around, began to assume a fantastic character. An uneasy vainglory, a desire to be always executing some feat or developing some new pretension, a restless strain after the histrionic and dramatic began to show themselves in him—as if he felt that his tenure somehow demanded a continued supply of such amusements for the people, who rushed to gaze and admire whatever he did, and filled the air with vivas: yet began secretly in their hearts, as Lo Popolo always does, to comment upon the extravagance of the Tribune, and the elevation over their heads of Janni the barber, for instance, who now rode about so grandly with a train of attendants, as if, instead of being popolo like themselves, he were one of the potenti whom his nephew Cola had cast down from their seats.

One of the first great acts which denotes this trembling of sound reason in the Tribune's soul was the fantastic ceremony by which he made himself a knight, to the wonder of all Rome. It was not, all the historians tell us, a strange or unheard-of thing that the City should create cavalieri of its own. Florence had done it, and Rome also had done it—in the case of Stefano Colonna and some others very shortly before—but with at least the pretence of an honour conferred by the people on citizens selected by their fellow-citizens. Nothing of the kind was possible with Cola di Rienzi, and no illusion was attempted on the subject. He was supreme in all things, and it pleased him to take this dignity to himself. No doubt there was an ambitious purpose hidden under the external ceremony, which from the outside looked so much like a dramatic interlude to amuse the people, and a satisfaction of vanity on his own part. Both these things no doubt had their share, but they were not all. He made extraordinary preparations for the success and éclat, of what was in reality a coup d'état of the most extraordinary kind. First of all he fortified himself by the verdict of all the learned lawyers in Rome, to whom he submitted the question whether the Roman people had the right to resume into their own hands, and exercise, the authority which had been used by tyrants in the name of the city—a question to which there could be but one answer, by acclamation. These rights had always been claimed as absolute and supreme by whatsoever leaders the people of Rome had permitted to speak for them, or whom, more truly, they had followed like sheep. Twenty years before, as we have seen, they had been by way of conferring the crown of the

Empire upon Louis of Bavaria. It was a pretension usually crushed in its birth as even Il Bavaro did by receiving the same crown a second time from his anti-Pope; but it was one which had been obstinately held, especially in the disorderly ranks of Lo Popolo, and by visionaries of all kinds. The Popes had taken that control out of the hands of Rome and claimed it for the Church with such success as we have attempted to trace; but that in one form or another the reigning city of the world had always a right to this supremacy was held by all. In both cases it had been in a great degree a visionary and unreal claim, never practically accepted by the world, and the cause of endless futile struggles to overcome might with (hypothetical) right.

Cola however, as we have seen, had as high a conception of those claims of Rome as Gregory had, or Innocent. He believed that in its own right the old Imperial race—which was as little Imperial by this time, as little assured in descent and as devoid of all royal qualities as any tribe of barbarians—retained still the sway over the world which had been enforced by the Imperial legions under the greatest generals in the world. The enthusiasts for this theory have been able to shut their eyes to all the laws of nature and government, and with the strangest superstition have clung to the ghost of what was real only by stress of superior power and force, when all force had departed out of the hands which were but as painted shadows of the past. It is strange to conceive by what possible reasoning a conflicting host of mediæval barons of the most mixed blood, this from the Rhine, that from the south of Italy, as Petrarch describes on more than one occasion, of no true patrician stock: and the remains of a constantly subject and enslaved people, never of any account except in moments of revolution—could be made to occupy the place in the world which Imperial Rome, the only conqueror, the sole autocrat of the world, had held. The Popes had another and more feasible claim. They were the heads of a spiritual Empire, standing by right of their office between God and the world, with a right (as they believed) to arbitrate and to ordain, as representatives of heaven; a perfectly legitimate right, if allowed by those subject to it, or proved by sufficient evidence. Cola, with a curious twist of intelligence and meaning, attempted to combine both claims. He was the messenger of the Holy Ghost as well as the Tribune of the City. Only by the immediate action of God, as he held, could such a sudden and complete revolution as that which had put the power into his hands have been accomplished: therefore he was appointed by God. But he was also the representative of the people, entrusted by Rome with complete power. The spheres of these two sublime influences were confused. Sometimes he acted as inspired by one, sometimes asserted himself as the impersonation of the other. Knight of the Holy Ghost, he was invested with the white robes of supernatural purity and right—Tribune of Rome, he held the mandate of the people and wielded the power which was its birthright. This was the dazzling, bewildering position and supremacy which he was now to claim before the world.

He had invited all the States of Italy to send deputations of their citizens to Rome, and the invitation had been largely accepted. From Florence, Sienna, Perugia, and many other lesser cities, the representatives of the people came to swell his train. The kings of France and England made answer by letter in tones of amity; from Germany Louis of Bavaria hailed the Tribune in friendly terms, requesting his intercession with the Pope. The Venetians, and "Messer Luchino il granne tyranno de Milano" also sent letters; and ambassadors came from Sicily and from Hungary, both claiming the help of Rome. Everything was joy and triumph in the city. It was the 1st of August—a great festival, the day of the Feriae Augusti— Feragosto, according to the Roman patois—among the populace which no longer knew what that meant; but Cola, who was better instructed, had chosen it because of its significance. He rode to the Lateran in the afternoon in great splendour. It was in the Church's calendar the vigil of San Pietro in Vincoli, the anniversary of the chains of the Apostle, which the Empress Eudoxia had brought with great solemnity to Rome. "All Rome," says the chronicler, "men and women rushed to St. John Lateran, taking places under the portico to see the festa, and crowding the streets to behold this triumph.

"Then came many cavaliers of all nations, barons and people, and Foresi with breastplates of bells, clothed in samite, and with banners; they made great festivity, and there were games and rejoicings, jugglers and buffoons without end. There sounded the trumpets, here the bagpipes, and the cannon was fired. Then, accompanied with music, came the wife of Cola on foot with her mother, and attended by many ladies. Behind the ladies came young men finely dressed, carrying the bridle of a horse gilt and ornamented. There were silver trumpets without number, and you could see the trumpeters blow. Afterwards came a multitude of horsemen, the first of whom were from Perugia and Corneto. Twice they threw off their silver robes.[7] Then came the Tribune with the Pope's Vicar by his side. Before the Tribune was seen one who carried a naked sword, another carried a banner over his head. In his own hand he bore a steel wand. Many and many nobles were with him. He was clothed in a long white robe, worked with gold thread. Between day and night he came out into the Chapel of Pope Benedict to the loggia and spoke to the people, saying, 'You know that this night I am to be made knight. When you come back you shall hear things which will be pleasing to God in heaven and to men on earth.' He spoke in such a way that in so great a multitude there was nothing but gladness, neither horror nor arms. Two men quarrelled and drew their swords, but were soon persuaded to return them to their scabbards.... When all had gone away the clergy celebrated a solemn service, and the Tribune entered into the Baptistery and bathed himself in the shell[8] of the Emperor Constantine which was of precious porphyry. Marvellous is this to say; and much was it talked of among the people. Then he slept upon a venerable bed, lying in that place called San Giovanni in Fonte within the circuit of the columns. There he passed the night, which was a great wonder. The bed and bedding were new, and as the Tribune got up from it some part of it fell to the ground in the silence of the night. In the morning he clothed himself in scarlet; the sword was girt upon him by Messer Vico degli Scotti, and the gold spurs of a knight. All Rome, and every knight among them, had come back to San Giovanni, also all the barons and strangers, to behold Messer Cola di Rienzi as a knight."

The chronicle goes on to tell us after this, how Cola went forth upon the loggia of Pope Benedict's Chapel, while a solemn mass was being performed, and addressed the people.

"And with a great voice he cited, first, 'Messer Papa Chimente' to return to his See in Rome, and afterwards cited the College of the Cardinals. Then he cited the Bavarian. Then he cited the electors of the Empire in Germany saying, 'I would see what right they have to elect,' for it was written that after a certain time had elapsed the election fell to the Romans. When this citation was made, immediately there appeared letters and couriers to carry them, who were sent at once on their way. Then he took the sword and drew it from its scabbard, and waved it to the three quarters of the world saying, 'This is mine; and this is mine; and this is mine.' The Vicar of the Pope was present, who stood like a dumb man and an idiot stupefied by this new thing. He had his notary with him, who protested and said that these things were not done by his consent, and that he had neither any knowledge of them, nor sanction from the Pope. And he prayed the notary to draw out his protest publicly. While the notary made this protest crying out with a loud voice, Messer Cola commanded the trumpets and all the other instruments to play, that the voice of the notary might not be heard, the greater noise swallowing up the lesser."

These were the news which Cola had promised to let the crowd know when they returned—news pleasing to God and to men. But there were no doubt many searchings of heart in the great crowd that filled the square of the Lateran, straining to hear his voice, as he claimed the dominion of the world, and called upon Pope and Emperor to appear before him. No wonder if the Pope's Vicar was "stupefied" and would take no part in these strange proceedings. It was probably the Notary of the Commune and not

Cola himself who published the citations, and the authority for them, set forth at length, which were enough to blanch the cheeks of any Vicar of the Pope.

"In the sanctuary, that is the Baptistery, of the holy prince Constantine of glorious memory, we have received the bath of chivalry; under the conduct of the Holy Spirit, whose unworthy servant and soldier we are, and for the glory of the Holy Church our mother, and our lord the Pope, and also for the happiness and advantage of the holy city of Rome, of holy Italy and of all Christendom, we, knight of the Holy Spirit, and as such clothed in white, Nicolas, severe and clement, liberator of the city, defender of Italy, friend of mankind, and august Tribune, we who wish and desire that the gift of the Holy Ghost should be received and should increase throughout Italy, and intend, as God enables us, to imitate the bounty and generosity of ancient princes, we make known: that when we accepted the dignity of Tribune the Roman people, according to the opinions of all the judges, lawyers, and learned authorities, recognised that they possessed still the same authority, power and jurisdiction over all the earth which belonged to them in primitive times, and at the period of their greatest splendour: and they have revoked formally all the privileges accorded to others against that same authority, power, and jurisdiction. Therefore in conformity with those ancient rights and the unlimited power which has been conferred upon us by the people in a general assembly, and also by our lord the Pope, as is proved by his bulls apostolical: and that we may not be ungrateful to the grace and gift of the Holy Spirit, or avaricious of this same grace and gift in respect to the Roman people and the peoples of Italy above mentioned: in order also that the rights and jurisdiction of the Roman people may not be lost: we resolve and announce, in virtue of the power and grace of the Holy Spirit, and in the form most feasible and just, that the holy city of Rome is the head of the world and the foundation of Christian faith: and we declare that all the cities of Italy are free, and we accord and have accorded to these cities an entire freedom, and from to-day constitute them Roman citizens, declaring, announcing, and ordaining that henceforward they should enjoy the privileges of Roman freedom.

"In addition, and in virtue of the same puissance and grace of God, of the Holy Spirit, and of the Roman people, we assert, recognise and declare that the choice of the Roman Emperor, the jurisdiction and dominion over all the holy empire, belongs to the Holy City itself, and to holy Italy by several causes and reasons; and we make known by this decree to all prelates, elected emperors, and electors, to the kings, dukes, princes, counts, and margraves, to the people, to the corporations, and to all others who contradict this and exercise any supposed right in respect to the choice of the empire, that they are called to appear to explain their pretensions in the Church of the Lateran, before us and the other commissioners of our lord the Pope between this and Pentecost of next year, and that after that time we shall proceed according to our rights and the inspiration of the Holy Ghost."

The instrument is very long drawn out and entangled in its sentences, but the claim set forth in it is very clear, and arrogant as that of any Forged Decretals or Papal Bull. Its tone makes every pretension of the Popes sound humble, and every assertion of their power reasonable. But there is no reason to doubt that it was perfectly sincere. Rome was a word which went to the heads of every one connected with that wonderful city. Nothing was too great for her; no exaltation too high. To transfer the election of the Emperor from the great German princes to the populace of Rome, fickle and ignorant, led by whoever came uppermost, was a fantastic imagination, which it is almost impossible to believe any sane man could entertain. Yet Cola thought it just and true, the only thing to be done in order to turn earth into a sort of heaven; and Petrarch, a more prudent man, thought the same. To the poet Cola's enterprise was the hope of Italy and of the world: and it was at this moment, when the Tribune was in the full flush of his triumph, that Petrarch addressed to him, besides a promise of a poem supposed to be fulfilled in the Spirito Gentil, a long letter, Esortatoria, in which he exhorts him to pursue the "happy success" of his "most glorious undertaking," by sobriety and modesty it is true, but also by gladness and triumph, in order that the city "chosen by all the world as the seat of empire," should not relapse into slavery. "Rome, queen of cities, lady of the world, head of the empire, seat of the great Pontiff," her claim to dominion was not doubted by those strange enthusiasts. She was an abstraction, an ideal wisdom and power personified—not even in a race, not in a great man or men, but in the city, and that ever wavering tumultuous voice of the populace, blown hither and thither by every wind. And Cola believed himself to hold in his hands the fortunes and interests of Christendom entire, the dominion of the whole world. No enthusiasm, no delusion, could be more extraordinary.

The ceremonies of August did not finish with this. Another prodigious ceremonial was celebrated on the day of the Assumption of the Virgin, the fifteenth of that month, also a great Roman holiday. On this day there was once more a great function in the Church of the Lateran. The Pope's Vicar refused to preside, awaiting in the meantime orders from headquarters. But this did not arrest these curious proceedings. This time it was the coronation of the Tribune that was in question. He had made himself a knight, and even had invented an order for himself, the order of those "Clothed in White," the Knights of the Holy Spirit. Now he was to be crowned according to his fashion. The chronicler of the life of Cola, however, takes no notice of this ceremony. It was begun by the Prior of St. John Lateran, who advanced to the Tribune and gave him a crown of oak-leaves, with the words, "Take this oaken crown because thou hast delivered the citizens from death." After him came the Prior of St. Peter's with a crown of ivy, saying, "Take this ivy because thou hast loved religion." The Dean of St. Paul's came next with a crown of myrtle, "Because thou hast done thy duty and preserved justice, and hast hated bribes." The Prior of St. Lorenzo brought a crown of laurel, he of Sta. Maria Maggiore one of olive, with the not very suitable address, "Take this, man of humble mind, because in thee humility has overcome pride." Finally the Prior of the hospital of Santo Spirito presented Cola with a silver crown and a sceptre, saying, "Illustrious Tribune, receive this crown and sceptre, the gifts of the Holy Spirit, along with the spiritual crown." This, one would suppose, must have been an interpolation; for Goffredo degli Scotti, who had belted on his sword as a knight, was present with another silver crown, given by the people of Rome, which was surmounted by a cross, and which was presented to Cola with the words: "Illustrious Tribune, receive this: exercise justice, and give us freedom and peace."

The reader will be tempted to imagine that Cola must have been weighed down by this pyramid of wreaths, like a French schoolboy in his moment of triumph. But in the midst of all these glorious surroundings his dramatic imagination had conceived a telling way of getting rid of them. By his side stood a man very poorly dressed and carrying a sword, with which he took off in succession every crown as it was placed upon the Tribune's head, "in sign of humility and because the Roman Emperors had to endure every incivility addressed to them in the day of their triumph." We find, however, the beggar man with all the crowns spitted upon his sword, a ridiculous rather than an expressive figure. The last of all, the silver crown, remained on the Tribune's brows, the Archbishop of Naples having the courtly inspiration of interposing when the ragged attendant would have taken it. All the different wreaths had classical or Scriptural meanings. They were made from the plants that grew wild about the Arch of Constantine; everything was symbolical, mystic—the seven gifts of the Spirit; and all pervaded by that fantastic mixture of the old and the new, of which the world was then full.

After this final assertion of his greatness Cola made a speech to the people confirming the assertions and high-flown pretensions of his former proclamation, and forbidding any emperor, king, or prince whatsoever, to touch the sacred soil of Italy without the consent of the Pope and the Roman people. He seems to have concluded by forbidding the use of the names of Guelf and Ghibelline—an admirable rule could it have been carried out.

While all Rome was thus swarming in the streets, filling up every available inch of space under the porticoes and in the square to see this great sight, a certain holy monk, much esteemed by the people, was found weeping and praying in one of the chapels of Sta. Maria Maggiore, while the Tribune in all his state was receiving crowns and homage. One of Cola's domestic priests, who officiated in the private chapel at the Capitol, asked Fra Guglielmo why in the midst of so much rejoicing he alone was sorrowful. "Thy master," said the monk, "has fallen from heaven to-day! Oh that such pride should have entered into his soul! With the help of the Holy Spirit he has driven the tyrants out of Rome without striking a blow, he has been raised to the dignity of a Tribune, and all the towns and all the lords of Italy have done him honour. Why is he so proud and so ungrateful towards the Most High, and why does he dare in an insolent address to compare himself to his Creator? Say to thy master that nothing will expiate such a crime but tears of penitence." Thus it will be seen that there were checks, very soon apparent, to the full flood of enthusiasm and faith with which the Tribune had been received.

Meanwhile there remained, outside of all these triumphs and rejoicings and the immense self-assertion of the man who in the name of Rome claimed a sort of universal dominion—a strong band of nobles still in possession of their castles and strongholds round the city, grimly watching the progress of affairs, and no doubt waiting the moment when the upstart who thus had pranked himself in all the finery and the follies of royalty, should take that step too far which is always to be expected and which should decide his fate. No doubt to old Stefano Colonna, with all his knowledge of men, this end would seem coming on very surely when he heard of, or perhaps witnessed, the melodrama of the knighthood, the farce of the coronation. Cola had been forced to take advantage of the services of these barons, even though he hated them. He had put an Orsini at the head of his troops against the Præfect Giovanni di Vico. He appointed Janni Colonna, his former patron, who had laughed at him so heartily, to lead the expedition against the Gaetani. Nowhere, it would seem, among the men who were popolari, of the people, was the ghost of a general to be found. The nobles had been at first banished from Rome; but their good behaviour in that great matter of the safety of the roads, or else the difficulty of acting against them individually, and the advice of Petrarch and others who advised great caution, had no doubt tacitly broken this sentence, and permitted their return. Many of them were certainly in Rome, going and coming, though none held any office; and we are told that old Stefano was present at the great dinner after Cola made himself a knight. Perhaps comments were made upon those ceremonies which reached the ears of the Tribune; perhaps there were whispers of growing impatience in the other party, or hints of plots among them. Or perhaps Cola, having exhausted all other methods of giving to himself and Rome a new sensation, bethought himself of these enemies of the Republic, always no doubt desirous of acting against her, whether they did so openly or not. His proceedings had now become so histrionic that it is permissible to surmise a motive which otherwise would have been unworthy a man of his genius and natural power; and in face of the curious tragi-comedy which followed it is difficult not to suspect something of the kind. One day in September the Tribune invited a number of the nobles to a great dinner. The list given in the Vita includes the noblest names in Rome. Stefano Colonna with three of his sons—Agapito and "the prosperous youth" Janni (grandson) and Stefanello, the eldest lay member of the family, along with a number of the Orsini, Luca de Savelli, the Conte di Vertolle, and several others. The feast would seem to have begun with apparent cordiality and that strained politeness and watchfulness on the part of the guests, which has distinguished many fatal banquets in which every man mistrusted his neighbour. Cola had done nothing as yet to warrant any downright suspicion of treachery, but most likely the barons had an evil conscience, and it might have been observed that the Tribune's courtesy also was strained.

"Towards evening the popolari who were among the guests began to talk of the defects of the nobles, and the goodness of the Tribune. Then Messer Stefano the elder began a question, which was best in a Ruler of the people, to be prodigal or economical? A great discussion arose upon this, and at the last Messer Stefano took up a corner of Cola's robe, and said, 'To thee, Tribune, it would be more suitable to wear an honest costume of cloth, than this pompous habit,' and saying this he showed the corner of the robe. When Cola heard this he was troubled. He called for the guard and had them all arrested. Messer Stefano the veteran was placed in an adjoining hall, where he remained all night without any bed, pacing about the room, and knocking at the door prayed the guards to free him; but the guards would not listen to him. Then daylight appeared. The Tribune deliberated whether he should not cut off their heads, in order to liberate completely the people of Rome. He gave orders that the Parlatorio should be hung with red and white cloth, which was the signal of execution. Then the great bell was rung and the people gathered to the Capitol. He sent to each of the prisoners a confessor, one of the Minor friars, that they might rise up to repentance and receive the body of Christ. When the Barons became aware of all these preparations and heard the great bell ringing, they were so frozen with fear that they could not speak. Most of them humbled themselves and made their penitence, and received the communion. Messer Rainallo degli Orsini and some others, because they had in the morning eaten fresh figs, could not receive, and Messer Stefano Colonna would not confess, nor communicate, saying that he was not ready, and had not set his affairs in order.

"In the meanwhile, several of the citizens, considering the judgment that was about to be made, used many arguments to prevent it in soothing and peaceful words. At last the Tribune rose from the council and broke up the debate. It was now the hour of Tierce. The Barons as condemned persons came down sadly into the Parlatorio. The trumpets sounded as if for their execution, and they were ranged in face of the people. Then the Tribune changed his purpose, ascended the platform, and made a beautiful sermon. He repeated the Pater Noster, that part which says 'Forgive us our debts.' Then he pardoned the Barons and said that he wished them to be in the service of the people, and made peace between them and the people. One by one they bowed their heads to the people. After this their offices were restored to them, and to each was given a beautiful robe trimmed with vair: and a new Gonfalon was made with wheatears in gold. Then he made them dine with him and afterwards rode through the city, leading them with him; and then let them go freely on their way. This that was done much displeased all discreet persons who said, 'He has lighted a fire and flame which he will not be able to put out.'"

"And I," adds the chronicler, "said this proverb," which was by no means a decorous one: its meaning was that it was useless to make a smell of gunpowder and shoot no one.

The Tribune's dramatic instincts had gone too far. He had indeed produced a thrilling sensation, a moment of extreme and terrible tragic apprehension; but he forgot that he was playing with men, not puppets, and that the mercy thus accorded after they had been brought through the bitterness of death, was not likely to be received as a generous boon by these shamed and outraged patricians, who were as much insulted by his mercy as they were injured by his fictitious condemnation. They must have followed him in that ride through Rome with hearts burning within them, the furred mantles which were his gifts like badges of shame upon their shoulders: and each made his way, as soon as they were free, outside the gates to their own castles, with fury in their hearts. These men were not of the kind upon whom so tragic a jest could be played. Old Stefano and his sons, having suffered the further indignity of being created by that rascal multitude patricians and consuls, went off to their impregnable Palestrina, and the Orsini to Marino, an equally strong place. Henceforward there was no peace possible between the Tribune and the nobles of Rome. "He drew back from the accomplishment of his treachery," says his modern biographer Papencordt. Did he ever intend to do more than was done? It seems to us very doubtful. He was a man of sensations, and loved a thrilling scene, which he certainly secured. He humiliated his foes to the very dust, and made a situation at which all Rome held its breath: the tribunal draped as for a sentence of death, the confessor at every man's elbow, the populace solemnly assembled to see the tyrants die, while all the while the robes with their border of royal minever were laid ready, and the banners worked with ears of wheat. There is a touch almost of the mountebank in those last details. Petrarch, it is curious to note, disapproved, not of the trap laid for the nobles, or the circumstances of the drama, but of the failure of Cola to take advantage of such an opportunity, "an occasion such as fortune never gave to an Emperor," when he might have cut off at a single blow the enemies of freedom. Perhaps the poet was right: but yet Cola in his folly would have been a worse man if he had been a wiser one. As it was his dramatic instinct was his ruin.

The barons went off fra denti minacciavano, swearing through their teeth, and it was not long before the Orsini, who had been, up to that tragic banquet, his friends and supporters, had entrenched themselves in Marino, and were in full rebellion, resuming all the ancient customs of their race, and ravaging the Campagna to the very gates of Rome. It was the time of the vintage, which for once it had seemed likely would be made in peace that first year of the republic, if never before. But already the spell of the short-lived peace was broken, and once more the raiders were abroad, carrying terror and loss to all the surrounding country. "So great was the folly of the Tribune," his primitive biographer resumes, losing patience, that instead of following the rebels at once to their lair, he gave them time to fortify Marino and set everything in order for defence, so that it proved a hard task when at last he bestirred himself and went against the stronghold with an army of unusual strength, chiefly raised among the irritated Romans themselves, with which he spoiled all the surrounding country, took a smaller fortress belonging to the Orsini, and so alarmed them that they offered to surrender on condition of having their safety secured. Cola would make no conditions, but he did not succeed in taking Marino, being urgently called back to Rome to meet the Legate of the Pope, who had been sent to deal with him with the severest threats and reprimands. The Tribune upon this returned to the city, raising the siege of Marino; and instantly on his arrival gave orders for the destruction of the palace of the Orsini, near the Castle of St. Angelo. He then went on to St. Peter's, where with his usual love of costume, and in the strange vanity which more and more took possession of him, he took from the treasury of the Chief of the Apostles the dalmatic usually worn by the Emperors during the ceremonies of their coronation, a garment of great price, "all embroidered," says the chronicler, "with small pearls." This he put on over his armour, and so equipped, and with the silver crown on his head which was his distinction as Tribune, and the glittering steel sceptre in his hand, went to the Papal palace, where the Legate awaited him. "Terrible and fantastic was his appearance," says his biographer; and he was in no mood to receive the Legate as so high a functionary expected. "You have come to see us—what is your pleasure?" he said. The Legate replied: "I have much to say to you from the Pope." When the Tribune heard these words, he spoke out loudly in a high voice, "What have you to say?" but when the Legate heard this rampant reply, he stood astonished and was silent; then the Tribune turned his back upon him.

Rampagnosa indeed was his air and manner, touched with that madness which the gods send to those whom they would destroy; and fantastico the appearance of the leader, unaccustomed to arms, with the Emperor's splendid mantle over the dust of the road, and the pacific simplicity of the little civic crown over his steel cap. Probably the stately Cardinal-Legate, accustomed to princes and statesmen, thought the Tribune mad; he must have been partially so at least, in the excitement of his first campaign, and the rising tide of his self-confidence, and the hurry and commotion of fate.

In the meantime, however, Marino was not taken, and another fire of rebellion had broken out among the Colonnas, who were now known to be making great preparations for a descent upon Rome. The Legate had retired to Monte Fiascone, whence he opened a correspondence with both divisions of these rebel nobles; and a formidable party was thus organised, from one point to another, against Rome: while the city itself began to send forth secret messengers on all sides, the populace changing its mind as usual, while the wealthy citizens were alarmed by their isolation, or offended by the arrogance of their chief. Cola, too, by this time had begun, it would seem, to feel in his sensitive person the reaction of so much excitement and exaltation, and was for a short time ill and miserable, feeling the horror of the gathering tempest which began to rise round him on every side. But he was reinvigorated by various successes in Rome itself and by the still greater encouragement given by the arrival of the first rebel, the Lord of Viterbo, Giovanni di Vico, who came in the guise of friendship and with offers of aid, but at the same time with airs of importance and pretension which Cola did not approve. He was promptly secured by the usual but too easy method of an invitation to a banquet, a snare into which the Roman nobles seem to have fallen with much readiness, and was imprisoned. Then Cola, fully restored to himself, prepared to meet his foes. It was winter weather, a dark and cold November, when the rumour rose that the Colonna were approaching Rome. Cola called together his army, which had been increased by some bands of allies from neighbouring cities, and was headed by several Orsini of another branch of the house. He had already encouraged the people by public addresses, in which he related the appearance to him first of St. Martin, who told him to have no fear, and secondly of St. Boniface, who declared himself the enemy of the Colonna, who wronged the Church of God. Such visions show something of the disturbed condition of the Tribune's mind vainly trying to strengthen himself in a confidence which he did not feel. On the twentieth of November, in the gray of the morning, the great bell rang, and the trumpets sounded for the approach of the enemy: and with his forces divided into three bands, one under his own command, the others led by Cola and Giordano Orsini, he set forth to meet the rebels who by the gate of St. Lorenzo were drawing near to Rome.

The enemy had no great mind for the battle. They had marched all night through the bitter rain and cold. Old Stefano had been attacked by fever and was trembling like a leaf. Agapito, his nephew, had had a bad dream in which he saw his wife a widow, weeping and tearing her hair. They arrived before the gate in indifferent heart and with divided counsels, though there had been information sent them of a conspiracy within, and that the gate would be opened to them without any struggle. Stefano Colonna the younger, who was general of the host, then rode up alone and demanded entrance. "I am a citizen of Rome. I wish to return to my house. I come in the name of the Buono Stato," he said. The Captain of the Gate replied with great simplicity. It is evident that Stefano had called some one by name, expecting admittance. "The guards to whom you call are not here. The guard has been changed. I have newly come with my men. You cannot by any means come in. The gate is locked. Do you not know in what anger the people are against you for having disturbed the Buono Stato? Do not you hear the great bell? I pray you for God's sake go away. I wish you no harm. To show you that you cannot enter here, I throw out the key." The key, which was useless on the outer side of the gate, fell into a pool made by the rain: but the noise of its fall startled the already troubled nerves of the leaders, and they held hasty counsel what to do. "They deliberated if they could retire with honour," says the chronicler. It is most curious to hear this parleying, and the murmur of the army, uneasy outside, not knowing what further step to take, in the miserable November dawn, after their night march. They had expected to be admitted by treachery, and evidently had not taken this contretemps into their calculations. "They resolved to retire with honour," says Papencordt: and for this purpose troop by troop advanced to the gate, and then turned to retreat: perhaps in obedience to some punctilio of ancient warfare. The third battalion contained the pride of the army (li pruodi, e le bene a cavallo, e tutta la fortezza), young Janni Colonna, at its head. One portion of Cola's army had by this time reached the same spot inside, and were eager for a sortie, but could not open the gate in the usual manner, the key being lost; they therefore broke open one portion of it with great clamour and noise. The right side opened, the left remained closed.

"Janni Colonna approached the gate, hearing the noise within, and considering that there had been no order to open it, he thought that his friends must have made that noise, and that they had broken the gate by force. Thus considering, Janni Colonna quickly crossed the threshold with his lance in rest, spurring his courser, riding boldly without precaution. He entered the gate of the city. Deh! how terrified were the people! Before him all the cavalry in Rome turned to fly. Likewise the Popolo retreated flying, for the space of half a turn. But not for this did his friends follow Janni, so that he remained alone there, as if he had been called to judgment. Then the Romans took courage, perceiving that he was alone: the greater was his misfortune. His horse caught its foot in an open cellar (grotta) which was by the left side of the gate, and threw him, trampling upon him. Janni perceiving his misfortune, called out to the people for quarter, adjuring them for God's sake not to strip him of his armour. How can it be said? He was stripped and struck by three blows and died. Fonneruglio de Trejo was the first to strike. He (Janni) was a young man of a good disposition. His fame was spread through every land. He lay there naked, wounded and dead, in a heap against the wall of the city within the gate, his hair all plastered with mud, scarcely to be recognised. Then was seen a great marvel. The pestilential and disturbed weather began to clear, the sun shone out, the sky from being dark and cloudy became serene and gay."

This, however, was but the first chapter of this dreadful tragedy. And still greater misery was to come.

"Stefano della Colonna, among the multitude outside in front of the gate, demanded anxiously where was his son Janni, and was answered: 'We know not what he has done or where he has gone.' Then Stefano began to suspect that he had gone in at the gate. He therefore spurred his horse and went on alone, and saw his son lying on the ground surrounded by many people, between the cellar and the pool of water. Seeing that, Stefano fearing for himself, turned back; he went out from the gate and his good sense abandoned him. He was confounded; the loss of his son overcame him. He said not a word, but turned back and again entered the gate, if by any means he might save his son. When he drew near he saw that his son was dead. The question now was to save his own life, and he turned back again sadly. As he went out of the gate, and was passing under the Tower, a great piece of stone struck him on the shoulder and his horse on the croup. Then followed lances, thrown from every side. The wounded horse threw out its heels, and the rider unable to keep his seat fell to the ground, when the Popolo rushed upon him in front of the gate, in that place where the image stands, in the middle of the road. There he lay naked in sight of the people and of every one who passed by. He had lost one foot and was wounded in many places, one terrible blow having struck him between the nose and the eyes. Janni was wounded only in the breast and in one of his feet. Then the people flung themselves forth from the gate furiously without order or leader, seeking merely whom to kill. They met the young Cavaliers, foremost of whom was Pietro of Agapito di Colonna who had been Præfect of Marseilles, and a priest. He had never used arms till that day. He fell from his horse and could not recover himself, the ground being so slippery, but fled into a vineyard close by. Bald he was, and old, praying for God's sake to be forgiven. But vain was his prayer. First his money was taken, then his arms, then his life. He lay in that vineyard naked, dead, bald, fat—not like a man of war. Near him lay another baron, Pandolfo of the lords of Belvedere. In a small space lay twelve of them; prostrate they lay. All the rest of the army, horsemen as well as footmen, flung their arms from them here and there, and without order, in great terror, turned their backs: and there was not one who struck a blow."

Thus ended the first attack upon the Tribune—horribly, vilely, with panic on both sides, and the rage of wild beasts among the victorious people, not one on either side, except those two murdered Colonnas, bearing himself like a man. The record of the struggle, so intense in its brevity, so brutal and terrible, with its background of leaden skies and falling rain, and the muddy earth upon which both horses and men slipped and fell, is placed before us like a picture: and the sudden clearing of the weather, the sun breaking out suddenly upon those white prostrate figures, white and red with horrible wounds. There could not be a more appalling scene—amid all the records of internecine warfare one of the most squalid, unredeemed even by any feat of arms; for poor young Janni walked into the snare unconscious, and a blind chance, horrible and unpremeditated, seemed to reign over all—all but the father, heart-broken, retiring by instinct in the first discovery of danger, then turning back to save, if it were possible, his dying boy, who had been so brutally struck down and cut to pieces. The old father of all, the great Stefano, too old for war, and trembling with fever, was borne along in the crowd of the flying, to hide his bereaved head in his old fortress and sternly lament his children lost.

Cola, the chronicle says, shared the consternation of the people when young Janni's noble figure appeared in the opening of the gate. The Tribune's banner was overturned in the backward rush of the people before that solitary invader: and he himself, raising his eyes to heaven, cried out no other word than this: "Ah, God, hast thou betrayed me?" But when the sudden rush of murder and pursuit was over he recovered all his dramatic instincts along with his courage. The silver trumpets were sounded, a wreath of olive was placed upon his head above the silver crown, he waved his steel wand in the now brilliant sunshine, and marched into Rome, triumphant—as indeed he had good reason to be—to the Church of the Ara Coeli, where he deposited the olive crown and the steel wand before the altar of the Virgin. "After this," says the indignant chronicler, "he never carried sceptre again, nor wore crown, nor had a banner borne over his head." Once more he addressed the people from the Parlatorio, with the intonation of victory in every word. Drawing his sword, he wiped it with his robe, and said: "I have cut off with this such a head as neither the Pope nor the Emperor could touch."

Meanwhile the three dead Colonnas had been carried into Rome to the chapel of their house in the Ara Coeli. "The Contesse (the relations, wives and sisters) came, attended by many women tearing their hair, to wail (ululare) over the dead," but Cola had them driven away and forbade any funeral honours. "If they trouble me any more about these accursed corpses," he said, "I will have them thrown into a ditch. They were perjurers—they were not worthy to be buried." The three dead knights were carried secretly by night to the Church of San Silvestro, and buried by the monks senza ululato, without any lament made over them. Thus ended the noble Colonna, the hopes of the house—and with them, though he knew it not, the extravagant hopes and miraculous good fortune of Cola di Rienzi, which began to fall from that day.

We have dwelt upon the details of this history, because there is scarcely any other which gives so clear a vision of the streets and palaces, the rushing of the Popolo, the uncertain counsels of the nobles, the mingled temerity and panic which prevailed among all on both sides. The confusion is extraordinary; the ignorant crowd with its enthusiast leader scarcely less ignorant of men and the just course of human affairs, who defied with a light heart the greatest powers in Christendom, and retreated before the terrific vision of one young warrior in the gate: the nobles with their army, which sought only how to get away again without disgrace when they found themselves in front of a defended gate, and fled before a rabble sortie, of men as much frightened as themselves, and brave only when pursuing another demoralised troop. Whether we look to one side or the other, the effect is equally vivid. The revelation, at first so romantic and splendid, if always fantastic and theatrical, falls now into a squalid horror and mad brag, and cowardice, and fury, in which the spectacle of the Tribune, wiping the sword guiltless of blood upon his mantle, reaches perhaps the highest point of tragic ridicule: while all the chivalry of Rome galloping along the muddy roads to their strongholds, flying before a civic mob, is its lowest point of humiliating misery. It seems almost impossible to believe that the best blood and highest names of Italy, as well as on the other side its most visionary aspirations, should come to such degrading confusion and downfall.

[PORTA DEL POPOLO (FLAMINIAN GATE)]

FOOTNOTES:

[6] *A necessary distinction when there were so many of the same name—i.e., Pietro the son of Agapito, nephew of old Stefano.*

[7] *Changed their dresses, throwing those which they took off among the people.*

[8] *The bath, or baptismal vase of Constantine (so-called) here referred to, still stands in the Baptistery of the Lateran.*

[THEATRE OF MARCELLUS]

After so strange and so complete a victory over one party, had the Tribune pushed his advantage, and gone against the other with all the prestige of his triumph, he would in all probability have ended the resistance of the nobles altogether. But he did not do this. He had no desire for any more fighting. It is supposed, with insufficient reason we think, that personally he was a coward. What is more likely is that so sensitive and nervous a man (to use the jargon of our own times) must have suffered, as any fine temperament would have done, from that scene at the gate of San Lorenzo, and poor young Janni Colonna lying in his blood; and that when he declared "he would draw his sword no more," he did so with a sincere disgust for all such brutal methods. His own ways of convincing people were by argument and elocution, and pictures on the walls, which, if they did not convince, did nobody any harm. The next scene, however, which he prepared for his audience does not look much like the horror for which we have given him credit. He had informed his followers before he first set out against the nobles that he was taking his son with him—something in the tone with which the presence of a Prince Imperial might be proclaimed to an army; and we now find the young Lorenzo placed still more in the foreground. The day after that dreadful victory Cola called together the militia of the city by the most touching argument. "Come with me," he said, "and afterwards you shall have your pay." They turned out accordingly to accompany him, wondering, but not knowing what he had in his mind.

"The trumpets sounded at the place where the fight (sconfitto) had taken place. No one knew what was to be done there. He went with his son to the very spot where Stefano Colonna had died. There was still there a little pool of water. Cola made his son dismount and threw over him the water which was still tinged with the blood of Stefano, and said to him: 'Be thou a Knight of Victory.' All around wondered and were stupefied. Then he gave orders that all the commanders should strike his son on the shoulder with their swords. This done he returned to the Capitol, and said: 'Go your ways. We have done a common work. All our sires were Romans, the country expects that we should fight for her.' When this was said the minds of the people were much exercised, and some would never bear arms again. Then the Tribune began to be greatly hated, and people began to talk among themselves of his arrogance which was not small."

This grotesque and horrible ceremony seems to have done Cola more harm than all that had gone before. The leader of a revolution should have no sons. The excellent instinct of providing for his family after him, and making himself a stepping stone for his children, though proceeding from "what is best within the soul," has spoiled many a history. Cola di Rienzi was a most conspicuous and might have been a great man: but Rienzo di Cola, which would have been his son's natural name, was nobody, and is never heard of after this terrible baptism of blood, so abhorrent to every natural and generous impulse. Did the gazers in the streets see the specks of red on young Lorenzo's dress as he rode along through the city from the Tiburtine gate, and through the Forum to the Capitol, where all the train was dismissed so summarily? As the Cavallerotti, the better part of the gathering, turned their horses and rode away offended, no doubt the news ran through quarter after quarter with them. The blood of Stefanello, the heir of great Colonna! And thoughts of the old man desolate, and of young Janni so brave and gay, would come into many a mind. They might be tyrants, but they were familiar Roman faces, known to all, and with some reason to be proud, if proud they were; not like this upstart, who called honest men away from their own concerns to do honour to his low-born son, and sent them packing about their business afterwards without so much as a dinner to celebrate the new knight!

This was all in November, the 20th and 21st: and it was on the 20th of May that Cola had received his election upon the Capitol and been proclaimed master of the destinies of the universe, by inference, as master of Rome. Six months, no more, crammed full of gorgeous pageants and exciting events. Then, notwithstanding the extraordinary character of his revolution, he had been believed in, and encouraged by all around. He had received the sanction of the Pope, the friendly congratulations of the great Italian towns, and above all the applause, enthusiastic and overflowing, of Petrarch the greatest of living poets. By degrees all these sympathies and applauses had fallen from him. Florence and the other great cities had withdrawn their friendship, the Pope had cancelled his commission, the Pope's Vicar had left the Tribune's side. The more his vanity and self-admiration grew, the more his friends had fallen from him. That very day—the day after the defeat of the Colonna, before the news could have reached any one at a distance, Petrarch on his way to Italy, partly brought back thither by anxiety about his friend, received from another friend a copy of one of the arrogant and extraordinary letters which Cola was sending about the world, and read and re-read it and was stupefied. "What answer can be made to it? I know not," he cries. "I see that fate pursues the country, and on whatever side I turn, I find subjects of grief and trouble. If Rome is ruined what hope remains for Italy? and if Italy is degraded what will become of me? What can I offer but tears?" A few days later, arrived at Genoa, the poet wrote to Rienzi himself in reproof and sorrow:

[AQUA FELICE]

"Often, I confess it, I have had occasion upon thy account to repeat with immense joy what Cicero puts in the mouth of Scipio Africanus:—'What is this great and delightful sound that comes to my ears?' And certainly nothing could be better applied to the splendour of thy name and to the frequent and joyful account of thy doings: and it was indeed good to my heart to speak to thee in that exhortation, full of thy praise and of encouragements to continue, which I sent thee. Deh! do nothing, I conjure thee, to make me now ask, whence is this great and fatal rumour which strikes my ear so painfully? Take care, I beseech thee, not thyself to soil thine own splendid fame. No man in the world except thyself can shake the foundations of the edifice thou hast constructed; but that which thou hast founded thou canst ruin: for to destroy his own proper work no man is so able as the architect. You know the road by which you have risen to glory: if you turn back you shall soon find yourself in the lowest place; and going down is naturally the quicker.... I was hastening to you and with all my heart: but I turn upon the way. Other than what you were, I would not see you. Adieu, Rome, to thee also adieu, if that is true which I have heard. Rather than come to thee I would go to the Indies, to the end of the world.... Oh, how ill the beginning agrees with the end! Oh, miserable ears of mine that, accustomed to the sound of glory, do not know how to bear such announcements of shame! But may not these be lies and my words false? Oh that it might be so! How glad should I be to confess my error!... If thou art indeed so little careful of thy fame, think at least of mine. You well know by what tremendous tempest I am threatened, how many are the crowd of faultfinders ready to ruin me. While there is still time put your mind to it, be vigilant, look well to what you do, guide yourself continually by good counsel, consider with yourself, not deceiving yourself, what you are, what you were, from whence you have come, and to what point, without detriment to the public weal, you can attain: how to attire yourself, what name to assume, what hopes to awaken, and of what doctrine to make open confession; understanding always that not Lord, but solely Minister, you are of the Republic."

The share which Petrarch thus takes to himself in Cola's fortunes may seem exaggerated; but it must be remembered that the Colonna were his chief patrons and friends, that it was under their protecting shadow that he had risen to fame, and that his warm friendship for Rienzi had already deeply affected the terms of his relationship with them. That relationship had come to a positive breach so far as his most powerful protector, the Cardinal Giovanni, was concerned, a breach of feeling on one side as well as of protection on the other. His letter to the Cardinal after this catastrophe, condoling with him upon the death of his brothers, is one of the coldest of compositions, very unlike the warm and eager affection of old, and consisting chiefly of elaborate apologies for not having written. The poet had completely committed himself in respect to the Tribune; he had hailed his advent in the most enthusiastic terms, he had proclaimed him the hope of Italy, he had staked his own reputation upon his friend's disinterestedness and patriotism; therefore this downfall with all its humiliating circumstances, the vanities and self-intoxication which had brought it about, were intolerable to Petrarch: his own credit as well as Cola's was concerned. He had been so rash as to answer for the Tribune in all quarters, to pledge his own judgment, his power of understanding men, almost his honour, on Cola's behalf; and to be proved so wrong, so little capable of estimating justly the man whom he believed himself to know so well, was bitterness unspeakable to him.

The interest of his tragic disappointment and sorrow is at the same time enhanced by the fact, that the other party to this dreadful quarrel had been the constant objects of the poet's eulogies and enthusiasm. It is to Petrarch that we owe most of our knowledge of the Colonna family at this remarkable period of a long history which is filled with the oft-repeated incidents of an endless struggle for power, either with the rebellious Romans themselves, or with the other little less great family of the Orsini who, unfortunately for themselves, had no Petrarch to bring them fully into the light of day. The many allusions in Petrarch's letters, his reminiscences of the ample and gracious household, all so friendly, and caressing, all of one mind as to his own poetical qualities, and anxious to heap honours upon him, light up for us the face of the much complicated story, and give interest to many an elaborate poetical or philosophical disquisition. Especially the figure of the father, the old Stefano with his seven sons and the innumerable tribe of nephews and cousins, not to say grandsons, still more cherished, who surrounded him—rises clear, magnanimous, out of the disturbed and stormy landscape. His brief appearances in the chronicle which we have quoted, with a keen brief speech here and there, imperative, in strong accents of common sense as well as of power, add a touch of energetic life to the many anecdotes and descriptions of a more elaborate kind. And the poet would seem never to have failed in his admiration for the old Magnanimo. At an earlier period he had described in several letters to the son Giovanni, the Cardinal, the reception given to him at Rome, and conversations, some of them very remarkable. One scene above all, of which Petrarch reminds Stefano himself in his bereavement, gives us a most touching picture of the noble old man.

"One day at sunset you and I alone were walking by that spacious way which leads from your house to the Capitol, when we paused at that point where it is crossed by the other road by which on one hand you ascend to the Arch of Camillus, and on the other go down to the Tiber: we paused there without interruption from any and talked together of the condition of your house and family, which, often assailed by the enmity of strangers, was at that time moved by grievous internal commotions:—when the discourse fell upon one of your sons with whom, more by the work of scandal-mongers than by paternal resentment, you were angry, and by your goodness it was given to me, what many others had not been able to obtain, to persuade you to receive him again to your good grace. After you had lamented his faults to me, changing your aspect all at once you said (I remember not only the substance of your discourse but the very words). 'This son of mine, thy friend, whom, thanks to thee, I will now receive again with paternal affection, has vomited forth words concerning my old age, of which it is best to be silent; but since I cannot refuse you, let us put a stone over the past and let a full amnesty, as people say, be conceded. From my lips I promise thee, not another word shall be heard.

"'One thing I will tell you, that you may make perpetual remembrance of it. It is made a reproach to my old age that I am mixed up with warlike factions more than is becoming, and more than there is any occasion, and that thus I will leave to my sons an inheritance of peril and hate. But as God is true, I desire you to believe that for love of peace alone I allow myself to be drawn into war. Whether it be the effect of my extreme old age which chills and enfeebles the spirit in this already stony bosom, or whether it proceeds from my long observation of human affairs, it is certain that more than others I am greedy of repose and peace. But fixed and immovable as is my resolution never to shrink from trouble though I may prefer a settled and tranquil life, I find it better, since fate compels me, to go down to the sepulchre fighting, than to submit, old as I am, to servitude. And for what you say of my heirs I have but one thing to reply. Listen well, and fix my words in your mind. God grant that I may leave my inheritance to my sons. But all in opposition to my desires are the decrees of fate (the words were said with tears): contrary to the order of nature it is I who shall be the heir of all my sons.' And thus saying, your eyes swollen with tears, you turned away."

At the corner where the Corso is crossed by the street which borders the Forum of Trajan, let whoso will pause amid the bustle of modern traffic and think for a moment of those two figures standing together talking, "without interruption from any one," in the middle of that open space, while the long level rays of the sunset streamed upon them from beyond the Flaminian gate. Was there some great popular meeting at the Capitol which had cleared the streets, the hum of voices rising on the height, but all quiet here at this dangerous, glorious hour, when fever is abroad and the women and children are all indoors? "I made light of it, I confess," says Petrarch, though he acknowledges that he told the story of this dreadful presentiment to the Cardinal, who, sighing, exclaimed, "Would to God that my father's prediction may not come true!" But old Stefano with his weight of years upon him, and his front like Jove, turned away sighing, stroking his venerable beard, unmoved by the poet's reassurances, with that terrible conviction in his heart. They were all young and he old: daring, careless young men, laughing at that same Cola of the little albergo, the son of the wine-shop, who said he was to be an emperor. But the shadow on the grandsire's heart was one of those which events cast before them. Young Janni was abolished, his property divided among his enemies. Never was a downfall more sudden or more complete.

Stefano Colonna and his friends re-entered Rome with little appearance of triumph. The remembrance of the Porta San Lorenzo was too recent for rejoicings, and it must be put to the credit of the old chief, bereaved and sorrowful, that no reprisals were made, that a general amnesty was proclaimed, and the peace of the city preserved. Cola's family, at least for the time, remained peaceably at Rome, and met with no harm. We hear nothing of the unfortunate young Knight of Victory who had been sprinkled with the blood of the Colonnas. The Tribune went down like a stone, and for the moment, of him who had filled men's mouths and minds with so many strange tidings, there was no more to tell.

Cola's absence from Rome lasted for seven years; of which time there is no mention whatever in the Vita, which concerns itself exclusively with things that happened in Rome; but his steps can be very clearly traced. We never again find our enthusiast, he who first ascended the Capitol in a passion of disinterested zeal and patriotism, approved by every honest visionary and every suffering citizen, a man chosen of God to deliver the city. That his motives were ever ill motives, or that he had begun to seek his own prosperity alone, it would be hard to say: but he appears to us henceforward in a changed aspect as the eager conspirator, the commonplace plotter and schemer, hungry for glory and plunder, and using every means, by hook or by crook, to recover what he has lost, which is a far more familiar figure than the ideal Reformer, the disinterested revolutionary. We meet with that vulgar hero a hundred times in the stormy record of Italian politics, a man without scruples, sticking at nothing. But Rienzi was of a different nature: he was at once a less and a greater sinner. It would be unjustifiable to say that he ever gave up the thought of the Buono Stato, or ceased to desire the welfare of Rome. But in the long interval of his disappearance from the scene, he not only plotted like the other, but used that higher motive, and the mystic elements that were in the air, and the tendency towards all that was occult, and much that was noble in the aspirations of the visionaries of his time, to further the one object, his return to power, to the Capitol, and to the dominion of Rome. A conspirator is the commonplace of Italian story, at every period: and the pretender, catching at every straw to get back to his unsteady throne, besieging every potentate that can help him, pleading every inducement from the highest to the lowest—self-interest, philanthropy, the service of God, the most generous and the meanest sentiments—is also a very well known figure; but it is rare to find a man truly affected by the most mystic teachings of religion, yet pressing them also into his service, and making use of what he conceives to be the impulses of the Holy Spirit for the furtherance of his private ends, without, nevertheless, so far as can be asserted, becoming a hypocrite or insincere in the faith which he professes.

This was the strange development to which the Tribune came. After some vain attempts to awaken in the Roman territory friends who could help him, his heart broken by the fickleness and desertion of the Popolo in which he had trusted, he took refuge in the wild mountain country of the Apennines, where there existed a rude and strange religious party, aiming in the midst of the most austere devotion at a total overturn of society, and that return of a primeval age of innocence and bliss which is so seductive to the mystical mind. In the caves and dens of the earth and in the mountain villages and little convents, there dwelt a severe sect of the Franciscans, men whose love of Poverty, their founder's bride and choice, was almost stronger than their love of that founder himself. The Fraticelli were only heretics by dint of holding their Rule more strictly than the other religious of their order, and by indulging in ecstatic visions of a renovated state and a purified people—visions less personal though not less sincere or pious, than those which inflicted upon Francis himself the semblance of the wounds of the Redeemer, in that passion of pity and love which possessed his heart. The exile among them, who had himself been aroused out of the obscurity of ordinary life by a corresponding dream, found himself stimulated and inspired over again by the teaching of these visionaries. One of them, it is said, found him out in the refuge where he thought himself absolutely unknown, and, addressing him by name, told him that he had still a great career before him, and that it should be his to restore to Rome the double reign of universal dominion, to establish the Pope and the Empire in the imperial city, and reconcile for ever those two joint rulers appointed of God.

It is curious to find that what is to some extent the existing state of affairs—the junction in one place of the two monarchs of the earth—should have been the dream and hope of religious visionaries in the middle of the fourteenth century. The Emperor to them was but a glorified King of Italy, with a vague and unknown world behind him; and they believed that the Millennium would come, when that supreme sovereign on the Capitol and the Holy Father from the seat of St. Peter should sway the world at their will. The same class, in the same order now—so much as confiscation after confiscation permits that order to exist—would fight to its last gasp against the forced conjunction, which its fathers before it thus thought of as the thing most to be prayed for, and schemed for, in the whole world.

When others beside the Fraticelli discovered Rienzi's hiding-place, and he found himself, or imagined himself, in some danger, he went to Prague to seek shelter with the Emperor Charles IV., and a remarkable correspondence took place between that potentate on one side and the Archbishop of Prague, his counsellor, and Rienzi on the other, in which the exile promised many splendours to the monarch, and offered himself as his guide to Rome, and to lend him the weight of his influence there with the people over whom Rienzi believed that he would yet himself preside with greater power than ever. That Charles himself should reply to these letters, and reason the matter out with this forlorn wanderer, shows of itself what a power was in his words and in the fervour of his purpose. But it is ill talking between a great monarch and a penniless exile, and Charles seems to have felt no scruple in handing him over, after full exposition of his views, to the archbishop as a heretic. That prelate transferred him to the Pope, to be dealt with as a man already excommunicated under the ban of the Church, and now once more promulgating strange doctrines, ought to be; and thus his freedom, and his wandering, and the comparative safety of his life came to an end, and a second stage of strange development began.

The fortunes of Rienzi were at a very low ebb when he reached Avignon and fell into the hands of his enemies, of those whom he had assailed and those whom he had disappointed, at that court where there was no one to say a good word for him, and where all that was best in him was even more greatly against him than that which was worst. In the dungeons of Avignon, in the stronghold of the Pope who had so much cause to regret having once sanctioned and patronised the Tribune, his cause had every appearance of being lost for ever. It was fortunate for him that there was no longer a Cardinal Colonna at that court; but there was, at the same time, no champion to take up his cause. Things indeed went so badly with him, that he was actually condemned to death as a heretic, himself allowing that he was guilty and worthy of death in some moment of profound depression, or perhaps with the hope of touching the hearts of his persecutors by humility as great as had been the pretensions of his brief and exciting reign. For poor Cola after all, if the affair at Porta San Lorenzo is left out—and that was no fault of his—had done nothing worthy of death. He had been carried away by the passion and madness of an almost impossible success; but he had scarcely ever been rebellious to the Church, and his vagaries of doctrine were rather due to the mingling together of the classical with the religious, and the inflation of certain not otherwise unorthodox ideas, than any real rebellion; but he carried his prevailing sentiment and character into everything, being lower than any in the depths of his downfall as he had been higher than any on the heights of his visionary pride and short-lived triumph.

He was saved from this sentence in a manner as fantastical as himself. It may be believed that it was never intended to be carried out, and that, especially after his acknowledgment of the justice of his sentence, means would have been found of preserving him from its execution; very likely, indeed, the curious means which were found, originated in some charitable whisper that a plausible pretence of a reason for letting him off would not be disagreeable to the Pope. He was saved by the suggestion that he was a poet! We have the story in full detail from Petrarch himself, who is not without a perception of its absurdity, and begins his letter by an indignant description of the foolish and pretended zeal for poetry of which this was so strange an example. "Poetry," he says, "divine gift and vouchsafed by heaven to so few, I see it, friend, if not prostituted, at least made into a vulgar thing.

"I feel my heart rise against this, and you, if I know you well, will not tolerate such an abuse for any consideration. Neither at Athens, nor at Rome, even in the lifetime of Horace, was there so much talk of poets and poetry as at the present day upon the banks of the Rhone—although there never was either time or place in which men understood it less. But now I will check your rising bile by laughter and show how a jest can come in the midst of melancholy.

"There has lately come to this court—or rather has not come but has been brought—a prisoner, Niccola di Lorenzo, once the formidable Tribune of Rome, now of all the men the most unhappy—and what is more, not perhaps worthy of the compassion which the misery of his present state calls forth. He might have ended his days gloriously upon the Capitol, but brought himself down instead, to the great shame of the Republic and of the Roman name, into the condition of a prisoner, first in Bohemia and now here. Unfortunately, many more than I now like to think of are the praises and encouragements which I myself have written to him. Lover of virtue as I am, I could not do less than exalt and admire the generous undertaking of the strong man: and thankful on account of Italy, hoping to see the Empire of Rome arise again and secure the peace of the whole world, my heart was inundated by such joy, on account of so many fine events, that to contain myself was impossible; and it seemed to me that I almost took part in his glory by giving encouragement and comfort to his enterprise: by which as both his messengers and his letters showed, he was himself set on fire—and always more and more willingly I set myself to increase this stimulus with every argument I could think of, and to feed the flame of that ardent spirit, well knowing that every generous heart kindles at the fire of praise and glory. For this reason with an applause which to some seemed extravagant but to me very just, I exalted his every act, encouraging him to complete the magnanimous task which he had begun. The letters which I then wrote went through many hands: and since I am no prophet and still less was he ever a prophet I am not ashamed of what I wrote: for certainly what he did in those days and promised to do, not in my opinion alone but to the praise and admiration of the whole world, were very worthy, and I would not abolish the memory of these letters of mine from my memory solely because he prefers an ignoble life to a glorious death. But it is useless to discuss a thing which is impossible; and however much I might desire to destroy them I could not do it. As soon as they come into the hands of the public, the writer has no more power over them. Let us return to our story.

"This man then, who had filled the wicked with terror, the good with expectation, and with joyful hope the universe, has come before this Court humiliated and abject; and he whom the people of Rome and all the cities of Italy exalted, was seen passing through our streets between two soldiers, affording a miserable spectacle to the rabble eager to see face to face one whose name they had heard to sound so high. He came from the King of Rome (a title of the Emperor) to the Roman Pontiff, oh marvellous commerce! As soon as he had arrived the Pope committed to three princes of the Church the charge of examining into his cause, and judging of what punishment he was guilty who had attempted to free the State."

The letter is too long to quote entire, and Petrarch, though maintaining the cause of his former friend, is perhaps too anxious to make it clear that, had Rienzi given due attention to his own letters, this great reverse would never have happened to him; yet it is on the whole a noble plea for the Tribune. "In this man," the poet declares, "I had placed the last hope of Italian liberty, and, having long known and loved him from the moment when he put his hand to this great work, he seemed to me worthy of all veneration and honour. Whatever might be the end of the work I cannot cease to hold as magnificent its beginning:" and he regrets with great indignation that it was this beginning which was chiefly brought against him, and that his description of himself as Nicolas, severe and clement, had more weight with his judges than his good government or the happy change that took place in Rome during his sway. We must hasten, however, to the irony of the Tribune's deliverance.

"In this miserable state (after so much that is sorrowful, here at last is something to laugh at), I learn from the letters of my friends that there is still a hope of saving him, and that because of a notion which has been spread abroad among the vulgar, that he is a famous poet.... What can we think of this? Truly I, more than I can say in words, comfort myself and rejoice in the thought that the Muses are so much honoured—and what is still more marvellous, among those who never knew anything about them—as to save from a fatal sentence a man who is shielded by their name. What greater sign of reverence could be given than that the name of Poetry should thus save from death a man who rightly or wrongly is abhorred by his judges, who has been convicted of the crime laid to his charge and has confessed it, and by the unanimous sentence of the tribunal has been found worthy of death? I rejoice, I repeat, I congratulate him and the Muses with him: that he should have such patrons, and they so unlooked-for an honour—nor would I to a man so unhappy, reduced to such an extreme of danger and of doubt, grudge the protecting name of poet. But if you would know what I think, I will say that Niccola di Lorenzo is a man of the greatest eloquence, most persuasive and ready of speech, a writer lucid and harmonious and of an elegant style. I do not remember any poet whom he has not read; but this no more makes him a poet than a man would be a weaver who clothed himself with garments woven by another hand. To merit the name of poet it is not enough to have made verses. But this man has never that I know written a single line."

There is not a word of all this in the Vita. To the chronicler, Rienzi, from the moment when he turned his face again towards Rome, was never in any danger. As he came from Germany to Avignon all the people in the villages came out to greet him, and would have rescued him but for his continual explanation that he went to the Pope of his own will; nor does his biographer seem to be aware that the Tribune ran any risk of his life. He did escape, however, by a hair's breadth only, and, as Petrarch had perfect knowledge of what was going on, no doubt in the very way described by the poet. But he was not delivered from prison until Cardinal Albornoz set out for Rome with the Pope's orders to pacify and quiet the turbulent city. Many and great had been its troubles in those seven years. It had fallen back into the old hands—an Orsini and a Colonna, a Colonna and an Orsini. There had been a temporary lull in the year of the Jubilee (1350), when all the world flocked to Rome to obtain the Indulgence, and to have their sins washed away in the full stream of Papal forgiveness. It is said that Rienzi himself made his way stealthily back to share in that Indulgence, but without making himself known: and the interest of the citizens was so much involved in peace, and it was so essential to keep a certain rule of order and self-restraint on account of the many guests who brought money to the city, that there was a temporary lull of its troubles. The town was no more than a great inn from Easter to Christmas, and wealth, which has always a soothing and quieting influence, poured into the pockets of the citizens, fully occupied as they were by the care of their guests, and by the continual ceremonials and sacred functions of those busy days. The Jubilee brought not only masses of pious pilgrims from every part of the world, but innumerable lawsuits—cases of conscience and of secular disputes—to be settled by the busy Cardinal who sat instead of the Pope, hearing daily what every applicant might have to say. There had been a new temporary bridge built in order to provide for the pressure of the crowd, and avoid that block of the old bridge of St. Angelo which Dante describes in the Inferno, when the mass of pilgrims coming and going broke down one of the arches. Other large if hasty labours of preparation were also in hand. The Capitol had to be repaired, and old churches furbished up, and every scrap of drapery and tapestry which was to be had employed to make the city fine. So that for one year at least there had been no thought but to put the best possible face on things, to quench internal disorders for the moment, and make all kinds of temporary arrangements for comfort and accommodation, as is often done in a family when important visitors force a salutary self-denial upon all; so that there were a hundred inducements to preserve a front of good behaviour and fit decorum before the world.

[THE TARPEIAN ROCK]

After the Jubilee however, things fell back once more into the old confusion: once more there was robbery and violence on every road to Rome; once more an Orsini and a Colonna balanced and struggled with each other as Senators, with no time to attend to anything but their personal interests, and no thought for the welfare of the people. In 1352, however, things had come to such a pass that a violent remedy had to be tried again, and the Romans once more took matters in their own hands and elected an official of their own, a certain Cerroni, in the place of the unworthy Senators. He however held the position a very short time, and being in his turn deserted by the people, gave up the thankless task. That year there was a riot in which the Orsini Senator was stoned to death at the foot of the stairs which lead to the Capitol, while his colleague Colonna, another Stefano, escaped by the other side. Then once more the expedient of a popular election was attempted and a certain Francesco Baroncelli was elected who styled himself the second Tribune of the people. The Pope had also attempted to do what he could, once by a committee of four Cardinals, constantly by Legates sent to guide and protect the ever-troubled city. The hopelessness of these repeated efforts was proved over and over again. Villani the historian writes with dismay that "the changes which took place in the ancient mother and mistress of the universe did not deserve to be recorded because of their frivolity and baseness." Baroncelli too fell after a short time, and it seemed that no government, and no reformation, could last.

In the meantime Pope Clement VI. died at Avignon, and Innocent VI. reigned in his stead. At the beginning of this new reign a new attempt to pacificate Rome, and to restore it to order and peace, was made. As it was the general feeling that a stranger was the safest ruler in the midst of the network of private and family interests in which the city was bound, the new Pope with a sincere desire to ameliorate the situation sent the Spanish Cardinal Albornoz to the rescue of Rome. All this was in the year 1353 when Rienzi, his death sentence remitted because of the illusion that he was a poet, lay in prison in Avignon. His story was well known: and it was well known too, that the people of Rome, after having deserted him, were eager to have him back, and had to all appearance repented very bitterly their behaviour to him. The Pope adopted the strong and daring expedient of taking the old demagogue from his prison and giving him a place in the Legate's council. There was no intention of replacing him in his former position, but he was eager to accept the secondary place, and to give the benefit of his advice and guidance to the Legate. All appearance of his old ambition seemed indeed to have died out of him. He went simply in the train of Albornoz to Montefiascone,[9] which had long been the headquarters of the Papal representative, and from whence the Legate conducted a campaign against the towns of the "Patrimony," each of whom, like the mother city, occasionally secured a gleam of uncertain independence, or else—which was oftener the case—fell into the clutches of some one of the band of nobles who had so long held Rome in fee. It is very likely that Rienzi had no ambitious motive, nor thought of a new revolution when he set out. He took part like the rest of the Cardinal's following in several of the expeditions, especially against his old enemy Giovanni di Vico, still as masterful and as dangerous as ever, but attempted nothing more.

FOOTNOTE:

[9] An amusing story used to be told in Rome concerning this place, which no doubt sprang from the legend of that old ecclesiastical inhabitation. It was that a bishop, travelling across the country (it is always a bishop who is the bon vivant of Italian story), sent a messenger before him with instructions to write on the wall of every town his opinion of the wine of the place, that his master might judge whether he should alight there or not. If it was good Est was to be the word. When the courier came to Montefiascone he was so delighted with the vintage there that he emblazoned the gate with a triple legend of Est, Est, Est. The bishop arrived, alighted; and never left Montefiascone more. The wine in its native flasks is still distinguished by this inscription.

[THE BORGHESE GARDENS]

CHAPTER V

THE SOLDIER OF FORTUNE

The short episode which here follows introduces an entirely new element into Rienzi's life. His nature was not that of a conspirator in the ordinary sense of the word; and though he had schemed and struggled much to return to Rome, it had lately been under the shield of Pope or Emperor, and never with any evident purpose of self-aggrandisement. But the wars which were continually raging in Italy, and in which every man's hand was against his neighbour's, had raised up a new agent in the much contested field, by whose aid, more than by that of either Pope or Emperor, principalities rose and fell, and great fortunes were made and lost. This was the singular institution of the Soldier of Fortune, the Free Lance, whose bands, without country, without object except pay and some vulgar version of fame, without creed or nationality or scruples of any kind, roamed over Europe, ready to adopt any cause or throw their weight on any side, and furnishing the very material that was necessary to carry on those perpetual struggles, which kept Italy in particular, and most other countries more or less, in constant commotion. These men took service with the utmost impartiality on whatever side was likely to give them the highest pay, or the best opportunity of acquiring wealth—their leaders occasionally possessing themselves of the lordship of a rich territory, the inferior captains falling into lesser fiefs and windfalls of all kinds, the merest man-at-arms apt to enrich himself, either by the terror he inspired, or the protection he could give. It was their existence indeed, it may almost be said, that made these endless wars, which were so generally without motive, demonstrations of vanity of one city against another, or attempts on the part of one to destroy the liberties and trade of another, which, had they been carried on by the citizens themselves, must have in the long run brought all human affairs to a deadlock, and become impossible: but which, when carried on through the agency of the mercenaries, were little more than an exciting game, more exciting than any Kriegsspiel that has been invented since. The men were themselves moving castles, almost impregnable, more apt to be suffocated in their armour than killed in honest fight, and as a matter of fact their campaigns were singularly bloodless; but they were like the locusts, the scourge of the country, leaving nothing but destruction and rapine behind them wherever they moved. The dreadful army known as La Grande Compagnia, of which Fra Moreale (the Chevalier de Monreal, but always bearing this name in Italy) was the head, was at this time pervading Italy—everywhere feared, everywhere sought, the cruel and terrible chief being at the same time a romantic and high born personage, a Knight Hospitaller, the equal of the great Seigneurs whom he served, and ready to be himself some time a great Seigneur too, the head of the first principality which he should be strong enough to lay hold of, as the Sforza had done of Milan. The services of such a man were of course a never-failing resource and temptation to every adventurer or pretender who could afford to procure the money to pay for them.

There is no proof that Rienzi had any plan of securing the dominion of Rome by such means; indeed his practice, as will be seen, leads to the contrary conclusion; but the transaction to which he became a party while he was in Perugia—under the orders of Cardinal Albornoz—shows that he was, for the moment at least, attracted by the strange possibilities put within his reach: as it also demonstrates the strangely business-like character and trade aspect of an agency so warlike and romantic. At Perugia and other towns through which he passed, the Tribune was recognised and everywhere followed by the Romans, who were to be found throughout the Patrimony, and who had but one entreaty to make to him. The chronicler recovers all his wonted energy when he resumes his narrative, leaving with delight the dull conflicts of the Roman nobles among themselves, and with the Legate vainly attempting to pacify and negotiate between them—for the living figure of the returned leader, and the eager populace who hailed him again, as their deliverer, as if it had been others and not themselves who had driven him away! Even in Montefiascone our biographer tells, there was such recourse of Romans to him that it was stupore, stupefying, to see them.

"Every Roman turned to him, and multitudes visited him. A great tail of the populace followed him wherever he went. Everybody marvelled, including the Legate, to see how he was followed. After the destruction of Viterbo, when the army returned, many Romans who were in it, some of them important men, came to Rienzi. They said, 'Return to thy Rome, cure her of her sickness. Be her lord. We will give thee help, favour, and strength. Be in no doubt. Never were you so much desired or so much loved as at present.' These flatteries the Romans gave him, but they did not give him a penny of money: their words however moved Cola di Rienzi, and also the glory of it, for which he always thirsted by nature, and he began to think what he could do to make a foundation, and where he would find people and money to go to Rome. He talked of it with the Legate, but neither did he supply him with any money. It had been settled that the people of Perugia should make a provision for him, giving him enough to live upon honourably; but that was not sufficient for raising an army. And for this reason he went to Perugia and met the Counsellors there. He spoke well and promised better, and the Counsellors were very eager to hear the sweetness of his words, to which they lent an attentive ear. These they licked up like honey. But they were responsible for the goods of the commune, and not one penny (Cortonese) could he obtain from them.

"At this time there were in Perugia two young gentlemen of Provence, Messer Arimbaldo, doctor of laws, and Messer Bettrom, the knight of Narba (Narbonne), in Provence, brothers; who were also the brothers of the famous Fra Moreale, who was at the head of La Grande Compagnia.... He had acquired much wealth by robbery and booty, and compelled the Commune of Perugia to provide for his brothers who were there. When Cola di Rienzi heard that Messer Arimbaldo of Narba, a young man who loved letters, was in Perugia, he invited him to visit him, and would have him dine at his hostel where he was.

While they were at table Cola di Rienzi began to talk of the greatness of the Romans. He mingled stories of Titus Livius with things from the Bible. He opened the fountain of his knowledge. Deh! how he talked—all his strength he put into his reasoning; and so much to the point did he speak that every man was overwhelmed by such wonderful conversation; every one rose to his feet, put his hand to his ear, and listened in silence. Messer Arimbaldo was astonished by these fine speeches. He admired the greatness of the Romans. The warmth of the wine raised his spirit to the heights. The fantastic understand the fantastic. Messer Arimbaldo could not endure to be absent from Cola di Rienzi. He lived with him, he walked with him; one meal they shared, and slept in one bed. He dreamt of doing great things, of raising up Rome, of restoring its ancient state. To do this money was wanted—three thousand florins at least. He pledged himself to procure the three thousand florins, and it was promised to him that he should be made a citizen of Rome and captain, and be much honoured, all which was arranged to the great despite of his brother Messer Bettrom. Therefore, Arimbaldo took from the merchants of Perugia four thousand florins, to give them to Cola di Rienzi. But before Messer Arimbaldo could give this money to Cola, he had to ask leave of his elder brother, Fra Moreale, which he did, sending him a letter in these words: 'Honoured brother,—I have gained in one day more than you have done in all your life. I have acquired the lordship of Rome, which is promised to me by Messer Cola di Rienzi, Knight, Tribune, who is much visited by the Romans and called by the people. I believe that such a plan cannot fail. With the help of your genius nothing could injure such a great State; but money is wanted to begin with. If it pleases your brotherly kindness, I am taking four thousand florins from the bank, and with a strong armament am setting out for Rome.' Fra Moreale read this letter and replied to it as follows:

"'I have thought much of this work which you intend to do. A great and weighty burden is this which you take upon you. I do not understand your intention; my mind does not go with it, my reason is against it. Nevertheless go on, and do it well. In the first place, take great care that the four thousand florins are not lost. If anything evil happen to you, write to me. I will come to your help with a thousand or two thousand men, and do the thing magnificently. Therefore do not fear. See that you and your brother love each other, honour each other, and make no quarrel between you.'

"Messer Arimbaldo received this letter with much joy, and arranged with the Tribune to set out for Rome."

Fra Moreale was a good brother and a far-seeing chief. He saw that the Signoria of Rome, if it could be attained, would be a good investment for his four thousand florins, and probably that Cola di Rienzi was an instrument which could easily be thrown away when it had fulfilled its end, so that it was worth while letting young Arimbaldo have his way. No prevision of the tragedy that was to come, troubled the spirit of the great brigand. He would no doubt have laughed at the suggestion, that his young brother's eloquent demagogue, the bel dicitore, a character always disdained of fighting men, could do him, with all his martial followers behind him, and his money in the bank, any harm.

The first thing that Rienzi did we are told, was to clothe himself gloriously in scarlet, furred with minever and embroidered with gold, in which garb he appeared before the Legate who had heretofore known him only in a sober suit of ordinary cloth—accompanied by the two brothers of Moreale and a train of attendants. There had been a report of more disorder than usual in Rome, a condition of things with which a recently appointed Senator, appointed as a stranger to keep the factions in order, was quite unable to cope: and there was therefore a certain reason in the request, when the Tribune in all his new finery, came into the presence of the Legate, although he asked no less than to be made Senator, undertaking, at the same time, to secure the peace of the turbulent city. The biographer gives a vivid picture of Rienzi in his sudden revival. "Splendidly he displayed himself with his scarlet hood on his shoulders, and scarlet mantle adorned with various furs. He moved his head back and forward, raising himself on his toes, as who would say 'Who am I?—I, who may I be?'" The Legate as usual was "stupefied" by this splendid apparition, but gave serious ear to his request, no doubt knowing the reality of his pretensions so far as the Roman people were concerned. He finally agreed to do what was required of him, no doubt like Fra Moreale, confident that the instrument, especially being so vain and slight a man as this, could easily be got rid of when he had served his turn.

Accordingly, with all the strength he could muster—a troop of 250 free lances, Germans and Burgundians, the same number of infantry from Tuscany, with fifty young men of good families in Perugia—a very tolerable army for the time—and the two young Provençals, along with other youths to whom he had promised various offices, the new Senator set out for Rome. He was now a legal official, with all the strength of the Pope and constituted authority behind him; not a penny of money it is true from the Legate, and only those four thousand florins in his treasury: but with all the taxes and offerings in Rome in front of him, and the highest promise of success. It was a very different beginning from that of seven years ago, when young, penniless, disinterested, with no grandeur to keep up, and no soldiers to pay, he had been borne by the shouting populace to the Capitol to an unlimited and impossible empire. He was now a sober man, experienced in the world, forty, and trained by the intercourse of courts, in other ways than those of his youth. He had now been taught how to scheme and plot, to cajole and flatter, to play one party against another, and change his plans to suit his circumstances. So far as we know, he had no motive that could be called bad, except that of achieving the splendour he loved, and surrounding himself with the paraphernalia of greatness. The devil surely never before used so small a bribe to corrupt a nature full of so many fine things. He meant to establish the Buono Stato, probably as sincerely as of old. He had learned that he could not put forth the same unlimited pretensions. The making of emperors and sway of the world had to be resigned; but there is no evidence that he did not mean to carry out in his new reign the high designs for his city, and for the peace and prosperity of the surrounding country, which he had so triumphantly succeeded in doing for that one happy and triumphant moment in his youth.

[TOMB OF CECILIA METELLA]

It was in the beginning of August 1354 that Rienzi returned to Rome. Great preparations had been made for his reception. The municipal guards, with all the cavalry that were in Rome, went out as far as Monte Mario to meet him, with branches of olive in their hands, "in sign of victory and peace. The people were as joyful as if he had been Scipio Africanus," our biographer says. He came in by the gate of the Castello, near St. Angelo, and went thence direct to the centre of the city, through streets adorned with triumphal arches, hung with tapestry, resounding with acclamations.

"Great was the delight and fervour of the people. With all these honours they led him to the Palazzo of the Capitol. There he made them a beautiful and eloquent speech, in which he said that for seven years he had been absent from his house, like Nebuchadnezzar; but by the power of God he had returned to his seat and was Senator by the appointment of the Pope. He added that he meant to rectify everything and raise up the condition of Rome. The rejoicing of the Romans was as great as was that of the Jews when Jesus Christ entered Jerusalem riding upon an ass. They all honoured him, hanging out draperies and olive branches, and singing 'Blessed is he that cometh.' When all was over they returned to their homes and left him alone with his followers in the Piazza. No one offered him so much as a poor repast. The following day Cola di Rienzi received several ambassadors from the surrounding country. Deh! how well he answered. He gave replies and promises on every side. The barons remained on the watch, taking no part. The tumult of the triumph was great. Never had there been so much pomp. The infantry lined the streets. It seemed as if he meant to govern in the way of the tyrants. Most of the goods he had forfeited were restored to him. He sent out letters to all the States to declare his happy return, and he desired that every one should prepare for the Buono Stato. This man was greatly changed from his former ways. It had been his habit to be sober, temperate, abstinent. Now he became an excessive drinker, and consumed much wine. And he became large and gross in his person. He had a paunch like a tun, triumphal, like an Abbate Asinico. He was full of flesh, red, with a long beard. His countenance was changed, his eyes were as if they were inflamed—sometimes they were red as blood."

This uncompromising picture of a man whom adversity had not improved but deteriorated, is very broad and coarse with those personalities which the mob loves. Yet his biographer does not seem to have been hostile to Rienzi. He goes on to describe how the new senator on the fourth day after his arrival sent a summons to all the barons to present themselves before him, and among others he summoned Stefanello Colonna who had been a child at the time of the dreadful rout of San Lorenzo, but was now head of the house, his noble old heart-broken grandfather being by this time happily dead. It was scarcely likely that the third Stefano should receive that summons in friendship. He seized the two messengers and threw them into prison, then after a time had the teeth of one drawn, an insulting infliction, and despatched the other to Rome to demand a ransom for them: following this up by a great raid upon the surrounding country, in which his lightly armed and flying forces "lifted" the cattle of the Romans as might have been done by the emissaries of a Highland chief. Rienzi seems to have rushed to arms, collecting a great miscellaneous gathering, "some armed, some without arms, according as time permitted" to recover the cattle. But they were misled by an artifice of the most transparent description, and stumbled on as far as Tivoli without finding any opponent. Here he was stopped by the mercenaries clamouring for their pay, which he adroitly obtained from the two young commanders, Arimbaldo and Bettrom, by representing to them that when such a difficulty arose in classical times it was met by the chief citizens who immediately subscribed what was necessary. The apparently simple-minded young men (Bettrom or Bertram having apparently got over his ill-temper) gave him 500 florins each, and so the trouble was got over for the moment, and the march towards Palestrina was resumed. But the expedition was quite futile, neither Rienzi nor the young men whom he had placed at the head of affairs knowing much about the science of war. There were dissensions in the camp, the men of Velletri having a feud with those of Tivoli; and the picture which the biographer affords us of the leaders looking on, seeing a train of cattle and provision waggons entering the town which they were by way of besieging, and inquiring innocently what it was, gives the most vivid impression of the ignorance and helplessness which reigned in the attacking party: while Stefanello Colonna, to the manner born, surrounded by old warriors and fighting for his life, defended his old towers with skill as well as desperation.

While the Romans thus lost their chances of victory and occupied themselves with that destruction of the surrounding country, which was the first word of warfare in those days—the peasants and the villages always suffering, whoever might escape—there was news brought to Rienzi's camp of the arrival in Rome of the terrible Fra Moreale himself, who had arrived in all confidence, with but a small party in his train, in the city for which his brothers were fighting and in which his money formed the only treasury of war. He was a bold man and used to danger; but it did not seem that any idea of danger had occurred to him. There had been whispers among the mercenaries that the great Captain entertained no amiable feelings towards the Senator who had beguiled his young brothers into this dubious warfare: and this report would seem to have come to Rienzi's ears: but that Fra Moreale stood in any danger from Rienzi does not seem to have occurred to any spectator.

One pauses here with a wondering inquiry what were his motives at this crisis of his life. Were they simply those of the ordinary and vulgar villain, "Let us kill him that the inheritance may be ours"?—was he terrified by the prospect of the inquiries which the experienced man of war would certainly make as to the manner in which his brothers had been treated by the leader who had attained such absolute power over them? or is it possible that the patriotism, the enthusiasm for Italy, the high regard for the common weal which had once existed in the bosom of Cola di Rienzi flashed up now in his mind, in one last and tremendous flame of righteous wrath? No one perhaps so dangerous to the permanent freedom and well-being of Italy existed as this Provençal with his great army, which held allegiance to no leader but himself—without country, without creed or scruple—which he led about at his pleasure, flinging it now into one, now into the other scale. The Grande Compagnia was the terror of the whole Continent. Except that it was certain to bring disaster wherever it went, its movements were never to be calculated upon. Whatever fluctuations there might be in state or city, this roving army was always on the side of evil; it lived by fighting and disaster alone; and to drive it out of the country, out of the world if possible, would have been the most true and noble act of deliverance which could have been accomplished. Was this the purpose that flashed into Rienzi's eyes when he heard that the head of this terror, the great brigand chief and captain, had trusted himself within the walls of Rome? With the philosophy of compromise which rules among us, and which forbids us to allow an uncomplicated motive in any man, we dare hardly say or even surmise that this was so; but we may allow some room for the mingled motives which are the pet theory of our age, and yet believe that something perhaps of this nobler impulse was in the mind of the Roman Senator, who, notwithstanding his decadence and his downfall, was still the same man who by sheer enthusiasm and generous wrath, without a blow struck, had once driven its petty tyrants out of the city. Whatever may be the judgment of the reader in this respect, it is clear that Rienzi dropped the siege of Palestrina when he heard of Fra Moreale's arrival, as a dog drops a bone or an infant his toys, and hastened to Rome; while his army melted away as was usual in such wars, each band to its own country. Eight days had been passed before Palestrina, and the country round was completely devastated: but no effectual advantage had been gained when this sudden change of purpose took place.

As soon as Rienzi arrived in Rome he caused Fra Moreale to be arrested, and placed him with his brothers in the prison of the Capitol, to the great astonishment of all; but especially to the surprise of the great Captain, who thought it at first a mere expedient for extorting money, and comforted by this explanation the unfortunate brothers for whose sake he had placed himself in the snare. "Do not trouble yourselves," he said, "let me manage this affair. He shall have ten thousand, twenty thousand florins, money and people as much as he pleases." Then answered the brothers, "Deh! do so, in the name of God." They perhaps knew their Rienzi by this time, young as they were, and foolish as they had been, better than their elder and superior. And no doubt Rienzi might have made excellent terms for himself, perhaps even for Rome; but he does not seem to have entertained such an idea for a moment. When the Tribune set his foot within the gates of the city the Condottiere's fate was sealed. The biographer gives us a most curious picture of the agitation and surprise of this man in face of his fate. When he was brought to the torture (menato a lo tormento) he cried out in a consternation which is wild with foregone conclusions. "I told you what your rustic villain was," he exclaimed, as if still carrying on that discussion with the foolish young brothers. "He is going to put me to the torment! Does he not know that I am a knight? Was there ever such a clown?" Thus storming, astonished, incredulous of such a possibility, yet eager to say that he had foreseen it, the dismayed Captain was alzato, pulled up presumably by his hands as was one manner of torture, all the time murmuring and crying in his beard, half-mad and incoherent in the unexpected catastrophe. "I am Captain of the Great Company," he cried; "and being a knight I ought to be honoured. I have put the cities of Tuscany to ransom. I have laid taxes on them. I have overthrown principalities and taken the people captive." While he babbled thus in his first agony of astonishment the shadow of death closed upon Moreale, and the character of his utterances changed. He began to perceive that it was all real, and that Rienzi had now gone too far to be won by money or promises. When he was taken back to the prison which his brothers shared he told them with more dignity, that he knew he was about to die. "Gentle brothers, be not afraid," he said. "You are young; you have not felt misfortune. You shall not die, but I shall die. My life has always been full of trouble." (He was a man of sentiment, and a poet in his way, as well as a soldier of fortune.) "It was a trouble to me to live, of death I have no fear. I am glad to die where died the blessed St. Peter and St. Paul. This misadventure is thy fault, Arimbaldo; it is you who have led me into this labyrinth; but do not blame yourself or mourn for me, for I die willingly. I am a man: I have been betrayed like other men. By heaven, I was deceived! But God will have mercy upon me, I have no doubt, because I came here with a good intention." These piteous words, full to the last of astonishment, form a sort of soliloquy which runs on, broken, to the very foot of the Lion upon the great stairs, where he was led to die, amid the stormy ringing of the great bell and rushing of the people, half exultant and half terrified, who came from all quarters to see this great and terrible act of that justice to which the city in her first fervour had pledged herself. "Oh, Romans, are ye consenting to my death?" he cried. "I never did you harm; but because of your poverty and my wealth I must die." The chronicler goes on reporting the last words with fascination, as if he could not refrain. There is a wildness in them, of wonder and amazement, to the last moment. "I am not well placed," he murmured, non sto bene, evidently meaning, I am not properly placed for the blow: as he seems to have changed his position several times, kneeling down and rising again. He then kissed the knife and said, "God save thee, holy justice," and making another round knelt down again. The narrative is full of life and pity; the great soldier all bewildered, his brain failing, overwhelmed with dolorous surprise, seeking the right spot to die in. "This excellent man (honestis probisque viris, in the Latin version), Fra Moreale, whose fame is in all Italy for strength and glory, was buried in the Church of the Ara Coeli," says our chronicler. His execution took place on the spot where the Lion still stands on the left hand of the great stairs. There Fra Moreale wandered in his distraction to find a comfortable place for the last blow. The association is grim enough, and others yet more appalling were soon to gather there.

This perhaps was the only step of his life in which Rienzi had the approbation of all. The Pope displayed his approval in the most practical way by confiscating all Fra Moreale's wealth, of which 60,000 gold florins were distributed among those who had suffered by him. The funds which he had in various cities were also seized, though we are told that of those in Rome Rienzi had but a small part, a certain notary having managed, by what means we are not told, to secure the larger sum. By the interposition of the Legate, the foolish Arimbaldo, whom Rienzi's fair words had so bitterly deceived, was discharged from his prison and permitted to leave Rome, but the younger brother Bettrom, or Bertram, who, so far as we see, was never a partisan of Rienzi, was left behind; and though his presence is noted at another tragic moment, we do not hear what became of him eventually. With the money he received Rienzi made haste to pay his soldiers and to renew the war. He was so fortunate as to secure the services of a noble and valiant captain, of whom the free lances declared that they had never served under so brave a man: and whose name is recorded as Riccardo Imprennante degli Annibaldi—Richard the enterprising, perhaps—and the war was pursued with vigour under him. Within Rome things did not go quite so well. Rienzi had to explain his conduct in respect to Fra Moreale to his own councillors. "Sirs," he said, "do not be disturbed by the death of this man; he was the worst man in the world. He has robbed churches and towns; he has murdered both men and women; two thousand depraved women followed him about. He came to disturb our state, not to help it, meaning to make himself the lord of it. And this is why we have condemned that false man. His money, his horses, and his arms we shall take for our soldiers." We scarcely see the eloquence for which Rienzi was famed in these succinct and staccato sentences in which his biographer reports him; but this was our chronicler's own style, and they are at least vigorous and to the point.

"By these words the Romans were partly quieted," we are told, and the course of the history went on. The siege of Palestrina went well, and garrisons were placed in several of the surrounding towns, while Rienzi held the control of everything in his hands. Some of his troops withdrew from his service, probably because of Fra Moreale; but others came—archers in great numbers, and three hundred horsemen.

"He maintained his place at the Capitol in order to provide for everything. Many were the cares. He had to procure money to pay the soldiers. He restricted himself in every expense; every penny was for the army. Such a man was never seen; alone he bore the cares of all the Romans. He stood in the Capitol arranging that which the leaders in their places afterwards carried out. He gave the orders and settled everything, and it was done—the closing of the roads, the times of attack, the taking of men and spies. It was never ending. His officers were neither slow nor cold, but no one did much except the hero Riccardo, who night and day weakened the Colonnese. Stefanello and his Colonnas, and Palestrina consumed away. The war was coming to a good end."

To do all this, however, the money of Moreale was not enough. Rienzi had to impose a tax upon wine, and to raise that upon salt, which the citizens resented. Everything was for the soldiers. His own expenses were much restricted, and he seemed to expect that the citizens would follow his example. One of them, a certain Pandolfuccio di Guido, Rienzi seized and beheaded without any apparent reason. He was said to have desired to make himself lord over the people, the chronicler says. This arbitrary step seems to have caused great alarm. "The Romans were like sheep, and they were afraid of the Tribune as of a demon."

[ANCIENT, MEDIÆVAL, AND MODERN ROME]

By this time Rienzi once more began to show signs of that confusion of mind which we call losing the head—a confusion of irritation and changeableness, the resolution of to-day giving place to another to-morrow—and the giddiness of approaching downfall seized upon every faculty. As had happened on the former occasion, this dizziness of doom caught him when all was going well. He displaced his Captain, who was carrying on the siege of Palestrina with so much vigour and success, for no apparent reason, and appointed other leaders whose names even the biographer does not think it worth while to give. The National Guard—if we may so call them—fifty for each Rione—who were the sole guardians of Rome, were kept without pay, while every penny that could be squeezed from the people was sent to the army. These things raised each a new enemy to the Tribune, the Senator, once so beloved, who now for the second time, and more completely than before, had proved himself incapable of the task which he had taken upon him. It was on the 1st of August, 1354, that he had entered Rome with a rejoicing escort of all its cavalry and principal inhabitants—with waving flags and olive branches, and a throng that filled all the streets, the Popolo itself shouting and acclaiming—and had been led to the Piazza of the Ara Coeli, at the foot of the great stairs of the Capitol. On the last day of that month, a sinister and tragic assembly, gathered together by the sound of the great bell, thronged once more to the foot of these stairs, to see the great soldier, the robber knight, the terror of Italy, executed. And it was still only September, the Vita says—though other accounts throw the catastrophe a month later—when the last day of Rienzi himself came. We know nothing of the immediate causes of the rising, nor who were its leaders. But Rome was in so parlous a state, seething with so many volcanic elements, that it must have been impossible to predict from morning to morning what might happen. What did happen looks like a sudden outburst, spontaneous and unpremeditated; but no doubt, from various circumstances which followed, the Colonna had a hand in it, who ever since the day of San Lorenzo had been Cola's bitterest enemies. This is how his biographer tells the tale:

"It was the month of September, the eighth day. In the morning Cola di Rienzi lay in his bed, having washed his face with Greek wine (no doubt a reference to his supposed habits). Suddenly voices were heard shouting Viva lo Popolo! Viva lo Popolo! At this sound the people in the streets began to run here and there. The sound increased, the crowd grew. At the cross in the market they were joined by armed men who came from St. Angelo and the Ripa, and from the Colonna quarter and the Trevi. As they joined, their cry was changed into this, Death to the traitor, Cola di Rienzi, death! Among them appeared the youths who had been put in his lists for the conscription. They rushed towards the palace of the Capitol with an innumerable throng of men, women and children, throwing stones, making a great clamour, encircling the palace on every side before and behind, and shouting, 'Death to the traitor who has inflicted the taxes! Death to him!' Terrible was the fury of them. The Tribune made no defence against them. He did not sound the tocsin. He said to himself, 'They cry Viva lo Popolo, and so do we. We are here to exalt the people. I have written to my soldiers. My letter of confirmation has come from the Pope. All that is wanted is to publish it in the Council.' But when he saw at the last that the thing was turning badly he began to be alarmed, especially as he perceived that he was abandoned by every living soul of those who usually occupied the Capitol. Judges, notaries, guards—all had fled to save their own skin. Only three persons remained with him—one of whom was Locciolo Pelliciaro, his kinsman."

This was the terrible awaking of the doomed man—without preparation, without the sound of a bell, or any of the usual warnings, roused from his day-dream of idle thoughts, his Greek wine, the indulgences to which he had accustomed himself, in his vain self-confidence. He had no home on the heights of that Capitol to which he had returned with such triumph. If his son Lorenzo was dead or living we do not hear. His wife had entered one of the convents of the Poor Clares, when he was wandering in the Apennines, and was far from him. There is not a word of any one who loved him, unless it might chance to be the poor relation who stood by him, Locciolo, the furrier, perhaps kept about him to look after his robes of minever, the royal fur. The cry that now surged round the ill-secured and half-ruinous palace would seem to have been indistinguishable to him, even when the hoarse roar came so near, like the dashing of a horrible wave round the walls: Viva lo Popolo! that was one thing. With his belle parole he could have easily turned that to his advantage, shouting it too. What else was he there for but to glorify the people? But the terrible thunder of sound took another tone, a longer cry, requiring a deeper breath—Death to the traitor:—these are not words a man can long mistake. Something had to be done—he knew not what. In that equality of misery which makes a man acquainted with such strange bedfellows, the Senator turned to the three humble retainers who trembled round him, and asked their advice. "By my faith, the thing cannot go like this," he said. It would appear that some one advised him to face the crowd: for he dressed himself in his costume as a knight, took the banner of the people in his hand, and went out upon the balcony:

"He extended his hand, making a sign that all were to be silent, and that he was about to speak. Without doubt if they had listened to him he would have broken their will and changed their opinion. But the Romans would not listen; they were as swine; they threw stones and aimed arrows at him, and some ran with fire to set light to the door. So many were the arrows shot at him that he could not remain on the balcony. Then he took the Gonfalone and spread out the standard, and with both his hands pointed to the letters of gold, the arms of the citizens of Rome—almost as if he said 'You will not let me speak;

but I am a citizen and a man of the people like you. I love you; and if you kill me, you will kill yourselves who are Romans.' But he could not continue in this position, for the people, without intellect, grew worse and worse. 'Death to the traitor,' they cried."

A great confusion was in the mind of the unfortunate Tribune. He could no longer keep his place in the balcony, and the rioters had set fire to the great door below, which began to burn. If he escaped into the room above, it was the prison of Bertram of Narbonne, the brother of Moreale, who would have killed him. In this dreadful strait Rienzi had himself let down by sheets knotted together into the court behind, encircled by the walls of the prison. Even here treachery pursued him, for Locciolo, his kinsman, ran out to the balcony, and with signs and cries informed the crowd that he had gone away behind, and was escaping by the other side. He it was, says the chronicler, who killed Rienzi; for he first aided him in his descent and then betrayed him. For one desperate moment of indecision the fallen Tribune held a last discussion with himself in the court of the prison. Should he still go forth in his knight's dress, armed and with his sword in his hand, and die there with dignity, "like a magnificent person," in the sight of all men? But life was still sweet. He threw off his surcoat, cut his beard and begrimed his face—then going into the porter's lodge, he found a peasant's coat which he put on, and seizing a covering from the bed, threw it over him, as if the pillage of the Palazzo had begun, and sallied forth. He struggled through the burning as best he could, and came through it untouched by the fire, speaking like a countryman, and crying "Up! Up! a glui, traditore! As he passed the last door one of the crowd accosted him roughly, and pushed back the article on his head, which would seem to have been a duvet, or heavy quilt: upon which the splendour of the bracelet he wore on his wrist became visible, and he was recognised. He was immediately seized, not with any violence at first, and taken down the great stair to the foot of the Lion, where the sentences were usually read. When he reached that spot, "a silence was made" (fo fatto uno silentio). "No man," says the chronicler, "showed any desire to touch him. He stood there for about an hour, his beard cut, his face black like a furnace-man, in a tunic of green silk, and yellow hose like a baron." In the silence, as he stood there, during that awful hour, he turned his head from side to side, "looking here and there." He does not seem to have made any attempt to speak, but bewildered in the collapse of his being, pitifully contemplated the horrible crowd, glaring at him, no man daring to strike the first blow. At last a follower of his own, one of the leaders of the mob, made a thrust with his sword—and immediately a dozen others followed. He died at the first stroke, his biographer tells us, and felt no pain. The whole dreadful scene passed in silence—"not a word was said," the piteous, eager head, looking here and there, fell, and all was over. And the roar of the dreadful crowd burst forth again.

The still more horrible details that follow need not be here given. The unfortunate had grown fat in the luxury of these latter days. Grasso era horriblimente. Bianco come latte ensanguinato, says the chronicler: and again he places before us, as at San Lorenzo seven years before, the white figure lying on the pavement, the red of the blood. It was dragged along the streets to the Colonna quarter; it was hung up to a balcony; finally the headless body, after all these dishonours, was taken to an open place before the Mausoleum of Augustus, and burned by the Jews. Why the Jews took this share of the carnival of blood we are not told. It had never been said that Rienzi was hard upon them; but no doubt at a period so penniless they must have had their full share of the taxes and payments exacted from all.

There is no moral even, to this tale, except the well-worn moral of the fickleness of the populace who acclaim a leader one moment, and kill him the next; but that is a commonplace and a worn-out one. If there were ever many men likely to sin in that way, it might be a lesson to the enthusiast thrusting an inexperienced hand into the web of fate, to confuse the threads with which the destiny of a country is wrought, without knowing either the pattern or the meaning of the weaving. He began with what we have every reason for believing to have been a noble and generous impulse to save his people. But his soul was not capable of that high emprise. He had the greatest and most immediate success ever given to a popular leader. The power to change, to mend, to make over again, to vindicate and to carry out his ideal was given him in the fullest measure. For a time it seemed that there was nothing in the world that Cola di Rienzi, the son of the wine-shop, the child of the people, might not do. But then he fell; the promise faded into dead ashes, the impulse which was inspiration breathed out and died away. Inspiration was all he had, neither knowledge nor the noble sense and understanding which might have been a substitute for it; and when the thin fire blazed up like the crackling of thorns under a pot, it blazed away again and left nothing behind. Had he perished at the end of his first reign, had he been slain at the foot of the Capitol, as Petrarch would have had him, his story would have been a perfect tragedy, and we might have been permitted to make a hero of the young patriot, standing alone, in an age to which patriotism was unknown. But the postscript of his second effort destroys the epic. It is all miserable self-seeking, all squalid, the story of any beggar on horseback, any vulgar adventurer. Yet the silent hour when he stood at the foot of the great stairs, the horrible mob silent before him, bridled by that mute and awful despair, incapable of striking the final blow, is one of the most intense moments of human tragedy. A large overgrown man, with blackened face and the rough remnants of a beard, half dressed, speechless, his head turning here and there—And yet no one dared to take that step, to thrust that eager sword, for nearly an hour. Perhaps it was only a minute, which would be less unaccountable, feeling like an hour to every looker on who was there and stood by.

No one in all the course of modern Roman history has so illustrated the streets and ways of Rome and set its excited throngs in evidence, and made the great bell sound in our very ears, a stuormo, and disclosed the noise of the rabble and the rule of the nobles, and the finery of the gallants, with so real and tangible an effect. The episode is a short one. The two periods of Rienzi's power put together scarcely amount to eight months; but there are few chapters in that history which is always so turbulent, yet lacks so much the charm of personal story and adventure, so picturesque and complete.

[LETTER WRITER]

[PIAZZA DEL POPOLO]

It is strange to leave the history of Rome at the climax to which the ablest and strongest of its modern masters had brought it, when it was the home of the highest ambition, and the loftiest claims in the world, the acknowledged head of one of the two powers which divided that world between them, and claiming a supreme visionary authority over the other also; and to take up that story again (after such a romantic episode as we have just discussed) when its rulers had become but the first among the fighting principalities of Italy, men of a hundred ambitions, not one of which was spiritual, carrying on their visionary sway as heads of the Church as a matter of routine merely, but reserving all their real life and energy for the perpetual internecine warfare that had been going on for generations, and the security of their personal possessions. From Innocent III. to such a man as Eugenius IV., still and always fighting, mixed up with all the struggles of the Continent, hiring Condottieri, marshalling troops, with his whole soul in the warfare, so continuous, so petty, even so bloodless so far as the actual armies were concerned—which never for a moment ceased in Italy: is a change incalculable. Let us judge the great Gregory and the great Innocent as we may, their aim and the purpose of their lives were among the greatest that have ever been conceived by man, perhaps the highest ideal ever formed, though like all high ideals impossible, so long as men are as we know them, and those who choose them are as helpless in the matter of selecting and securing the best as their forefathers were. But to set up that tribunal on earth—that shadow and representation of the great White Throne hereafter to be established in the skies—in order to judge righteous judgment, to redress wrongs, to neutralise the sway of might over right—let it fail ever so completely, is at least a great conception, the noblest plan at which human hands can work. We have endeavoured to show how little it succeeded even in the strongest hands; but the failure was a greater thing than any lesser success—certainly a much greater thing than the desire to be first in that shouting crowd of Italian princedoms and commonwealths, to pit Piccinino and Carmagnola against each other, to set your honour on the stake of an ironbound band of troopers deploying upon a harmless field, in wars which would have been not much more important than tournaments; if it had not been for the ruin and murder and devastation of the helpless peasants and the smitten country on either side.

But the pettier rôle was one of which men tired, as much as they did of that perpetual strain of the greater which required an amount of strength and concentration of mind not given to many, such as could not (and this was the great defect of the plan) be secured for a line of Popes any more than for any other line of men. The Popes who would have ruled the world failed, and gave up that forlorn hope; they were opposed by all the powers of earth, they were worn out by fictions of anti-Popes, and by real and continual personal sufferings for their ideal:—and they did not even secure at any time the sympathy of the world. But when among the vain line of Pontiffs who not for infamy and not for glory, but per se lived, and flitted, a wavering file of figures meaning little, across the surface of the world—there arose a Pope here and there, forming into a short succession as the purpose grew, who took up consciously the aim of making Rome—not Rome Imperial nor yet Rome Papal, which were each a natural power on the earth and Head of nations, but Rome the City—the home of art, the shrine of letters, in another way and with a smaller meaning, yet still meaning something, the centre of the world—their work and position have always attracted a great deal of sympathy, and gained at once the admiration of all men. English literature has not done much justice to the greater Popes. Mr. Bowden's life of Gregory VII. is the only work of any importance specially devoted to that great ruler. Gregory the Great to whom England owes so much, and Innocent III., who was also, though in no very favourable way, mixed up in her affairs, have tempted no English historian to the labours of a biography. But Leo X. has had a very different fate: and even the Borgias, the worst of Papal houses, have a complete literature of their own. The difference is curious. It is perhaps by this survival of the unfittest, so general in literature, that English distrust and prejudice have been so crystallised, and that to the humbler reader the word Pope remains the synonym of a proud and despotic priest, sometimes Inquisitor and sometimes Indulger—often corrupt, luxurious, or tyrannical—a ruler whose government is inevitably weak yet cruel. The reason of this strange preference must be that the love of art is more general and strong than the love of history; or rather that a decorative and tangible external object, something to see and to admire, is more than all theories of government or morals. The period of the Renaissance is full of horror and impurity, perhaps the least desirable of all ages on which to dwell. But art has given it an importance to which it has no other right.

Curious it is also to find that of all the cities of Italy, Rome has the least native right to be considered in the history of art. No great painter or sculptor, architect or even decorator, has arisen among the Roman people. Ancient Rome took her art from Greece. Modern Rome has sought hers over all Italy—from Florence, from the hills and valleys of Umbria, everywhere but in her own bosom. She has crowned poets, but, since the days of Virgil and Horace, neither of whom were Romans born, though more hers than any since, has produced none. All her glories have been imported. This of course is often the case with her Popes also. Pope Martin V., to whom may be given the first credit of the policy of rebuilding the city, was a native-born Roman; but Pope Eugenius IV., who took up its embellishment still more seriously, was a Venetian, bringing with him from the sea-margin the love of glowing colour and that "labour of an age in pilëd stones" which was so dear to those who built their palaces upon the waters. Nicolas was a Pisan, Pope Leo, who advanced the work so greatly, was a Florentine. But their common ambition was to make Rome a wonder and a glory that all men might flock to see. The tombs of the

Apostles interested them less perhaps than most of their predecessors: but they were as strongly bent as any upon drawing pilgrims from the ends of the earth to see what art could do to make those tombs gorgeous: and built their own to be glories too, admired of all the world. These men have had a fuller reward than their great predecessors. Insomuch as the aim was smaller, it was more perfectly carried out; for though it is a great work to hang a dome like that of St. Peter's in the air, it is easier than to hold the hearts of kings in your hand, and decide the destiny of nations. The Popes who made the city have had better luck in every way than those who made the Papacy. Neither of them secured either the gratitude or even the consent of Rome herself to what was done for her. But nevertheless almost all that has kept up her fame in the world for, let us say, the last four hundred years, was their work.

[MODERN ROME: SHELLEY'S TOMB]

This period of the history of the great city began when Pope Martin V. concluded what has been called the schism of the West, and brought back the seat of the Papacy from Avignon, where it had been exiled, to Rome. We have seen something of the moral and economical state of the city during that interregnum. Its physical condition was yet more desolate and terrible. The city itself was little more than a heap of ruins. The little cluster of the inhabited town was as a nest of life in the centre of a vast ancient mass of building, all fallen into confusion and decay. No one cared for the old Forums, the palaces ravaged by many an invasion, burned and beaten down, and quarried out, by generations of men to whom the meaning and the memory of their founders was as nothing, and themselves only so many waste places, or so much available material for the uses of the vulgar day. Some one suggests that the early Church took pleasure in showing how entirely shattered was the ancient framework, and how little the ancient gods had been able to do for the preservation of their temples; and with that intention gave them over to desolation and the careless hands of the spoiler. We think that men are much more often swayed by immediate necessities than by any elaborate motive of this description. The ruins were exceedingly handy—every nation in its turn has found such ruins to be so. To get the material for your wall, without paying anything for it, already at your hand, hewn and prepared as nobody then working could do it—what a wonderful simplification of labour! Everybody took advantage of it, small and great. Then, when you wanted to build a strong tower or fortress to intimidate your neighbours, what an admirable foundation were those old buildings, founded as on the very kernel and central rock of the earth! For many centuries no one attempted to fill up those great gaps within the city walls, in which vines flourished and gardens grew, none the worse for the underlying stones that covered themselves thickly with weeds and flowers by Nature's lavish assistance. Buildings of various kinds, adapted to the necessities of the moment, grew up by nature in all kinds of places, a church sometimes placed in the very lap of an ancient temple. Indeed the churches were everywhere, some of them humble enough, many of great antique dignity and beauty, almost all preserving the form of the basilica, the place of meeting where everything was open and clear for the holding of assemblies and delivery of addresses, not dim and mysterious as for sacrifices of faith.

So entirely was this state of affairs accepted, that there is more talk of repairing than of building in the chronicles; at all times of the Church, each pious Pope undertook some work of the kind, mending a decaying chapel or building up a broken wall; but we hear of few buildings of any importance, even when the era of the builders first began. Works of reparation must have been necessary to some extent after every burning or fight. Probably the scuffles in the streets did little harm, but when such a terrible inundation took place as that of the Normans, and still worse the Saracens, who followed Robert Guiscard in the time of Gregory VII., it must have been the work of a generation to patch up the remnants of the place so as to make it in the rudest way habitable again. It was no doubt in one of these great emergencies that the ancient palaces, most durable of all buildings, were seized by the people, and converted each into a species of rabbit-warren, foul and swarming. It does not appear however that any plan of restoring the city to its original grandeur, or indeed to any satisfactory reconstruction at all, was thought of for centuries. In the extreme commotion of affairs, and the long struggle of the Popes with the Emperors, there was neither leisure nor means for any great scheme of this kind, nor much thought of the material framework of the city, while every mind was bent upon establishing its moral position and lofty standing ground among the nations. As much as was indispensable would be done: but in these days the requirements of the people in respect to their lodging were few: as indeed they still are to an extraordinary extent in Italy, where life is so much carried on out of doors.

It is evident, however, that Rome the city had never yet become the object of any man's life or ambition, or that a thought of anything beyond what was needful for actual use, for shelter or defence, had entered into the thoughts of its masters when the Papal Court returned from Avignon. The churches alone were cared for now and then, and decorated whenever possible with rich hangings, with marbles and ancient columns generally taken from classical buildings, sometimes even from churches of an older date; but even so late as the time of Petrarch so important a building as St. John Lateran, the Papal church par excellence, lay roofless and half ruined, in such a state that it was impossible to say mass in it. The poet describes Rome itself, when, after a long walk amid all the relics of the classical ages, his friend and he sat down to rest upon the ruined arches of the Baths of Diocletian, and gazed upon the city at their feet—"the spectacle of these grand ruins." "If she once began to recognise of herself the low estate in which she lies, Rome would make her own resurrection," he says with a confidence but poorly merited by the factious and restless city. But Rome, torn asunder by the feuds of Colonna and Orsini, seizing every occasion to do battle with her Pope, only faithful to him in his absence, of which she complained to heaven and earth—was little likely to exert herself to any such end.

This was the unfortunate plight in which Rome lay when Martin V., a Roman of the house of Colonna, came back in the year 1421, with all the treasures of art acquired by the Popes during their stay in France, to the shrine of the Apostles. The historian Platina, whose records are so full of life when they approach the period of which he had the knowledge of a contemporary, gives a wonderful description of her. "He found Rome," says the biographer of the Popes, "in such ruin that it bore no longer the aspect of a city but rather of a desert. Everything was on the way to complete destruction. The churches were in ruins, the country abandoned, the streets in evil state, and an extreme penury reigned everywhere. In fact it had no appearance of a city or a sign of civilisation. The good Pontiff, moved by the sight of such calamity, gave his mind to the work of adorning and embellishing the city, and reforming the corrupt ways into which it had fallen, which in a short time were so improved by his care that not only Supreme Pontiff but father of his country he was called by all. He rebuilt the portico of St. Peter's which had been falling into ruins, and completed the mosaic work of the pavement of the Lateran which he covered with fine works, and began that beautiful picture which was made by Gentile, the excellent painter." He also repaired the palace of the twelve Apostles, so that it became habitable. The Cardinals in imitation of him executed similar works in the churches from which each took his title, and by this means the city began to recover decency and possible comfort at least, if as yet little of its ancient splendour.

"As soon as Pope Martin arrived in Rome," says the chronicle, Diarium Romanum, of Infessura, "he began to administer justice, for Rome was very corrupt and full of thieves. He took thought for everything, and especially to those robbers who were outside the walls, and who robbed the poor pilgrims who came for the pardon of their sins to Rome." The painter above mentioned, and who suggests to us the name of a greater than he, would appear to have been Gentile da Fabriano, who seems to have been employed by the Pope at a regular yearly salary. These good deeds of Pope Martin are a little neutralised by the fact that he gave a formal permission to certain other of his workmen to take whatever marbles and stones might be wanted for the pavement of the Lateran, virtually wherever they happened to find them, but especially from ruined churches both within and outside of the city.

Eugenius IV., who succeeded Pope Martin in the year 1431, was a man who loved above all things to "guerrare e murare"—to make war and to build—a splendid and noble Venetian, whose fine and commanding person fills one of his biographers, a certain Florentine bookseller and book-collector, called Vespasiano, with a rapture of admiration which becomes almost lyrical, in the midst of his simple and garrulous story.

"He was tall in person, beautiful of countenance, slender and serious, and so venerable to behold that there was no one, by reason of the great authority that was in him, who could look him in the face. It happened one evening that an important personage went to speak with him, who stood with his head bowed, never raising his eyes, in such a way that the Pope perceived it and asked him why he so bowed his head. He answered quickly that the Pope had such an aspect by nature that none dared meet his eye. I myself recollect often to have seen the Pope with his Cardinals upon a balcony near the door of the cloisters of Sta Maria Novella (in Florence) when the Piazza de Sta Maria Novella was full of people, and not only the Piazza, but all the streets that led into it. And such was the devotion of the people that they stood entranced (stupefatti) to see him, not hearing any one who spoke, but turning every one towards the Pontiff: and when he began according to the custom of the Pope to say the Adjutorium nostrum in nomine Domini the Piazza was full of weeping and cries, appealing to the mercy of God for the great devotion they bore towards his Holiness. It appeared indeed that this people saw in him not only the vicar of Christ on earth, but the reflection of His true Divinity. His Holiness showed such great devotion, and also all his Cardinals round him, who were all men of great authority, that veritably at that moment he appeared that which he represented."

There is much refreshment to the soul in the biographies of Vespasiano, who was no more than a Florentine bookseller as we have said, greatly employed in collecting ancient manuscripts, which was the special taste of the time, with a hand in the formation of all the libraries then being established, and in consequence a considerable acquaintance with great personages, those at least who were patrons of the arts and had a literary turn. Pope Eugenius is not in ordinary history a highly attractive character, and the general records of the Papacy are not such as to allure the mind as with ready discovery of unknown friends. But the two Popes whom the old bookman chronicles, rise before us in the freshest colours, the first in stately serenity and austerity of mien, dazzling in his aspetto di natura, as Moses when he came from the presence of God—moving all hearts when he raised his voice in the prayers of the Church, every listener hanging on his breath, the crowd gazing at him overwhelmed as if upon Him whom the Pope represented, though no man dared face his penetrating eyes. It is a great thing for the most magnificent potentate to have such a biographer as our bookseller. Eugenius was as kind as he was splendid, according to Vespasiano. One day a poor gentleman reduced to want went to the Pope, appealing for charity "being in exile, poor, and fuori della patria," words which are more touching than their English synonyms, out of his country, banished from all his belongings: an evil which went to the very hearts of those who were themselves at any moment subject to that fate, and to whom la patria meant an ungrateful fierce native city—never certain in its temper from one moment to another. The Pope sent for a purse full of florins, and bade the exile take from it as much as he wanted. "Felice, abashed, put in his hand timidly, when the Pope turned to him laughing and said, 'Put in your hand freely, I give it to you willingly.'" This being his disposition we need not wonder that Vespasian adds:— "He never had much supply of money in the house; according as he had it, quickly he expended it." Remembering what lies before us in history (but not in this broken record of men), soon to be filled with Borgias and such like, the reader would do well to sweeten his thoughts on the edge of the horrors of the Renaissance, with Vespasian's kind and humane tales. Platina takes up the story in a different tone.

"Among other things Eugenius, in order that it might not seem that he thought of nothing but fighting (his wars were perpetual, guerrare winning the day over murare; he built like Nehemiah with the sword in his other hand), canonized S. Nicola di Tolentino of the order of S. Augustine, who did many miracles. He built the portico which leads from the Church of the Lateran to the Sancta Sanctorum, and remade and enlarged the cloister inhabited by the priests, and completed the picture of the Church begun under Martin by Gentile. He was not easily moved by wrath, or personal offence, and never spoke evil of any man, neither by word of mouth nor hand of write. He was gracious to all the schools, specially to those of Rome, where he desired to see every kind of literature and doctrine flourish. He himself had little literature, but much knowledge, especially of history. He had a great love for monks, and was very generous to them, and was also a great lover of war, a thing which seems marvellous in a Pope. He was very faithful to the engagements he made—unless when he saw that it was more expedient to revoke a promise than to fulfil it."

Martin and Eugenius were both busy and warlike men. They were involved in all the countless internal conflicts of Italy; they were confronted by many troubles in the Church, by the argumentative and persistent Council of Bâle, and an anti-Pope or two to increase their cares. The reign of Eugenius began by a flight from Rome with one attendant, from the mob who threatened his life. Nevertheless it was in these agitated days that the first thought of Rome rebuilt, as glorious as a bride, more beautiful than in her climax of classic splendour, began to enter into men's thoughts.

[FOUNTAIN OF TREVI]

The reign of their immediate successor, the learned and magnificent Nicolas V., who was created Pope in 1447, was, however, the actual era of this new conception. It is not necessary, we are thankful to think, to enter here into any description of the Renaissance, that age so splendid in art, so horrible in history—when every vice seemed let loose on the earth, yet the evil demons so draped themselves in everything beautiful, that they often attained their most dangerous and terrible aspect, that of angels of light. The Renaissance has had more than its share in history; it has flooded the world with scandals of every kind, and such examples of depravity as are scarcely to be found in any other age; or perhaps it is that no other age has commanded the same contrasts and incongruities, the same picturesque accessories, the splendour and external grace, the swing of careless force and franchise, without restraint and without shame. To many minds these things themselves are enough to attract and to dazzle, and they have captivated many writers to whom the brilliant society, the triumphs of art, the ever shifting, ever glittering panorama with its startling succession of scenes, spectacles, splendours, and tragedies, have made the more serious and more worthy records of life appear sombre, and its nobler motives dull in comparison. When Thomas of Sarzana was born in Pisa—in a humble house of peasants who had no surname nor other distinction, but who managed to secure for him the education which was sufficiently easy in those days for boys destined to the priesthood—the age of the Renaissance was coming into full flower. Literature and learning, the pursuit of ancient manuscripts, the worship of Greece and the overwhelming influence of its language and masterpieces, were the inspiration of the age, so far as matters intellectual were concerned. To read and collate and copy was the special occupation of the literary class. If they attempted any original work, it was a commentary: and a Latin couplet, an epigram, was the highest effort of imagination which they permitted themselves. The day of Dante and Petrarch was over. No one cared to be volgarizzato—brought down in plain Italian to the knowledge of common men. The language of their literary traffic was Latin, the object of their adoration Greek. To read, and yet to read, and again to go on reading, was the occupation of every man who desired to make himself known in the narrow circles of literature; and a small attendant world of scribes was maintained in every learned household, and accompanied the path of every scholar. The world so far as its books went had gone back to a period in which gods and men were alike different from those of the existing generation; and the living age, disgusted with its own unsatisfactory conditions, attempted to gain dignity and beauty by pranking itself in the ill-adapted robes of a life totally different from its own.

Between the classical ages and the Christian there must always be the great gulf fixed of this complete difference of sentiment and of atmosphere. And the wonderful contradiction was more marked than usual in Rome of a world devoted outside to the rites and ceremonies of religion, while dwelling in its intellectual sphere in the air of a region to which Christianity was unknown. The routine of devotion never relaxing—planned out for every hour of every day, calling for constant attention, constant performance, avowedly addressing itself not to the learned or wise, avowedly restricting itself in all those enjoyments of life which were the first and greatest of objects in the order of the ancient ages— yet carried on by votaries of the Muses, to whom Jove and Apollo were more attractive than any Christian ideal—must have made an unceasing and bewildering conflict in the minds of men. No doubt that conflict, and the evident certainty that one or the other must be wrong, along with the strong setting of that tide of fashion which is so hard to be resisted, towards the less exacting creed, had much to do with the fever of the time. Yet the curious equalising touch of common life, the established order whatever it may be, against which only one here and there ever successfully rebels, made the strange conjunction possible; and the final conflict abided its time. Such a man as Nicolas V. might indeed fill his palace with scholars and scribes, and put his greatest pride in his manuscripts: but the affairs of life around were too urgent to affect his own constitution as Pope and priest and man of his time. He bandied epigrams with his learned convives in his moments of leisure: but he had himself too much to do to fall into dilettante heathenism. Perhaps the manuscripts themselves, the glory of possessing them, the busy scribes all labouring for that high end of instructing the world: while courtiers never slow to catch the tone that pleased, celebrated their sovereign as the head of humane and liberal study as well as of the Church—may have been more to Nicolas than all his MSS. contained. He remained quite sincere in his mass, quite simple in his life, notwithstanding the influx of the heathen element: and most likely took no note in his much occupied career of the great distance that lay between.

Nicolas V. was the first of those Pontiffs who are the pride of modern Rome—the men who, by a strange provision, or as it almost seems neglect of Providence, appear in the foremost places of the Church pre-occupied with secondary matters, when they ought to have been preparing for that great Revolution which, it was once fondly hoped, was to lay spiritual Rome in ruins, at the very moment when material Rome rose most gloriously from her ashes. But, notwithstanding that he was still troubled by that long-drawn-out Council of Bâle, it does not seem that any such shadow was in the mind of Nicolas. He stood calm in human unconsciousness between heathendom at his back, and the Reformation in front of him, going about his daily work thinking of nothing, as the majority of men even on the eve of the greatest of revolutions so constantly do. Nicolas was, like so many of the great Popes, a poor man's son, without a surname, Thomas of Sarzana taking his name from the village in which he was brought up. He had the good fortune, which in those days was so possible to a scholar, recommended originally by his learning alone, to rise from post to post in the household of bishop and Cardinal until he arrived at that of the Pope, where a man of real value was highly estimated, and where it was above all things important to have a steadfast and faithful envoy, one who could be trusted with the often delicate negotiations of the Holy See, and who would neither be daunted nor led astray by imperial caresses or the frowns of power.

"He was very learned, dottissimo, in philosophy, and master of all the arts. There were few writers in Greek or in Latin of any kind that he had not read their works, and he had the whole of the Bible in his memory, and quoted from it continually. This intimate knowledge of the Holy Scriptures gave the greatest honour to his pontificate and the answers he was called upon to make." There were great hopes in those days of the reunion of the Greek Church with the Latin, an object much in the mind of all the greater Popes: to promote which happy possibility Pope Eugenius called a Council in Ferrara in 1438, which was also intended to confound the rebellious and heretical Council of Bâle, as well as to bring about, if possible, the desired union. The Emperor of the East was there in person, along with the patriarch and a large following; and it was in this assembly that Thomas of Sarzana, then secretary and counsellor of the Cardinal di Santa Croce—who had accompanied his Cardinal over i monti on a mission to the King of France from which he had just returned—made himself known to Christendom as a fine debater and accomplished student. The question chiefly discussed in the Council of Ferrara was that which is formally called the Procession of the Holy Spirit, the doctrine which has always stood between the two Churches, and prevented mutual understanding.

"In this council before the Pope, the Cardinals, and all the court of Rome, the Latins disputed daily with the Greeks against their error, which is that the Holy Spirit proceeds from the Father only not from the Son: the Latins, according to the true doctrine of the faith, maintaining that He proceeds from the Father and the Son. Every morning and every evening the most learned men in Italy took part in this discussion as well as many out of Italy, whom Pope Eugenius had called together. One in particular, from Negroponte, whose name was Niccolo Secondino: wonderful was it to hear what the said Niccolo did; for when the Greeks spoke and brought together arguments to prove their opinion, Niccolo Secondino explained everything in Latin de verbo ad verbum, so that it was a thing admirable to hear: and when the Latins spoke he expounded in Greek all that they answered to the arguments of the Greeks. In all these disputations Messer Tommaso held the part of the Latins, and was admired above all for his universal knowledge of the Holy Scriptures, and also of the doctors, ancient and modern, both Greek and Latin."

[ON THE PINCIO]

Messer Tommaso distinguished himself so much in this controversy that he was appointed by the Pope to confer with certain ambassadors from the unknown, Ethiopians, Indians, and "Jacobiti,"—were these the envoys of Prester John, that mysterious potentate? or were they Nestorians as some suggest? At all events they were Christians and persons of singularly austere life. The conference was carried on by means of an interpreter, "a certain Venetian who knew twenty languages." These three nations were so convinced by Tommaso, that they placed themselves under the authority of the Church, an incident which does not make any appearance in more dignified history. Even while these important matters of ecclesiastical business were going on, however, this rising churchman kept his eyes open as to every chance of a new, that is an old book, and would on various occasions turn away from his most distinguished visitors to talk apart with Messer Vespasiano, who once more is our best guide, about their mutual researches and good luck in the way of finding rare examples or making fine copies. "He never went out of Italy with his Cardinal on any mission that he did not bring back with him some new work not to be found in Italy." Indeed Messer Tommaso's knowledge was so well understood that there was no library formed on which his advice was not asked, and specially by Cosimo dei Medici, who begged his help as to what ought to be done for the formation of the Library of S. Marco in Florence—to which Tommaso responded by sending such instructions as never had been given before, how to make a library, and to keep it in the highest order, the regulations all written in his own hand. "Everything that he had," says Vespasian in the ardour of his admiration, "he spent on books. He used to say that if he had it in his power, the two things on which he would like to spend money would be in buying books and in building (murare); which things he did in his pontificate, both the one and the other." Alas! Messer Tommaso had not always money, which is a condition common to collectors; in which case Vespasian tells us (who approved of this mode of procedure as a bookseller, though perhaps it was a bad example to be set by the Head of the Church) he had "to buy books on credit and to borrow money in order to pay the scribes and miniaturists." The books, the reader will perceive, were curious manuscripts, illustrated by those schools of painters in little, whose undying pigments, fresh as when laid upon the vellum, smile almost as exquisitely to-day from the ancient page as in Messer Tommaso's time.

There is an enthusiasm of the seller for the buyer in Vespasian's description of the dignified book-hunter which is very characteristic, but at the same time so natural that it places the very man before us, as he lived, a man full of humour, facetissimo, saying pleasant things to everybody, and making every one to whom he talked his partisan.

"He was a man open, large and liberal, not knowing how to feign or dissimulate, and the enemy of all who feigned. He was also hostile to ceremony and adulation, treating all with the greatest friendliness. Great though he was as a bishop, as an ambassador, he honoured all who came to see him, and desired that whoever would speak with him should do so seated by his side, and with his head covered; and when one would not do so (out of modesty) he would take one by the arm and make one sit down, whether one liked or not."

A delightful recollection of that flattering compulsion, the great man's touch upon his arm, the seat by his side, upon which Vespasian would scarcely be able to sit for pleasure, is in the bookseller's tone; and he has another pleasant story to tell of Giannozzo Manetti, who went to see their common patron when he was Cardinal and ambassador to France, and tried hard, in his sense of too much honour done him, to prevent the great man from accompanying him, not only to the door of the reception room, but down stairs. "He stood firm on the staircase to prevent him from coming further down: but Giannozzo was obliged to have patience, being in the Osteria del Lione, for not only would Messer Tommaso accompany him down stairs, but to the very door of the hotel, ambassador of Pope Eugenius as he was."

We must not, however, allow ourselves to be seduced into prolixity by the old bookseller, whose account of his patron is so full of gratitude and feeling. As became a scholar and lover of the arts, Nicolas V. was a man of peace. Immediately after his elevation to the papacy, he declared his sentiments to Vespasian in the prettiest scene, which shines like one of the miniatures they loved, out of the sober page.

"Not long after he was made Pope, I went to see him on Friday evening, when he gave audience publicly, as he did once every week. When I went into the hall in which he gave audience it was about one hour of the night (seven o'clock in the evening); he saw me at once, and called to me that I was welcome, and that if I would have patience a little he would talk to me alone. Not long after I was told to go to his Holiness. I went, and according to custom kissed his feet; afterwards he bade me rise, and rising himself from his seat, dismissed the court, saying that the audience was over. He then went to a private room where twenty candles were burning, near a door which opened into an orchard. He made a sign that they should be taken away, and when we were alone began to laugh, and to say 'Do the Florentines believe, Vespasiano, that it is for the confusion of the proud, that a priest only fit to ring the bell should have been made Supreme Pontiff?' I answered that the Florentines believed that his Holiness had attained that dignity by his worth, and that they rejoiced much, believing that he would give Italy peace. To this he answered and said: 'I pray God that He will give me grace to fulfil that which I desire to do, and to use no arms in my pontificate except that which God has given me for my defence, which is His cross, and which I shall employ as long as my day lasts.'"

The cool darkness of the little chamber, near the door into the orchard, the blazing candles all sent away, the grateful freshness of the Roman night—come before us like a picture, with the Pope's splendid robes glimmering white, and the sober-suited citizen little seen in the quick-falling twilight. It must have been in the spring or early summer, the sweetest time in Rome. Pope Eugenius had died in the month of February, and it was on the 16th of March, 1447, that Nicolas was elected to the Holy See.

A few years after came the jubilee, in the year 1450, as had now become the habit, and the influx of pilgrims was very great. It was a time of great profit not only to the Romans who turned the city into one vast inn to receive the visitors, but also to the Pope. "The people were like ants on the roads which led from Florence to Rome," we are told. The crowd was so immense crossing the bridge of St. Angelo, that there were some terrible accidents, and as many as two hundred people were killed on their way to the shrine of the Apostles. "There was not a great lord in all Christendom who did not come to this jubilee." "Much money came to the Apostolical See," continues the biographer, "and the Pope began to build in many places, and to send everywhere for Greek and Latin books wherever he could find them, without regard to the price.

"He also had many scribes from every quarter to whom he gave constant employment; also many learned men both to compose new works, and to translate those which had not been translated, making great provision for them, both ordinary and extraordinary; and to those who translated books, when they were brought to him, he gave much money that they might go on willingly with that which they had to do. He collected a very great number of books on every subject, both in Greek and Latin, to the number of five thousand volumes. These at the end of his life were found in the catalogue which did not include the half of the copies of books he had on every subject; for if there was a book which could not be found, or which he could not have in any other way, he had it copied. The intention of Pope Nicolas was to make a library in St. Peter's for the use of the Court of Rome, which would have been a marvellous thing had it been carried out; but it was interrupted by death."

Vespasian adds for his own part a list of these books, which occupies a whole column in one of Muratori's gigantic pages.

Another anecdote we must add to show our Pope's quaint ways with his little court of literary men.

"Pope Nicolas was the light and the ornament of literature, and of men of letters. If there had arisen another Pontiff after him who would have followed up his work, the state of letters would have been elevated to a worthy degree. But after him things went from bad to worse, and there were no prizes for virtue. The liberality of Pope Nicolas was such that many turned to him who would not otherwise have done so. In every place where he could do honour to men of letters, he did so, and left nobody out. When Messer Francesco Filelfo passed through Rome on his way to Naples without paying him a visit, the Pope, hearing of it, sent for him. Those who went to call him said to him, 'Messer Francesco, we are astonished that you should have passed through Rome without going to see him.' Messer Francesco replied that he was carrying some of his books to King Alfonso, but meant to see the Pope on his return. The Pope had a scarsella at his side in which were five hundred florins which he emptied out, saying to him, 'Take this money for your expenses on the way.' This is what one calls liberal! He had always a scarsella (pouch) at his side where were several hundreds of florins and gave them away for God's sake, and to worthy persons. He took them out of the scarsella by handfuls and gave to them. Liberality is natural to men, and does not come by nobility nor by gentry: for in every generation we see some who are very liberal and some who are equally avaricious."

But the literary aspect of Pope Nicolas's character, however delightful, is not that with which we are chiefly concerned. He was the first Pope to conceive a systematic plan for the reconstruction and permanent restoration of Rome, a plan which it is needless to say his life was not long enough to carry out, but which yet formed the basis of all after-plans, and was eventually more or less accomplished by different hands.

It was to the centre of ecclesiastical Rome, the shrine of the Apostles, the chief church of Christendom and its adjacent buildings that the care of the Builder-Pope was first directed. The Leonine city, or Borgo as it is more familiarly called, is that portion of Rome which lies on the left side of the Tiber, and which extends from the castle of St. Angelo to the boundary of the Vatican gardens—enclosing the church of St. Peter, the Vatican Palace with all its wealth, and the great Hospital of Santo Spirito, surrounded and intersected by many little streets, and joined to the other portions of the city by the bridge of St. Angelo. Behind the mass of picture galleries, museums, and collections of all kinds, which now fill up the endless halls and corridors of the Papal palace, comes a sweep of noble gardens full of shade and shelter from the Roman sun, such a resort for the

"learnèd leisure Which in trim gardens takes its pleasure"

as it would be difficult to surpass. In this fine extent of wood and verdure the Pope's villa or casino, now the only summer palace which the existing Pontiff chooses to permit himself, stands as in a domain, small yet perfect. Almost everything within these walls has been built or completely transformed since the days of Nicolas. But then as now, here was the heart and centre of Christendom, the supreme shrine of the Catholic faith, the home of the spiritual ruler whose sway reached over the whole earth. When Nicolas began his reign, the old church of St. Peter was the church of the Western world, then as now, classical in form, a stately basilica without the picturesqueness and romantic variety, and also, as we think, without the majesty and grandeur of a Gothic cathedral, yet more picturesque if less stupendous in size and construction than the present great edifice, so majestic in its own grave and splendid way, with which through all the agitations of the recent centuries, the name of St. Peter's has been identified. The earlier church was full of riches, and of great associations, to which the wonderful St. Peter's we all know can lay claim only as its successor and supplanter. With its flight of broad steps, its portico and colonnaded façade crowned with a great tower, it dominated the square, open and glowing in the sun without the shelter of the great existing colonnades or the sparkle of the fountains. Behind was the little palace begun by Innocent III. to afford a shelter for the Popes in dangerous times, or on occasion to receive the foreign guests whose object was to visit the Shrine of the Apostles. Almost all the buildings then standing have been replaced by greater, yet the position is the same, the shrine unchanged, though everything else then existing has faded away, except some portion of the old wall which enclosed this sacred place in a special sanctity and security, which was not, however, always respected. The Borgo was the holiest portion of all the sacred city. It was there that the blood of the martyrs had been shed, and where from the earliest age of Christianity their memory and tradition had been preserved. It is not necessary for us to enter into the question whether St. Peter ever was in Rome, which many writers have laboriously contested. So far as the record of the Acts of the Apostles is concerned, there is no evidence at all for or against, but tradition is all on the side of those who assert it. The position taken by Signor Lanciani on this point seems to us a very sensible one. "I write about the monuments of ancient Rome," he says, "from a strictly archæological point of view, avoiding questions which pertain, or are supposed to pertain, to religious controversy."

"For the archæologist the presence and execution of SS. Peter and Paul in Rome are facts established beyond a shadow of doubt by purely monumental evidence. There was a time when persons belonging to different creeds made it almost a case of conscience to affirm or deny a priori those facts, according to their acceptance or rejection of the tradition of any particular Church. This state of feeling is a matter of the past at least for those who have followed the progress of recent discoveries and of critical literature. There is no event of the Imperial age and of Imperial Rome which is attested by so many noble structures, all of which point to the same conclusion—the presence and execution of the Apostles in the capital of the empire. When Constantine raised the monumental basilicas over their tombs on the Via Cornelia and the Via Ostiensis: when Eudoxia built the Church ad Vincula: when Damasus put a memorial tablet in the Platonia ad Catacombos: when the houses of Pudens and Aquila and Prisca were turned into oratories: when the name of Nymphæ Sancti Petri was given to the springs in the catacombs of the Via Nomentana: when the 29th June was accepted as the anniversary of St. Peter's execution: when sculptors, painters, medallists, goldsmiths, workers in glass and enamel, and engravers of precious stones, all began to reproduce in Rome the likeness of the apostle at the beginning of the second century, and continued to do so till the fall of the Empire: must we consider them as labouring under a delusion, or conspiring in the commission of a gigantic fraud? Why were such proceedings accepted without protest from whatever city, whatever community—if there were any other—which claimed to own the genuine tombs of SS. Peter and Paul? These arguments gain more value from the fact that the evidence on the other side is purely negative."

This is one of those practical arguments which are always more interesting than those which depend upon theories and opinions. However, there are many books on both sides of the question which may be consulted. We are content to follow Signor Lanciani. The special sanctity and importance of Il Borgo originated in this belief. The shrine of the Apostle was its centre and its glory. It was this that brought pilgrims from the far corners of the earth before there was any masterpiece of art to visit, or any of those priceless collections which now form the glory of the Vatican. The spot of the Apostle's execution was indicated "by immemorial tradition" as between the two goals (inter duas metas) of Nero's circus, which spot Signor Lanciani tells us is exactly the site of the obelisk now standing in the piazza of St.

Peter. A little chapel, called the Chapel of the Crucifixion, stood there in the early ages, before any great basilica or splendid shrine was possible.

[IN THE CORSO: CHURCH DOORS]

This sacred spot, and the church built to commemorate it, were naturally the centre of all those religious traditions which separate Rome from every other city. It was to preserve them from assault, "in order that it should be less easy for the enemy to make depredations and burn the church of St. Peter, as they have heretofore done," that Leo IV., the first Pope, whom we find engaged in any real work of construction built a wall round the mount of the Vatican, the "Colle Vaticano"—little hill, not so high as the seven hills of Rome—where against the strong wall of Nero's circus Constantine had built his great basilica. At that period—in the middle of the ninth century—there was nothing but the church and shrine—no palace and no hospital. The existing houses were given to the Corsi, a family which had been driven out of their island, according to Platina, by the Saracens, who shortly before had made an incursion up to the very walls of Rome, whither the peoples of the coast (luoghi maritimi del Mar Terreno) from Naples northward had apparently pursued the Corsairs, and helped the Romans to beat them back. One other humble building of some sort, "called Burgus Saxonum, Vicus Saxonum, Schola Saxonum, and simply Saxia or Sassia," it is interesting to know, existed close to the sacred centre of the place, a lodging built for himself by Ina, King of Wessex, in 727. Thus we have a national association of our own with the central shrine of Christianity. "There was also a Schola Francorum in the Borgo." The pilgrims must have built their huts and set up some sort of little oratory—favoured, as was the case even in Pope Nicolas's day, by the excellent quarry of the circus close at hand—as near as possible to the great shrine and basilica which they had come so far to say their prayers in; and attracted too, no doubt, by the freedom of the lonely suburb between the green hill and the flowing river. Leo IV. built his wall round this little city, and fortified it by towers. "In every part he put sculptures of marble and wrote a prayer," says Platina. One of these gates led to St. Pellegrino, another was close to the castle of St. Angelo, and was "the gate by which one goes forth to the open country." The third led to the School of the Saxons; and over each was a prayer inscribed. These three prayers were all to the same effect—"that God would defend this new city which the Pope had enclosed with walls and called by his own name, the Leonine City, from all assaults of the enemy, either by fraud or by force."

This was then from the beginning the citadel and innermost sanctuary of Rome. It was not till much later, under the reign of Innocent III., that the idea of building a house for the Pope within that enclosure originated. The same great Pope founded the vast hospital of the Santo Spirito—on the site of a previous hospice for the poor either within or close to its walls. Thus it came to be the lodging of the Sovereign Pontiff, and of the scarcely less sacred sick and suffering, as well as the most holy and chiefest of all Christian sanctuaries. Were we to be very minute, it might be easily proved that almost every Pope contributed something to the existence and decoration of the Leonine city, the imperium in imperio; and specially, as was natural, to the great basilica.

The little Palazzo di San Pietro being close to St. Angelo, the stronghold and most safe resort in danger, was occupied by the court on its return from Avignon, and probably then became the official home of the Popes; though for some time there seems to have been a considerable latitude in that respect. Pope Martin afterwards removed to the Palace of the Apostles. Another of the Popes preferred to all others the great Palazzo Venezia, which he had built: but the name of the Vatican was henceforth received as the title of the Papal court. The enlargement and embellishment of this palace thus became naturally the great object of the Popes, and nothing was spared upon it. It is put first in every record of achievement even when there is other important work to describe. "Nicolas," says Platina, "builded magnificently both in the Vatican, and in the city. He rebuilt the churches of St. Stefano Rotondo and of St. Teodoro," the former most interesting church being built upon the foundations of a round building of classical times, supposed, Mr. Hare tells us, to have belonged to the ancient Fleshmarket, as we should say, the Macellum Magnum. S. Teodoro is also a rotondo. It would seem that there were different opinions as to the success of these restorations in the fifteenth century such as arise among ourselves in respect to almost every work of the same kind. A certain "celebrated architect," Francesco di Giorgio di Martino, of Sienna, was then about the world, a man who spoke his mind. "Hedifitio ruinato," he says of St. Stefano, with equal disregard to spelling and to manners. "Rebuilt," he adds, "by Pope Nichola; but much more spoilt:" which is such a thing as we now hear said of the once much-vaunted restorations of Sir Gilbert Scott. Our Pope also "made a leaden roof for Sta. Maria Rotonda in the middle of the city, built by M. Agrippa as a temple for all the gods and called the Pantheon." He must have been fond of this unusual form; but whether it was a mere whim of personal liking, or if there was any meaning in his construction of these round temples, we have no information. Perhaps Nicolas had a special admiration of the solemn and beautiful Pantheon, in which we completely sympathise. The question is too insignificant to be inquired into. Yet it is curious in its way.

These were however, though specially distinguished by Platina, but a drop in the ocean to the numberless undertakings of Pope Nicolas throughout the city; and all these again were inferior in importance to the great works in St. Peter's and the Vatican, to which his predecessors had each put a hand so long as their time lasted. "In the Vatican," says Platina, "he built those apartments of the Pontiff, which are to be seen to this day: and he began the wall of the Vatican, great and high, with its incredible depth of foundation, and high towers, to hold the enemy at a distance, so that neither the church of St. Peter (as had already happened several times) nor the palace of the Pope should ever be sacked. He began also the tribune of the church of St. Peter, that the church might hold more people, and might be more magnificent. He also rebuilt the Ponte Molle, and erected near the baths of Viterbo a great palace. Having the aid of much money, he built many parts of the city, and cleansed all the streets." Great also in other ways were his gifts to his beloved church and city—"vases of gold and silver, crosses ornamented with gems, rich vestments and precious tapestry, woven with gold and silver, and the mitre of the Pontificate, which demonstrated his liberality." It was he who first placed a second crown on the mitre, which up to this time had borne one circlet alone. The complete tiara with the three crowns was adopted in a later reign.

The two previous Popes, his predecessors, had been magnificent also in their acquisitions for the Church in this kind; both of them being curious in goldsmiths' work, then entering upon its most splendid development, and in their collections of precious stones. The valuable work of M. Muntz, Les Arts à la cour des papes, abounds in details of these splendid jewels. Indeed his sober records of daily work and its payment seem to transport us out of one busy scene into another as by the touch of a magician's wand, as if Rome the turbulent and idle, full of aimless popular rushes to and fro, had suddenly become a beehive full of energetic workers and the noise of cheerful labour, both out of doors in the sun, where the masons were loudly at work, and in many a workshop, where the most delicate and ingenious arts were being carried on. Roman artists at length began to appear amid the host of Florentines and the whole world seems to have turned into one great bottega full of everything rich and rare.

[SANTA MARIA DEL POPOLO]

The greatest, however, of all the conceptions of Pope Nicolas, the very centre of his great plan, was the library of the Vatican, which he began to build and to which he left all the collections of his life. Vespasian gives us a list of the principal among those 5,000 volumes, the things which he prized most, which the Pope bequeathed to the Church and to Rome. These cherished rolls of parchment, many of them translations made under his own eyes, were enclosed in elaborate bindings ornamented with gold and silver. We are not, however, informed whether any of the great treasures of the Vatican library came from his hands—the good Vespasian taking more interest in the work of his scribes than in

Codexes. He tells us of 500 scudi given to Lorenzo Valle with a pretty speech that the price was below his merits, but that eventually he should have more liberal pay; of 1,500 scudi given to Guerroni for a translation of the Iliad, and so forth. It is like a bookseller of the present day vaunting his new editions to a collector in search of the earliest known. But Pope Nicolas, like most other patrons of his time, knew no Greek, nor probably ever expected that it would become a usual subject of study, so that his translations were precious to him, the chief way of making his treasures of any practical use.

The greater part, alas! of all this splendour has passed away. One pure and perfect glory, the little chapel of San Lorenzo, painted by the tender hand of Fra Angelico, remains unharmed, the only work of that grand painter to be found in Rome. If one could have chosen a monument for the good Pope, the patron and friend of art in every form, there could not have been a better than this. Fra Angelico seems to have been brought to Rome by Pope Eugenius, but it was under Nicolas, in two or three years of gentle labour, that the work was done. It is, however, impossible to enumerate all the undertakings of Pope Nicolas. He did something to re-establish or decorate almost all of the great basilicas. It is feared—but here our later historians speak with bated breath, not liking to bring such an accusation against the kind Pope, who loved men of letters—that the destruction of St. Peter's, afterwards ruthlessly carried out by succeeding Popes was in his plan: on the pretext, so constantly employed, and possibly believed in, of the instability of the ancient building. But there is no absolute certainty of evidence, and at all events he might have repented, for he certainly did not do that deed. He began the tribune, however, in the ancient church, which may have been a preparation for the entire renewal of the edifice; and he did much towards the decoration of another round church, that of the Madonna delle Febbre, an ill-omened name, attached to the Vatican. He also built the Belvedere in the gardens, and surrounded the whole with strong walls and towers (round), one of which according to Nibby still remained fifty years ago; which very little of Nicolas's building has done. His great sin was one which he shared with all his brother-Popes, that he boldly treated the antique ruins of the city as quarries for his new buildings, not without protest and remonstrance from many, yet with the calm of a mind preoccupied and seeing nothing so great and important as the work upon which his own heart was set.

This excellent Pope died in 1455, soon after having received the news of the downfall of Constantinople, which is said to have broken his heart. He had many ailments, and was always a small and spare man of little strength of constitution; but "nothing transfixed his heart so much as to hear that the Turk had taken Constantinople and killed the Europeans, with many thousands of Christians," among them that same "Imperadore de Gostantinopli" whom he had seen seated in state at the Council of Ferrara, listening to his own and other arguments, only a few years before—as well as the greater part, no doubt, of his own clerical opponents there. When he was dying "being not the less of a strong spirit," he called the Cardinals round his bed, and many prelates with them, and made them a last address. His pontificate had lasted a little more than eight years, and to have carried out so little of his great plan must have been heavy on his heart; but his dying words are those of one to whom the holiness and unity of the Church came before all. No doubt the fear that the victorious Turks might spread ruin over the whole of Christendom was first in his mind at that solemn hour.

"'Knowing, my dearest brethren, that I am approaching the hour of my death, I would, for the greater dignity and authority of the Apostolic See, make a serious and important testament before you, not committed to the memory of letters, not written, neither on a tablet nor on parchment, but given by my living voice that it may have more authority. Listen, I pray you, while your little Pope Nicolas (papa Niccolajo) in the very instant of dying makes his last will before you. In the first place I render thanks to the Highest God for the measureless benefits which, beginning from the day of my birth until the present day, I have received of His infinite mercy. And now I recommend to you this beautiful spouse of

Christ, whom, so far as I was able, I have exalted and magnified, as each of you is well aware; knowing this to be to the honour of God, for the great dignity that is in her, and the great privileges that she possesses, and so worthy, and formed by so worthy an Author, who is the Creator of the Universe. Being of sane mind and intellect, and having done that which every Christian is called to do, and specially the Pastor of the Church, I have received the most sacred body of Christ with penitence, taking from His table with my two hands, and praying the Omnipotent God that he would pardon my sins. Having had these sacraments I have also received the extreme unction which is the last sacrament for the redeeming of my soul. Again I recommend to you, as long as I am able, the Roman Church, notwithstanding that I have already done so; for this is the most important duty you have to fulfil in the sight of God and men. This is that true Spouse of Christ which He bought with his blood. This is that robe without seam, which the impious Jews would have torn but could not. This is that ship of St. Peter, Prince of the Apostles, agitated and tossed by varied fortunes of the winds, but sustained by the Omnipotent God, so that she can never be submerged or shipwrecked. With all the strength of your souls sustain her and rule her: she has need of your good works, and you should show a good example by your lives. If you with all your strength care for her and love her, God will reward you, both in this present life and in the future with life eternal; and to do this with all the strength we have, we pray you: do it diligently, dearest brethren.'

"Having said this he raised his hands to heaven and said, 'Omnipotent God, grant to the Holy Church, and to these fathers, a pastor who will preserve her and increase her; give to them a good pastor who will rule and govern thy flock the most maturely that one can rule and govern. And I pray for you and comfort you as much as I know and can. Pray for me to God in your prayers.' When he had ended these words, he raised his right arm and, with a generous soul, gave the benediction—Benedicat vos Deus, Pater et Filius et Spiritus Sanctus—speaking with a raised voice and solemnly, in modo Pontificale."

[MODERN DEGRADATION OF A PALACE]

These tremulous words, broken and confused by the weakness of his last hours, were taken down by the favourite scribe, Giannozzo Manetti, in the chamber of the dying Pope: with much more of the most serious matter to the Church and to Rome. His eager desire to soften all possible controversies and produce in the minds of the conclave about his bed, so full of ambition and the force of life, the softened heart which would dispose them to a peaceful and conscientious election of his successor, is very touching, coming out of the fogs and mists of approaching death.

In the very age that produced the Borgias, and himself the head of that band of elegant scholars and connoisseurs, everything but Christian, to whom Rome owes so much of her external beauty and splendour, it is pathetic to stand by this kind and gentle spirit as he pauses on the threshold of a higher life, subduing the astute and worldly minded Churchmen round him with the tender appeal of the dying father, their Papa Niccolajo, familiar and persuasive—beseeching them to be of one accord without so much as saying it, turning his own weakness to account to touch their hearts, for the honour of the Church and the welfare of the flock.

CHAPTER II

CALIXTUS III—PIUS II—PAUL II—SIXTUS IV

It is not unusual even in the strictest of hereditary monarchies to find the policy of one ruler entirely contradicted and upset by his successor; and it is still more natural that such a thing should happen in a succession of men, unlike and unconnected with each other as were the Popes; but the difference was more than usually great between Nicolas and Calixtus III., the next occupant of the Holy See, elected 1455, died 1458, who was an old man and a Spaniard, and loved neither books nor pictures, nor any of the new arts which had bewitched (as many people believed) Pope Nicolas and seduced him into squandering the treasure of the Papacy upon unnecessary buildings, and still more unnecessary decorations. Calixtus was a Borgia, the first to introduce the horror of that name: but he was not in himself a harmful personage. "He spent little in building," says Platina, "for he lived but a short time, and saved all his money for the undertaking against the Turks," an enterprise which had become a very real and necessary one, now that Constantinople had fallen; but which had no longer the romance and sentiment of the Crusades to inspire it, though successive Pontiffs did their best to rouse Christendom on the subject. The aged Spanish Cardinal threw himself into it with all the fervour of his nature, which better than many others knew the mettle of the Moor. His short term of power was entirely occupied with this. A little building went on, which could not be helped: the walls had always to be looked to; but Pope Nicolas's army of scribes were all turned off summarily; the studios were closed, the artist people turned away about their business; all the great works put a stop to. Worse even than that—for Calixtus was a short-lived interruption, and perhaps might only have stopped the progress of events for some three years or so—Pope Nicolas's great plan, which was so complete, went out of sight, and was lost in the limbo of good intentions. His workmen were dispersed, and the fashion to which he had accustomed the world, changed. It was only resumed with earnestness after several generations, and never quite in the great lines which he had laid out. Neither did the new Pope get his Crusade, which might have been a better thing. Yet Calixtus was a person assai generoso, Platina tells us; in any case he occupied his great post for a very short time.

His successor, Pius II., 1458, on the other hand, was such a man as might well have inherited the highest purpose. He is almost better known as Eneas Silvius, a famous traveller and writer—not the usual peasant monk without a surname as so many had been, but one of the Piccolomini of Sienna, a great house, though ruined or partially ruined in his day. He was a man who had travelled much, and was known at all the courts; at one time young, heretical, adventurous, and ready to pull down all authorities, the life and soul of that famous Council of Bâle which took upon itself to depose Pope

Eugenius; but not long after that outburst of independent youthfulness and energy was over, we find him filling the highest offices, the Legate of Eugenius and a very rising yet always much-opposed Cardinal. He it was who travelled to a remote and obscure little country called Scotland, in the Pope's name, to arrange matters there; and found the people very savage, digging stones out of the earth to make fires of them: but having plenty of fish and flesh, and surprisingly comfortable on the whole. He was one of the ablest men who ever sat on the Papal throne, but too reasonable, too moderate, too natural for the position. He loved literature, or at least he loved books, which is not always the same thing, and himself wrote a great many on various subjects; and he was so fortunate as to have the historian of the Popes, Platina—our guide, who we would have wished might live for ever—for his librarian, who was worth all the marble tombs in the world and all the epitaphs to a man whom he liked, and worse than any heathen conqueror to the man who was unkind to him.

Platina gives us a beautiful character of Pope Pius. He is very lenient to the faults of his youth, as indeed most historians are in respect to personages afterwards great, finding in their peccadilloes, we presume, a welcome and picturesque relief to the perfections that become a Pope. Yet Pius II. was never too perfect. He was a man who disliked the narrowness of a court, and loved the fresh air, and to give audience in his garden, and to eat his modest meal beside the tinkling of a fountain or under the shade of trees. He loved wit and a joke, and even gave ear to ridiculous things and to the excellent mimicry of a certain Florentine, who "took off" the courtiers and other absurd persons, and made his Holiness laugh. And he was hasty in temper, but bore no malice, and paid no attention to evil reports raised about himself. "He never punished those who spoke ill of him, saying that in a free city like Rome, every one should speak freely what he thought." He hated lying and story-tellers, and never made war unless he was forced to it. Whenever he was freed from the trials of business he took his pleasure in reading or in writing. "Books were more dear to him than sapphires or emeralds," says Platina, with a shrewd prick by the way at his successor, Paul, as we shall afterwards see, "and he was used to say that his chrysolites and other jewels were all enclosed in them." He never took a meal alone if he could help it, but loved a lively companion, and to make his little feasts in his garden as we have said, shocking much the scandalised courtiers, who declared that no other Pope had ever done such a thing; for which Pope Pius cared nothing at all. He wrote upon all kinds of subjects; from a grammar which he made for the little King of Hungary, to histories of various kingdoms, and philosophical disquisitions. Indeed the list of his subjects is like that of a series of popular lectures in our own day. "He wrote many books in dialogue— upon the power of the Council of Bâle, upon the sources of the Nile, upon hunting, upon Fate, upon the presence of God." If he had been a University Extension lecturer, he could scarcely have been more many-sided. And he wrote largely upon peace, no less than thirty-two orations "upon the peace of kings, the concord of princes, the tranquillity of nations, the defence of religion, and the quiet of the world." There was neither peace among kings, concord among princes, nor tranquillity among nations when Pope Pius delivered and collected his orations. They ought to have had all the greater effect; but we fear he was too wise a man to put much faith in any immediate result. His greatest work, however, was his Commentaries, an enlarged and philosophical study of his own times, which he did not live long enough to finish.

This Pontiff carried on the work of his predecessor more or less, but without any great zeal for it. "He collected manuscripts, but with discretion; he built, but it was in moderation," Bishop Creighton says. Platina, with more warmth, tells us that "he took great delight in building," but he seems to have confined himself to his own immediate surroundings, working at the improvement of St. Peter's, building a chapel, putting up a statue, restoring the great flight of stairs which then as now led up to the portico which previous Popes had adorned; and adding a little to the defences and decoration of the Vatican. He is suspected of having had a guilty liking for the Gothic style in architecture which greatly shocked the Roman dilettanti; and certainly expressed his admiration for some of the great churches in Germany with enthusiasm. One great piece of architectural work he did, but it was not at Rome. It was in the headquarters of his family at Sienna, and specially in the little adjacent town of Corsignano, where he was born, one of those little fortified villages which add so much to the beauty of Italy. This little place he made glorious with beautiful buildings, forgetting his native wisdom and discretion in the foolishness of that narrow but intense patriotism which bound the Italian to his native town, and made it the joy of the whole earth to his eyes. It gives a charm the more to his interesting character that he should have been capable of such a folly; though not perhaps that he should have changed its name to Pienza, a reflection of his own pontifical name.

With this, however, we have nothing to do, and not very much altogether with the great Piccolomini, though he is one of the most interesting and sympathetic figures which has ever sat upon the papal throne. His death was a strange and painful conclusion to a life full of work, full of admirable sense and intelligence without exaggeration or pretence. He followed the policy of his predecessors in desiring to institute a Crusade, one more strenuously called for perhaps than any which preceded it, since Constantinople had now fallen into the hands of the Turks, and Christendom was believed to be in danger. It is scarcely possible to imagine that his full and active life should have been much occupied by this endeavour: nor can we think that this great spectator and observer of human affairs was consumed with anxiety in respect to a danger about which the civilised world was so careless: but in the end of his life he seems to have taken it up with tragical earnestness, perhaps out of compunction for previous indifference. The impulse which once moved whole nations to take the cross had died out; and not even the sight of the beautiful metropolis of Eastern Christianity fallen into the hands of the infidel, and so splendid a Christian temple as St. Sophia turned into a mosque had power to rouse Europe. The King of Hungary was the only monarch who showed any real energy in the matter, feeling his own safety imperilled, and Venice, also for the same reason, was the only great city; and except in these quarters the remonstrances and entreaties of Pius had no success. In these circumstances the Pope called his court about him and announced to them the plan he had formed, a most unlikely plan for such a man, yet possible enough if there was any remorseful sense of carelessness in the past. The Duke of Burgundy had promised to go if another prince would join him. The Pope determined that in the absence of any other he himself would be that prince. Old as he was, and sick, and no warrior, and perhaps with but little of the zeal which makes such a self-devotion possible, he would himself go forth to repel the infidel. "We do not go to fight," he said, with faltering voice. "We will imitate those who, when Israel fought against Amalek, prayed on the mountain. We will stand on the prow of our ship or upon some hill, and with the holy Eucharist before our eyes, we will ask from our Lord victory for our soldiers." After a pause of alarm and astonishment the Cardinals consented, and such preparations as were possible were made. It was published throughout all Christendom that the Pope was to sail from Ancona at a certain date, and that every one who could provide for the expenses of the journey should meet him there. He invited the old Doge of Venice to join with himself and the Duke of Burgundy, also an old man. "We shall be three old men," he said, "and our trinity will be aided by the Trinity of Heaven." A kind of sublimity was in the suggestion, a sublimity almost trembling on the borders of the ridiculous; for the enterprise was no longer one which accorded with the spirit of the time, and all was hesitation and difficulty. A miscellaneous host crowded to Ancona, where the Pope, much suffering, was carried in his litter, quite unfit for a long journey; but the most of them had no money and had to be sent back; and the Venetian galleys engaged to transport those who were left did not arrive till the pilgrims had waited long, and were worn out with delay and confusion. They arrived at last a day or two before Pope Pius died, when he was no longer capable of moving—and with his death the ill-fated Crusade fell to pieces and was heard of no more. It was the most curious end, in an enthusiasm founded upon anxious calculation, of a man who was never an enthusiast, whose eyes were always too clear-sighted to permit him to be led away by feeling, a man of letters and of thought, rather than of romantic-solemn enterprises or the zeal of a martyr. That he was a kind of martyr to the strong conviction of a danger which threatened Christendom, and the forlorn hope of repelling it, there can be no doubt.

Pius II. was succeeded in 1464 by Paul II., also in his way a man of more than usual ability and note. He was a Venetian, the nephew of the last Venetian Pope, Eugenius; and it was he who built, to begin with, the fine palace still called the Palazzo Venezia, with which all visitors to Rome are so well acquainted. It was built for his own residence during his Cardinalate, and remained his favourite dwelling, a habitation still very much more in the centre of everything, as we say, than the remote and stately Vatican. The reader will easily recall the imposing appearance of this fine building, placed at the end of the straight street—the chief in Rome—in which were run the many races which formed part of the carnival festivities, a recent institution in Pope Paul's day. The street was called the Corso in consequence; and it is not long since the last of these races, one of horses without riders, was abolished. The Palazzo Venezia commanded the long straight street from its windows, and all the humours and wonders of the town, in which the Pope took pleasure. It was Paul's fate to make himself an implacable enemy in the often contemned, but—as regards the place in history of either pope or king—all-important class of writers, which it must have seemed ridiculous indeed for a Sovereign Pontiff to have kept terms with, on account of any power in their hands. But this was a shortsighted conclusion, unworthy the wisdom of a Pope. And the result of the Pontiff's ill-treatment of the historian Platina, to whom we are so much indebted, especially for the lives of those Popes who were his contemporaries, has been a lasting stigma upon his character, which the researches of the impartial critics of a later age have shown to be partly without foundation, but which until quite recently was accepted by everybody. In this way a writer has a power which is almost absolute. We have seen in our own days a conspicuous instance of this in the treatment by Mr. Froude of the life of Thomas Carlyle. Numbers of Carlyle's friends made instant protest against the view taken by his biographer; but they did so in evanescent methods—in periodical literature, the nature of which is to die after it has had its day—while a book remains. Very likely many of Pope Paul's friends protested against the coolly ferocious account of his life given by the aggrieved and revengeful author; but it is only quite recently, in the calm of great distance, that people have come to think—charitably in respect to Pope Paul II—that perhaps Platina's strictures might not be true.

Platina, however, had great provocation. He was one of the disciples of the famous school of Humanists, the then new school of learning, literature, and criticism, which had arisen under the papacy and patronage of Pope Nicolas V., and had continued to exist, though with less encouragement, under his successors. Pius II. had not been their patron as Nicolas was, but he had not been hostile to them, and his tastes were all of a kind congenial to their work. But Paul looked coldly upon the group of contemptuous scholars who had made themselves into an academy, and vapoured much about classical examples and the superiority of ancient times. He had no quarrel with literature, but he persuaded himself to believe that the academy which talked and masqueraded under classic names, and played with dangerous theories of liberty, and criticism of public proceedings, was a nest of conspirators and heretics scheming against himself. There was no foundation whatever for his fears, but that mattered little in those arbitrary days. This is Platina's own account of the matter:

"When Pius was dead and Paul created in his place, he had no sooner grasped the keys of Peter, than he proceeded—whether in consequence of a promise to do so, or because the decrees and proceedings of Pius were odious to him—to dismiss all the officials elected by Pius, on the ground that they were useless and ignorant (as he said): and deprived them of their dignity and revenues without permitting them to say a word in their own defence, though they were men who for their erudition and doctrine had been gathered together from all the ends of the world, and attracted to the court of Rome by the promise of great reward. The College was full of men of letters and virtuous persons learned in the law both divine and human. Among them were poets and orators who gave no less ornament to the court than they received from it. Paul sent them all away as incapable and as strangers, and deprived them of everything, although those who had bought their offices were allowed to retain them. Those who suffered most attempted to dissuade him from this intention, and I, who was one of them, begged earnestly that our cause might be committed to the judge of the Rota. Then he fixed on me his angry eyes. 'So,' he said, 'thou wouldst appeal to other judges against the decision we have made! Know ye not that all justice and law are in the casket of our bosom? Thus I will it to be. Begone, all of you! for, whatever you may wish I am Pope, and according to my pleasure can make and unmake.'"

After hearing this determined assertion of right, the displaced scholars withdrew, but continued to plead their cause by urgent letters, which ended at last in an unwise threat to make the continental princes aware how they were treated, and to bring about the Pope's ears a Council, to which he would be obliged to give account. The word Council was to a Pope what the red flag is to a bull, and in a transport of rage Paul II. threw Platina into prison. He never in his life did a more foolish thing. The historian was kept in confinement for two years, and passed one long winter without fire, subjected to every hardship; but finally was set free by the intercession of Cardinal Gonzaga, and remained, by order of the Pope, under observation in Rome, where watching with a vigilant eye all that went on, he laid up his materials for that brief but scathing biography of Paul II. which forms one of the keenest effects in his work, and from which the Pope's memory has never recovered. It is a dangerous thing to provoke a man of letters who has a keen tongue and a gift of recollection, especially in those days when such men were not so many as now.

Nevertheless Platina did a certain justice to his persecutor. "He built magnificently," he says, "splendidly in St. Marco, and in the Vatican." The Church of St. Marco is close to the Palazzo Venezia where Paul chiefly lived; he had taken his title as Cardinal from his native saint. Both in St. Peter's and in the Vatican he carried on the works begun by his predecessors, and though he was unkind to the scholars, he was not so in every case. "He expended his money liberally enough," says Platina, "giving freely to poor Cardinals and bishops, and to princes and persons of noble houses when cast out of their homes, and especially to poor women and widows, and the sick who had no one else to think of them. And he also took great trouble to secure that corn and other things necessary to life should be furnished in abundance, and at lower prices than had been known ever before." These were good and noble qualities which his enemy did not attempt to disguise.

The special service done by Pope Paul to the city would seem, however, to have been the restoration of some of those ancient monuments which belonged to imperial Rome, of which none of his predecessors had made much account. If he still helped himself freely, like them, from the great reservoir of the Colosseum, he bestowed an attention and care, which they had not dreamed of, upon some of the great works of classic art, the arches of Titus and of Septimus Severus in particular, and the famous statue of Marcus Aurelius. M. Muntz comments with much spirit on the reason why this Pope's works of restoration have been so little celebrated. His taste was toward sculpture rather than painting. "To the eyes of the world," says the historian of the arts, "the smallest fresco is of more account than the finest monuments of architecture, or of sculpture. Nicolas V. did better for his fame in engaging Fra Angelico than in undertaking the reconstruction of St. Peter's. Pius II. owes a sort of posthumous celebrity to the paintings in the library of the cathedral of Sienna."

The same classical tastes of which he thus gave token made Pope Paul a great collector of bronzes, cameos, medals, intaglios, the smaller precious objects of ancient art; the love of which he was the first to bring back as a special study and pursuit. His collection of these was wonderful for his time, and great for any time. All the other adornments of ancient art were dear to him, and his palace, which, after all, is his most complete memorial in Rome, was adorned like a bride with every kind of glory in carved and inlaid work, in vessels of gold and silver, embroideries and tapestries. He had the still more personal and individual characteristic of a love for fine clothes, which the gorgeous costumes of the popedom permitted him to indulge in to a large extent: and jewels, which he not only wore like an Eastern prince, but kept about him unset in drawers and cabinets for his private delight, playing with them, as Platina tells us, in the silent hours of the night. Some part at least of these magnificent tastes arose no doubt from the fact that he was himself a magnificent specimen of manhood, so distinguished in personal appearance that he had the naïve vanity of suggesting the name of Formosus for himself when elected Pope, though he yielded the point to the scandalised remonstrances of the Cardinals. This simplicity of self-admiration, so undoubting as to be almost a moral quality, no doubt gave meaning to the glorious mitres and tiara encrusted with the richest jewels, which it gave him so much pleasure to wear, and which take rank with the other great embellishments of Rome, though their object was more personal than official. The habits of his life were strange, for he slept during the day, and performed the duties of life during the night, the reason assigned for this being that he was tormented by a cough which prevented him from sleeping at the usual hours. "It was difficult to come to speech of him," Platina says, for this reason. "And when, after long waiting, he opened the door, you were obliged rather to listen than to speak; for he was very copious and long in speaking. In everything he desired to be thought astute, and therefore his conversation was in very intricate and ambiguous language He liked many sorts of viands on his table, all of the worst taste; and took much pleasure in eating melons, crawfish, pastry, fish, and salt pork, from which, I believe, came the apoplexy from which he died." Thus the prejudices of his enemy penetrated the most private details of the Pope's life. The venom of hatred defeats itself and becomes ridiculous when carried so far.

His fine collection was seized by his successor and broken up, as is the fate of such treasures; and his works in St. Peter's, as we shall see, had much the same fate, along with the great works of his predecessor for the embellishment of the same building, all of which perished or were set aside in the fever of rebuilding which ensued. But there is still a sufficient memorial of him in the sombre magnificence of his Venetian palace, to recall to us the image of a true Renaissance Pope, mingling the most exquisite tastes with the rudest, the perfection of personal vanity—for he loved to see himself in a procession, head and shoulders over all the people—with the likings of a gondolier. Thus we see him in the records of his contemporaries, watching from his windows the strange sports in the long street newly named the Corso, races of men and of horses, and carnival processions accompanied by all the cumbrous and coarse humour of the period; or a stranger sight still, seated by night in his cabinet turning over his wealth of sparkling stones, enjoying the glow of light in them and twinkle of many colours, while the big candles flared, or a milder light shone from the beaks of the silver lamps. Notwithstanding which strange humours, tastes, and vanities, he remains in all these records a striking and remarkable figure, no intellectualist, but an effective and notable man.

It is not the intention of these chapters to enter at all into the political life of the Popes of this period. They were still a power in Christendom, perhaps no less so that the Papacy had ceased to maintain those great pretensions of being the final arbiter in all disputes among the nations. But the papal negotiations, as always, came to very little when not aided by the events which are in no man's hand. Matthias of Hungary, though supported by all the influence and counsels of Pope Paul, made little head against the heretical George Podiebrad of Bohemia, until death suddenly overtook that prince, and left a troubled kingdom without a head, at the mercy of the invaders, an event such as constantly occurred to overturn all combinations and form the crises of history under a larger providence than that of human effort. And Paul no more than Pius could move Christendom against the Turk, or form again, when all its elements had crumbled, and the inspiration of enthusiasm was entirely gone, a new crusade. So far as our purpose goes, however, the Venetian Palace, the Church of St. Marco attached to it, and certain portions of the Vatican, better represent the life of this Pope, to whom the picturesque circumstances of his life and the rancour of a disappointed man of letters have given a special place of his own in the long line, than any summary we could give of the agitated sea of continental politics. The history of Rome was working up to that climax, odious, dazzling, and terrible, to which the age of the Renaissance, with all its luxury, its splendour, and its vice, brought the great city, and even the Church so irrevocably bound to it. Nicolas, Pius, and Paul at the beginning of that period, yet but little affected by its worst features, give us a pause of satisfaction before we get further. They were very different men. Pope Nicolas, with his crowd of copyists forming a ragged regiment after him, and the noise of all the workshops in his ears; and Paul, alone in his chamber pouring from one hand to another the stream of glowing and sparkling jewels which threw out radiance like the waterways of his own Venice under the light, afford images as unlike as it is possible to conceive; while the wise and thoughtful Pius, with those eyes "which had kept watch o'er man's mortality," stands over both, the perennial spectator and commentator of the world. They were all of one mind to glorify Rome, to make her a wonder in the whole earth, as Jerusalem had been, if not to pave her streets with gold, yet to line them with noble edifices more costly than gold, and to build and adorn the first of Christian churches, the shrine to which every Christian came. Alas! by that time it was beginning to be visible that all Christians would not long continue to come to the one shrine, that the pictorial age of symbols and representations was dying away, and that Rome had not learned at all how to meet that great revolution. It was not likely to be met by even the most splendid restoration of the fated city, any more than the necessities of the people were to be met by those other resurrections of institutions dead and gone, attempted by Rienzi, and his still less successful copyist Porcaro; but how were these men to know? They did their best, the worst of them not without some noble meaning, at least at the beginning of their several careers; but they are all reduced to their place, so much less important than they believed, by the large sweep of history, and the guidance of a higher hand.

Paul II. died in August 1471. Another order of man now succeeded these remarkable personages, the first of the line of purely secular princes, men of the world, splendid, unprincipled, and more or less vicious, although in this case it is once more a peasant, without so much as a surname, Sixtus IV., who takes his place in the scene, and who has left his name more conspicuously than any of his predecessors upon the later records of Rome. So far as the reader is concerned, the inscription at the end of the life of Pope Paul is a more melancholy one than anything that concerns that Pope. "Fin qui, scrisse il Platina," says the legend. We miss in the after-records his individual touch, the hand of the contemporary, in which the frankness of the chronicler is modified by the experience and knowledge of an educated mind. The work of Panvinio, scriba del Senato e popolo Romano, who completes the record, is without the same charm.

We have said that Pope Sixtus IV. was a man without a surname, Francesco of Savona, his native place furnishing his only patronymic: but there was soon found for him—probably for the satisfaction of the nephews who took so large a place in his life—a name which bore some credit, that of a family of gentry in which it is said the young monk had fulfilled the duties of tutor in the beginning of his career. By what imaginary pedigree this was brought about we are not told; but it is unlikely that the real della Roveres would reject the engrafting of a great Pope into their stock, and it soon became a name to conjure with throughout Italy. Although he also vaguely made proposals about a Crusade, and languidly desired to drive back the Turk, he was a man much more interested in the internal squabbles of Italy, and in his plans for endowing and establishing his nephews, than in any larger purpose. But he was also a man of boundless energy and power, cooped up for the greater part of his life, but now bursting forth like the strong current of a river. Whether it was from a natural inclination towards beauty and splendour, or because he saw it to be the best way in which to distinguish himself and make his own name as well as that of his city glorious, matters little to the result. He was, in the fullest sense of the words, one of the chiefest of the Popes who made the modern city of Rome, as still existing and glorious in the sight of all the world.

It was still a confused and disorderly place, in which narrow streets and tortuous ways, full of irregularities and projections of all kinds, threaded through the large and pathetic desert of the ancient city, leaving a rim of ruin round the too-closely clustered centre of life where men crowded together for security and warmth after the custom of the mediæval age—when Sixtus began to reign; and this it was which specially impressed King Ferdinand of Naples when he paid his visit to the Pope in the year 1475, and had to be led about by Cardinals and other high officials, sometimes, it would appear, by his Holiness himself, to see the sights. The remarks he made upon the town were very useful if not quite civil to the seat of Roman influence and authority. Infessura gives this little incident vividly, so that we almost see the streets with their outer stairs crowded with bystanders, their balconies laden with bright tapestries and fair women, and every projecting gable and pillared doorway pushing out into the pavement at its own unfettered will. The course of sightseeing followed by the King, conducted by the Pope and Cardinals, is fully set forth in these quaint pages. King Ferrante came to make his devotions allo perdono, probably the Jubilee of 1475, and offered to each of the three churches of St. Peter, St. John Lateran, and St. Paul, a pallium of gold for each, besides many other gifts.

"He went over all Rome to see the great buildings, and to Santa Maria Rotonda, and the columns of Antonius and of Trajan; and every man did him great honour. And when he had seen all these things he turned back to the palace, and talking to Pope Sixtus said that he (the Pope) could never be the lord of the place, nor ever truly reign over it, because of the porticoes and balconies which were in the streets; and that if it were ever necessary to put men at arms in possession of Rome the women in the balconies, with small bombs, could make them fly; and that nothing could be more easy than to make barricades in the narrow streets; and he advised him to clear away the balconies and the porticoes and to widen the streets, under pretence of improving and embellishing the city. The Pope took this advice, and as soon as it was possible cast down all those porticoes, and balconies, and widened the ways under pretence of improving them. And the said King remained there three days, and then went away."

This story and the spirit in which the suggestion was made recall Napoleon's grim whiff of grapeshot, and the policy which has made the present Paris a city of straight lines which a battery of artillery could clear in a moment, instead of all the elbows and corners of the old picturesque streets. Pope Sixtus appreciated the suggestion, knowing how undisciplined a city he had to deal with, and what a good thing it might be to fill up those hornets' nests, with all their capabilities of offence. Probably a great many picturesque dwellings perished in the destruction of those centres of rebellion, which recall to us so vividly the scenes in which Rienzi the tribune fluttered through his little day, and which were continually filled with the rustle and tumult of an abounding populace. We cannot be so grateful to King Ferdinand, or so full of praise for this portion of the work of Pope Sixtus, as were his contemporaries, though no doubt it gave to us almost all the leading thoroughfares we know. It was reserved for his kinsman-Pope to strike Rome the severest stroke that was possible, and commit the worst of iconoclasms; but we do not doubt that the destruction of the porches, and stairheads, and balconies must have greatly diminished the old-world attraction of a city—in which, however, it was the mediæval with all its irregularities that was the intruder, while what was new in the hand of Sixtus and his architects linked itself in sympathy with the most ancient, the originator yet survivor of all.

It was with the same purpose and intentions that the Pope built in place of the Ponte Rotto—which had lain long in ruins—a bridge over the Tiber, which he called by his own name, and which still remains, affording a second means of reaching the Borgo and the Sanctuaries, as a relief to the bridge of St. Angelo, upon which serious accidents were apt to happen by reason of the crowd. Both the chroniclers, Infessura and Panvinio, the continuator of Platina, describe the bridge as being a rebuilding of the actual Ponte Rotto itself. "It was his intention to mend this bridge," says the former authority, and he takes the opportunity to point out the presumptuous and proud attempt of Sixtus to preserve his own name and memory by it, a fault already committed by several of his predecessors; "he accordingly descended to the river and placed in the foundations by the said bridge a square stone on which was written: Sixtus Quartus Pontifex Maximus fecit fieri sub Anno Domini 1473. Behind this stone the Pope placed certain gold medals bearing his head, and afterwards built that bridge, which after this was no longer called Ponte Rotto, but Ponte Sisto, as is written on it." It is a wonderful point of view, commanding as it does both sides of the river, St. Peter's on one hand and the Palatine on the other, with all the mass of buildings which are Rome. The Scritte on the Ponte Sisto begs the prayers of the passer-by for its founder, who certainly had need of them both for his achievements in life and in architecture. There is still, however, a Ponte Rotto further up the stream.

Besides the work of widening the streets, which necessitated much pulling down and rebuilding of houses, and frequent encounters with the inhabitants, who naturally objected to proceedings so summary—and removing the excrescences, balconies, and porticoes, "which occupied, obscured, and made them ugly (brutte) and disorderly:" Pope Sixtus rebuilt the great Hospital of the Santo Spirito, which had fallen into disrepair, providing shelter in the meantime for the patients who had to be removed from it, and arranging for the future in the most grandfatherly way. This great infirmary is also a foundling hospital, and there was a large number of children to provide for. "Seeing that many children both male and female along with their nurses were thrown out on the world, he assigned them a place where they could live, and ordained that the marriageable girls should be portioned and honestly married, and that the others who would not marry should become the nurses of the sick. He also arranged that there should be (in the new hospital) more honourable rooms and better furnished for sick gentle-folks, so that they might be kept separate from the common people": an arrangement which is one of the things (like so many ancient expedients) on which we now pride ourselves as an invention of our own age, though the poor gentle-folks of Pope Sisto were not apparently made to pay for their privileges. This hospital in some of its details is considered the most meritorious of the Pope's architectural work.

Sixtus IV. was a man of the most violent temper, which led him into some curious scenes which have become historical. When one of the unfortunate proprietors of a house which stood in the way of his improvements resisted the workmen, Sixtus had him cast into prison on the moment, and savagely stood by to see the house pulled down before he would leave the spot. He delighted, the chroniclers say, in the ruins he made. A more tragic instance of his rage was the judicial murder of the Protonotary Colonna, who paid with his life for crossing the will of the Pope. But this masterful will and impetuous temper secured an incredible swiftness in the execution of his work.

The prudent suggestion of Ferdinand resulted in the clearance of those straight streets which led from the Flaminian Gate—now called the Porta del Popolo, which Sixtus built or restored, as well as the church of Sta. Maria del Popolo, which stands close by—to all the principal places in the city; the Corso being the way to the Capitol, the Ripetta to St. Angelo and the Borgo. He repaired once more the church and ancient palace of the Lateran, which had so long been the home of the Popes, and was still formally their diocesan church to which they went in state after their election. It is unnecessary, however, to give here a list of the many churches which he repaired or rebuilt. His work was Rome itself, and pervaded every part, from St. Peter's and the Vatican to the furthest corners of the city. The latter were, above all, the chief objects of his care, and he seems to have taken up with even a warmer ardour, if perhaps with a less cultivated intelligence, the plan of Nicolas V. in respect to the Palace at least. Like him he gathered a crowd of painters, chiefly strangers, around him, so that there is scarcely a great name of the time that does not appear in his lists; but he managed these great craftsmen personally like a slave-driver, pushing them on to a breathless speed of execution, so that the works produced for him are more memorable for their extent than for their perfection.

The fame of a sanitary reformer before his time seems an unlikely one for Pope Sixtus, yet he seems to have had no inconsiderable right to it. Nettare and purgare are two words in constant use in the record of his life. He restored to efficient order the Cloaca Maxima. He brought in, a more beautiful office, the Acqua Vergine, a name of itself enough to glorify any master-builder, "remaking," says the chronicler, "the aqueducts, which were in ruins, from Monte Pincio to the fountain of Trevi." Here is perhaps a better reason for blessing Pope Sixtus than even his bridge, for those splendid and abundant waters which convey coolness and freshness and pleasant sound into the very heart of Rome were brought hither by his hand, a gift which may be received without criticism, for not upon his name lies the guilt of the prodigious construction, a creation of the eighteenth century, through which they now flow. The traveller from the ends of the earth who takes his draught of this wonderful unfailing fountain, rejoicing in the sparkle and the flow of water so crystal-clear and cold even in the height of summer, and hoping to secure as he does so his return to Rome, may well pour a libation to Papa Sisto, who, half pagan as they all were in those days, would probably have liked that form of recollection quite as much as the prayers he invokes according to the formal requirements of piety and the custom of the Church. However, they found it quite easy to combine the two during that strange age. The chief thing of all, however, which perpetuates the name of Sixtus is the famous Sistine chapel, although its chief attraction is not derived from anything ordained by him. Some of the greatest names in art were concerned in its earlier decorations—Perugino, Botticelli, Ghirlandajo, along with many others. Michael Angelo was not yet, neither had Raphael appeared from the Umbrian bottega with his charm of grace and youth. But the Pope collected the greatest he could find, and set them to work upon his newly-built walls with a magnificence and liberality which deserved a more lasting issue. The reader will shiver, yet almost laugh with consternation and wonder, to hear that several great pictures of Perugino were destroyed on these walls by the orders of another Pope in order to make room for Michael Angelo. There could not be a more characteristic token of the course of events in the Papal succession, and of the wanton waste and destruction by one of the most cherished work of another.

Sixtus was none the less a warlike prince, struggling in perpetual conflict with the princes of the other states, perhaps with even a fiercer strain of ambition, fighting for wealth and position with which to endow the young men who were as his sons—as worldly in his aims as any Malatesta or Sforza, as little scrupulous about his means of carrying them out, shedding blood or at least permitting it to be shed in his name, extorting money, selling offices, trampling upon the rights of other men. Yet amid all these distractions he pursued his nobler work, not without a wish for the good of his people as well as for his own ends, making his city more habitable, providing a lordly habitation for the sick, pouring floods of life-giving water into the hot and thirsty place. The glory of building may have many elements of vanity in it as well as the formation of galleries of art, and the employment of all the greatest art-workmen of their time. But ours is the advantage in these latter respects, so that we may well judge charitably a man who, in devising great works for his own honour and pleasure, has at the same time endowed us, and especially his country and people, with a lasting inheritance. Perhaps, even in competition with these, it is most to his credit that he fulfilled offices which did not so much recommend themselves to his generation, and cleansed and cleared out and let in air and light like any modern sanitary reformer. The Acqua Vergine and the Santo Spirito Hospital are as fine things as even a Botticelli for a great prince's fame. He may even be forgiven the destruction of the balconies and all the picturesque irregularities which form the charm of ancient streets, in consideration of the sewerage and the cleaning out. The pictures, the libraries, and all the more beautiful things of life, in which we of the distant lands and centuries have our share of benefit, are good deeds which are not likely to be forgotten.

It is however naturally the beautiful things of which it is most pleasant to think. The chroniclers, whom we love to follow, curiously enough, have nothing to say about the pictures, perhaps because it was not an art favoured by the Romans, or which they themselves pursued, except in its lower branches. Infessura mentions a certain Antonazzo Pintore, who was the author of a Madonna, painted on the wall near the church of Sta. Maria, below the Capitol at the foot of the hill, which on the 26th of June, in the year 1470, began to do miracles, and was afterwards enshrined in a church dedicated to our Lady of Consolations. Antonazzo was a humble Roman artist, whose name is to be found among the workmen in the service of Pope Paul II., who was not much given to pictures. Perhaps he is mentioned because he was a Roman, more likely because he had the good luck to produce a miraculous Madonna. The same writer makes passing mention of I Fiorentini, under which generic name all the bottegas were included.

"He renewed the Palace of the Vatican, drawing it forth under great colonnades," says, picturesquely, the chronicler Panvinio, working probably from Platina's notes, "and making under his chapel a library": which was the finest thing of all, for he there reinstated Platina, who had been kept under so profound a shadow in the time of Paul II., and called back the learned men whom his predecessor had discouraged, sending far and near through all Europe for books, and thus enlarging the library begun by Pope Nicolas which is one of the most celebrated which the world possesses, and to which he secured a revenue, "enough to enable those who had the care of it to live, and even to buy more books." This provision still exists, though it is no longer sufficient for the purpose for which it was dedicated. The Cardinals emulated the Pope both in palace and church, each doing his best to leave behind him some building worthy of his name. Ornament abounded everywhere; sometimes rather of a showy than of a refined kind. There is a story in Vasari of how one of the painters employed on the Sistine, competing for a prize which the Pope had offered, piled on his colours beyond all laws of taste or harmony, and was laughed at by his fellows; but proved the correctness of his judgment by winning the prize, having gauged the knowledge and taste of Sixtus better than the others whose attempt had been to do their best—a height entirely beyond his grasp.

All these buildings, however, were fatal to the remnants still existing of ancient Rome. The Colosseum and the other great relics of antiquity were still the quarries out of which the new erections were built. The Sistine Bridge was founded upon huge blocks of travertine brought directly from the ruins of the Colosseum. The buildings of the Imperial architects thus melted away as we are told now everything in the world does, our own bodies among the rest, into new combinations, under a law which if just and universal in nature is not willingly adopted in art. The wonder is how they should have supplied so many successive generations, and still remain even to the extent they still do. Every building in Rome owes something to the Colosseum—its stones were sold freely in earlier ages, and carried off to the ends of the earth; but it has remained like the widow's cruse, inexhaustible: which is almost more wonderful than the fact of its constant use.

There is a picture in the Vatican gallery, which though not one of the highest merit is very interesting from a historical point of view. We quote the description of it from Bishop Creighton.

"It represents Sixtus IV. founding the Vatican library. The Pope with a face characterised by mingled strength and coarseness, his hands grasping the arms of his chair, sits looking at Platina, who kneels before him, a man whose face is that of a scholar, with square jaw, thin lips, finely cut mouth, and keen glancing eye. Cardinal Giuliano stands like an official who is about to give a message to the Pope, by whose side is Pietro Riario with aquiline nose and sensual chin, red-cheeked and supercilious. Behind Platina is Count Girolamo with a shock of black hair falling over large black eyes, his look contemptuous and his mien imperious."

These were the three men for whom the Pontiff fought and struggled and soiled his hands with blood, and sold his favour to the highest bidder. Giuliano della Rovere and Pietro Riario were Cardinals: Count Girolamo or Jeronimo was worse—he was of the rudest type of the predatory baron, working out a fortune for himself with the sword, the last man in the world to be the henchman of a Pope. They were but one step from the peasant race, without distinction or merit which had given them birth, and all three built upon that rude stock the dissolute character and grasping greed for money, acquired by every injustice, and expended on every folly, which was so common in their time. They were all young, intoxicated with their wonderful success and with every kind of extravagance to be provided for. They made Rome glitter and glow with pageants, always so congenial to the taste of the people, seizing every opportunity of display and magnificence. Infessura tells the story of one of these wonderful shows, with a mixture of admiration and horror. The Cardinal of San Sisto, he tells us, who was Pietro Riario, covered the whole of the Piazza of the Santi Apostoli, and hung it with cloth of arras, and above the portico of the church erected a fine loggia with panels painted by the Florentines for the festa of San ... (the good

Infessura forgets the name with a certain contempt one cannot but feel for the foreign painters and their works), and in front made two fountains which threw water very high, as high as the roof of the church. This wonderful arrangement was intended for the delectation of the royal guest Madonna Leonora, daughter of King Ferrante for whom he and his cousin Girolamo made a great feast.

"After the above banquet was seen one of the finest things that were ever seen in Rome or out of Rome: for between the banquet and the festa, several thousands of ducats were spent. There was erected a buffet with so much silver upon it as you would never have believed the Church of God had so much, in addition to that which was used at table: and even the things to eat were gilt, and the sugar used to make them was without measure, more than could be believed. And the said Madonna Leonora was in the aforesaid house with many demoiselles and baronesses. And every one of these ladies had a washing basin of gold given her by the Cardinal. Oh guarda! in such things as these to spend the treasure of the Church!"

Next year the Cardinal Riario died at twenty-eight, "poisoned," Infessura says: "and this was the end of all our fine festas." Another day it was the layman among the nephews who stirred all Rome, and the world beyond, with an immeasurable holiday.

"On St. Mark's Day, 1746, the Count Jeronimo, son, or nephew of Pope Sixtus, held a solemn tournament in Navona, where were many valiant knights of Italy and much people, Catalans and Burgundians and other nations; and it was believed that at this festivity there were more than a hundred thousand people, and it lasted over Friday, Saturday, and Sunday. And there were three prizes, one of which was won by Juliano Matatino, and another by Lucio Poncello, and the third by a man of arms of the Kingdom (Naples, so called until very recent days), and they were of great value."

[FOUNTAIN OF TREVI]

The Piazza Navona, the scene of this tournament, was made by Pope Sixtus the market-place of Rome, where markets were held once a month, an institution which still continues. The noble Pantheon occupies the end of this great square, as when Count Jeronimo with his black brows, marshalled his knights within the long enclosure, so fit for such a sight. We have now come to a period of history in which all the localities are familiar, and where we can identify every house and church and tower.

"Sixtus," says the chronicler, "left nothing undone which he saw to be for the ornament or comfort of the city. He defended intrepidly the cause of the Romans and the dignity of the Holy See." The first of these statements is more true perhaps than the last; and we may forgive him his shortcomings and his nephews on that great score. He ended his reign in August 1484, having held the Pontificate thirteen years.

CHAPTER III

JULIUS II—LEO X

It is happily possible to pass over the succeeding pontificates of Innocent VIII. and Alexander VI. These Popes did little for Rome except, especially the last of them, to associate the name of the central city of Christendom with every depravity. The charitable opinion of later historians who take that pleasure in upsetting all previous notions, which is one of the features of our time, has begun to whisper that even the Borgias were not so black as they were painted. But it will take a great deal of persuasion and of eloquence to convince the world that there is anything to be said for that name. Pope Innocent VIII. continued the embellishment of the Vatican, which was his own palace, and completed the Belvedere, and set Andrea Mantegna to paint its chambers; but this was not more than any Roman nobleman might have done for his palace if he had had money enough for decorations, which were by no means so costly in those days as they would be now, and probably indeed were much cheaper than the more magnificent kinds of arras or other decorative stuffs fit for a Pope's palace. Alexander, too, added a splendid apartment for himself, still known by his name; and provided for possible danger (which did not occur however in his day) by making and decorating another apartment in the castle of St. Angelo, whither he might have retired and still managed to enjoy himself, had Rome risen against him. But Rome, which often before had hunted its best Popes into the strait confinement of that stronghold, left the Borgia at peace. We are glad to pass on to the next Pope, whose footsteps, almost more than those of any other of her monarchs, are still to be seen and recognised through Rome. He gave more to the city than any one who had preceded him, and he destroyed more than any Pope before had permitted himself to do.

Julius II., della Rovere, the nephew of Pope Sixtus, for whom and for his brother and cousin that Pope occupied so much of his busy life, was a violent man of war, whose whole life was occupied in fighting, and who neither had nor pretended to have any reputation for sanctity or devotion. But passionate and unsparing as he was, and fiercely bent on his own way, the aim of his perpetual conflicts was at all events a higher one than that of his uncle, in so far that it was to enrich the Church and not his own family that he toiled and fought. He was the centre of warlike combinations all his life—League of Cambrai, holy League, every kind of concerted fighting to crush those who opposed him and to divide their goods; but the portion of the goods which fell to the share of Pope Julius was for the Church and not for the endowment of a sister's son. He was not insensible altogether to the claims of sister's sons; but he preferred on the whole the patrimony of St. Peter, and fought for that with unfailing energy all round. There are many books in which the history of those wars and of the Renaissance Popes in general may be read in full, but the Julius II. in whom we are here interested is not one who ever led an army or signed an offensive league: it is the employer of Bramante and Michael Angelo and Raphael, the choleric patron who threatened to throw the painter of the Sistine chapel from his scaffolding, the dreadful iconoclast who pulled down St. Peter's and destroyed the tombs of the Popes, the magnificent prince who bound the greatest artists then existing in Italy, which was to say in the world, to his chariot wheels, and drove them about at his will. Most of these things were good things, and give a favourable conception of him; though not that which was the most important of all.

[OLD ST. PETER'S]

How it was that he came to pull down St. Peter's nobody can say. He had of course the contempt which a man, carried on the highest tide of a new movement, has by nature for all previous waves of impulse. He thought of the ancient building so often restored, the object of so much loving care, with all the anxious expedients employed by past Popes to glorify and embellish the beloved interior, giving it the warmest and most varied historical interest—with much the same feeling as the respectable churchwarden in the eighteenth century looked upon the piece of old Gothic which had fallen into his hands. A church of the fourteenth century built for eternity has always looked to the churchwarden as if it would tumble about his ears—and his Herculean efforts to pull down an arch that without him would have stood till the end of time have always been interpreted as meaning that the ancient erection was about to fall. Julius II. in the same way announced St. Peter's to be in a bad way and greatly in need of repair, so as scarcely to be safe for the faithful; and Bramante was there all ready with the most beautiful plans, and the Pope was not a patient man who would wait, but one who insisted upon results at once. This church had been for many hundreds of years the most famous of Christian shrines; from the ends of the world pilgrims had sought its altars. The tomb of the Apostles was its central point, and many another saint and martyr inhabited its sacred places. It had seen the consecration of Emperors, it had held false Popes and true, and had witnessed the highest climax of triumph for some, and for some the last solemnity of death.[10] But Bramante saw in that venerable temple only the foundations for a new cathedral after the fashion of the great Duomo which was the pride of Florence; and his master beheld in imagination the columns rising, and the vast arches growing, of such an edifice as would be the brag of Christendom, and carry the glory of his own name to the furthest ends of the earth: a temple all-glorious in pagan pride, more classical than the classics, adorned with great statues and blank magnificence of pilasters and tombs rising up to the roof—one tomb at least, that of the della Roveres, of Sixtus IV. and Julius II., which should live as long as history, and which, if that proud and petulant fellow Buonarotti would but complete his work, would be one of the glories of the Eternal City.

The ancient St. Peter's would not seem to have had anything of the poetic splendour and mystery of a Gothic building as understood in northern countries: the rounded arches of its façade did not spring upwards with the lofty lightness and soaring grace of the great cathedrals of France and Germany. But the irregular front was full of interest and life, picturesque if not splendid. It had character and meaning in every line, it was a series of erections, carrying the method of one century into another, with that art which makes one great building into an animated and varied history of the times and ages through which it has passed, taking something from each, and giving shelter and the sense of continuance to all. There is no such charm as this in the most perfect of architectural triumphs executed by a single impulse. But this was the last quality in the world likely to deter a magnificent Pope of the fifteenth century, to whom unity of conception and correctness of form were of much more concern than any such imaginative interest. However Julius II. must not have greater guilt laid upon him than was his due. His operations concerned only the eastern part of the great church: the façade, and the external effect of the building remained unchanged for more than a hundred years; while the plan as now believed, was that of Pope Nicolas V., only carried out by instalments by his successors, of whom Julius was one of the boldest.

It is, however, in the fame of his three servants, sublime slaves, whose names are more potent still than those of any Pontiff, that this Pope has become chiefly illustrious. His triumphs of fighting are lost from memory in the pages of the historians, where we read and forget, the struggle he maintained in Italy, and the transformations through which that much troubled country passed under his sway—to change again the morrow after, as it had changed the day before the beginning of his career. To be sure it was he who finally identified and secured the Patrimony of St. Peter—so that the States of the Church were not henceforward lost and won by a natural succession of events once at least in the life of every Pope. But we forget that fact, and all that secured it, the tumultuous chaos of European affairs being as yet too dark to be penetrated by any certainty of consolidation. The course of events was in large what the history of the fortunes of St. John Lateran, for example, was in small. From the days of Pope Martin V. until those of Sixtus IV. a change of the clergy there was made in almost each pontificate. Eugenius IV. restored the canons regular, or monks: who were driven forth by Calixtus III., again restored by Paul II., and so forth, until at length Sixtus, bringing back the secular priests for the third time, satisfied the monks by the gift of his new church of Sta. Maria della Pace. The revolution of affairs in Italy was almost as regular, and it is only with an effort of the mind that the reader can follow the endless shifting of the scenes, the combinations that disperse and reassemble, the whirl of events for ever coming round again to the point from which they started. But when we put aside the Popes and the Princes and the stamping and tumult of mail-clad warriors—and the crowd opening on every side gives us to see a patient, yet high-tempered artisan mounting day by day his lofty platform, swung up close to the roof, where sometimes lying on his back, sometimes crouched upon his knees, he made roof and architrave eloquent with a vision which centuries cannot fade, nor any revolution, either of external affairs or of modes of thought, lessen in interest, a very different feeling fills the mind, and the thoughts, which were sick and weary with the purposeless and dizzy whirl of fact, come back relieved to the consoling permanence of art. The Pope who mounted imperious, a master of the world, on to those dizzy planks, admired, and blasphemed and threatened in a breath; but with no power to move the sturdy painter, who, it was well known, was a man impossible to replace. "When will you have done?" said the Pope.

"When I can," replied the other. The Pontiff might rage and threaten, but the Florentine painted on steadily; and Pope Julius, on the tremulous scaffolding up against the roof of his uncle's chapel, is better known to the world by that scene than by all his victories. Uncle and nephew, both men of might, warlike souls and strong, that room in the Vatican has more share in their fame than anything else which they achieved in the world.

Another and a gentler spirit comes in at the same time to glorify this fortunate Pope. His predecessors for some time back had each done something for the splendour of the dwelling which was their chief residence, even the least interested adding at least a loggia, a corridor, a villa in the garden, as has been seen, to make the Vatican glorious. Alexander VI. had been the last to embellish and extend the more than regal lodging of the Pontiffs; but Julius II. had a hatred of his predecessor which all honest men have a right to share, and would not live in the rooms upon which the Borgias had left the horror of their name. He went back to the cleaner if simpler apartments which Nicolas V. had built and decorated by the hands of the elder painters. Upon one of these he set young Raphael to work, a young man with whom there was likely to be no such trouble as that he had with the gnarled and crabbed Florentine, who was as wilful as himself. Almost as soon as the young painter had begun his gracious work the delighted Pope perceived what a treasury of glory he had got in this new servant. What matter that the new painter's master, Perugino, had been there before him with other men of the highest claims? The only thing to do was to break up these old-fashioned masters, to clear them away from the walls, to leave it all to Raphael. We shiver and wonder at such a proof of enthusiasm. Was the young man willing to get space for his smooth ethereal pictures with all their heavenly grace, at such a price? But if he made any remonstrance—which probably he did, for we see him afterwards in much trouble over St. Peter's, and the destruction carried on there—his imperious master took little notice. Julius was one of the men who had to be obeyed, and he was always as ready to pull down as to build up. The destruction of St. Peter's on one hand, and all those pictures on the other, prove the reckless and masterful nature of the man, standing at nothing in a matter on which he had set his heart. In later days the pictures of Perugino on the wall of the Sistine chapel were demolished, as has been said, to make place for the Last Judgment of Michael Angelo; but Pope Julius by that time had passed into another sphere.

Most people will remember the famous portrait of this Pope by Raphael, one of the best known pictures in the world. He sits in his chair, an old man, his head slightly bowed, musing, in a pause of the endless occupations and energy which made his life so full. The portrait is quite simple, but full of dignity and a brooding power. We feel that it would not be well to rouse the old lion, though at the moment his repose is perfect. Raphael was at his ease in the peacefulness of his own soul to observe and to record the powerful master whose fame he was to have so great a share in making. It would have been curious to have had also the Julius whom Michael Angelo knew.

He died in the midst of all this great work, while yet the dust of the downfall of St. Peter's was in the air. Had it been possible that he could have lived to see the new and splendid temple risen in its place, we could better understand the wonderful hardihood of the act; but it would be almost inconceivable how even the most impious of men could have executed such an impulse, leaving nothing but a partial ruin behind him of the great Shrine of Christendom, did we not know that a whole line of able rulers had carried on the plan to gradual completion. It was not till a hundred and fifty years later that the new St. Peter's in its present form, vast and splendid, but apparently framed to look, to the first glance, as little so as possible, stood complete, to the admiration of the world. In the violence of destruction a great number of the tombs of the Popes perished, by means of that cynical carelessness and profanity which is more cruel than any hostile impulse. Julius preserved the grave of his uncle Sixtus, where he was himself afterwards laid, not in his own splendid tomb which had been in the making for many years, and which is now to be seen in the church of San Pietro in Vincoli from which he took his Cardinal's title. He had therefore little good of that work of art as he well deserved, and it was itself sadly diminished, cut down, and completed by various secondary hands; but it is kept within the ken of the spectator by Michael Angelo's Moses and some other portions of his original work, though it neither enshrines the body nor marks the resting place of its imperious master. Julius died in 1513, "more illustrious in military glory than a Pope ought to be." Panvinio says: "He was of great soul and constancy, and a powerful defender of all ecclesiastical things: he would not suffer any offence, and was implacable with rebels and contumacious persons. He was such a one as could not but be praised for having with so much strength and fidelity preserved and increased the possessions of the Church, although there are a few to whom it appears that he was more given to arms than was becoming a holy Pope." "On the 21st of February 1513, died Pope Julius, at nine hours of the night," says another chronicler, Sebastiano Branca; "he held the papacy nine years, three months, and twenty-five days. He was from Savona: he acquired many lands for the Church: no Pope had ever done what Pope Julius did. The first was Faenza, the others Forli, Cervia, Ravenna, Rimini, Parma, Piacenza, and Arezzo. He gained them all for the Church, nor ever thought of giving them to his own family. Pesaro he gave to the Duke of Urbino, his nephew, but no other. Thirty-three cardinals died in his time. And he caused the death in war of more than a hundred thousand people." There could not be a more grim summary.

It is curious to remark that the men who originated the splendour of modern Rome, who built its noblest churches and palaces, and emblazoned its walls with the noblest works of art, and filled its libraries with the highest luxury of books, were men of the humblest race, of peasant origin, born to poverty and toil. Thomas of Sarzana, Pope Nicolas V., Francesco and Giuliano of Savona, Popes Sixtus IV. and Julius II.: these men were born without even the distinction of a surname, in the huts where poor men lie, or more humbly still in some room hung high against the rocky foundations of a village, perched upon a cliff, after the fashion of Italy. It was they who set the fashion of a magnificence beyond the dreams of the greatest princes of their time.

It was not so, however, with the successor of Julius II., the Pope in whose name all the grandeur and magnificence of Rome is concentrated, and of whom we think most immediately when the golden age of ecclesiastical luxury and the splendour of art is named. Leo X. was as true a son of luxury as they were of the soil. The race of Medici has always been fortunate in its records. The greatest painters of the world have been at its feet, encouraged and cherished and tyrannised over. Literature such as was in the highest esteem in those days flattered and caressed and fawned upon them. Lorenzo, somewhat foolishly styled in history the Magnificent,—in forgetfulness of the fact that il Magnifico was the common title of a Florentine official,—is by many supposed to be the most conspicuous and splendid character in the history of Florence. And Leo X. bears the same renown in the records of Papal Rome. We will not say that he was a modern Nero fiddling while Rome was burning, for he showed himself in many ways an unusually astute politician, and as little disposed to let slip any temporal advantage as his fighting predecessors—but the spectacle is still a curious one of a man expending his life and his wealth (or that of other people) in what was even the most exquisite and splendid of decorations, such wonders of ornamentation as Raphael's frescoes—while the Papacy itself was being assailed by the greatest rebellion ever raised against it. To go on painting the walls while the foundations of the building are being ruined under your feet and at any moment may fall about your ears, reducing your splendid ornaments to powder, is a thing which gives the most curious sensation to the looker on. The world did not know in those days that even to an institution so corrupt superficially as the Church of Rome the ancient promise stood fast, and not only the gates of hell, but those more like of heaven, should not prevail against her. Out of Italy it was believed that the Church which had but lately been ruled over by a Borgia, and which was admittedly full of wickedness in high places, must go down altogether under the tremendous blow. A great part of the world indeed went on believing so for a century or two. But in the midst of that almost universal conviction nothing can be more curious than to see the life of Papal Rome going on as if nothing had happened, and young Raphael and all his disciples coming and going, cheerful as the day, about the great empty chambers which they were making into a wonder of the earth. Michael Angelo, it is true, in grim discontent hewed at those huge slaves of his in Florence, working wonderful thoughts into their great limbs; but all that Roman world flowed on in brightness and in glory under skies untouched by any threatening of catastrophe.

[MODERN ROME: THE GRAVE OF KEATS]

The Italian chroniclers scarcely so much as mention the beginnings of the Reformation. "At that time in the furthest part of Germany the abominable and infamous name of Martin Luther began to be heard," says one. The elephant which Emmanuel of Portugal sent to his Holiness, and which was supposed to be a thousand years old, takes up as much space. The sun shone on in Rome. The painters sang and whistled at their work, and their sublime patron went and came, and capped verses with Venetian Bembo, and the unique Aretino. They were not, it would seem, in the least afraid of Luther, nor even cognisant of him except in a faint and far-off way. He was so absurd as to object to the sale of indulgences. Now the sale of indulgences was not to be defended in theory, as all these philosophers knew. But to buy off the penances which otherwise they would at all events have been obliged to pretend to do, was a relief grateful to many persons who were not bad Christians, besides being good Catholics. Perhaps, indeed, in the gross popular imagination these indulgences might have come to look like permissions to sin, as that monster in Germany asserted them to be; but this did not really alter their true character, any more than other popular mistakes affected doctrine generally. And how to get on with that huge building of St. Peter's, at which innumerable workmen were labouring year after year, and which was the most terrible burden upon the Papal funds, without that method of wringing stone and mortar and gilding and mosaic out of the common people? Pope Leo took it very easily. Notwithstanding the acquisitions of Pope Julius, and the certainty with which the historians assure us that from his time the Patrimony of St. Peter was well established in the possession of Rome, some portion of it had been lost again, and had again to be recovered in the days of his successor. That was doubtless more important than the name, nefando, execrabile of the German monk. And so the wars went on, though not with the spirit and relish which Julius II. had brought into them. Leo X. had no desire to kill anybody. When he was compelled to do it he did it quite calmly and inexorably as became a Medici; but he took no pleasure in the act. If Luther had fallen into his hands the Curia would no doubt have found some means of letting the pestilent fellow off. A walk round the loggie or the stanze where the painters were so busy, and where Raphael, a born gentleman, would not grumble as that savage Buonarotti did, at being interrupted, but would pause and smile and explain, put the thought of all troublesome Germans easily out of the genial potentate's head. It was the Golden Age; and Rome was the centre of the world as was meet, and genius toiled untiringly for the embellishment of everything; and such clever remarks had never been made in any court, such witty suggestions, such fine language used and subtle arguments held, as those of all the scholars and all the wits who vied with each other for the ear and the glance of Pope Leo. The calm enjoyment of life over a volcano was never exhibited in such perfection before.

We need not pause here to enumerate or describe those works which every visitor to Rome hastens to see, in which the benign and lovely art of Raphael has lighted up the splendid rooms of the Vatican with something of the light that never was on sea or shore. We confess that for ourselves one little picture from the same hand, to be met with here and there, and often far from the spot where it was painted, outvalues all those works of art; but no one can dispute their beauty or importance. Pope Leo did not by so much as the touch of a pencil contribute to their perfection, yet they are the chief glory of his time, and the chief element in his fame. He made them in so far that he provided the means, the noble situation as well as the more vulgar provision which was quite as necessary, and he has therefore a right to his share of the applause—by which he is well rewarded for all he did; for doubtless the payment of the moment, the pleasure which he sincerely took in them, and the pride of so nobly taking his share in the lasting illumination of Rome were a very great recompense in themselves, without the harvest he has since reaped in the applause of posterity. Nowadays we do not perhaps so honour the patron of art as people were apt to do in the last century. And there are, no doubt, many now who worship Raphael in the Vatican without a thought of Leo. Still he is worthy to be honoured. He gave the young painter a free hand, believing in his genius and probably attracted by his more genial nature, while holding Michael Angelo, for whom he seems always to have felt a certain repugnance, at arm's length.

We will not attempt to point out in Raphael's great mural paintings the flattering allusions to Leo's history and triumph which critics find there, nor yet the high purpose with which others hold the painter to have been moved in those great works. Bishop Creighton finds a lesson in them, which is highly edifying, but rather beyond what we should be disposed to look for. "The life of Raphael," he says, "expresses the best quality of the spirit of the Italian Renaissance, its belief in the power of culture to restore unity to life and implant serenity in the soul. It is clear that Raphael did not live for mere enjoyment, but that his time was spent in ceaseless activity animated by high hopes for the future." How this may be we do not know: but lean rather to the opinion that Raphael, like other men of great and spontaneous genius, did what was in him and did his best, with little ulterior purpose and small thought about the power of culture. It was his, we think, to show how art might best illustrate and with the most perfect effect the space given him to beautify, with a meaning not unworthy of the gracious work, but no didactic impulse. It was his to make these fine rooms, and the airy lightness of the brilliant loggie beautiful, with triumphant exposition of a theme full of pictorial possibilities. But what it should have to do with Luther, or how the one should counterbalance the other, it is difficult to perceive. Goethe on the other hand declares that going to Raphael's loggie from the Sistine chapel "we could scarcely bear to look at them. The eye was so educated and enlarged by those grand forms and the glorious completeness of all the parts that it could take no pleasure" in works so much less important. Such are the differences of opinion in all ages. It is the glory of this period of Roman history that at a time when the Apostolic See had lost so much, and when all its great purposes, its noble ideals, its reign of holiness and inspired wisdom had perished like the flower of the fields—when all that Gregory and Innocent had struggled their lives long to attain had dissolved like a bubble: when the Popes were no longer holy men, nor distinguished by any great and universal aim, but Italian princes like others, worse rather than better in some cases: there should have arisen, with a mantle of glory to hide the failure and the horror and the scorn, these two great brethren of Art—the one rugged, mournful, self-conscious, bowed down by the evil of the time, the other all sweetness and gladness, an angel of light, divining in his gracious simplicity the secrets of the skies.

Leo the Pope was no such noble soul. He was only an urbane and skilful Medici, great to take every advantage of the divine slaves that were ready for his service—using them not badly, encouraging them to do their best, if not for higher motives yet to please him, the Sommo Pontefice, surely the best thing that they could hope for; and to win such share of the ducats which came to him from the sale of the offices of the Vatican, the cardinals' hats, the papal knighthoods, and other trumpery, as might suffice for all their wants. He sold these and other things, indulgences for instance, sown broadcast over the face of the earth and raising crops of a quite different kind. But on the other hand he never sold a benefice. He remitted the tax on salt; and he gave liberally to whoever asked him, and enjoyed life with all his heart, in itself no bad quality.

[A BRIC-A-BRAC SHOP]

"The pontificate of Leo was the most gay and the most happy that Rome ever saw," says the chronicler. "Being much enamoured of building he took up with a great soul the making of San Pietro, which Julius, with marvellous art, had begun. He ennobled the palace of the Vatican with triple porticoes, ample and long, of the most beautiful fabrication, with gilded roofs and ornamented by excellent pictures. He rebuilt almost from the foundations the church of our Lady of the Monte Coelio, from which he had his title as cardinal, and adorned it with mosaics. Finally there was nothing which during all his life he had more at heart or more ardently desired than the excellent name of liberal, although it was the wont ordinarily of all the others to turn their backs upon that virtue of liberality, and to keep far from it. He judged those unworthy of high station who did not with large and benign hand disperse the gifts of fortune, and above all those which were acquired by little or no fatigue. But while he in this guise governed Rome, and all Italy enjoyed a gladsome peace, he was by a too early death taken from this world although still in the flower and height of his years."

He died forty-five years old on December 1, 1521.

The great works which one and another of the Popes thus left half done were completed—St. Peter's by Sixtus V. 1590, and Paul V. 1615. The Last Judgment completing the Sistine chapel was finished by Michael Angelo in 1541 under Clement VII. and Paul III. And thus the Rome of our days—the Rome which not as pilgrims, but as persons living according to the fashion of our own times, which compels us to go to and fro over all the earth and see whatever is to be seen, we visit every year in large numbers— was left more or less as it is now, for the admiration of the world. Much has been done since, and is doing still every day to make more intelligible and more evident the memorials of an inexhaustible antiquity—but in the Rome of the Popes, the Rome of Christendom, History has had but little and Art not another word to say.

FOOTNOTE:

[10] See the death of Pope Leo IX., p. 199.

Margaret Oliphant – A Short Biography

Margaret Oliphant Wilson was born on April 4th, 1828 to Francis W. Wilson, a clerk, and Margaret Oliphant, at Wallyford, near Musselburgh, East Lothian.

She spent her childhood at Lasswade, near Dalkeith, Glasgow before moving to Liverpool.

Her youth was spent in establishing a writing style so much so that, in 1849, she had her first novel published: Passages in the Life of Mrs. Margaret Maitland based on the Scottish Free Church movement. It met with some success and was a good start to her career.

Two years later, in 1851, her third book Caleb Field was published. It was also now that she met the publisher William Blackwood in Edinburgh and was asked to contribute to his well-received Blackwood's Magazine. It was to be a lifelong endeavor. Over the course of the relationship she would have well over 100 articles published.

In May 1852, Margaret married her cousin, Frank Wilson Oliphant, at Birkenhead, and they settled at Harrington Square, Camden, London. He was an artist working primarily in stained glass. With the marriage she became Margaret Oliphant Wilson Oliphant.

Their marriage produced six children but three tragically died in infancy.

When her husband developed signs of the dreaded consumption (tuberculosis) they moved, on the advice of doctors, to warmer climes. In January 1859 it was to Florence, and then to Rome where, sadly, he died.

Margaret was naturally devastated but was also now left without support and only her income from her writing. She returned to England and took up the task of supporting her three remaining children by her literary activity.

By now she was being published both as an established novelist and regularly in Blackwood's Magazine, amongst several others. Her incredible and prolific work rate increased both her commercial reputation and the size of her reading audience.

Against this her domestic life continued to be tragic, full of sorrow and disappointment.

In January 1864 her only remaining daughter, Maggie, died and was buried in her father's grave in Rome. Her brother, who had emigrated to Canada, was shortly afterwards involved in financial ruin. Margaret generously offered a home to him and his children, adding another demand to her already heavy responsibilities.

In 1866 she settled at Windsor to be closer to her sons, who were being educated at near-by Eton School. That year, her second cousin, Annie Louisa Walker, came to live with her as a companion-housekeeper. Windsor was now to be her home for the rest of her life.

Her literary career for three decades was one of constant delivery and success. Whether she wrote historical works or across several genres in fiction: domestic realism, historical, romance or supernatural she was successful.

For more than thirty years she pursued a varied literary career but family life continued to bring problems.

The literary ambitions she wished for her sons were unfulfilled. Cyril Francis, the eldest, died in 1890, leaving a Life of Alfred de Musset, which was later incorporated in his mother's Foreign Classics for English Readers. The younger, Francis, who she nicknamed 'Cecco', collaborated with her in the Victorian Age of English Literature and won a position at the British Museum, but was rejected by Sir Andrew Clark, a famous physician. Cecco died in 1894.

With the last of her children now lost to her, she had but little further interest in life. Her health steadily and inexorably declined.

Margaret Oliphant Wilson Oliphant died at the age of 69 in Wimbledon on 20th June 1897. She is buried in Eton beside her sons.

At her death, Margaret was still working on Annals of a Publishing House, a record of Blackwood's Magazine with which she had enjoyed such a successful relationship.

Her Autobiography and Letters, which present a thoughtful picture of her domestic anxieties, was published in 1899. Only parts were written with a wider audience in mind: she had originally intended the Autobiography for her son, but he died before she could finish it.

Opinions on Oliphant's work are split, with some critics seeing her as a 'domestic novelist', while others recognize her work as influential and important to the Victorian literature canon. Critical reception from her contemporaries is also divided. John Skelton took the view that Oliphant wrote too much and too quickly. Writing a Blackwood's article called 'A Little Chat About Mrs. Oliphant', he asked, "Had Mrs. Oliphant concentrated her powers, what might she not have done? We might have had another Charlotte Brontë or another George Eliot." However not all of the contemporary reception was negative. The esteemed M. R. James admired Oliphant's supernatural fiction, concluding that "the religious ghost story, as it may be called, was never done better than by Mrs. Oliphant in 'The Open Door' and 'A Beleaguered City'. Mary Butts lavished praise on Oliphant's ghost story 'The Library Window', describing it as "one masterpiece of sober loveliness".

More modern critics of Oliphant's work include Virginia Woolf, who asked in 'Three Guineas' whether Oliphant's autobiography does not lead the reader "to deplore the fact that Mrs. Oliphant sold her brain, her very admirable brain, prostituted her culture and enslaved her intellectual liberty in order that she might earn her living and educate her children."

Whatever the merits of their cases Margaret Oliphant has been shamefully neglected in modern years. She is now becoming more widely recognised as a leading writer of her day.

Margaret Oliphant – A Concise Bibliography

A canon of more than 120 works, including novels, travel books, histories, and volumes of literary criticism.

Novels
Margaret Maitland (1849)
Merkland (1850)
Caleb Field (1851)
John Drayton (1851)
Adam Graeme (1852)
The Melvilles (1852)
Katie Stewart (1852)
Harry Muir (1853)
Ailieford (1853)
The Quiet Heart (1854)
Magdalen Hepburn (1854)
Zaidee (1855)
Lilliesleaf (1855)
Christian Melville (1855)
The Athelings (1857)
The Days of My Life (1857)
Orphans (1858)
The Laird of Norlaw (1858)
Agnes Hopetoun's Schools and Holidays (1859)
Lucy Crofton (1860)
The House on the Moor (1861)
The Last of the Mortimers (1862)
Heart and Cross (1863)
Salem Chapel (1863)

The Rector (1863)
Doctor's Family (1863)
The Perpetual Curate (1864)
Miss Marjoribanks (1866)
Phoebe Junior (1876)
A Son of the Soil (1865)
Agnes (1866)
Madonna Mary (1867)
Brownlows (1868)
The Minister's Wife (1869)
The Three Brothers (1870)
John: A Love Story (1870)
Squire Arden (1871)
At his Gates (1872)
Ombra (1872
May (1873)
Innocent (1873)
The Story of Valentine and His Brother (1875)
A Rose in June (1874)
For Love and Life (1874)
Whiteladies (1875)
An Odd Couple (1875)
The Curate in Charge (1876)
Carità (1877)
Young Musgrave (1877)
Mrs. Arthur (1877)
The Primrose Path (1878)
Within the Precincts (1879)
The Fugitives (1879)
A Beleaguered City (1879)
The Greatest Heiress in England (1880)
He That Will Not When He May (1880)
In Trust (1881)
Harry Joscelyn (1881)
Lady Jane (1882)
A Little Pilgrim in the Unseen (1882)
The Lady Lindores (1883)
Sir Tom (1883)
Hester (1883)
It Was a Lover and his Lass (1883)
The Lady's Walk (1883)
The Wizard's Son (1884)
Madam (1884)
The Prodigals and Their Inheritance (1885)
Oliver's Bride (1885)
A Country Gentleman and His Family (1886)
A House Divided Against Itself (1886)
Effie Ogilvie (1886)

A Poor Gentleman (1886)
The Son of His Father (1886)
Joyce (1888)
Cousin Mary (1888)
The Land of Darkness (1888)
Lady Car (1889)
Kirsteen (1890)
The Mystery of Mrs. Biencarrow (1890)
Sons and Daughters (1890)
The Railway Man and His Children (1891)
The Heir Presumptive and the Heir Apparent (1891)
The Marriage of Elinor (1891)
Janet (1891)
The Cuckoo in the Nest (1892)
Diana Trelawny (1892)
The Sorceress (1893)
A House in Bloomsbury (1894)
Sir Robert's Fortune (1894)
Who Was Lost and is Found (1894)
Lady William (1894)
Two Strangers (1895)
Old Mr. Tredgold (1895)
The Unjust Steward (1896)
The Ways of Life (1897)

Short stories
Neighbours on the Green (1889)
A Widow's Tale and Other Stories (1898)
That Little Cutty (1898)
The Open Door (1918)

Selected Articles
Mary Russel Mitford (Blackwood's Magazine, Vol. 75, 1854)
Evelin and Pepys (Blackwood's Magazine, Vol. 76, 1854)
The Holy Land (Blackwood's Magazine, Vol. 76, 1854)
Mr. Thackeray and his Novels (Blackwood's Magazine, Vol. 77, 1855)
Bulwer (Blackwood's Magazine, Vol. 77, 1855)
Charles Dickens (Blackwood's Magazine, Vol. 77, 1855)
Modern Novelists—Great and Small (Blackwood's Magazine, Vol. 77, 1855)
Modern Light Literature: Poetry (Blackwood's Magazine, Vol. 79, 1856)
Religion in Common Life (Blackwood's Magazine, Vol. 79, 1856)
Sydney Smith (Blackwood's Magazine, Vol. 79, 1856)
The Laws Concerning Women (Blackwood's Magazine, Vol. 79, 1856)
The Art of Caviling (Blackwood's Magazine, Vol. 80, 1856)
Béranger (Blackwood's Magazine, Vol. 83, 1858)
The Condition of Women (Blackwood's Magazine, Vol. 83, 1858)

The Missionary Explorer (Blackwood's Magazine, Vol. 83, 1858)
Religious Memoirs (Blackwood's Magazine, Vol. 83, 1858)
Social Science (Blackwood's Magazine, Vol. 88, 1860)
Scotland and her Accusers (Blackwood's Magazine, Vol. 90, 1861)
The Chronicles of Carlingford (Blackwood's Magazine 1862–1865)
Girolamo Savonarola (Blackwood's Magazine, Vol. 93, 1863)
The Life of Jesus (Blackwood's Magazine, Vol. 96, 1864)
Giacomo Leopardi (Blackwood's Magazine, Vol. 98, 1865)
The Great Unrepresented (Blackwood's Magazine, Vol. 100, 1866)
Mill on the Subjection of Women (The Edinburgh Review, Vol. 130, 1869)
The Opium-Eater (Blackwood's Magazine, Vol. 122, 1877)
Russian and Nihilism in the Novels of I. Tourgeniéf (Blackwood's Magazine, Vol. 127, 1880)
School and College (Blackwood's Magazine, Vol. 128, 1880)
The Grievances of Women (Fraser's Magazine, New Series, Vol. 21, 1880)
Mrs. Carlyle (The Contemporary Review, Vol. 43, May 1883)
The Ethics of Biography (The Contemporary Review, July 1883)
Victor Hugo (The Contemporary Review, Vol. 48, July/December 1885)
A Venetian Dynasty (The Contemporary Review, Vol. 50, August 1886)
Laurence Oliphant (Blackwood's Magazine, Vol. 145, 1889)
Tennyson (Blackwood's Magazine, Vol. 152, 1892)
Addison, the Humorist (Century Magazine, Vol. 48, 1894)
The Anti-Marriage League (Blackwood's Magazine, Vol. 159, 1896)

Biographies
Edward Irving (1862)
Francis of Assisi (1871)
Count de Montalembert (1872)
Dante (1877)
Cervantes (1880)
Life of Sheridan in the English Men of Letters series (1883)
John Tulloch (1888)
Laurence Oliphant (1892)

Historical & Critical Works
Historical Sketches of the Reign of George II (1869)
The Makers of Florence (1876)
A Literary History of England from 1760 to 1825 (1882)
The Makers of Venice (1887)
Royal Edinburgh (1890)
Jerusalem (1891)
The Makers of Modern Rome (1895)
William Blackwood and his Sons (1897)
The Sisters Brontë. In: Women Novelists of Queen Victoria's Reign (1897)

www.ingramcontent.com/pod-product-compliance
Lightning Source LLC
Chambersburg PA
CBHW052020020726

47501CB00004B/1157